Dead North

Nina DeGraff

First paperback edition February 2025

Book design by Nina C. DeGraff
"Fantastic Milky Way in the New Year's Eve" cover photo:
Standret/shutterstock.com

*Poem excerpt, acknowledgments page:
Lowenstein, Tom, translator. *Eskimo Poems from Canada and Greenland*, by Knud Rasmussen, University of Pittsburgh Press, 1973.

ISBN 979-8-9888-3696-4 (paperback)
ISBN 979-8-9888-3697-1 (ebook)

Round Pond Publishing, LLC
54 State Street, Suite 804 #9162
Albany, NY 12207

www.roundpondpublishing.com

If I kill you,
I will offer
handsome presents
to your soul:
hides for kamiks,
moss for wicks.
Come happily,
towards me!
Come!

Orpingalik*

1

I don't suppose any story of mine will ever begin with, "There I was, minding my own business." With my neighbors and best friends immersed in exciting vacations in distant lands and my state trooper boyfriend in the midst of completing an out-of-town training drill for a couple of days, I planned to do nothing *but* delve into the business of others.

It was all I could think about on that early November night as I locked the front door of the Corner Pocket, the singularly wonderful gourmet and necessities store where I was filling in as a part-time clerk while the owners were away. With cookies, milk, and powdered cocoa tucked into my bag, I looked forward to a long night of cross-checking my biological father's private journals with the instances of theft, arson, suspicious deaths, and drug-related crimes that he'd circled on a map of Maine.

So far, none of the clues could be tied to the last words that Raymond French ever wrote after sitting down at his kitchen table to sip coffee and shake off the cold with a snack of cinnamon toast.

Sleet, snow, wind — it's quite a mess out there tonight, he'd written at roughly nine p.m. the previous year on February 5th. *No surprise the power is out. Just before I cranked up the generator, I heard a snowmobile whining on one of my trails. Whoever it is has to be crazy to be out in this kind of weather.*

Crazy was just for starters. Someone had trekked through a raging blizzard to kill my father and stage the scene to make it look like an accident. Premeditated murder took planning and ice-cold calculation. I had grit and determination on my side. Come what may, I would unearth the circumstances that had escalated to the point where I'd needed to add my father's name and address to his map of crime scenes.

First, I had to check in with Norris Bolton to see if I needed to stop by his son's house before I headed home. With my phone in hand, I settled Luke, my plus-sized King Shepherd adopted mutt, in the back seat of my car, where his panting began fogging up the frosty windows.

"Norris?" I said, cranking up the heat as I backed away from the canary yellow storefront. "Did June feed Dan's fish?"

"I didn't reach her just now, so it's possible she conked out at home and went to bed on the early side," Norris said of his wife of thirty years. "I'm sure the fish can wait until morning."

"A few are new to the tank. I'll swing by to make sure they're not belly-up or half-eaten by the resident fish." I closed my eyes, aware that I might be projecting my tribulations onto innocent animals. "Enough about my boring night. How are things going down there?"

"Well, active shooter training is not a path to calm, if you get my drift," Norris said of the multi-agency exercise underway in an unknown location in southern Maine. "Dan is in the shower, then we're having a late dinner with some of his colleagues."

"I'm glad you're there to lend support," I said.

"Should I tell Dan to give you a call?" Norris asked.

"No, let him de-stress," I said. "We'll catch up tomorrow."

"Thank you, Sonny."

State Trooper Daniel Bolton had summoned a SWAT response on my behalf on two separate occasions during recent months when I'd landed in the wrong place at the wrong time, so I was determined to step up for him in return whenever I got the chance. His mother, June, tended to fix me with concerned glances when she figured I wasn't looking, but I didn't blame her for thinking I might be more trouble than I was worth. In time, she would come to trust my deep commitment to her son.

Beyond the tiny village of Gracious, Maine, the unlit road wound past rural businesses and historic homes where festive lights framed every door and electric candles flickered in the windows. Luke started to whine with anticipation as he caught onto where we were heading.

Behind me in the cargo area, a set of antique sleigh bells faintly jingled every time my car hit a bump on the wooded road. Friends had convinced me to sign up for the local "Farm Crawl," an event in February where people were invited to visit small operations across the region for a taste of country fun. It was a way to build interest in orchards, cheesemakers, sheep breeders, and other kinds of farms that were often operating on life support. My strawberry fields wouldn't be a fun place to visit until the berries ripened next summer, so my contribution to the event would be to offer sleigh rides on my wooded trails. I smiled every time I pictured the moment when I would shake the reins and send Dodge, my Belgian draft horse, into a lively walk through the deep snow, with his hooves thudding, and the bells jingling on his shoulders and haunches.

After the last few turns on the secluded road, Luke's whining reached a crescendo, complete with biscuit-scented breath. In Dan, he'd found a coach who tasked him with the ins and outs of fetching, seeking, and protection skills. "He's a King Shepherd cross," Dan had explained. "He's built to work. His mind needs the satisfaction of a job."

Luke wasn't the only one. My current life was a patchwork of tackling any freelance photo shoots that came my way. On the local front, *Coast & Candle* magazine offered the kind of work I loved the most, with a focus on New England cuisine, handmade crafts, country décor, and rural traditions. If the bills started piling up, I would be obliged to head to my old stomping ground in Boston to carry out the wishes of my former boss, whose raison d'être was stripping the world of depth and meaning one advertising campaign at a time. For the foreseeable future, the money he tossed my way would be too good to turn down.

With the headlights illuminating the scattered flakes of a light snowfall, I was about to pull into Dan's driveway when a reflected glint on my left caught my eye. I shifted into reverse and retraced my path far enough to study a dark van that was tucked into the long-abandoned logging trail on the opposite side of the road from Dan's property.

Aside from the unfamiliar van, all looked quiet in the neighborhood of scattered homes. Dan had outfitted his house and garage with so many floodlights that I pictured astronauts puzzling over the bright spot as they swept through the heavens on the space station.

Sensing my concern, Luke went from whining in anticipation of seeing Dan to stone-cold silent and rigid with attention, his keen eyes assessing the unknown vehicle as if he, too, had noticed that the windows on the back door were frosted over from the inside.

"The engine is off," I said. "Maybe the driver ran out of gas."

Luke pawed at the door. He wanted to check it out.

"Give me a minute," I said. "It's important to assess things first."

I knew that Dan had caught two teenagers necking in a sedan in that spot last month. Maybe they'd upgraded to a van.

With my phone in hand, I opened the window, letting in a burst of cold air, and took a photo of the license plate. Below the bumper was a wallet and a keyring with a fob. I reversed my car and pulled to the side of the road with my headlights illuminating the van.

Unlike Dan, I didn't have a tactical vest. I had a fishing vest from my father's closet. I pulled it from my camera bag and slipped it over my jacket. With roomy styling and a range of inventive compartments, it had become my go-to means of carrying memory cards and other photography essentials, plus it allowed me to secure my phone in a mesh pocket with the lens facing out in case I needed to record events fast.

Next, I snugged on my neoprene half-gloves that added oomph to my knuckles but freed my fingertips. From the side door, I pulled out a metal flashlight with a beam that could illuminate objects as far away as 120 yards, all the while thinking, *Look at me cope. I can do this.*

I stretched my neck on both sides, stepped out into the frosty night, and crossed to the wallet and keys. The wooded trail led steeply upward into a forest of maple trees and pines. Unnerved by the bare branches rattling in a passing breeze, I swept the beam over the van from fender to fender. Traces of frost on the front hood told me the engine had been off for a while. With a thudding heart, I trained my light on the wallet and flipped it open, and then with my phone in hand, I got a few clear shots of the driver's license. The owner, Gerald Leblanc, was a fiftyish man who had foiled the DMV's predilection for turning a smile into a grimace. The key fob on the ground was from "Polk Realty & Storage."

Emboldened by the stillness and lack of hidden threats, I stepped to the van's back windows and illuminated the interior through narrow gaps in the frost, which had formed from an inside source.

Seeing bolt cutters, plastic ties, and other items scattered about, I held my breath as an object directly next to the back doors resolved into a man dressed in the sort of camouflage shirt and matching pants that hunters used. Alarmed that he'd pulled up the trail to sleep off a bender, which put him in danger of getting hypothermia, I tested the handle and found that the back doors were unlocked. As they swung wide, I realized too late that the angle of the trail would tip the man toward me. I struggled to catch him, but he flopped to the ground with a sad thud.

It didn't sound right, the way the man had landed.

Luke appeared to agree, yipping and barking as he raked my car's interior with his front paws. My mind narrowed into pinpoint clarity as my flashlight illuminated the cable ties on the stranger's wrists and ankles, and then my heart constricted into a painful, non-pumping weight in my chest when I saw the fixed expression on the man's face.

Gerald Leblanc wasn't drunk.

He was dead.

2

"This is a dream or a cruel hoax," I said, waiting in vain to jerk awake in my bedroom overlooking my beautiful strawberry farm. "Because another murder scene would mean fate *really* has it in for me."

Yet there the stranger lay, ashen in the face and neck, with his features drawn and spent, as if regrets had plagued him in the end.

With grim resolve, I knelt on the roadside, paused for a moment, and checked Gerald Leblanc's neck, finding no sign of warmth, no sign of life. He'd stopped breathing long enough ago for his skin to have achieved the same temperature as the winter air. Between my rubbery legs and my sudden dizziness, climbing to my feet felt like rising and falling at the same time. Over the sound of my slamming heart and Luke's barking, I heard muffled sounds coming from behind me in Dan's house.

Turning in place — really it was more of a confused stagger — I realized the floodlights that Dan had strategically positioned around his house, attached garage, and yard had suddenly shut down and all the interior lamps he'd outfitted with timers had gone dark.

For a second, I stood in the beam of my car's headlights like a stage performer who'd forgotten her character's pivotal lines, and then the icy touch of snowflakes on my face brought a vivid clarity to the shrill noise of a woman screaming for all she was worth.

"June?" I managed.

Paralysis left me. I surged across the road and cut through Dan's yard with the flashlight gripped in my hand, desperate to reach his mother before the awful picture in my mind became a reality.

Midway to his garage, I glimpsed a masked figure closing in on my right. Pitching forward into a calculated tumble, as Dan had taught me to do, I rolled and struck the assailant's ankle bone with the flashlight: a swift, fierce hit that had him screaming and dropping fast. Scrambling after him across the icy grass, I followed through with a glancing blow across his masked head, which caused my flashlight to shut off.

No matter. Fury and the need to end the battle fast drove me forward with a rain of precise blows to his knee as he rolled, then his elbow, his shoulder, and his back as he desperately tried to crawl away. Horrified to see a familiar gleam of metal on his hip, I snatched the sidearm from its holster and held it toward my car's headlights until I figured out how to eject the magazine, which I tossed away into the weeds.

The assailant lurched toward the van, limping and clutching his arm. Saving June was my priority. With the empty weapon tucked into my vest pocket, I raced onward, hearing squawks and walkie-talkie static coming from the fleeing burglar and someone inside the house. Multiple French-speaking players were communicating through radios.

Slowing my pace, I neared the side door of the garage with my heart thudding and sweat beading on my brow. My winter jacket was an impediment. I made quick work of shedding it and re-zipped myself into the fishing vest. June's hollering was muffled. I couldn't tell if her mouth had been taped, or if someone was holding her jaw shut.

In a crouch, I reached up and opened the side door of the garage, revealing that June's car was parked inside, which she might naturally do on a winter night with snow in the air. I was confused not to hear sirens in the distance, and then shock blazed through my mind.

I hadn't called 911.

With trembling fingers, I made the call and kept the line open as I returned my phone to my vest's mesh pocket with the lens facing outward. I conveyed Dan's badge number and a recap of events.

"I've got 911 on the line," I hollered into the garage, "The police are on the way, so you should hit the road while you can!"

Hearing a door bang open behind the house, I paused, elated that I'd inspired them to leave, and then I slowly crept into the garage.

"*Mmm!*" June managed as if to warn me.

Seeing a shadow close in, I swung the flashlight in that direction, but lost ground as the attacker used his weight to knock me off balance and secure my arms. He was muscled, tactical, and strong.

"Please don't hurt me," I said, changing my approach on the fly. "The guy in the yard broke my arm. I just want to live."

He gripped my throat, his eyes framed by a balaclava. "You have two seconds to tell me the combination for the safe."

"The safe?" I asked. "Umm … 6-4-3-4."

I yelped as he gripped my vest and hauled me through the dark garage. Feebly protesting, I snagged my right toe on the handle of a carpet stapler that would be his worst nightmare if I managed to take him off guard. When he paused for breath, I used my left toe to pinion the handle all the more. On he dragged me, and then he shoved me into a heap against June, whose tearful eyes showed signs of flagging spirits.

"Please don't hurt us," I said. "Take what you want and go!"

"*Shhh.*"

With a sharp jab, the man silenced my babbling and used a shoulder radio to relay the combination for the safe to whoever had pretended to exit through the back door. In black military gear that was all too familiar after my last harrowing arc, the man appeared to have gray eyes, but it was tough to get a true sense of him in the dark.

Inch by inch, I drew the stapler closer with my toes, moaning about my sore arm, and claiming to have broken ribs as well.

"What do you want from us?" I wailed. "Please don't hurt us!"

"*Shhh,*" he hissed. "Arms out front."

As he tried to bind my wrists, I dove in the direction of the stapler. If it was the jammed tool destined for the trash I was cooked, but I grabbed the handle and adjusted my grip. Cursing and sweating, he paused as he touched the empty sidearm that I'd tucked into my fishing vest.

His eyes met mine, his thought obvious.

Who in the hell is this woman?

I swung Dan's tool around and shot a heavy-duty staple into the soft divot between the man's chest and shoulder tip. His wail was extreme, his roll immediate. With what can only be described as a feral growl, I lurched after him and planted another staple in his ass.

"Que diable?" the third guy growled as he arrived.

"Get out," I hollered. "I'm still on the line with 911."

Sirens were approaching from all directions, sharpening in clarity as the cruisers crested hills along the heavily wooded roads, but I knew that help and support weren't closing in by any stretch.

The third guy either didn't know, or he didn't care.

Without pause, he shouldered his wounded comrade toward the door. Cursing and struggling, they lurched away into the night. At last, I could focus on pulling the tape from June's mouth. While she gasped and sputtered thanks, I found tin snips and freed her bound wrists.

"Are you injured?" I asked.

"Just bruised," she managed. "If you hadn't come—"

"Don't think about that," I said. "You're safe."

Beyond the front yard, the van's doors slammed shut and the tires shrieked on the road as the assailants peeled away. June was shivering. Not sure if further surprises awaited us inside the house, I ushered her outside, bundled her into my coat, and continued conveying information to 911 as I raced over the snow-slick grass to fetch Luke. After slipping and sliding a few times on the return journey, I handed the leash to Dan's shivering mother and signaled for Luke to keep her warm.

Breathless, but determined to forge on, I pulled out my phone and instructed June to continue updating the dispatcher.

"Where are you going?" she asked as I turned to the house.

"I think I hear a noise," I said. "I need to check it out."

"Alison Littlefield, don't you dare!" June hollered.

Ignoring her, I dashed back into the garage, skirted past June's station wagon, and paused to orient myself as I stepped into Dan's house. In the darkness, all the power cords, toolboxes, and piles of lumber formed tripping hazards across the kitchen and living room. Over eighteen months had passed since Dan had picked up a sledgehammer and demolished the walls. Shocked to his core, and blind with grief, he'd needed a solitary, physical means of processing the death of his childhood friend, Aaron Pierce, who'd succumbed to despair after a divorce and other hardships. Details were slow to emerge, but I knew that if not for that awful pass, Dan would never have signed onto undercover work.

He'd come a long way since the covert stint ended in August. Every newly installed board and spackled nail hole symbolized healing, an indication that his mind was on the mend. Now his upward climb would be upended by men who didn't know right from wrong.

With that in mind, I grabbed two sandwich bags and a butter knife from a drawer. In Dan's bedroom closet, I shoved his shirts down the pole to expose the clothing that he hadn't touched since he'd invited me into his private world. Checking the pockets, I confirmed that every receipt and business card pointed to the Canadian border, where his secret stint had taken place. Once the documents were secured in a bag, I flipped his boots to scrape dried mud from the treads into the second bag.

It felt like a long shot, but there had to be a scientist who could help me target the specific region where Dan had worked. If further attacks came out of the blue and he disappeared, I wasn't about to sit on my heels until the police figured things out. I needed a solid plan.

I paused, hearing a whisper of activity in the bathroom down the hallway. Had one of the culprits looped back, or stayed behind?

I crept forward with the empty sidearm in hand, pausing to hold my breath and listen. Maybe the baseboard heat had made the noise. Along the way, I confirmed with a glance that the burglars had opened Dan's decoy safe in the living room. Instead of grabbing evidence or whatever they'd hoped to find, they'd risked everything to cart off some cash, bogus paperwork, and a flash drive that was a tracking device.

Near the bathroom, I stepped forward in shock, seeing that the towel warmer covering Dan's *real* safe had been pulled from the wall.

Caught in mid-step, I gulped as a man extracted the weapon from my hand and spun me into a locked position in one swift motion. As he set the gun aside, my split-second advantage turned into a mistake as he pulled me into a straitjacket hold with his strong arms wrapped around me from behind and my wrists secured from opposite sides.

Cursing my lapse of attention, I struggled to free myself, and then the mixed message of his flexed muscles and calm breathing plunged me into confusion. At no point had any bout with a bad guy involved a moment of quiet. With his warmth against my back, I sensed that he was careful and strategic, in keeping with Dan's training, but it wasn't Dan.

"We are peaceful and composed?" he asked.

"What's going on?" I demanded.

"I am hoping to not be stabbed," he said.

"I don't have a knife, and the gun was empty," I said. "I'm dating Dan. That's why I'm here. Your turn. Who are you?"

His clean-shaven face arrived next to my ear. "Does the name Antoine ring any bells?" he said softly, casting the scent of mint gum across my face. "I can tell that it does, which means our mutual friend has been naughty, telling tales. No wonder things went to shit."

"If you're a good guy, let go," I said, picking up on his French accent, and daring to hope that he truly was Dan's colleague.

"It's curious that you returned to the scene," he said.

"The burglars were gone," I said. "I thought it was safe."

"Unhand her, you rascal villain!" June hollered behind us.

Without pause, Antoine spun me out of the hold with the verve and grace of a dance pro and retrieved the weapon he'd taken from me. Once he verified that the sidearm was unloaded, he turned the butt toward me and offered it back. Moonlight defined his jawline and bold features, revealing a subtle smile and expressive eyebrows. His hazel eyes were keen and intense, assessing me as I assessed him.

"It's a shame that you didn't wear gloves," he said, signaling that his hands were covered. "It's ok for you to tell Dan that his colleague, Antoine, was here, but nobody else, understand?"

In a knitted sweater with a pine tree theme on the lower edge, June stepped forward and brandished her favorite soup ladle.

"No funny moves, Mister," she said. "The police are on their way."

"I am a friend, not a foe," he said calmly.

"You are Antoine?" I asked. "The undercover guy who landed Dan in a car crash up north? It left him with two black eyes."

Antoine's sigh reflected disappointment in Dan for oversharing, and then he knelt to secure the panel that covered the safe.

I stepped closer and nudged his arm. "It's confusing to find you here. How did you know Dan's house would be attacked?"

"I am good at my job," Antoine said.

"How did you know the safe was in here?" I asked.

"I am *very* good at my job," he said.

None of my questions, jabs, or swats to get his attention had the slightest effect in derailing Antoine's focus on covering the safe. As he stood, he gently grasped my shoulders to steer me to one side, and then he reached for a stack of folders that he'd set aside on a shelf.

"Wait, what are those?" I asked.

"I'm not sure, but since you are a puzzle to sort out …" Antoine flipped open the top folder. "Any thoughts?"

I stared in shock as I recognized my father's handwriting. "Those are my father's notes. What are they doing here?"

Antoine studied me in the near darkness.

"Once again, your surprise is genuine," he said. "I'll leave it to Dan to explain their presence here. I need to head out."

"Those papers belong to me," I insisted.

"If so, I will return them," Antoine said, smoothly removing the ladle from June's hand when she attempted to clock him. "Again, it's fine to let Dan know that I was here, but you won't help matters by telling anyone else." A fit man, in a tight button-up shirt and a ponytail, Antoine paused and fixed me with his keen gaze. "I heard their radio chatter, but it's good to verify facts. Was one of them a woman? Could you tell?"

"It was three men," I said. "I'm positive."

"She's right," June agreed. "It was three men."

Antoine nodded. "Bonne nuit, mesdames."

"You can't take those folders," I said, catching at his arm. "They're not connected to Dan's work up north. Antoine, stop. *Wait.*"

As he slipped away, the sirens increased in sound, and touches of blue flashing lights were starting to play over the walls.

"If only I hadn't left Luke in the yard," June said. "I thought you were coming in to snoop, but apparently, you did hear a noise."

I cast about in the bathroom, tempted to leave the unloaded weapon somewhere in the house, but too many surprises had unfolded that night. I tucked it into my fishing vest, and then glanced at June, who was heaving sighs and shaking her head as she looked at me.

"Did you spark what happened here?" she demanded.

I gaped. "Of course not. I came to feed the fish."

"That's why I came," June said. "I had it covered."

"You can't imagine I was involved," I said.

"Not directly, of course," June said. "But Norris let me in on the giant secret that your father's death wasn't an accident. Dan has been upending the world to solve the case so you don't land in the crosshairs."

"I've been giving the matter a wide berth," I insisted.

"That's baloney and nonsense," June said. "You inherited Raymond's drive to get answers, even though you two never met. At some point, he pushed the wrong button with the wrong sort. That's why my son is now in harm's way. It's as plain as the nose on my face."

The situation was anything but plain, but I didn't want to argue.

"Did you reach Dan?" I asked.

"I sure did, and I talked to Detective Allen as well," June said. "Prepare to get your butt kicked for returning to the crime scene."

I groaned and closed my eyes.

3

Detective Roy Allen had gained a few pounds since our last meeting at a crime scene back in September, and his cropped hair was noticeably grayer. His efforts to stretch a kink out of his neck and rub his weary eyes told me that he'd been woken up out of a sound sleep. His dicey, high-speed ride down winding wooded roads had further dampened his sense of humor, and nixed any latitude he might otherwise extend to me.

"There are blood smears in the garage and in the yard," Roy said with his pen entrusting notes to a pad. "None of it is yours?"

"No, I'm unscathed," I said.

"You came here to feed the fish," he said. "Same as June."

With a sigh, I said, "I've already told you all this."

Roy's upward glance, which did not involve the slightest movement of his head, instructed me to answer his questions, with no back talk.

"Yes, I stopped by to check the fish. There was confusion over whether or not June had remembered to do it." I closed my eyes. "The fact that you asked about the blood means I didn't explain things clearly. I think I'm experiencing a block. A snag in facing how I handled getting jumped. You know my history. It's happened before. Getting kidnapped. The shock and horror of it. So, this time … I clocked the first guy. I'll be stunned if my flashlight isn't dented. It shut off when I hit his head. Or his knee. I hit him a *lot*. June was screaming. I dove in to rescue her. I'm sure you can imagine how fast it all went. I disarmed his weapon."

"The first guy was *armed?*" Roy prompted.

"Don't worry, I disarmed the weapon straight away. I tossed the magazine over there." I waved in the direction of the trees, where Dan's holiday lights sparkled with twinkling icy light. "Look, the electricity is back on. It shut off when my back was turned."

"Alison, *where* is the weapon?" Detective Allen asked.

"In my pocket," I said.

State troopers who'd been standing nearby were prompted forward. I was instructed to hold my arms straight out while the sidearm was removed from my fishing vest and bagged as evidence.

"I shot the other guy with a stapler," I said.

Roy paused. "You made contact with the tool?"

"I got him right here," I said, pointing to my shoulder. "He screamed and tried to flee. I sort of stapled him in the butt."

"You 'sort of' stapled him in the butt …?"

"No, I totally did. Hence, the smears of blood. This is what I'm saying. How do I live with this? I've never caused bodily harm before. Granted, I fought off all kinds of murderers back in May. September as well. I guess the die was cast then. Is this who I *am* now?"

"Sonny …"

"I saw your frown when I mentioned the dead hunter who fell out of the van," I said. "It's bizarre that they took his body with them, isn't it? Given their rush to escape? Maybe you don't believe that part, but it was for real. It's like a picture in my head that I can't erase."

How Gerald Leblanc's skin had felt when I'd checked for a pulse, icy and lifeless, his hands and ankles bound with plastic ties, and his eyes fixed in a permanent stare. I'd opened the van's back doors without thinking, causing his body to land on the roadside gravel with a ghastly, leaden thud. Where had he been going in his hunting camouflage? A weekend trip? An outing with friends? With all I'd been through in recent months, the other deaths I'd witnessed, wasn't I due for a break? Why did I have to be the one to find the lifeless corpse of Gerald Leblanc?

The scene of officers staring at me blurred, the way the night had vanished into a dark fog when I'd found a human skeleton hand on my farm. Dan had been there to catch me when I'd started to faint. I desperately needed his strong arms and solid presence to lean against now, but he was having a late dinner with his father in a distant town.

"*Sonny.*"

Detective Allen gripped my arms and steadied me, pulling my gaze to his eyes, which had switched from impatient to kind.

"We'll take a breather," he said. "Do you want coffee?"

"No, let's get this finished," I managed. "I took photos."

Roy paused. "Of the body?"

"No, of the license plate, wallet, and keys," I said.

Once I transferred the photos to Roy's phone, I was instructed to stay put while the details that I'd provided were discussed. June Bolton had returned my jacket to me before she'd been swept away to be supported elsewhere. I pulled the zipper to my chin, though the warmth the jacket provided was marginal. Amidst a fresh round of snowflakes that landed on my shoulders with a soft tickle of sound, I was desperate to reconnect with my dog. Luke had behaved admirably so far and was now being adored by a police tech near the property's edge.

"Thank you for keeping him company," I said, crossing to the woman and reaching for Luke's leash. "Hopefully, he's been a good boy."

"He's a gem," she enthused, in no hurry to return him to me. "A King Shepherd, if I'm not mistaken. What's his name?"

I hesitated, thrown by her French accent and the disconnect between her bold gaze and her exaggerated smile. She was pretty and fit, dressed in dark clothes. With flowing, shoulder-length hair that curtained her face, she playfully grimaced when I didn't respond.

"His name is Luke, right?" she prompted.

"None of the technicians I know would need to ask," I said. "And I'm noticing that your identification isn't visible. Can I see it?"

"You want my phone number?" she purred. "That's fast."

A flicker of surprise touched her eyes when I showed her *my* meaning of fast, pulling out my phone and taking a burst of photos that documented her reaction, from impish to angry as she abruptly stood.

"I need help over here," I hollered.

Once she glanced over my shoulder and saw that my plea for assistance was unheard, she pouted on my behalf in mock sympathy.

"Who are you?" I demanded.

"I'm a friend," she said. "Not a foe."

As I paused, hearing the same words Antoine had used, my confused reaction appeared to please her all the more.

On her way past me, she whispered, "Ask Dan who I am."

If she'd meant to silence me long enough for her to melt away into the night, she'd achieved her objective with precision and ease.

Gripping Luke's leash, I raced toward a group of officers, and then I halted in place, paralyzed by the element of Dan's undercover work. It was supposed to be locked down, never to be discussed with just anyone. With trembling hands, I regrouped and called him, figuring he would pick up right away since we had yet to touch base. He didn't answer.

I cast about, looking for Detective Roy Allen, and saw him talking to two fiftyish men dressed in casual business attire.

"Back up a second, Mr. Polk," Roy said. "Gerald is still in your employ at Polk Realty and Storage, but he didn't show up today?"

"That is correct," Mr. Polk said.

"He's a trusted employee?" Roy asked.

"I was leery at first, knowing he'd spent time in prison," Mr. Polk said. "But it's important to give people a second chance."

"What about Gerald's cousins?" Roy asked.

"They're the reason Gerald got into trouble," Mr. Polk said. "He's a bit gullible, but Gerald has turned his life around under my guidance. He collects toys for needy children. I don't see him in handcuffs here, by the way. What makes you think he's involved?"

"It's possible there isn't a link," the detective said.

"You're cross-checking tips, that sort of thing?" Mr. Polk asked.

"Exactly," Roy said. "Mr. Munroe, anything to add?"

"The Boltons are clients at the bank," the second man said. "If offering a reward for information would help, let me know."

"Excellent," Roy said. "Thanks for weighing in."

As the men shook hands with the detective and retreated to a barricade twenty or more yards away, I stepped in that direction, puzzled to see fire trucks from local towns parked nearby, as if ready to rush in. I'd assumed from previous crime scenes that only one fire department was needed to cover the off chance of an unexpected event. Why did the scene at Dan's house demand the presence of four rigs and crews?

My gaze snagged on a thirtyish man standing amongst the inevitable crowd of concerned neighbors who'd been drawn to the scene by the fuss and chaos. With a cigarette in hand and a slow smile, he stepped into the light of the police strobes, took a long last drag, causing the tip to flare in the night, and then he tossed the butt to the roadside without snuffing the ember with his work boot. There it lay, smoldering and only half-consumed, which pretty much described my lingering hostility toward Haydn Pike whenever we crossed paths.

"You've still got your guard up," he called over. "I apologized ten times since I messed up. You sure take a grudge to the limits."

How Pike could inflate two halfhearted apologies into ten, I couldn't imagine. His own bad judgment had gotten him fired from the sheriff's department back in May, but that didn't stop him from blaming me. He'd blamed Dan as well for reporting his behavior.

In seconds flat, Haydn Pike was added to the list of people who might arrange a hit on Dan's house. I crossed to him with Luke padding by my side. Flecks of sawdust on Pike's plaid shirt suggested he was working in the lumber trade, in keeping with what I'd heard.

"Nice dog," he said. "Except for the growling."

With a quick signal, I told Luke to sit and settle.

"You put some hurt on the bad guys," Pike said. "That's a new twist."

"What's your interest in being here?" I asked.

"Sirens stir my heart," Pike said. "I pulled a fast turn and followed them in, especially when I heard the address over the scanner."

"You wanted to gloat?" I asked.

"Of course not, Dan is a good guy. He's messed up in the head around you," Pike added. "Keeping your butt out of danger all the time."

"Like the time you cornered and threatened me," I said.

"I acted on false information," Pike said. "I focused on getting justice, and it went wrong. Truth be told, I'm thrilled to be out in the woods instead of risking my life for zero thanks. On that note, I'm grateful to hear you'll be helping Dan put things right with the house he inherited from Aaron Pierce. I appreciate the spirit of it. We all do."

I raised my eyebrows. "By 'we' you mean …?"

"I'm still friends with ninety percent of my former colleagues," he said, indicating the nearby troopers and sheriff's deputies. "Every one of us is tested to the max by police work. We can't get it right every time. Dan is clearly on somebody's shit list."

"We don't discuss his work," I said.

"Not even the time he put handcuffs on your father?" Pike asked.

I hesitated, hating that he'd landed a shock.

"Lord in heaven, he didn't *tell* you about it?" Pike asked.

"We've been dating for seven weeks, not seven years," I said.

"Come on, it started six months ago, but I get what you're saying. Dan was away June, July, and August tackling a secret assignment that nobody's supposed to know about," Pike added, enjoying his noxious version of small talk. "Back to your father, the dearly departed Raymond French. You know Raymond drank for a bit after his wife died. He took a swing at a guy in a bar. Dan responded to the call and applied the handcuffs, but in *that* instance, he treated a fellow officer with respect. Instead of making an arrest, he got your father home safe and sound."

"That's a great story about Dan," I said. "He didn't tell me because he knew it would be upsetting to hear about a sad chapter in Raymond's life. I'm waiting for you to have an ah-ha moment."

"Your giant naïve streak is what you ought to be worried about." With a glance at his watch, Haydn Pike added, "It's late. I'm up at dawn these days. Speaking of which, I've heard you're clearing trails for sleigh rides this winter. I'm real handy with a chainsaw."

"Dan is helping with chores on my farm," I said.

"That only applies if he's *around* to help," Pike said, and then he rolled his eyes at my hard glare. "I'm talking about your chances on the love front. I saw your back-and-forth with that hot chick a minute ago. In comparison, you're a hot mess. I feel for you."

"Have a nice night, Haydn," I said.

With a wince, he said, "If only you meant it."

I watched as he fist-bumped a few firefighters and deputies on his way to his truck, confirming his claim to still be on good terms with his former colleagues. Dan had made no mention of him one way or the other after he'd returned from his stint up north, but the need to direct my attention elsewhere was forewarned by approaching footfalls.

"I'm fairly certain I instructed you to stay put over there," Detective Allen said, reaching out to take Luke's leash from me and handing it to an officer who was standing nearby. "We need to revisit your activities in the house. Where you went, and what you touched."

"Can't it wait?" I asked.

"We'll wrap up soon," Roy said. "This way."

Ushered forward with his firm grip on my arm, I used my remaining brain cells to formulate an excuse for searching Dan's pockets and scraping dried mud from the cleats of his boots. Panic rose in me like a hot helium balloon as I pictured how Dan would react, though his mother had spelled it out clearly enough: *prepare to get your butt kicked.*

Detective Allen leaned around me to open the house's heavy wooden door and antique knocker, and then we crossed the living room past the couch and matching armchairs that were still covered with plastic to spare the leather from daily doses of construction sawdust. The same way that Luke balked and scrambled when confronted by a bath, I shortened my steps to faltering hops and half-turns as we neared the bedroom.

"This is unfair," I said. "I want a lawyer."

"In you go," Roy said.

I was propelled through the doorway, where the fish tank transfixed me for a second, with its gentle, bubbling noise and my photo of a coral reef adding a realistic blue backdrop. Together, Dan and I had picked out an array of bright fish that provided a resting spot for our gazes as we lay in bed in the dark of night, caressing each other until weariness tugged at our eyes. I always let Dan fall asleep first, pleased to see that my influence had delivered a means of restoring peace to his life.

"Sonny?" Dan said.

I focused on him standing there in the denim shirt that I'd bought for him, looking concerned by my distracted stare.

"You're here?" I managed. "How are you here?"

"How can you not be injured?" Dan asked, checking my face and arms for signs of damage. "Those guys were pros."

"I made it out," I said. "I'm ok."

"They didn't hurt you?" Dan asked, unzipping my jacket and tossing it aside. "Why are you wearing a fishing vest?"

"Why are you lurking in your bedroom?" I asked.

"My whereabouts are need-to-know for the short term," he said. "But I had to assess the scene, and I wanted to see you."

I dove forward, elated to have his arms around me and his assurances in my ear. He kissed away my confusion and trauma, allowing me to think of nothing else for a stretch of heartbeats, and then he searched my face as if he still didn't believe I'd come out of the ordeal alive. I gripped his shirt and tugged until his lips returned to mine, but it was a complex moment. I had worries and burdens to share, and he sensed it.

"Sonny," Dan whispered. "Why did you re-enter the house?"

"I'll fill you in when we get to my place."

"That's not possible," Dan said. "You'll need to stay in a safe spot with my parents for a few days. I know it'll be tough—"

"Where will you be?" I asked.

"Up north, possibly," he said.

"No way," I said. "You are *not* going undercover again."

"Not as deep as before," Dan said. "I'll be with a team."

"Including Antoine?" I asked.

"No," Dan said. "We haven't been in touch in months."

"He was here," I whispered. "Tonight."

Dan gaped. "He was one of the three?"

"No, he came in after they left, and I caught a woman petting Luke in the yard," I said, handing him my phone.

Dan turned away, softly cursing as he scrolled through the photos that showed the woman's gaze flaring with hostility.

"What did she say?" Dan prompted.

"She made a veiled hint that you know her," I said.

"Typical Nicole," he muttered.

"Clearly, you do know her," I said. "Who is she?"

"Antoine's girlfriend, more or less," Dan said, handing back my phone. "She plays the field, depending on her goals."

Nicole's parting shot hinted at some kind of involvement with Dan up north, but just then I needed to focus on recapping the night, starting with my shock when Gerald Leblanc fell out of the van.

Listening attentively, Dan nodded when I conveyed that Gerald's employer, Paul Polk of Polk Realty & Storage, was questioned by Detective Allen outside in the yard, along with another man.

"That was Isaac Munroe," Dan said. "It's not surprising that he came out of concern. He supports the police in a big way."

As I described my conversation with Haydn Pike, Dan's tight expression took on a familiar, protective edge.

"I know where your thoughts are headed," I said. "I've proven that I can handle myself. Plus, I promised Sue and Kate that I would help at the Corner Pocket while they're away."

"Sonny," Dan said. "You made yourself a target tonight."

"The store is a safe spot," I said. "I can sleep there if necessary."

Just then, a man in dark fatigues and loaded down with gear signaled that he needed a word with Dan. Listening to their hushed conversation with rapt attention, I learned that Liam was part of a two-man bodyguard team devoted to Dan's safety until further notice. The van had been found wiped clean, without Gerald's body inside, but the contents of Dan's fake safe were in the cargo area. In short order, the burglars had figured out that the flash drive they'd stolen was a tracker.

"Damn it," Dan seethed.

"Get in gear," Liam said. "Two minutes."

My heart threatened to implode. Ever since Dan had stepped into my life, I'd been plagued by nightmares where he was wrenched from my arms and sucked back into high-stakes undercover work. There had to be a path where he stepped aside and let others handle the burden.

"Uh-oh, I'm about to throw up," I said.

With a pointed glare, I conveyed that we needed a private word. Dan caught on and thankfully didn't indulge his usual need for details upfront. Once the bathroom door was closed, he looked on with concern as I made a few heaving sounds to add a note of realism.

"Antoine opened the safe in here," I whispered, hitting the flush lever to mask a recap of my back-and-forth with Antoine earlier that night. "I can't believe you took my father's files."

"To keep you out of harm's way," Dan said. "Mimic being sick again. I need to check the safe to see if Antoine left a note."

"That's my cue to butt in," Detective Allen said, opening the door with a pleased smile. "I knew it would pay off to put you together."

Roy's smile died as Liam stepped in with a colleague named Bart, who was Liam's twin in terms of size and tactical gear. With the news that they needed to be present to assess the safe, they maneuvered their broad shoulders, ballistic vests, handcuffs, sidearms, and tactical gear past us in the cramped bathroom, creaking and clacking and thumping and rustling and sniffing until they settled to rest with their thumbs looped on their belts. Stealth was absolutely out of their wheelhouse.

"Hang on, let's think this through," Liam said. "Nothing personal, Detective Allen, but local police efforts can complicate matters more than help. Maybe it's best if you step out."

"The hell I will," Roy said. "Clearly, Dan's covert gig went south up north. You know what I mean. Now it's landed on my turf."

"All right, restricted access," Liam said. "Just the five of us."

"Sonny shouldn't be here," Dan said.

"I already saw the contents of the safe," I pointed out. "I can provide details, if any questions or concerns arise."

"Makes sense," Liam said. "Let's get to it."

For Dan to unlatch the towel warmer cover, we needed to reassemble ourselves again. Bart, the colleague, had to stand in the tub.

Dan opened the safe and studied the contents.

"Most of what I'd tucked away is here," he said. "My phone and wallet from up north. All Antoine took were some folders that relate to the death of Sonny's father, Raymond French."

"Did you tell Antoine about this safe?" Roy asked.

"No, but—" Dan closed his eyes, looking pained. "At one point he showed me the blueprints for a bathroom safe."

"So, however long ago, Antoine planted the idea for this hidey-hole in your mind," Roy marveled. "You took the bait."

"Thanks for being kind about it," Dan muttered.

Roy massaged his chin and nodded in understanding.

"So, you put a phony safe in your living room," he said. "In the open, easy to find, with the same combination as this safe. When Sonny hollered the combination and it worked on the fake safe, the perpetrators figured they'd landed some kind of big prize. Antoine knew better. He came in after the coast was clear and opened the safe in here."

"Why didn't he help Dan's mother?" I asked.

"Anything he might have tried got nixed when you showed up," Dan said. "I think it was Antoine who cut the power to get your attention and give you an advantage. If so, it worked."

"Is there a third safe?" Detective Allen asked. "Because I'm not grasping what they were after. It had to be something big."

"There's nothing that would warrant a strike along these lines," Dan insisted. "I left the covert gig with the shirt on my back. This phone from up north is dead. I took out the sim card."

"We can conjecture all day," Roy said. "We need facts and answers. I want Antoine in front of me. Are we clear?"

"Out of the question," Liam said.

"This is a crime scene," Roy said. "Make it happen."

"You need to trust the track record," Dan cut in. "Deep agents like Antoine have leeway because they get results. To be honest, he's our best bet for unearthing what sparked tonight's raid."

"If so, you don't need to be involved," I said.

"I can't sit it out," Dan said softly. "The more we delve into this, the more it's clear that Sonny needs protection."

"You have a hundred grand tucked away?" Liam asked. "It's Sonny's choice." Seeing me nod, he added, "Dearly Beloved, we are gathered here to witness these two agreeing to the reality at hand. Trooper Bolton, do you hereby commit to the job a hundred percent?"

"All right, I get it," Dan grumbled.

"Boom," Liam said. "Done."

"I want daily updates," Roy said on his way out.

"Of course," Liam promised. "Yes, Sir."

Once the detective's back was turned, Liam's roll of eyes said that Roy would be getting zero updates in the days to come.

"Say goodbye, Juvénile." Liam clapped Dan on the back as he lumbered out in his heavy gear. "We have work to do."

"Did he call you a juvenile?" I asked.

"The border team was fond of nicknames," Dan said tiredly. "When I first landed in front of Antoine, he decided I wasn't edgy enough to pull off a deep role. I worked in a bar. Eyes and ears."

I started to ask about Nicole, and then I remembered our pact. I had a past. Dan had a past. All that mattered was the present.

"This is awful," I said. "We can't catch a break."

"The bad guys made mistakes," Dan said. "They'll have to dodge and weave their way north. We'll catch them."

"Then why make your parents leave town?" I asked.

"That's about what will happen once the crime scene tape is taken off," Dan said. "Mom has been smothering me ever since I got back in August. On top of the daily meal drops and cleaning, she'll be here rifling through my pockets, trying to figure things out."

I shook my head. "Parents, huh?"

Dan smoothed his thumb over my lower lip and brushed his fingers across my cheek while I searched his brown eyes and rested my hand over his steady heartbeats. We'd been through multiple traumas together in a short span of months, so there was a constant need to convince ourselves that we'd made it out of the dark woods alive and well.

"Who will feed your fish?" I asked.

"My colleagues will handle it," he said.

"We were supposed to see fish in the wild," I said. "Tropical paradise. Walks on a beach, and sinking our feet into the sand."

"It will happen," Dan said. "Keep the faith."

As always, Dan sent his lips into action to seal the deal, taking me on a ride that went nowhere in space, but everywhere below skin level, and then he switched gears and put a flip phone into my palm.

"This is a specialized helpline for emergency use," Dan said. "If your life is under threat, press the call button. It will sound as if you've reached a store. To verify the threat level, say, 'I'm sorry, I meant to call my doctor's office.' Hang up and shelter in place."

Nodding, I said, "Doctor's office. Shelter in place. Got it."

"As an added element," Dan said. "If you have intel to share—"

"So, it's not a regular phone," I said.

"Sonny, please focus."

"Sorry," I said. "Go ahead."

"If you have intel to share, you should say 'I'm coming in to pick up my wet-dry vacuum.' Then name a time."

"Wet-dry vacuum," I said. "Name a time. Got it."

"Wait two hours, and then go to the store," Dan said.

I paused. "What store?"

"They'll choose a real store," Dan said. "A public place."

"Less iffy than a dark alley?" I asked.

"Exactly. Please don't need to use the phone."

"Please come back to me, safe and sound," I said.

"Sonny, I won't let you land in the crosshairs because of my job," Dan said. "I will shut it down where it started. Up north."

We crushed together, kissing and hugging, setting our passion aflame, and it never took long. Even with clothes between us, I felt all the chemical elements that never failed to consume us for delicious, mindless hours in our bedrooms and occasional cabins, anywhere we could make the world go away. A few times under a sky of stars. Now it was winter, with snow showers in the forecast and the shortest, darkest day of the year ahead.

I steeled myself to get through it. Somehow.

4

I know when I've pushed a man's patience too far. The brooding and lack of eye contact. Pretending I didn't exist. That night, my go-to methods for smoothing a lapse of judgment fell short. Apologies. Promises to never let him down again. All I got in return was a chilly glance that said, "Who do you think you're dealing with? Don't insult my intelligence."

"I forgave you when you chewed up my camera strap," I pointed out.

Silence. More brooding.

"Yes, I should have brought you in to bond with Dan," I told Luke as I neared my driveway on the lightless wooded road. "Maybe it wouldn't have slipped my mind if you hadn't let Nicole, a stranger with an iffy vibe, pet you. She implied things about Dan and left her noxious perfume on your fur. A classic, passive-aggressive move."

An escort car had been provided to ensure that I didn't fall asleep at the wheel or come to bodily harm once I'd been cleared to leave the crime scene. Through the deep forests and rustic environs of Gracious, Maine, the deputy maintained a uniform distance from my bumper until I pulled into my driveway, stepped out, and crossed to my mailbox.

With a wave, he surged away to get on with his life.

For months, the family who lived across the road had kept my spirits afloat. Now, Joan and her teens were away in South Carolina for the week after Joan's husband had begged her to reconsider their impending divorce.

He'd quit his seafaring job as a merchant mariner and now worked in a shipping yard. A landlocked job was an improvement, but Joan was unlikely to buckle since her husband's affairs had sparked the split.

My mailbox contained the first oil bill of the winter season and a package of cards that I'd ordered under the giddy influence of a high note. The front featured my photo of a patch of frost shaped like a palm tree: a wry choice for my holiday cards. Amidst the bills was a postcard from my best friend, Arlene, who was midway through a bucket-list trip to China. In my car, I paused to study her cheering note and the photo of a temple perched amidst misty, forested land. When it came to arranging surprises, Arlene's husband could be counted on to not spring a murdered hunter, armed burglars, and undercover agents into her path.

The tires rumbled over loose gravel as I drove onward under a belt of sheltering, sixty-foot pines, and then my headlights led the way toward the house and barn at the top of the hill. On my right, the long paths of the strawberry field were silvered by moonlight, curving westward around the slope to the edge of an orchard of apple, plum, nectarine, and pear trees. On my left, past a rail fence and fieldstone wall that bordered the driveway, my sheep were nibbling unmeasurable stubs of grass. Even the slightest hint of chlorophyll in the stems temped them into action.

Dodge, my Belgian draft horse, bellowed a whinny as I drove past him under the stars. On massive, thudding hooves, he flanked my progress up the hill on the other side of the fence, and then he pawed the ground as I parked and let Luke out to explore his favorite spots, especially near the barn that formed a black silhouette against the night sky, slightly askew here and there along the roofline. Built of thick, rough-hewn timber that spoke of ancient hardwood trees that were more and more rare, the barn was full of strange air currents as warmth from the hay loft mixed with the stalls on the first floor. I stared toward the dark doorway where I'd collided with an assailant on a similarly jarring night. No weapons were involved that time. His visit had to do with a human skeleton hand.

Dodge nudged me with his soft muzzle as I arrived at the fence to pat his warm neck, and my sheep drifted toward me on dainty hooves that whispered against the frozen ground. In the crystalline stillness of the November night, I could hear the chuckling, rippling current of the stream that flickered in and out of view at the bottom of the hill before it disappeared into the forest straight ahead and on my right.

Faintly gleaming on the forest's edge was a white cross that marked the final resting place of Bubbah, my father's old ram, who'd grown frail with shocking speed. It took two visits from the veterinarian to convince me the moment of parting had come. Now, especially after finding a murdered stranger, I recalled my father's words about loss.

Midnight is a lonely hour, Raymond wrote in one of his journals. *Under the moon, I knelt by the stream and marveled at the frogs and fireflies tucked away underground. Frozen in the months to come, just shy of death, but come spring they'll be stirred by the warming sun and longer days. Why can't it be like that for us? Why does our end have to be permanent?*

Now it was me feeling restless under the moon.

Nine months ago, I'd been loosely engaged to a dentist, working as a photographer for a Boston design firm, and believed that my father was Donald Littlefield III, an insufferable tyrant who'd died when I was ten. Then, in the wake of a blizzard in February, a lawyer dropped the news that I'd inherited a thirty-acre strawberry farm in the town of Gracious, Maine from a stranger named Raymond French, whose rugged vibe and commitment to law enforcement stood in stark contrast to my mother's upper-crust origins in Newton, Massachusetts. The details of their secret tryst were veiled in mystery, but I'd narrowed the circumstances to a rebellious period during my mother's college years. I cast a dark glance toward Paris, France, where she was on a shopping spree, thriving as a pillar of taste and decorum, even after her secret had been outed.

Having her occupied in a different time zone spared me from a fresh round of "I told you so" lectures on how my life would turn to ruin if I insisted on living in rural Maine. I was an expert on the new doorways that shock could open in a person's mind, starting with the moment I'd seen Raymond's photograph for the first time. Who was the man whose blue eyes and wavy hair were nearly identical to my own?

For one thing, my father had left a map of cold case crimes that I'd vowed to piece together until they were solved. I fetched it from my car, along with the cookies and milk that had turned to ice. I left the milk on the ground for the wild cats, and then I squinted as headlights stabbed toward me from the road. Once the minivan halted, the armed, serious-looking driver stepped out and opened the door for Dan's father. Dressed in khakis and a cable knit sweater, Norris pulled me into a hug.

"Bless you for saving June," he said of his wife of thirty years. "Who knew that feeding fish would lead to a nightmare?"

"How is she coping?" I asked.

"She's asleep in the car," Norris said. "Dan is sending us to whatever location he's decided is best. You're welcome to join us."

"I'm working at the Corner Pocket, and I want to tackle the cleaning in Aaron's house," I said. "I forgot to get the key from Dan."

"Here's mine," Norris said, slipping it from his keyring. "Without Dan acting as referee, you'll need to be patient with Aaron's father. Kevin's job as a probation officer has added to his tough-guy spirit over time. Don't take it personally. He's still bogged down with grief."

"I've met Kevin," I said. "We'll get along fine."

Over a year and a half had gone by since Dan's friend, Aaron Pierce, had taken his own life after a tough divorce put his life in a tailspin. The shock of it drove Dan into an undercover stint up north, leaving Aaron's house to sit in silence, but now Dan was facing the need to move on.

"I'll get started on the cleanup tomorrow," I said. "I'm working at the store in the morning, but my afternoons are free."

As I hugged Norris in parting, I hesitated, seeing a man waving to me from the near darkness of my porch. Leaning forward into the moonlight, Antoine held a finger to his lips, directing me not to disclose his presence, and then he motioned for me to come to the house.

"Umm ..."

"Something else?" Norris asked.

"No, I was just ... it's been a long night," I said.

Once Norris returned to the minivan, where June was wrapped in a comforter and fast asleep, their hired driver reversed the vehicle downhill to the lightless, wooded road. All the while, Luke sat nearby with his eyes shining in eager anticipation of playing fetch.

"Hello," I said. "There's a stranger on the porch."

Luke picked up his lobster toy and flipped it towards me.

I sighed. "At least I know where I stand."

Not seeing Antoine on the porch, I approached my house with a flutter of nerves and cautious, sideways steps so I was poised to run if he turned out to be a threat. The old stairs creaked underfoot, and then I scanned the darkness as I continued toward the kitchen door.

"What are you doing?" Antoine asked behind me.

"*Shit.*" I sagged and gripped my chest. "What is the matter with you, sneaking up on a person in the dark of night?"

"It is my job." Turning to Luke's adoring gaze, Antoine said, "That is a nice lobster toy. Give it here. You are a gem."

"Yes, do play with my dog while I finish having a heart attack," I said.

"Allow me," Antoine said. "You have had a long night."

Nimble and courteous, he opened the door, indicating that I should precede him inside, then he flipped on the light.

Squinting, I made my way toward the kitchen table in the center of the room with my hand pawing at the brightness as if it was a solid substance that could be dispelled like cobwebs or filmy gauze.

I stopped in my tracks and turned.

"How did you open the door?" I asked.

"I found your spare keys," Antoine said.

"They were *inside* the house," I said. "In a drawer."

"Hmm." Antoine frowned. "That's puzzling."

"Plus, where did you park?" I asked. "There's no car out front."

"You are burning a lot of oil, which puts money in the wrong pockets," he said, indicating the baseboards that were ticking as they warmed the kitchen and living room. "Crisp air is healthier."

"I'm exhausted," I said. "What are you doing here?"

"I am building a picture of you."

All the while we talked, Antoine fell into constant motion, studying the room with his thumbs looped on the front pockets of his threadbare jeans, which cupped his butt. His dark button-up shirt was tight as well, as if to make for fast escapes since folds would invite snags. His sun-streaked curls were pulled into a loose ponytail that ended at the nape of his neck, an unruly counterpoint to his shrewd gaze and air of intense thought. I wanted to photograph him in that moment, to capture his aura of contained intrigue, but I knew better than to even ask.

Luke wagged his tail with an eager gaze, thinking a biscuit was in order for his superb behavior. With a roll of eyes, I tossed him two.

"This color scheme is noteworthy," Antoine said, motioning toward the sherbert-orange kitchen walls posed next to the Caribbean blue color beaming from the living room. "Not your taste, surely?"

"No," I said. "It's thanks to one of my cousins here in Maine, a misguided effort to cheer up my biological father during a bad stretch. Charlotte and her brother are difficult. They hate me because they'd hoped to inherit the farm, but they're family. I try to be tolerant."

"You are a treasure, Berrichon," Antoine said.

I frowned. "Is that a kind of cheese?"

"It's a breed of sheep," he said. "A proper shepherdess would know."

"One of Dan's bodyguards called him Juvénile," I said. "There was a brother vibe to it. Dan didn't seem to mind."

"I'm glad you see it that way," Antoine said. "Nicknames can be a stress reliever within a team, a sign of a person's hidden worth."

"Lucky me," I said. "I'm a sheep."

"No, Berrichon is lovely and melodic," Antoine insisted. "Plus, you are the opposite of a sheep who follows the trodden path."

"An ironic nickname," I said. "I get it."

Antoine plucked my father's favorite cap from a shelf. Over time, Raymond had hooked his best hand-made fishing flies on the browband, creating a work of art that he'd worn during his forays to streams and rivers. I carefully returned his cap to the shelf.

"Your father made those flies?" Antoine asked.

"Yes," I said. "But it wasn't about catching fish."

With a pensive frown, I explained what I'd learned from reading my father's journals: with fanciful names like Painted Lady, Blue Winged Olive, and Wooly Worm, each of his creations had a different feel when he'd cast his line into space and the feathered hook touched the surface of the river. It was a dance, an art form, a conversation with water. The icy current lapping against his waders. The rolling gurgle of the rapids. The soft purr of the reel. The feel of the rod moving through space again and again. A rhythm that calmed my father, and centered him. I likened it to how I felt when I practiced yoga and tai chi. Without meeting him, or any direct experience with fishing, our passions connected us.

When I turned, Antoine was next to me, standing perfectly still with his arms folded, watching me with keen attention.

"You had nothing to do with tonight's raid," he murmured.

"My description of fishing convinced you?" I asked.

"Ninety percent," he said. "Tell me more."

I closed my eyes. He'd dropped in without warning to gain the upper hand. As of that moment, his advantage ended.

"Does Nicole have a nickname?" I asked.

Antoine heaved a sigh. "Juvénile knows better than to talk shop and drop names with civilians. No wonder he became a target."

"Most of Dan's undercover stint is locked down," I said. "He described Nicole as your girlfriend 'more or less.' She strays and plays the field depending on her goals. Doesn't that bother you?"

Chewing gum as he paced, Antoine plucked a letter opener from the bookshelf and slowly rotated it in his right hand, immersed in thought as he pondered how to respond to my comment.

"Now and then you will see a hawk in the sky with a tether dangling from its ankle," he said. "Born wild, then held captive, then escaped. Fierce and beautiful. A creature of the wind and the sky, but broken, deep down. Neither wild nor tamed."

"That's Nicole?" I asked.

"It is a captivating puzzle for men," Antoine said.

I braced myself, and then asked, "Including Dan?"

"Jealousy is a dangerous foe," he said. "Never let it take hold."

Antoine strolled past the windows that faced the driveway, paused to study the plaid couch that was more comfortable than it looked, and then continued to the wood stove that I never used, afraid I would stack the logs wrong and cause a fire. Using his right arm as a horizontal perch for his left elbow, he rested his chin on his thumb and forefinger, as he might do in a museum, and studied the trophy buck on the wall.

"I know you and Dan met in May," Antoine said. "He helped you with a personal matter, though you had no history together."

"We hit it off," I said. "There were sparks."

"Your personal matter was resolved?" he asked.

I paused, striving to avoid getting bogged down with the particulars of the week-long experience of being kidnapped, shot at, and nearly condemned to join other victims in a shallow grave.

"Yes," I said. "It was resolved."

"Dan left to finish the border assignment," Antoine said. "No contact for months. You reconnected when he got home?"

"There was a delay while Dan dialed down from the undercover work," I said. "He had insomnia, and an ex was in town. You probably know he was briefly married. Anyway, it was a shock to know that he'd delayed getting in touch, but … will you *please* stop that," I said of Antoine's winces as I told the story. "You're as transparent as Dan."

"Mon Dieu, let's hope not," Antoine said.

Rolling one hand, I said, "Go ahead, express your thoughts."

"Perhaps the delay signaled he was weighing the two paths," Antoine said. "How could he re-engage with you, if …?"

"Nicole had a hold on his heart? Is that what you're saying? You're wrong. He would have told me about it," I said, snatching a stick of gum from the package Antoine had left on the table and madly chewing the minty wad as I paced. "Our bond is deep. It's special."

"I'm sure it is," Antoine soothed.

"Nicole got in my face for a reason tonight—"

I gulped as Antoine spun me to face him, his eyes ablaze with attention. "You told me a woman wasn't present," he said.

I explained the gist of my encounter with Nicole, how I'd found her petting my dog, and what little she'd said to me.

"I assumed you'd come as a team," I said.

"No," he said. "We work apart more than not."

With a frown, Antoine pondered the situation out loud.

"The same whispers that brought me here could have reached Nicole. Perhaps she arrived late, when the scene was already under control. It's not entirely out of bounds for her to delay reaching out. Deep stealth is a factor in our work from time to time."

"Or, maybe she's behind the strike tonight," I said.

"That notion is biased, an example of jealousy at work," Antoine said tiredly. "I learned a long time ago that true love is a myth, a fantasy that can lead to ruin, but if you remain a believer, Dan will come back to you. Nicole will get bored. He'll need someone to lick his wounds."

"I'm not licking anything if he cheats on me," I said. "But you've got it wrong. He was playing a role up north. A false front."

"You love him?" Antoine asked. "You're true to him?"

"Definitely," I agreed. "Like I said—"

I gulped, pulled forward into a heated, dreamy kiss that had an addling effect, intense and soulful, and then all of a sudden Antoine exchanged our wads of gum with his tongue. I gathered my wits, shoved him away with both hands and glared at him with outrage.

"That was *totally* inappropriate," I said.

"From my side," he said, "you enjoyed it for a count of five."

"I'm in shock," I said. "You took advantage."

"This is what we face in the dark alleys of the world," Antoine said crossly. "I was demonstrating how a smooth operator like Nicole can catch a person off guard. If she gets her way with Dan, you'll need to be strong. I'm not saying it will happen. I will urge Nicole to exercise restraint if I get the chance, but there is no room for naiveté."

Stung by his lecture, I folded my arms and pushed down the insecurity that had dogged me for most of my life. The sense that I wouldn't win a tug-of-war over a man's heart. I wasn't alluring enough. Loveable enough. I blamed Donald Littlefield, who'd made a pact with my mother to pretend that I was a product of his DNA, but over time he'd grown more and more intolerant. He couldn't stand the sight of me, the blue eyes and curly hair that outed me as the daughter of another man.

"Berrichon," Antoine said. "You tangled with an armed crew and sent them packing. Where is the fierce warrior I saw tonight?"

"Right here," I said. "You promised to return the folders you took from Dan's safe. I'll be needing them in the days to come."

"They're on the shelf," Antoine said.

"Excellent," I said. "Thank you."

Tucking the folders into a safe spot, I abruptly turned.

"Regarding tonight, spillover from up north is only one angle to look into," I said. "Someone killed my father during a blizzard and made it look like an accident. That's why Dan was looking into these cases. My gut says tonight's raid has to do with my father's murder."

Antoine paused with a thoughtful gaze.

"It did strike me that the crew of three was out of the norm in terms of what we dealt with on our task force," he said. "Wrong accent. Different gear. You might be right, but your father's death is a matter for the local police. I need to work with Dan and his team."

"If necessary, I'll tackle both angles on my own." With a flourish, I pulled the bag of business cards and receipts from my pocket. "You asked why I returned to the house after the burglars left. I collected these from the clothes Dan wore up north."

"Show some sense," Antoine chided, snatching the bag away. "These should be destroyed, not waved around."

"I'm open to training," I said. "I want to help."

Antoine pondered the situation with a pensive frown, chewing the wad of gum he'd taken from my mouth, which meant I was now chewing *his* wad of gum. I cupped my hand and spit it out.

"Berrichon," he said. "That's not nice."

"There's no flavor in it anymore," I said.

"You are a bad liar," Antoine said, looking conflicted as he continued evaluating my plea. With a groan, he said, "My parents and sister were murdered long ago, so I understand your plight. I will put my ear to the ground on your behalf if I get the chance, but my first priority is learning who planted the micro detonator tonight."

I hesitated. "The micro *what?*"

"In Dan's basement, I found scored wires," Antoine said. "Along with a remote trigger designed to set them aflame at some point."

"A part of the intent for the break-in was to *kill* Dan?" I asked.

"Without a doubt," Antoine said gravely.

I stared, suddenly grasping why multiple fire departments had responded to the scene. I'd been right to wonder about it.

"Hopefully you see why it's not safe to blunder around?" Antoine said. "At some point, your beau sparked tonight's raid. Here? Up north? While we're in this delicate early phase, drop your inquiries. Asking the wrong questions could drive guilty parties underground. Your chances of getting justice for your father would be all the more remote."

"I hear what you're saying. I'll endeavor to be careful but …" I paused and winced. "It's come to light that things can spiral out of control despite my best efforts to stay in my own lane. Dan jokingly calls it the Sonny effect. Well, I guess it's not a joke to him."

"One moment, let's check the record." After a search on his phone, Antoine began pacing with his hand clapped to his forehead. "Your personal problem in May was finding a skeleton hand? *Merde.* Lies, treachery, death in the woods. Et ce n'est pas tout."

"If you're saying it's a lot to process," I said. "I get it."

"In September it began again," Antoine said, reading whatever record he'd found online. "Murder, mayhem …"

"It all got sorted out," I said. "Here I am, safe and sound."

Tucking his phone away, Antoine looked at me anew.

"Indeed, here you are, not just unscathed, but as bright as a penny," he said. "A miracle? Perhaps, but also something else."

"I'm highly observant," I said. "Mostly, and I have other skills."

"In alchemy, what is this called?" Antoine murmured with narrowed eyes, lost in his train of thought. "A synergist is able to change base materials into gold. Volatile and malleable. Very rare."

"By 'malleable' I hope you don't mean—"

"Forgive my wording." Antoine grasped my shoulders and settled my worries with his calm gaze. "I was delving into the way people think. They crave attention. You're empathetic beyond the norm, which could attract the wrong sort. It's good to know this element. I'll keep my eye on it. First thing, I'll make sure the trouble isn't spillover from the task force. If the trail runs cold, we'll try a different approach."

"You and Dan, you mean," I said. "I'm out in the cold."

"I see it's a part of your nature to assume the worst," he said softly. "It's a trait that I happen to share. I apologize for my wrong assumptions coming in. For testing you after a jarring experience."

"I get the need for it," I said. "The stakes are high."

"Is there anything else to keep in mind?" Antoine asked.

"No more kissing me without warning," I said.

"Bon. What kind of warning do you prefer?"

"Kissing is off the table," I said. "I'm not cut out to cheat."

"If only you hadn't exchanged our wads of gum," Antoine said, adding a wry smile when I inhaled to protest. "We share a sense of humor as well, non? What else has you looking troubled?"

"The holidays are around the bend," I said. "A happy time, but people can get overcommitted and stressed. Myself, for example. Be careful when you ask around. That's all I'm saying."

"Oui, bien sûr," he said. "I will set things in motion."

I hesitated. "What kind of things?"

"The usual steps that fit a highly-charged matter of this sort," Antoine said, opening the kitchen door and pausing with the view of stars visible and cold air rushing in. "A bit of protection, since armed men are involved. Expect the first ghost at noon."

I paused. "What does that mean?"

"Au revoir, chérie," Antoine said. "Sleep well."

I frowned once the door was closed, dimly aware that during every moment of our exchange, I'd failed to maintain the power seat. I lunged forward and grappled with the knob, but with a deft move, Antoine had flipped the deadbolt. At last, I spun the lock and surged out onto the frosty, moonlit porch. Aside from the soft shapes of the sheep on the other side of the fence rails, and Dodge swishing his tail at imaginary flies, the winter night was silent and still. I hesitated, wondering if a whisper of leaves was Antoine heading for a vehicle he'd stowed along the road, but it was a gust of wind coming straight out of Canada.

A north wind. I might have guessed.

5

I groaned as my alarm clock woke me out of a dead sleep.

Face down, in the sprawled position I'd landed in after testing my endurance with online searches last night, I scanned my bedroom in the darkness, absorbing all the sweet touches, like the pink walls and the vanity with carved roses and hearts around the mirror. I'd found Raymond's journal entry describing how he'd bumped into my mother and me in a coastal town when I was ten. He'd taken one look at my face and grasped with a bolt of wonder that I was his daughter. Once the shock wore off, Raymond and his wife, Ella, had decorated the room with frilly pillows, toy horses, and nature books on the hope that I could visit "once the dust settled." Thanks to my mother's refusal to allow him a space in my life, I'd never seen the view from the window until last February.

Insomnia had taken hold after I'd visited the Polk Realty & Storage website. In one photo, Gerald Leblanc and his coworker, Sal, wore inviting grins as they posed in front of a small moving truck with the caption: *If your dreams come true, we'll get you where you're going. If your dreams go bust, we'll set you up nice and neat in one of the storage bays!*

As I showered and dressed, adding a fleece vest that I wouldn't need as the day warmed, I fell into gloom, knowing the hardworking team had been split up for reasons that wouldn't add up, no matter how many of the pieces of the crime were put together by the police.

With Luke in the car and my father's folders tucked into my bag, I stifled yawns as I navigated the winter dawn at 6:45 a.m.

Thanks to my father's journals, I drove through the village with some knowledge of the settlers who'd come to the region in search of farmland in the 1800s — hardy, enterprising families who'd endured Maine's winters by balancing stores of vegetables with staples like salt pork, sausage, and cheese. Local lore had touted the place as a haven of virtue, free of capital crimes. Of course, that notion had been wrong.

Downtown Gracious was marked by a grassy common, with four roads branching off in all directions. Some of the homes that had been built in the 1800s still stood along the connecting roads, with flags out front and flower boxes that were now decorated with pine boughs and twinkling lights. Here and there were weathered outbuildings that had been updated to hold anything from boats to seasonal antique shops.

Perched around the common were a brick post office, a firehouse, a real estate office, and a B&B with a white picket fence and gate. My destination was the Corner Pocket, a former pool hall that Sue Black and Kate McKenna had painted canary yellow and converted into a convenience store with a small gas pump out front. Vintage photographs of pool-playing locals lined the walls that framed gleaming oak aisles of gourmet items, necessities, and baked goods. In one corner, tables offered a place to read and sip coffee or tea, with a constant cloud of enticing aromas in the air, from fresh apple pie to brownies and hot chocolate.

I slowed my car and groaned, seeing that Mr. and Mrs. Brooks, my co-workers for the week, had arrived a while ago: a mantle of frost was already glistening on the front hood of their car. I slipped into the adjacent parking space, shouldered my bag, and led Luke to a strip of grass for a last pee before he was relegated to the office out back.

A tiny bell jingled above me as I opened the door.

"You're *late*," Mrs. Brooks said from the front counter. "And I see you have that creature with you again. He's not a service animal."

"My usual pet sitters are away," I said for the third morning in a row. "Sue and Kate gave me permission to bring Luke."

In sneakers that squeaked on the polished floor, she marched toward me in her pink sweater and came to a stop under my nose.

"You of all people should know how busy the store gets after a crime," she said. "Thomas and I came early. We're seniors, you realize."

As he stacked fresh bread on a shelf, her husband, Thomas, cast me a look of sympathy. The previous day, he'd confided what I already knew: being put in charge had gone to his wife's head.

"Out with it." She snapped her fingers. "What am I to tell folks?"

Per the dictates of the store's ethically minded owners, customers were told only a crisp summary of local crimes. Scurrilous details were forbidden, lest local gossips, like my cousins, ruin reputations and further traumatize innocent victims with false narratives.

"It was a burglary," I said. "June Bolton and I had a bit of a fright, but we scared the bad guys into fleeing. The culprits were careless and left evidence. Anyone with information should step forward. The police are working nonstop to get answers."

"Anything else?" Mrs. Brooks prompted.

"Happy holidays to all," I said.

"Our first delivery of baked goods has arrived," Mrs. Brooks said of the wonderful smells in the air, thanks to an arrangement Sue and Kate had with a couple who churned out pies, breads, and stews throughout the day, depending on whatever season was unfolding in the larger world. "Start warming the apple pie, mix the cocoa—"

"I know the drill, Mrs. Brooks," I interrupted.

"Stop dawdling," she said. "Off you go."

Once Luke and I exchanged an eye-roll befitting the moment, I led him forward down the oak aisle where cookies and snacks were neatly stacked. With sleek shelving, tuck-away cubbies, a table that morphed into a cot, and other means of getting the most out of a relatively small space, the office out back was a model of efficiency.

The computer and high-speed internet beckoned to me from the desk. Somewhere in Sue and Kate's search history had to be a contact where I could send the trace evidence from Dan's shoes, though my methods were far from ideal: the sandwich bag of dirt had sprung a leak. I taped the hole and then swept the particles into the office waste bin.

I paused, staring at the gum wrappers in the bin that should have been emptied by the cleaning crew after closing time.

Reaching for the store's warbling landline, I picked up the receiver. "Hello? Er, Corner Pocket. How can I help you?"

"It is me, Berrichon," a man with a sexy French accent said.

I straightened. "Antoine?"

"You found my wrappers," he said. "I am watching you right now."

Turning in place, I stared at the camera aimed my way. "You were *here* last night? How did you breach the security system?"

"Sue and Kate told me the code," he said.

I paused. "You know them?"

"I know a friend of a friend," Antoine said. "All is well."

"What's the latest?" I asked. "Have you learned anything?"

"I have learned that you're holding a mysterious bag of dirt," he said.

"That's, umm, from my strawberry field …"

"I believe we covered this point last night," Antoine said.

I closed my eyes. "Fine, I'll toss the dirt, but there's a serious issue." I took my father's notes from my bag and held them in front of the camera. "The thick folder I saw at Dan's house is missing."

"Oui, a manuscript about local explorers," he said.

I stepped closer, freshly excited. "Raymond was writing a book?"

"No, and it's too delicate to discuss over the phone. Don't drop hints or test theories with friends. I must go. Au revoir."

Click.

"Well, that's just great," I said. "Have a nice day."

Before I'd left home, I'd discovered that Dan had deleted the photos I'd taken of Nicole. It made sense that he would want to protect the identity of a fellow undercover agent, but the news had sparked scenes in my head, like Dan waking up to the surprise of finding Nicole snuggling close to him in a surveillance van. Men could be clueless about certain kinds of women, letting a moment like that slip under the radar. The next thing anyone knew, it would become an accepted routine.

"Alison!" Mrs. Brooks barked from somewhere in the store.

"Right here," I said. "I'm coming."

While Luke plopped onto his bed and focused on gnawing a rawhide chew stick into oblivion, I started assembling trays that would make quick work of refilling the coffee makers in the snack area, and then I followed through on the chores that Sue and Kate had entrusted to a list. A happy couple with extrasensory capabilities, they'd known it would be tough for a mortal like myself to step into their shoes.

By mid-morning, the continuously jingling bell over the door told me it was time to get the microfiber mop ready for making quick sweeps of the floor since last night's dusting of snow spelled the possibility of mud. According to Mrs. Brooks, muddy footprints could not be tolerated in a place of business. With my waves and curls tamed into a ponytail, I mostly kept my head down as I re-stocked shelves and made discrete passes with the mop whenever customer traffic thinned.

Once the mop was stowed in the back office, I paused on my way to the coffee bar, seeing a familiar man signaling to me.

In casual business attire, Kevin Pierce looked to be the most world-weary man in the state of Maine, and no wonder, given the heavy caseload, inadequate resources, and other reasons probation officers were prone to burnout. On top of that stress, he'd weathered the shocking sudden death of his only son, Aaron. Dan had warned me that Kevin might be among the local law enforcement professionals who would take a dim view of my penchant for landing in the wrong place at the wrong time, but Kevin had shown restraint along those lines when we'd met at the Fall Fest a few months ago. His affection for Dan carried a lot of weight.

"What'd the culprits get last night?" he asked.

"I'm not sure," I said. "June and I scared them away."

"Multiple agencies were on scene," Kevin said. "It makes sense with a trooper's house in the crosshairs. No harm done?"

"Dan is confident the burglars will be caught soon," I said.

Kevin nodded. "Norris sent word that you'll be tackling the cleaning and painting in Aaron's house while Dan is caught up with the case. Last year I would have pushed back on outside help, but at this point, I think the situation could use a gentle nudge."

"Dan has been extra busy on the work front," I said carefully.

"All that matters is turning the page," Kevin said. "Back to the house, after Aaron's divorce, he wasn't inclined to tidy up. It's a bit of a mess. You met my wife, Peg? She's still on the fragile side."

"Of course," I said. "I'll keep it in mind."

"It's one of the reasons Aaron left the house to Dan," Kevin confided. "To spare us the hassle that comes with inheriting property. It's painful to know that my son wasn't thinking clearly in some regards. Dan is the one with business sense. Aaron saw that."

"I'm grappling with loss myself," I said.

"Of course you are," Kevin said. "I'm glad to see you thriving."

"Are there items I should set aside?" I asked.

"Yeah, I'll swing by with a list of things that Peg and I will want to find amidst the chaos and keep." Kevin paused, having tuned in on a familiar-looking fiftyish man in a button-up, plaid wool jacket who'd been hovering nearby. "What is it, Sal?"

Hesitating, Sal said, "Sorry to interrupt."

"Out with it," Kevin said. "I'm due at work."

"Have you seen Gerald?" Sal asked. "We were supposed to go bowling last night. He's vanished, and not answering his phone."

"He's been off my radar for a long time," Kevin said, alluding to the murdered man's brushes with the law and time served. "Last I heard, you're both on Paul's payroll at his storage facility."

"This is the thing," Sal said. "Gerald and I are a team."

"If he doesn't show up in a day or two, let me know." Kevin turned to me. "Thank you for helping, Sonny. I'll check in soon."

"I wouldn't want his job," Sal said as he watched Kevin head for the door. "Or his bad luck. I heard you talking about his son. Handsome kid. Aaron was smart and likeable, and just starting out in life. You never know what's going on with folks deep down."

I extended my hand. "I'm Sonny. Nice to meet you."

"Salvatore Hall. I'm not Italian," he confessed. "My parents liked how the name brought to mind an important building, something like that."

"It does sound that way," I said.

"I don't suppose you've seen Gerald," Sal prompted.

"I'm new in town," I said. "So, I never met him."

I looked down and studied my shoes. Without a body to identify, the police were viewing that part of my statement as hearsay, yet to be confirmed. Detective Allen's admonition that I not spill the beans had been forcefully delivered, with growled warnings of possible consequences that included having me deported to the North Pole.

"Gerald and I go way back," Sal confided. "All the way to grade school. Best buds forever, but don't lump me in with the trouble he got into with his cousins. They're into all kinds of things."

When he hesitated, I said, "Such as …?"

"Such as …" With a look that showed he regretted raising the subject, Sal motioned with one hand. "You know, I never heard specifics. They're good guys. *Great* guys. I'm talking out of turn."

"So, Gerald hasn't been in touch for a bit?" I asked.

"Gosh, you really are Raymond's girl, with intense blue eyes," Sal said. "It's awful that you never met him. A darned shame."

"I'm getting to know him through his friends," I said.

"Uh-oh, Paul at five o'clock, Paul at five o'clock." Sal shifted position to use me as a shield as a man in business attire stepped into the store and headed toward the coffee nook. "Help me out, he's my boss," Sal said. "I'm supposed to be manning the desk at his realty office."

"Nobody else can cover for you?" I asked.

"No, it's down to me and Gerald. Paul pays well," Sal added. "Mostly, he's been good to us, but if you do business with him, watch your wallet, if you know what I mean. His smile is a flash of teeth."

"Listen, if you calm down—"

"I wasn't here, all right?" Sal said. "Catch you later."

Far from aiding his effort to hide, his dodging and bobbing had caused his employer to look toward us and frown. Sal doubled down on doing the wrong thing by scurrying away along the bread aisle and diving toward the front door. The bell jingled, which quite possibly made Salvatore Hall the worst escape artist in the state of Maine.

As Thomas joined me, I said, "What's your sense of Paul Polk?"

"He fancies himself the local real estate king," Thomas said. "Always on the lookout for prime property, and he came up with the notion that when folks buy and sell, they need a place to stash their stuff. Next to his realty office, he's got a building of storage bays. Sal and Gerald do all the odd jobs, from helping folks move to manning the desk."

Thomas joined me in watching the fiftyish realtor pour coffee into a paper cup next to a second man in business attire. I'd seen both of them last night talking to Detective Allen outside Dan's house.

"That's Isaac Munroe," Thomas whispered. "Banker, up and coming in local politics. Those two used to pal around and cause trouble in middle school. There's a story of them scaring Sal out in the woods so bad that the poor kid peed his pants."

With their backs to us, unaware that they were being observed as they opened packets of sugar over their cups of coffee, the two men fell into a heated exchange that amounted to speaking to each other out of the sides of their mouths. As Mr. Polk snorted and made an impatient dismissive gesture, Isaac Munroe gripped him by the collar.

"You want to get sued?" Isaac demanded. "Is that it?"

Stepping from behind the register, Mrs. Brooks bore down on them. "I will take a rolled-up newspaper to the two of you if you don't cut it out," she said crossly. "Where are your manners?"

Isaac let go. "We're good. Sports bet gone wrong."

"You spilled coffee," she said. "That'll cost you five dollars each."

"You're a genuine hustler, Mrs. Brooks," Isaac said.

"It takes one to know one," she said. "Thomas, where's the mop?"

"Sadly, I'm due at a showing," Paul Polk said, gingerly stepping over the mess. "I don't want to leave my client hanging."

"We'll catch up later," Isaac tossed at Paul's retreating back, then he darkly muttered when the realtor left without paying, "Slick bastard, gliding along like rules are meant for everyone else."

At any other time, I would pitch in with the clean-up, but I wanted to meet the man who had a beef with Gerald Leblanc's employer. As Isaac secured his coffee with a lid, I stepped up to meet him.

"Excuse me," I said. "I'm helping a friend get a house ready for sale. If you don't mind me asking, is Mr. Polk a good choice for the listing? I'm Sonny Littlefield," I added, shaking his hand.

Fit and attractive, with dark hair and clothes that were drycleaned and sharp, he relished being seen as an authority on a business matter.

"With buyers, Paul will distract clients from honing in on the flaws of a place, from squirrels in the attic to a funny odor in the air, but in selling a house, his tactics might be agreeable." Isaac paused and narrowed his eyes. "It's uploading all at once, why your face is familiar. You're Raymond French's daughter, the house you're inquiring about is the place that Dan Bolton inherited from Aaron Pierce, *and* you were on the scene in the aftermath of the burglary at Dan's house last night."

"I was feeding his fish," I said. "Wrong place at the wrong time."

Isaac's wince said he'd witnessed how I'd been hauled into Dan's house like a perp, asking for a lawyer, and begging for mercy.

"I brushed paths with the burglars," I said quietly. "I'm not supposed to talk about it. Back to your sense of Mr. Polk—"

"You're a pet sitter, that kind of thing?" he asked.

"No," I said. "Dan and I have been dating since September."

He raised his eyebrows. "And …?"

"That's sort of a complete sentence," I said slowly.

"I'm running late, but I will share my opinion on Paul as a seller agent," Isaac said. "He isn't the right fit for Aaron's house, given the sensitive history there. My guess is, you already know that."

"I've never met Mr. Polk, so …"

"Take care, Miss Littlefield," Isaac said. "Have a nice day."

"You, too," I said. "Thanks for your advice."

As he stepped around me, his parting glance hinted that he had a giant "decline" stamp on his desk in the event that anyone of my ilk, a shop girl with a notorious reputation, applied for a loan at his bank.

"That looked uncomfortable," Thomas said as he rejoined me.

"It went a little sideways," I agreed.

"There's a story I need to share," Thomas whispered, signaling that he was delving into the forbidden territory of gossip. "Many months ago, a hunter came upon Gerald and Sal while they were washing up in a stream out in the forest. They were covered head to toe with white powder as if they'd been in a bakery explosion. Their splashing masked the hunter's approach, so he got to listen in for a while."

"The water must have been cold," I said.

"Darned cold," Thomas said. "There they were, stripped down to their skivvies, hollering to each other over the churning water, scared out of their minds about getting an overdose of the drug on their clothes. Something had gone awry. They were terrified."

"What kind of drug was it?" I asked.

Thomas shrugged. "Meth? Heroin? It was unclear. By the time we heard the story here at the store, a whole winter had gone by after snow and rain storms. The police checked for traces along the stream and questioned Sal and Gerald. They said they were camping in the woods for fun, and got careless with the flour in making pancakes."

"That sounds fishy," I said.

"*Alison*," Mrs. Brooks chided behind us.

"Catch you later," Thomas whispered as he melted away.

"We're due a quick break now and then," I said.

"Never mind that." Mrs. Brooks held a can so close to my nose that I couldn't focus on the label. "Anyone with sense would know that creamed corn is *not* two hundred dollars per unit."

I blinked. "What …?"

"You got the labels wrong," she said. "It's causing a panic."

I sighed. "Mrs. Brooks, this is the last straw. I have no idea—" Alerted to a flash of movement behind her, I saw Thomas waving his hands with a look that begged me not to out his error with the label gun. "No idea how I did that," I said tightly.

"You've always got your head in the clouds," she said. "It's close to the end of your shift, but you're staying put until it's fixed."

Handed the label gun, I cast Thomas a dark look as I headed to the front of the store where canned essentials enjoyed a prominent location for people to grab in the coming months when winter snow storms threatened to cut power. Sure enough, all the neatly stacked cans of creamed corn were marked $200 on the lid. The peas were mismarked as well. I adjusted the label gun and started correcting Thomas's mistake.

"I'm sorry," he said, looking abashed as he joined me. "We're in tight quarters here all day. I had a weak moment."

"No worries, it won't take long."

"Before you head out, I wanted to loop back on Mr. Munroe," Thomas said. "He went to college on a soccer scholarship and had a brief stint as a pro. Busted his whatchamacallit tendon and had to quit."

"Why is that important?" I asked.

"Given the soccer legacy, his son goes by the nickname 'Kick.'"

While we talked, I adjusted the label gun to reflect the price for the peas indicated on the sign attached to the shelf.

"His nickname fits his approach in life?" I asked.

"No, he seems a good lad," Thomas said. "Kick aspires to be a private investigator. You might find him useful."

"I'm supposed to be steering clear of crimes for Dan's sake."

"But will the crimes steer clear of you?" Thomas asked dubiously.

"I have a problem," I admitted. "I think it's genetic."

We turned as the bell over the door jingled. Just shy of noon, the sun was beaming through the front windows, casting angled light around the twenty-something man who paused in the doorway. In jeans and a T-shirt that offered zero warmth on a winter day, he smoothed his tousled hair, a move that brought definition to his broad shoulders and arm muscles, all of which tapered down to a magnificently toned waist.

"Is Sonny Littlefield around?" he asked in a husky voice.

My hand reacted, shooting ten labels onto the floor.

"Right here," Thomas said.

"Yes, here I *am*," I purred. "Er … do I know you?"

Prompted forward, he walked toward us in sneakers, and then he loomed there with a charming, puppylike expression that was so at odds with his manly physique, he fell into the category of Nature's personal best when it came to tempting good women into ruin.

"I'm here about the arrangement," he said. "Staying with you."

Pieces of the past twenty-four hours slammed into the void that his unexpected appearance had created in my mind. One of Antoine's cryptic comments involved arranging, "A bit of protection since armed men are in the picture. Expect the first ghost at noon." I'd expected a grizzled former cop with a cigar clenched in his teeth.

"How about it?" the puppy hunk inquired.

"Umm, how about *what*?" I asked.

"The arrangement," he said.

"You specialize in undercover work?" I whispered.

He paused. "You want me to sleep with you?"

"Of course not. *No.*" I closed my eyes and summoned a businesslike tone befitting a job interview, "I meant, are you a police officer?"

"I'm just a guy," he said.

"You don't have protection skills?" I asked.

"Ok, it sounds like we're back to sleeping together."

"*Bodyguard* skills," I said with increasing ire. "Fighting skills."

"Oh," he said. "Brumby and I got into scuffles a time or two. Angry husbands looking to mess him up, that sort of thing."

I paused. "Brumby Jones?"

"Yeah, he's my older brother. I'm Jeremy."

Thomas leaned close and whispered, "Brumby has a brother?"

"Apparently, he does," I said.

Jake "Brumby" Jones was always an arresting figure in his black Stetson, tight jeans, and hand-tooled leather boots. In bright shirts that set off his tan, a result of his thirty-odd years of toughening up under the sun, Brumby was known for his skill in shoeing and trimming horse hooves, and also for his notorious philandering. At the moment, Brumby was away in Vermont giving seminars at a high-end horse barn.

"You have an American accent," I said. "Brumby is from Australia."

"That's thanks to our different moms," Jeremy said. "Most of us are born right here in the United States. After I tracked down Brumby, I got to looking up ancestry stuff online, figuring there were lots of us. So far there's five, and counting."

"Any girls in the family?" Mrs. Brooks asked, having stepped from the front counter to listen to the exchange with folded arms.

"No, my dad was clear about wanting boys. I guess he got his way."

"He traveled the world, did he?" she asked.

"Yup," Jeremy said. "Rodeo circuit. Anyway, I know Brumby has spent a night or two on your couch, Sonny. You'll be aware that he rents out his apartment through an online app. I'm without a roof for a short stretch, so I called your landline. A guy with a funny accent picked up and said you were in need of a house guest. It's perfect timing."

"When was this?" I asked.

"Last night," Jeremy said. "Nine o'clock or so."

I calculated that nine p.m. was *hours* before I'd gotten home from the crime scene. Antoine had wasted no time in heading to my farm after we'd "bumped into" each other in Dan's house.

"What's your job experience?" Mrs. Brooks asked. "Never mind, all we need is a strong helper who'll get down to work instead of dreaming the day away. There's a delivery of dry goods coming in. If you're available and willing, grab an apron. You're hired."

"Jeremy is here for a job with me," I said.

"You snooze, you lose," she said. "Our afternoon clerk called to say she got free tickets for a stay at the casino. I was steamed as heck, thinking we were in a pickle. This kid showing up is an act of God."

Free tickets to the casino out of the blue? All things considered, my gut said it wasn't an act of God. It was an act of Antoine.

"This is great," Jeremy said. "Once we clock out, I'll turn to guarding Sonny. From casting about for my next big move in life, I've landed *two* jobs in one minute. My brothers won't believe it."

As Mrs. Brooks ushered Jeremy down the aisle into her world of strict rules, zero nonsense, and constant motion, I calmed myself by grasping how Jeremy's arrival might amount to an upgrade in my hectic life as well. He could fill in at the store while I addressed any errands that arose, and once he'd proven himself as an asset, he could pitch in at Aaron's house in exchange for the roof I was providing over his head.

"Antoine, you're a genius," I murmured.

"Toss the dirt, Berrichon," Antoine said over the speaker attached to the front camera. "We will meet again soon."

6

My jarring night and hectic morning fell away as I pulled into Aaron Pierce's driveway on a quiet, tree-lined street on the outskirts of the village. The ranch-style house had been vacant for over eighteen months. The lawn had suffered from the sporadic mowing of a landscaping service that had left a patchwork of uneven grass and overgrown shrubs.

With my bag in hand, I led Luke onto the front stoop, sank the key into the lock, and paused for a moment to brace myself for the silence that would greet me on the other side of the door. When I'd accompanied Dan on his visit to drop off painting supplies, I'd watched his face as he'd cast an agonized gaze toward the garage, where his childhood friend had ended his depression with his service firearm. A single shot to the heart.

"You need to be a good boy in there," I whispered to Luke.

He sat down and regarded me with a somber gaze, a genius when it came to reading my moods and lending support.

"Here we go."

It was chilly in the living room, but once I adjusted the thermostat the furnace ignited in the basement with a low rumble, and the baseboards started ticking with a surge of heat. The sheer curtains and cell shades were dusty. Divots in the carpeting indicated where a couch and armchairs had been stationed until recent weeks when Aaron's friends and colleagues had come to fetch the items to put them to good use. Stacked near the door were new cans of paint that were in keeping with the present color scheme: a soft taupe for the living room, a warm white in the kitchen and hallway, and a misty bluish-green for the bathrooms.

I planned to start with cleaning and bringing garbage to the curb. Nicknacks, photos, trophies from high school and college, and other keepsakes would be tucked into boxes and bins and set aside. At some point, Dan, Kevin, and his wife, Peg, would need to make the hard choices involved with deciding what should be kept or donated.

First, I collected shirts and pants from the floor and brought the load to the laundry nook down the hallway, since discarding Aaron's clothes didn't feel right. While the machine spun into action, I fetched trash bags and began collecting toiletries from the master bathroom. Opening the medicine cabinet, I felt a stab of unease as I encountered several bottles of antidepressants. For the moment, I put them in his bedroom.

On to the kitchen, which was separated from the living room by an island with four bar stools. Most of the food in the cabinets was long expired, which had the garbage bags filling up fast. The waste bin under the sink included receipts that caught my eye as they cascaded out.

Aaron had taken to online betting to one degree or another. I'd seen more than one news report about how sports gambling was becoming a scourge for young men who got hooked and played until there was nothing left. I floundered with the knowledge for a moment, and then I brought the receipts to the bedroom to leave with the antidepressants.

I continued dumping expired food, hauled the bags to the bins outside the garage, and rolled them to the curb. While heading back to the house, I saw a woman staring at me from the driver's seat of a hybrid car parked nearby along the curb. In her late twenties or early thirties, she stepped out and crossed to me in smart-looking business attire.

"Vivian Vandorne," she crisply announced as she extended her chilly hand. "Human Resources Director at Westdale College. I tried to reach Trooper Bolton through the state police and encountered a disheartening runaround. I'm told you're the one to speak to about arranging a meeting. In-person or virtual. Can you set it up?"

I donned a polite smile and folded my arms. As it happened, I'd heard about her place of employment through my best friend's father, who was a history professor in Boston. Situated on a hill with stone buildings and uplifting signs, Westdale College was a bastion of favoritism, infighting, and other foibles that often ruined the larger world.

"What might the meeting entail?" I asked.

"I'm told that you're working together to 'resolve' your father's concerns over a matter that was a painful chapter for me," she said. "Meanwhile, Trooper Bolton's house is an epicenter of crime. One would imagine his time would be better spent keeping his own affairs in order. As a woman, I've had to work hard to build my career. I'm sure you've faced challenges in whatever it is that you're doing," Vivian added, motioning toward my cleaning clothes. "Perhaps you and I can sort out the issue here and now. What is it that you need to know?"

"Well," I said, "I'll need a clear sense of the painful chapter and related details. Names, dates, and facts from your perspective."

"You don't know the information outright?" she asked.

"My father was pursuing a range of matters," I said. "It's important to know which instance of wrongdoing to look toward."

"I was *free* of wrongdoing," Vivian insisted.

"Maybe that was the wrong word," I said.

"You have no idea what I'm talking about," Ms. Vandorne murmured with an absent, puzzled frown. "That means people have put ideas in my head, which is troubling and odd. Why would they do that?"

"Ok, let's start over," I said softly. "If someone is giving you a wrong sense of Dan's inquiries, I'm happy to sort it out."

"Not if it opens a door that's been long closed."

"Vivian, I'm concerned for you," I said. "You're pale and rattled. I'm a good listener. If you come inside—"

"No, I'm jumping the gun before getting my ducks in a row," she said. "If you're free later in the week, that might work."

"That's perfect," I said, adding her name and number to my phone's contact list. "What day is good for you?"

"I'll check my schedule," Vivian promised.

"I'm sure we can sort things out," I said.

"Undoubtedly," she said. "Of course we can."

As I reached the front stoop, Vivian was in the driver's seat of her car, engaged in a heated phone conversation. She gunned the engine, tossed her phone aside, and conducted a fast change of direction from the curb, which put her in the path of a truck that skidded to a halt with a screech of tires. Vivian balled her fist at the other driver, though she was clearly at fault, and then she surged away down the road.

"Crazy bitch," the driver hollered, and then he leaned toward me with his arm on the widow frame. "What was that about?"

I closed my eyes. It was Haydn Pike.

"She almost clipped my bumper," he added.

"Maybe you were driving too fast," I said.

"Point taken," Haydn said. "How's it going in there?"

"As you can imagine," I said. "It's sad and tough."

"Sounds like your dearly departed guest." When I frowned in confusion, Haydn added, "Vivian Vandorne. She's sad and tough. Word around town is that she murdered a guy in cold blood a few years ago. Right up your alley. Is that why she stopped by?"

"Haydn," I said. "I'm busy with the work."

"You're extra cute when you're flushed," he said.

With disgust, I said, "You make a comment like that here?"

"Aaron would flirt with you to get under Dan's skin," he said. "With that in mind, give me a call if you're lonesome."

Sometimes, closing a door makes a point better than words.

Through the sheer curtains, I watched him drum his fingers on the truck door as if he was weighing his options, and then an approaching car decided for him. As his truck glided away, I wondered if his presence in the neighborhood was a coincidence. For all I knew, he lived nearby and was following a known pattern that he stuck to every day.

I wondered if Aaron truly had been a flirt. In the guest bedroom, I paused in my effort to stow items in bins and leafed through a photo album. One page offered a snapshot of Dan and Aaron during their teens. Grinning at the camera with tools on the ground and their hands grimy, they'd been tuning up a dirt bike in a suburban yard.

They'd played sports together, tested the limits of sense together, and rebuilt motorcycles together. After college, they'd tossed their engineering degrees aside to tackle police work thanks to a trooper they'd admired. Dan had dropped hints that he and Aaron had drifted apart after college. Nothing dramatic. Just a quiet turn down different paths in life. Dan was human. Caught up with his own ambitions and problems, he'd missed signs of distress in his friend at the worst possible time.

Once I finished gathering miscellaneous items, I stacked the bins in the center of each room and flipped open sheets of plastic to cover the desk in the office, plus the bedroom furniture so I could launch into the painting process without pause the next time I stopped in.

In the kitchen, I snugged on rubber gloves, filled a bucket with warm, sudsy water, and knelt in front of the refrigerator to scrub the shelves. Bits of dried parsley and traces of orange peels told me that Aaron had maintained a healthy diet for a single man. A divorced man. A sheriff's deputy, as opposed to Dan's path of being a trooper. What went into decisions like that? According to the gossip I'd overheard, Aaron had married a "difficult" woman, but with that sort of label attached to my name, I was not about to put stock in any opinion until I understood the specifics.

When I'd met Aaron's mother, Peg, at the Fall Fest some weeks ago, she'd warmly hugged Dan, reflecting their deep bond. He'd blinked back tears and collected himself immediately, and then Peg had warmly hugged me. In the Corner Pocket, Kevin had described Peg as fragile, but I sensed a core of strength in her, despite her lingering grief.

Chilled by the icy air in the refrigerator, I sat on my heels and closed my eyes against the jarring memory of Gerald Leblanc's body in the back of the van, where he'd been left to be "dealt with" later on. Had he still been alive at that same moment twenty-four hours ago? Whatever the cause of death, I hadn't seen any trace of blood.

Filled with unease, I did not need the shock of Luke suddenly scrambling to his feet and trotting into the living room. Fixing his alert gaze and pricked ears toward the door, he stopped and softly growled.

Seeing Isaac Munroe climbing out of a gleaming luxury car in the driveway, I struggled to remove the rubber gloves, snapped off one with a spray of bubbles, and then was left to stand there with the other glove intact as Isaac tapped a few times and opened the door.

I straightened, dripping, and smoothed my hair.

"Mr. Munroe," I said. "This is a surprise."

"Sorry to interrupt," Isaac said. "Is your dog friendly?"

With a quick signal, I told Luke to sit and settle.

"If you're looking for Kevin, he's not here," I said.

"No, I came to apologize for being abrupt in the store," he said "Turns out you saved June Bolton's life. Selfless and brave."

"I heard her screaming," I said. "Instinct kicked in."

"Roy made it look like you were a culprit, hauling you into the house," Isaac said. "I'm shocked that he didn't strike the right tone."

"No worries," I said. "It's been sorted out."

Relieved to not be faced with another awkward back-and-forth, I relaxed out of my tense state and wrenched off the second glove. Too soon, perhaps. Isaac rubbed his neck, signaling concerns.

"If you get down to the bank where I work, you'll see it's a nice historic building," he said. "Pillars, stone floor, the works. It creates a kind of amphitheater effect. My office faces the high ceiling," Isaac went on, "So, the gossip I overhear booms around the place and has an afterlife of echoes. If your cousin, Charlotte Bergley, is in the lobby ..."

"She's angry that Raymond left his farm to me," I said.

"I'm aware she had big plans for the property," Isaac agreed. "There's often a supporter who comes to your defense, but last night's trouble has inspired a new arc of echoes that revolve around you tackling the work here instead of hiring professionals."

"Are the new echoes attached to a name?" I asked.

"Haydn Pike," Isaac said. "As a friend of Aaron's, he's worried to see you hauling trash to the curb without the family involved."

I closed my eyes, unable to grasp why I was surprised.

"He's stirring up trouble without cause," Isaac said.

"It's heartening that you agree," I said.

"My son, Kick, is a financial analyst at the bank," Isaac went on. "He's set up a side hustle helping people whose records get compromised from scammers and careless mistakes. There's been a rash of it in recent years. Even Raymond fell victim to it one time when he clicked on a link in a bogus email, supposedly sent from a colleague."

I frowned. "This is the first I've heard of it."

"Because it got resolved," Isaac said. "Everything is about marketing these days. Take this moment. Heiress up to her elbows in soap suds to do another good deed after chasing away bad guys."

"Actually, I'm uncomfortable with that label," I said. "I've peeled away from the Littlefield empire, so … you looked me up?"

"It's my job to know who is who on the money front, and I'm hoping you'll open an account one day," Isaac said. "To eclipse Haydn's narrative, I can send my son to the rescue at your convenience. He can sort through Aaron's records and shred items that might be a problem."

"I only just met you," I said carefully.

"Dan, his folks, and the Pierces are clients at the bank," Isaac assured me. "We've got direct knowledge of Aaron's affairs." When I continued to hesitate, he added, "Haydn is saying that your motive in helping out is to dig into records and profit from it. If you don't counterbalance the story, people like your cousin will pitch it as the truth."

"It's kind of you to worry," I said. "I've got my hands full today, but if Kevin is ok with your son's help, let's arrange it."

"Excellent," he said. "I'll reach out to Kevin."

At first blush, I was taken off guard by his concern over documents that had sat in an empty house for over a year and a half, though a part of me grasped the problem. In another world, I might question the motives of a woman who was seen by some as a troublesome unknown.

"Sorry if I wasn't clear," Isaac said. "I'm told I'm emotionally unaware at times. My ex-wife is another voice I've heard echoing in the bank. There's a litany of things I'm apparently doing wrong."

His smile invited me to congratulate him for being a modern guy, able to absorb criticism. I nodded, lest I dent his ego.

"If you're all set, I'll leave you to it," he said.

"Thank you for stopping in," I said.

Isaac ducked out and headed to his car, leaving me with a sense of unease over what had seemed a straightforward process. From that moment onward, I would let Kevin haul the garbage to the curb. I left him a voicemail that recapped Isaac's concerns, and his proposed solution. I'd come to understand that Aaron had left his house to Dan to spare his parents from a transaction that would amount to a time-consuming business matter. It made sense on the logic front. Dan was tackling the burden with grim determination, but he'd told Kevin and Peg that they were in charge of figuring out what possessions to keep and what to toss.

Hopefully, my careful sorting system would help.

As the washer buzzed, I crossed down the hallway and put Aaron's clothes into the dryer, and then I knelt in front of the oven and focused on scrubbing away caked-on grease from a casserole cooked during bygone days. Luke brought me a squeak-toy that he'd found in a corner and attempted to cheer me up with its funny sound.

"I'm good," I told him. "This first day was bound to be hard."

* * *

After three and a half hours of work, the kitchen and bathrooms in Aaron's house gleamed, which brought on a note of irony as I parked next to my own house, where dust bunnies roamed over the hardwood floors and tiny cobwebs existed in corners. Out front, the weeds that I hadn't had time to trim engulfed the latticework that still bore the marks of a shocking attack I'd survived in the dark of night. At times, I couldn't comprehend the math. How could that have happened seven weeks ago?

I let Luke out of the car and reached into the cargo area to pull out the antique sleigh bells that I'd bought as a festive addition to Dodge's harness. Each four-inch bell was wrought with embellishments and fastened to a leather strap. I shook them on my way to the barn to hang them on a peg, loving their mellow notes, and then I crossed to the pasture in the twilight. With the sheep dozing nearby, I reached up to scratch the topline of Dodge's dramatic, blonde mane. With a quiet nicker, he tugged at my hair with his lips, a gentle, playful expression of affection that had his long whiskers tickling my face. I smiled and patted his neck.

"You're the best," I said softly.

Inside the house, with the coffee maker gurgling, I ate crackers on the fly as I dug my father's notes out of my bag, and was surprised to find that each folder contained only a lone page of scribbled notes. Raymond was a meticulous man. He would surely have included at least some supporting documentation for each case. I was already fuming at Dan for taking the folders out of my father's secret floorboard hiding place, leaving me to find cash tucked away, and not much else. Now I pictured him shredding any police reports that Raymond had obtained outside "normal" police procedures and channels. That left me in the dark in deciphering the initials and abbreviations my father had relied on when he'd circled locations on his map of Maine. No matter. I would start with the basic information, and check for elements that narrowed into connection points.

"Ok, listen up," I said to Luke as I spread the map on the table and started landing my finger on each of the circled locations. "We've got a case of arson that was never solved. We've got a suspicious death on the coast. We've got a makeshift meth lab in the woods with no arrests. We've got a case of two deaths by carbon monoxide poisoning. Over here we have circles around a property with cryptic letters." I smoothed a fold that had marred my father's handwriting, and read, "Recent focus for DC … 5ARCHST … 2CMPST … 5EH … Chk D-footage …"

I straightened and stared across the kitchen.

"Check drone footage?" I asked.

I lurched from the chair and rushed to my father's bedroom down the hallway, certain that I'd seen a box for a drone at some point. For once, it was a good thing to have left his forest green room as an untouched shrine. The drone wasn't in his closet or under the bed.

Pulled up short by the growl of an old truck coming up the driveway, I rushed to the kitchen, wrenched open the door, and unceremoniously pulled Brumby's brother, Jeremy, into the hunt.

"You're looking for what?" the puppy hunk asked.

"A drone. The box is this big." I demonstrated. "Check the basement. Hi, by the way. This is a great help."

Upstairs, I searched my stepmother's sewing room and saw the box in a corner next to her knitting basket.

"I found it!" I hollered.

Rushing down the stairs, with Luke scampering behind me, I grabbed my camera bag and pulled out my device for opening memory cards, and drummed my fingers while my laptop powered up.

"I brought lasagna from the store," Jeremy said.

"Excellent, I'm starving. You can sleep over there," I said, waving toward the plaid couch on the far wall. "It's comfier than it looks."

"It's perfect for guarding the door," Jeremy said.

I nodded. "Exactly."

The aroma of lasagna filled the air as I downloaded the memory card and fast-forwarded through the videos that had been taken as the drone traveled along streams, hovered over fields, and wove through forests. One of the forest videos was shot as the drone hovered over a square area that was dug to a consistent depth with yellow tape around the perimeter and string arranged in a precise grid from side to side.

"Were *bodies* found there?" Jeremy said, leaning his broad shoulders and shaved face into my personal space.

When I looked at him, he seemed abashed.

"Sorry, I figured there'd be a chance to get a grip on what to expect," he said. "I'm flying by the seat of my pants."

"I thought I'd made a breakthrough," I explained, indicating the map. "But I'm as lost as before. The footage isn't tied to any of the locations. It's an uphill climb, unscrambling what my father wrote."

"*Well,*" Jeremy said. "Antoine, the guy who hired me, has a full agenda lined up for tomorrow. You and him. A road trip."

I paused. "He stopped by the store?"

"No, he talked to me through the security camera. I guess it's normal. Anyway, Mrs. Brooks says I'm to take over as clerk."

"My arrangement is with the owners, Sue and Kate," I said.

"Well," Jeremy said. "Mrs. Brooks says I'm in, and you're out."

I closed my eyes. "Unbelievable."

"Antoine will get you home by nightfall, more or less," Jeremy said. "He'll meet you at the Corner Pocket at 8 a.m. Oh, and a giant other thing. There's breaking news you'll want to see. A bust up north."

"Already?" I asked. "Why didn't you lead with that?"

Soon, I found a news item featuring a scene that had unfolded on the border between Maine and Quebec. Filmed from a helicopter, the clip showed four shadows tossing a canister into a cabin. A moment later, a guy staggered out and flopped to the ground. Zooming in as the man was handcuffed, I smiled at the buff, tactical figure that I knew to be Dan, only to see him fist bump Nicole. No matter. With one of the culprits in custody, Dan's team would have leverage in tracking down the two who remained at large. Maybe that promising start had convinced Antoine to check my father's cases as possible connecting points.

With Jeremy's back turned my way, I assessed him anew, tempted to find an alternate address for him that week. If I made progress on any of the cases at hand, he might land in harm's way.

"Antoine says I'm *his* hire," Jeremy said in response to my gaze. "If you pitch me out, I am to spend the icy hours on your doorstep."

"Antoine put it that way?" I asked.

"I'm up for it," Jeremy declared. "Just say the word."

His qualifications as a bodyguard were iffy, but his presence would be a comfort when the inevitable rustlings and trills started unfolding in the paddock between midnight and three a.m. The capture was a win, my progress in Aaron's house was a win, Antoine's plan for a crime-scene road trip was a win, and the impending meal of lasagna was a win.

"Look at me cope," I declared.

While we ate, Jeremy shared that he was downcast to know that he wasn't cut out to be a social media trendsetter like some of his friends back home in Ohio. Even worse, Brumby couldn't seem to make up his mind about wanting Jeremy in his inner circle or not.

"Give him time," I said.

Hunched over his plate, Jeremy looked at me shyly. "Brumby says you're a lesson a minute. You're not to be messed with."

I smiled. "And don't you forget it."

7

By 9 a.m., an hour into our joint venture of assessing crime locations, the questions that Antoine deflected with sideways musings started piling up. So, you *do* have a car? Where did you stow it the other night? Is it a rental, or a police-issue sort of deal? Why make me park at the Corner Pocket instead of picking me up at my farm? Aren't you worried about slipping on ice in a pair of light sneakers? Getting cold without a jacket? Running out of gum? Falling asleep from a lack of coffee?

All right, that was a question I was asking myself, having imagined our day would begin with a chat over a plate of pastries.

Once again that week, I was wrong.

In the passenger seat of his dark sedan, I concluded from the new car aroma and leather seats that Antoine was not averse to indulging himself now and then. His face was closely shaved and his ponytail gave off a fresh scent, which spoke of a hotel room and a suitcase with an endless supply of tight dark shirts and butt-cupping threadbare jeans. He'd looked rested and focused as he'd studied my father's map in the parking lot of the Corner Pocket at 8 a.m., and then he'd pulled onto the road with an air of knowing where to start. My photographer's wiring had me framing his handsome profile in my mind, with the background blurred and the light subdued, but his eyes sharply defined. Add a gold mantle and embroidered robe, and he would look like a king from a bygone era.

"Listen," I said. "I don't suppose …"

"Not even with your phone," Antoine said.

"You're psychic?" I asked.

"At times," he said. "In this instance, you are obvious."

"I was elated to hear Dan's team caught at least one member of the burglary crew," I said. "What about the other two?"

"The bust you saw in the news was a false lead," Antoine said with a rueful twist of eyebrows. "All three culprits remain at large."

I absorbed the news in silence, grasping that it didn't serve me well to ask why Antoine had included me in his fact-finding efforts. I'd assumed it was because Dan's team had made progress.

"We've blown past several of the properties," I said.

"Four looked promising," Antoine said. "I had to choose."

"What do you make of the drone footage?" I asked, having walked him through the files I'd uploaded to my cloud account. "There's a video of a forest location that looks like a taped-off crime scene."

"No, the tape was the kind used for surveying," Antoine said. "On the map the forest location is marked as 'ARCHST,' your father's abbreviation for several archaeological sites. You didn't read his notes?"

"I absorbed the gist of the notes, but my best thinking happens when I check a location in person," I said. "Plus, the 'Sonny effect' phenomenon I told you about kept me busy yesterday."

I explained my work at Aaron's house and how Isaac Munroe had stopped by after our strained encounter at the Corner Pocket.

"At first, I was leery of giving him access to Aaron's financial records," I said. "I alerted Kevin Pierce about the plan, so nothing will happen without the family's consent. It's best to be careful."

Emerging from my recollections, I held my breath as the sign for Polk Realty & Storage loomed ahead along the road.

"Drive past it," I prompted. "Keep going."

"I need directions," Antoine said.

"We can ask elsewhere," I said. "Hit the gas!"

Antoine raised an eyebrow. "You are bossy this way with Juvénile?"

"No. Maybe." I closed my eyes. "Gerald Leblanc, the deceased hunter I saw in the van, worked at Polk Realty & Storage."

"I understand your concern," Antoine said. "Stay in the car and shield your face. I will ask directions, and nothing more."

"Not with my father's map," I said. *"Wait—"*

Too late. Antoine stepped out with the map in hand, looking at ease as he headed for the business office at the end of the row of storage bays. I shrank down, hoping the sedan's dark windows would obscure my presence in the passenger seat. After a minute or two, Antoine reappeared, indicating with a quick wave that he'd gotten directions. Following him out in an agreeable fashion, Sal stood in the office doorway and called out to Antoine that it was a nice day for a country drive.

"If I kin adjust t'th cold," Antoine said, sounding like he was from the deep south. "Thanks a bunch, Mister … what's yer name ag'in?"

"Salvatore Hall. I'm not Italian," Sal confessed for the second time in two days as if following a worn pattern. "My parents liked how the name brought to mind an important building, something like that."

"Love it," Antoine replied. "See y'all around."

"What was that?" I hissed as he slipped in.

"I was curtailing his ability to identify us."

"You only asked for directions?" I asked.

"Oui," Antoine said. "All is well."

He secured his seatbelt, taking pains to adjust the strap so it fit across his shoulders, and then he swung out and rejoined the road.

"I truly am grateful for your help," I said. "Dan is great in many ways, but I'm steamed at him for taking my father's folders. We're both driven to get justice, and I tend to get impatient with a double standard. Things blew up in September. First, he got mad, then I got mad."

"You forgave each other in the end?" Antoine asked.

"Yes," I said. "We worked it out."

With glances, I studied the man Dan had worked with on the Canadian border since it helped fill in some of the blanks of that time in Dan's life. Antoine's hands were not fixed at ten and two o'clock on the steering wheel per the dictates of driving science. First, his right hand was pressed into action for a stretch of time, then his left hand, then his right hand as if he was using the drive as a weightlifting exercise for his exceptionally toned biceps and his mind. He chewed gum with the same steady rhythm, working the minty wad with his molars until a bubble formed and it snapped. All the while, Antoine maintained his amiable air of detachment from ordinary concerns like stomach ulcers and bodily harm.

"Are you allowed to tell me your full name?" I asked.

"For you, I will confess anything," he said, tossing me a captivating smile that he seemed to use sparingly. "Antoine Chamailard."

"That's got a ring to it," I said.

He smiled. "As does your name, Berrichon."

"Except my name is Sonny," I said tiredly.

"Bon," he said. "Sonn*eee*."

"No, Sonny, like—" I glowered as he grinned at me.

"You are fun to tease," he said. "Plus, fair is fair. Back home, my name is not pronounced Án-twan, but rather Ohntuán."

"I hear the difference," I said. "Ohntuán …"

"Perfect," he said. "As if you are making love to my name."

His grin grew all the brighter as I turned pink.

"Was a prank what you had in mind when you sent Brumby's younger brother to my house to serve as my protection detail?" I asked. "Granted, Jeremy looks the part. Often, a show of force is all it takes, and I believe he would step up on my behalf if trouble hits the fan. He's a lost soul. I think I can make the arrangement work."

Antoine drove on with an air of focus and calm.

"Well?" I prompted.

"Your sense of it is flawless," he said. "There is nothing to add."

"Ok, this looks familiar," I said as Antoine turned at a fork in the road with a sign that was tipped toward the sky. "It's thanks to this map that I landed at a murder scene a few months ago. At the time, I didn't know my father had circled a farmer's previous address. It's a sad story. The house and barn were torched by arsonists … there it is," I said as we swept past the charred ruin. "It's on the list. We need to check it out."

"We will look at it another day," Antoine said.

"You're suddenly driving a little fast," I said, clutching the passenger door as we rocketed down a hill and blew through a yield sign.

"I love pastoral lanes," he said. "Il y a un air de carnaval, non?"

"I'd prefer less of a carnival feel," I said.

The road's faded yellow lines had taken us through stands of pines and stretches of open farmland where cows rested on muddy hillsides near red barns and ancient silos. Antoine's car offered a surprisingly smooth ride over the crumbled, ribboned results of years of savage cold and thundering plow trucks, but the twists and turns pitched me from one side of the seat to the other. Every so often we crested a hill with a spectacular view of dried cornfields awaiting their turn to be harvested by a farmer's combine, with a backdrop of distant mountains that had been reduced to a bluish haze, and then the car plunged straight down in a trajectory that released me from gravity and pitched my stomach into swirling confusion.

"Antoine," I said, "I'm reminded that you were at the wheel when Dan ended up in a wreck that resulted in two black eyes."

"Yes, with naughty criminals on our tail. A back road similar to this one, except it was dark and snowy. I rolled the car intentionally," Antoine assured me. "At just the right spot."

"A roll isn't on today's agenda, right?" I asked.

"Only if we stir up a nest of criminals," Antoine said.

At last, he pulled into a gravel turnout where the shimmering ocean was framed by pine trees on either side. I'd been so caught up in studying my guide that I hadn't realized he'd been heading toward the coast. My heart raced as I stared at the vivid scene, linking it to one of the locations my father had circled on his map with a note saying a geologist had fallen to his death under suspicious circumstances.

"In terms of creating a timeline, this is the first incident that Raymond flagged," I said. "It happened over two years ago."

"A cold case, all but forgotten now," Antoine said.

I climbed out and stretched my legs, savoring the misty salt air that smelled of seaweed and carried the distant chug of lobster boats. Pointing out red poison ivy leaves I should avoid, Antoine led the way along a sandy path flanked by bayberry bushes and purple asters with yellow disks. As always, the light along Maine's coast was stunning on a clear day, adding glints to the rugged gray outcrop and the frothing, thundering waves that churned toward us at high tide.

"Mind the edge in case it's slippery," Antoine said.

First, we veered down a path that led to the area where the victim had landed after falling from a height of fifteen or more feet. My father's notes described how tourists who'd spotted his body some hours after the incident pulled him away from the water's edge, leaving the police investigators to guess at the circumstances that led to his fall.

Squinting against the sun's bright glare, Antoine appeared to be assessing various trajectories of how the incident might have happened, and then he led the way up the path to the higher point.

At the tip of the overhang, uneven ridges in the rock could be tripping hazards, but for the most part, it offered a wide stretch of solid footing. Crime scene or not, I indulged a moment of joy in the view as I felt the crisp breeze on my face, and watched the waterfowl that Dan had pointed out on an early trip to the coast: black guillemots and bay ducks slipping into the churning surf to fetch crustaceans and small fish.

"This is a wonderful spot," I said.

"Perhaps those were the victim's last words."

Gently, Antoine secured my shoulders and guided me back a few steps so I was standing a safe distance from the edge.

"Imagine if it was unwise to trust me," he said softly.

With my mind back in gear, I studied my father's notes. Phone data indicated that the victim had arrived at the outcrop at 9 p.m. There were reports of a bad breakup with VV and the autopsy confirmed alcohol in the geologist's blood. VV was questioned about her whereabouts that night and was cleared of involvement by an alibi from PP.

"Maybe PP signifies Paul Polk," I said, then I looked up. "A woman named Vivian Vandorne came to see me."

Antoine paused. "When?"

"Yesterday afternoon at Aaron's house," I said. "Someone told her that Dan was following up on Raymond's casework. When she grasped that I didn't know what she was talking about, she frowned and made a comment about being misled. We agreed to meet later in the week," I added, pulling out my phone. "Let's see if I can learn more."

Leaning close, Antoine raised an eyebrow when the number I dialed reached the front desk of a dry cleaner.

"She must have changed her mind at the last second," I said. "I'll leave it for now. I don't want her to feel pushed."

"That's always a good rule of thumb when dealing with rattled persons of interest." Antoine studied me thoughtfully. "I picked this location based on the next location. Did anyone else reach out?"

I recapped why Haydn Pike's reappearance was a concern: he'd lost his job at the sheriff's department after Dan reported him for harassing me. Antoine gravely listened as I described Haydn's comments outside Dan's house, and our interaction after Vivian's visit, including the former deputy's misuse of the term "dearly departed guest" in describing Vivian, and his implication that she'd murdered a guy in cold blood.

"Shortly afterward, Isaac Munroe stopped by," I said.

"All in the space of a half hour," Antoine murmured.

"You're seeing the Sonny effect in real-time," I said.

Smiling, Antoine said, "Indeed, I am."

"Hopefully, the payoff will be catching Raymond's killer," I said. "My father and I never met, but through videos, I've gotten a sense of how he spoke and carried himself. It's brought vivid clarity to nightmares I've had about his death. Even if Raymond was taken off guard, he must have had awareness and pain. Imagine lying in the snow, lashed by wind and gripped by sub-freezing cold, half conscious and confused."

"Try not to picture it," Antoine said softly.

"Picturing things is my go-to lane in life," I said.

"Come," Antoine said. "We have a lot of ground to cover."

I scarcely saw the road on the drive to the next property, torn between the beauty of the rock ledge, and the horror of a man possibly being pushed to his death. With an effort, I put the awful image aside as Antoine pulled into a gravel driveway with granite pillars at the entrance, with classy light fixtures on top. The quaint, two-story cape was well maintained, painted royal blue, but the grass hadn't been mowed in months.

Following Antoine's lead, I stepped out next to a for-sale sign showing Paul Polk's photo and details. Now that we were inland, surrounded by leafless trees, a chill in the air had me zipping my light jacket up to my chin. Antoine didn't seem affected by the cold. With his thumbs looped in his front pockets, he began an attentive inspection of the house and yard. I continued my attentive inspection of Antoine. Even the sunlight seemed captivated by his stillness, resting on his shoulders as he paused to gaze at the bare branches of a maple tree. He narrowed his eyes and looked down the road as if calculating a distance in his head.

"This is a lovely stretch of land," he said.

"Eleven acres," I said, reading my father's notes out loud. "Owned by 'DC.' Recent upgrades. Partial solar. Raymond saw him as innocent when he was accused of misusing funds at—" I stopped and stared at Antoine. "The owner of this house taught archaeology at Westdale College, where Vivian works. Do you know what DC stands for?"

"Doctor Bertrand Clark," Antoine said.

"The geologist who fell to his death at the coast was *also* a professor at the college," I said. "Dr. Clark was accused and later cleared, but the hints of financial misconduct tanked his career. As HR Director, Vivian was the one to draw up a termination contract. Raymond was outraged. His notes say Bertrand got a pittance for keeping his mouth shut. I've always mistrusted the use of non-disclosure agreements."

Antoine nodded. "Crushing a person's right to speak seems at odds with your country's First Amendment."

"Raymond's notes say that Bertrand reported being hounded by mystery assailants," I said. "Chased through the woods, and blocked from getting another job. The police didn't buy it."

"It is a tale of shattered dreams," Antoine said.

"Where is Dr. Clark now?" I asked.

"He disappeared," Antoine said. "Some see it as a sign of guilt."

"Maybe he's in hiding somewhere." I frowned at the notes. "My father didn't include the geology professor's name."

"I'm not sure it's necessary to know during this early phase," Antoine said. "You've been drawn into nearly ten instances of tragic death in a short span of time. Spare yourself from overload."

"I wish I'd stopped months ago," I said. "I've got enough baggage from knowing my name should be Alison French."

"I looked through your father's journals the other night," Antoine said. "Even the best of men can have blind spots. He imagined you had a gilded life, which I gather was not the case."

Preferring to stick to the present, I pondered my father's notes.

"We've got an elderly woman whose identity was stolen, a family who called 911 about scary sounds at night," I said. "There's the arson case we drove past. An instance of car theft, but the tables turned when the car was found with drugs inside. The owner railed about being set up. Besides the coastal location and this house, I don't see any connection to Westdale College." Seeing Antoine's twist of eyebrows calling me an impatient neophyte, I sighed. "Sorry. Let's keep moving."

"Bon," he said. "Two properties to go."

Once again, I was treated to a zero-gravity ride on a wooded road, soaring in space for seconds at a time as the wheels lost their connection to planet Earth. Dizzied by pressure changes in my ears, I winced every time it seemed unlikely that we would remain upright, and then reminded myself that the tradeoff was getting the insights of a highly-trained undercover operative. Not to mention our high-speed arc would enable us to cover a lot of ground in one day. In short order, Antoine slowed for the next address my father had circled on the map.

"This will be more of a challenge," he said.

I thoroughly agreed. Not long ago, I'd assumed the best of untamed woods, loving the sheltering peace under the canopy of trees, and then I was almost pitched into a shallow grave, a jarring memory that demanded an extra level of assessment. I leaned forward and saw similarities to the notorious forest where I'd almost perished. Not more than twenty feet past the muddy entrance, a narrow trail disappeared into a thicket of briars and shrubs, followed by a dark wall of hemlocks, pines, maples, and just about every other kind of tree jammed tightly together. It was the sort of place a criminal gang or extraterrestrial hoard would look at and say, "This is where we'll plot out the end of the world."

"Paul Polk owns this land," I said, reading my father's notes. "Fifty acres, mostly forest. Lots of hardwood trees still intact. Apparently, Gerald and Sal set up a rustic 'glamping' experience for tourists."

"This was in the realty office," Antoine said, handing me a brochure showing wooden platforms that offered a view of the forest. "When I asked about it, Sal said the tents were vandalized."

"Glamping is a high-end concept," I said. "They'd be lucky to get even one week when mosquitoes weren't a major issue."

"In town, Gerald and Sal are described as big on dreams, and short on sense," Antoine said. "It's a shame if their glamping enterprise went bust. People benefit from contact with nature."

The brochure listed the longtime friends as the main contacts under the umbrella of Polk Realty & Storage. A map on the back panel showed the tent platforms perched near a winding stream.

"If we head west, we'll be closer to the … *Antoine,*" I said as he stepped out. "This side of the property looks iffy."

"Come and stretch your legs," he said.

I joined him beyond the hood of the car, relieved not to hear the rapid-fire blasts of someone honing their aim with a pump-action shotgun. All was quiet, except for the bright chatter of chickadees and nuthatches flitting through the trees. In the sunshine, my jacket was too warm, but as Antoine led the way into the forest the breeze felt chilly, which had me alternately pulling the zipper down and then wrenching it upward again.

"You are very loud, Berrichon," Antoine said.

"Why is it necessary to hike in?" I asked. "I've noticed that you don't carry a sidearm. One would think it would come in handy."

"I loathe the confusion of hollering warnings and getting peppered with gunfire. It's far better to travel light, and … *shhh,*" he prompted, motioning for me to take cover behind him. "I heard a rustle of plastic. That can mean only one thing."

"Someone is wrapping up a body?" I asked.

"Bon. It points to two possible things."

"What's that smell in the air?" I asked. "Marijuana?"

"Oui," he said. "It is legal in Maine."

"Only if it's grown in small quantities," I whispered. "We're here without any backup. For now, we're done."

"We are done when we have answers, capiche?" Antoine asked.

"Don't start confusing things with Italian," I said.

"Terminaremos cuando tengamos respuestas," Antoine replied, seamlessly rolling his r's and rounding his vowels. "Wir sind fertig, wenn wir antworten haben. My zakonchim, kogda poluchim otvety."

"What in the heck is all that?" I whispered.

"I am saying 'we are done when we have answers' in Spanish, German, and Russian. You did beg me to help you, non?"

I sighed. "All right, let's see what they're up to."

Music was playing up ahead, loud enough to mask the soft crackle of our footfalls in the leaves, and then two men were suddenly visible in a twenty-foot area that had been stripped of trees and undergrowth to accommodate a makeshift plastic greenhouse. With a quick signal, Antoine directed me to take cover behind a sapling that would protect my belly button and little else, and then he slipped forward through the shadows, freezing when the men looked his way, his dark shirt merging into the undergrowth. In less than a minute he cut a zigzag path that brought him to the makeshift growing operation, which appeared to run on solar energy and a heater hooked up to a tank of propane. Given the time of year, it was no surprise they were dismantling the equipment, stowing trays and other supplies in cardboard boxes next to an ATV.

One of the men froze, seeing me standing there in my blue coat.

"Duck Berrichon!" Antoine hollered.

I dove forward in time to hear a hard object whistle over my head. I scrambled through the leaves and took cover behind a barrel.

Thuds and crashing sounds unfolded for a moment, and then all was quiet, except for the pained groans of the two men. When I risked a peek around the barrel, Antoine was ejecting the magazine from a sidearm and instructing a third man to sit with his fellow growers. Lying around here and there were zip ties they'd used to fasten tarps to poles. Antoine repurposed the ties to secure the wrists of the men.

One by one, he gripped each of their hands and pressed their thumbs against a thin device he attached to his phone, and then he touched his brow with an air of drama in response to their lengthy records.

"Antoine," I said. "Ask them about—"

"Hush, Berrichon," he prompted. "Let me work."

First, he got in their faces and grilled them with questions from inches away. No matter how they shrank down, he followed their evasions with precision and intensity, reminiscent of the way I'd seen flocks of starlings funneling themselves into twists and turns in the London sky. At last, the grilling appeared to be over. As Antoine switched gears and stood, one man in particular looked desperate to be set free.

"Hey, listen," he said. "We found that gun. It isn't ours. Paul looks the other way on our hobby out here. Are you the reason Gerald is in hiding? He's our cousin, but we're not close. Maybe he's muscling in on your operation? We have zero interest in heroin or whatever Gerald and Sal are up to. You flashed a badge, but which side are you on?"

"When did you last see Gerald?" Antoine asked in a Southern drawl.

"Like, two or three days ago. We're not close."

"C'est triste, si tu es de la famille," Antoine said.

"Shit," the man said. "You're French Canadian?"

"Why would that be a problem?" Antoine asked.

"Because of the, umm, hockey rivalry."

With a sharp hiss, one of his cohorts urged him to shut up.

"Anything else on your mind?" Antoine prompted.

"No, I'm done," the man murmured.

With his phone in hand, Antoine blocked his number as he reported the pot operation to the sheriff's department. He briefly argued with the dispatcher that longitude and latitude coordinates were normal means of reporting a location, and then with a roll of eyes, he hung up.

Kneeling in front of Gerald's cousins, Antoine looked like a coach gearing them up for a championship game, but his gestures were along the lines of threats. First, his index finger unfurled, then the next finger, and the next, until his open hand represented five reasons for them to fear him for the rest of their lives. After grimacing their way through the list, they bowed their heads and nodded. For all I knew, they were signing onto nicknames that involved breeds of sheep.

Antoine clapped his knees with an air of completion, brushed off his jeans as he stood, and returned to me with a pleased smile.

"On to the next property," he said. "Let's look at the map."

I gaped at him for a moment because gaping — an essential element of participating in a bizarre unexpected event that involved criminals, guns, and drugs — had gotten tossed to the wayside.

"We can't just leave," I said.

"The police are on the way," he said. "All is well."

"What about the weapon you took?" I asked.

"Here." Antoine patted his waistband where the gun was tucked. "Is it your wish to be present if your beau shows up?"

"He'll find out anyway," I said.

"All the growers know is that a man with a southern accent arrived with a woman named Berrichon who was difficult to see," Antoine said. "No such name will be found in the police database."

I paused. "So, all this time …"

"Come," he said. "Delays are costly."

Breathless, I jogged after Antoine with some preliminary questions in mind. He spoke fluent English, French, Spanish, German, and Russian? Obviously. What was his training, exactly? I was starting to imagine he'd spent time in the military. Was he truly from Canada, or was that supposedly known element a part of an effort to spin contrails of mystery around himself, too fast and elusive for anyone to get close?

With a sideways look, and possibly an amused glint in his eyes, he opened the door for me and gently closed it once I was seated as if we were in evening clothes headed for a night on the town instead of filthy from crawling through the forest. In the distance, a siren wailed, but he took his time stowing the captured weapon in the trunk. He crossed around to his door, slipped in, and tossed me a reassuring smile.

"Paul Polk owns this land?" I asked, buckling my seatbelt.

"Apparently so." Antoine's right hand almost clipped my chin as he spread my father's map across the dashboard. He fluffed out the folds and studied the roads. "There is one more location to check, but a drive past the other properties will be useful. It might take hours."

"Let's narrow the search," I said. "The sun sets early this time of year."

"No worries," he said. "I have brought flashlights."

Antoine started the engine and reversed out of the turnout, and then we surged down the road at a respectable speed. A moment later, a sheriff's car whooshed past us in the opposite lane, which meant my questions truly had almost landed us in the soup. Still, now that I could catch my breath, I felt it was important to clarify a few points.

"Antoine, you have leeway thanks to your job," I said. "I'm a regular person. There are rules and laws. I don't want to land in jail."

"On what grounds?" he asked. "You are free of wrongdoing."

"Leaving a crime scene is frowned upon," I said.

"In undercover work, staying is frowned upon," he said.

Nodding, I said, "I guess that makes sense."

Antoine pulled out a package of gum, unwrapped a fresh piece with one hand, and then his methodical chewing began anew.

"Ok, let's recap," I said. "Those guys have family ties with Gerald, who was murdered in recent days, and they're operating in a location circled on Raymond's map. Marijuana is a gateway drug. They think Gerald is mixed up in the heroin trade. If we find similar operations, we'll have unearthed a possible reason Raymond was targeted. Dan as well."

"In what sense?" Antoine asked.

"Drugs, obviously," I said. "All the locations on the map are rural. Ideal for operating in secret. There's a story of Gerald and Sal being covered in white powder. Heroin needs to be processed."

"Up north, our task force focused on fentanyl," Antoine said.

As the car wound through the shadows of trees in the afternoon light, I waited in vain for him to disclose further details.

"You go from seemingly calm and carefree to intense in a matter of minutes," I said. "Which Antoine is the real deal?"

"I could ask you the same. You balk and worry, fret and pause. In the next heartbeat, you find the courage to tackle an armed burglar." Antoine glanced at me. "What do you know about tourmaline?"

"The gem?" I asked. "That's an odd segue."

Steering with one hand, Antoine held a four-inch piece of watermelon tourmaline in a ray of sunlight, bringing depth and luster to the gemstone that was named after its pink center and green outer edge. Recognizing the unique contours and coloring, and grasping that he'd borrowed it from my father's house, I waited to hear why it was relevant.

"Tourmaline is a marvel of geological forces," Antoine said. "A mix of heat, vapor, minerals, and pressure deep underground. In its liquid state, the elements slip into fissures, any place where crystals can form. This particular kind of tourmaline is thought to nourish confidence, restore inner balance, and meld a person's conflicted selves."

"I need to carry a pound of it," I said.

Antoine smiled. "Yes, you truly do."

"What's the context?" I asked.

"The geologist who fell to his death gave lectures on tourmaline, with strictly a scientist's approach," Antoine said. "When prompted to weigh in on the gem's healing powers, he rolled his eyes with disdain. Perhaps someone in the audience took offense."

"You're not posing that as a motive to murder him?" I asked.

Antoine shrugged. "I am conjecturing to keep my first impressions in check. For all we know a bird flew at him on the ledge."

"You described the case as all but forgotten," I said. "That means his death has been a barren statistic for over two years. Vivian didn't seem sad. She talked about the incident like it was an annoyance."

Antoine glanced at me with a look of concern.

"This is why I urged you to tap the brake," he said. "Early in my career, I anticipated being shocked by the diversity of the cases I would face. Instead, it's the sameness of treachery that confounds me. I don't want your father's death to be about drugs. I don't want the foe to be anyone who turned against a friend, or acted out of love, or breathes air. Breathing implies the presence of a heart that should know better."

"You've encountered awful things," I said softly.

"Too many times to count," he said.

"You mentioned that your parents and sister died," I said.

Slowly chewing his gum, Antoine deliberated over whether or not to disclose the details, and then his wry expression said my scrutiny of him was having an effect that he couldn't resist.

"My parents were murdered when I was six, more or less," he said. "A needless, petty dispute over drugs. Years later, I strove to right the wrong by becoming a cop. My sister chose the opposite path."

"Drugs?" I asked softly. "Did she find a way to heal?"

"No, she indulged her last high alone, in the dark of night."

Antoine's driving had slowed, and his pensive frown, awash in bursts of sunlight, told me he didn't mind talking about it.

"I'm sorry to hear it," I said. "What was her name?"

"Chloé," Antoine said.

"I can tell her death still haunts you," I said.

"Our last conversation was a tough talk," Antoine said. "A day I came to regret. When she died, I wanted every factor to be dug out and understood. I was unpleasant to Chloé's boyfriend."

"He was an addict as well?" I asked.

"He was blameless in that regard," Antoine said. "They'd collaborated on a project, but Chloé liked fun more than she liked work. The boyfriend grew tired of her antics and ended their agreement. The compensation he offered was spent in wild ways. In my perspective at the time, he'd all but signed her death warrant. He should have known better."

"You conveyed that message to him?" I asked.

"I hounded him for a month or so, wanting him to think harder about his choices." Antoine glanced at me. "I wasn't a thug about it if that's what you're asking. The real menace was her dealer. I tracked him down. Made the arrest, but even that was a hollow victory."

"I wish we could eliminate the drug trade," I said.

"I have asked that of fate a thousand times," Antoine said. "Release the hounds on a different plane. Give me a supernatural foe."

"Wouldn't that be worse?" I asked.

"Only a lightning strike would be worse," he said.

Antoine had a knack for bringing gooseflesh to my arms.

"It's good if you got justice for your sister," I said.

"Sadly, her dealer emerged from his prison stint with new skills and a devotion to succeeding at crime." With a troubled frown, Antoine regarded me in the angled light. "Your statement paints the crew in Dan's house as careless, caught off guard, and eager to escape."

"That's the basic arc," I agreed.

"In the Corner Pocket, none of the customers sparked panic in asking where ice cream might be?" he asked. "A shiver you couldn't explain?"

"I'm getting a shiver now," I said.

"Focus, Berrichon," Antoine said. "This is important."

"Trust me, I'm on high alert in case the burglars land in front of me," I said. "The store is a great place to assess new faces."

"The forest as well," Antoine said. "If Gerald's cousins were the crew in Dan's house, you would have reacted, non?"

I paused with wide eyes, seeing my inclusion on the day's ride, plus the decision to visit the forest location, in a new light.

"I can still vividly recall that night," I said. "A few times, I heard the crew speaking in English with inflections indicating their native language was French. Gerald's cousins have Maine accents."

"Any other differences?" Antoine asked.

"The guys from the crew were younger than Gerald's cousins," I said. "Mid-thirties at most. Fit and lean, with no signs of extra pounds. Gerald's cousins have beer bellies. Wider, shorter, and slower. There's no way any of them were on the crew from Dan's house."

Antoine smiled. "Great observations. Well done."

"The growers are a group of three connected to Gerald," I said. "Why didn't the police put them in a lineup for me to review?"

"Perhaps they will get around to it," Antoine said.

"I can tell it's painful, knowing that Chloé's dealer is out there," I said. "When was the last time you encountered him?"

Antoine's eyebrows twisted as he calculated in his head. "Eighteen months, six days, and twenty-three hours."

"That's precise," I said.

"How long ago was your life under threat?" he asked.

"I prefer to not keep track," I said. "My focus has been on having the harsh reality be an outlier, rather than the norm."

Antoine nodded. "I will help all I can."

8

Antoine's driving slowed, as if he was timing upcoming events down to the minute. I was more and more intrigued by his unique ways.

"Do you have a military background, by any chance?" I asked.

He tossed me a raised eyebrow. "Why do you ask?"

"You're skilled and experienced beyond the norm," I said. "With your fluency in different languages, the other possibility is a covert role. Is there a Canadian equivalent of the CIA?"

Antoine closed his eyes, as if with disdain.

"By any rational measure, that acronym should indicate the Canadian Intelligence Agency," he said. "Two CIAs would be confusing, so we have the Canadian Security Intelligence Service. I find it annoying. Three letters are better."

"Did you work for them at some point?" I asked.

"You flatter me, Berrichon." He reached into the cup holder. "Gum?"

When we got to the next property, a sliver of sun was still visible on the horizon, winking like an orange cat eye, and casting its fiery glow into the clear night until the light blended with the blackness and shining stars above us. Antoine's bold profile and ponytail were crisply defined against the dramatic horizon as he studied the one-story house where an elderly couple had died from carbon monoxide poisoning a few years ago.

"Bud and Birdie Orland," I said, reading my father's notes. "Raymond suspected foul play. The house and land were bought by an entity called Pintail Holdings. That sounds like a developer to me."

"The new owner is adept at handling legalities and contracts," Antoine said. "It's not always a sign of iffy intentions. I would submerge my name in secrecy if a property had special meaning to me."

"I'm seeing the sale as a blow for wildlife," I said. "The Orland family protected this land for generations as a habitat for turtles. A ninety-year-old, sixty-five-pound male snapping turtle was 'murdered' by hooligans a hundred years ago. Raymond used that word."

"Rightly so," Antoine murmured. "They are splendid creatures."

"The family saw it as a wild pet. The trauma of finding it dead sparked their protection efforts. Hence, the turtle-crossing signs on the road. Birdie was the Orland descendant. Bud took her last name instead of the usual tradition when people marry. You won't find many men who would do that. Raymond was impressed. They were friends. Bud worked as a welder at the Iron Works down on the coast."

I stowed the folder in the car and zipped up my jacket.

"I'm ready whenever you are," I said.

"I have been meaning to ask …" Antoine's hand rested on the small of my back, and then slid downward. "What is this?"

"It's my butt," I said.

"You know I mean the second phone," he said.

"Dan gave it to me to use in an emergency," I said.

"Bon," Antoine said. "He learned from me after all."

"Your hand is still on my butt," I said.

"I am warming you on a chilly night," he said. "It helps, non?"

"Non, nein, uh-uh, and in plain old English, *no*."

With a playful smile, Antoine resumed his assessment of the house and forest. He leaned close and pointed into the dusk.

"There is a stream near the tree line," he said. "Be careful of mud."

"It'll be dark in the house," I said. "No electricity."

Antoine nodded. "All the better."

"But—" I closed my eyes. "Whatever you say."

We were silent as we approached the dwelling, other than the faint swish of our legs and shoes parting the overgrown grass. We paused on the front walkway's tilted pavers, which threatened to turn my ankles. There was a spooky, hovering silence across the unlit property, and the forest sent wafts of fragrant balsam-scented air our way, with a damp chill I associated with the process of ice forming on a stream.

Antoine assessed the dark building. "No rear exits. Wait here while I check the interior. Remain alert, but silent."

"You're not using your flashlight," I said.

"Nor should you," Antoine said.

I flipped my hands as he walked forward and disappeared into the murk that the overgrown bushes provided near the front door. Reduced to a black silhouette, Antoine rattled the knob, and then with a subtle move, he used a quick jerk to loosen the old lock.

At that same moment, a whine of hinges behind the house said he'd missed the mark in his conclusion that there wasn't a second door.

"Antoine," I hissed.

Too late, he was inside the house.

No sidekick in the world could hold her head high if she missed a chance to play a critical role, so I crept around the ramshackle cottage, cursing as thorns caught at my legs, and then I tripped over a rusted fender engulfed in the tall grass. Staggering, but not slowed down, I honed in on a dark figure dashing from the back door toward the forest. Cursing as my right shoe was sucked off by mud, I rushed toward the figure at top speed, only to see Antoine tackle him from my left.

They struggled for a moment, and then a zipping sound told me that Antoine had secured the man's wrists with plastic ties.

"Well done, Berrichon," he said.

"How did you outflank me?" I asked, resting my hands on my knees to catch my breath. "Did you know he was here?"

"Oui, I felt his presence," Antoine said.

"Why not loop me in?" I asked. "I don't understand."

"In my youth, I had a spaniel like you," he said. "Unruly and impossible to train, but she flushed more grouse than any other dog I ever owned."

"Let's avoid the word 'owned,'" I said darkly.

"Of course," Antoine said. "Now, look who we have here."

Hauled upward, Salvatore Hall glared at us, splattered with mud, with his pants sinking into the wet ground near the stream.

"I have permission to be here," Sal growled.

"From whom, and for what purpose?" Antoine asked.

"To fetch the furnace, I guess," Sal said.

"The heater, you mean?" Antoine asked.

Squinting, Sal said, "Same thing, isn't it?"

"How was the message conveyed?" Antoine asked.

"It was sort of a text," Sal said

"Not a note?" Antoine asked. "Left under a rock?"

Sal stared at him, clearly startled that a secret means of communication had been outed, and then he hunched his shoulders.

"You were directed to come tonight?" Antoine asked.

"That part wasn't clear," Sal said. "I figured it was best to wait for my work buddy, Gerald, to get back. He's away, I guess. Then you showed up and spooked me with that map with all the circles on it."

I flipped my hands. Antoine hadn't stopped at Polk Realty & Storage that morning to get directions. Checking out the property last, in the dark of night, had been a part of his plan all along.

"Describe the note system," Antoine prompted.

"You're not going to leave it alone, are you?" Sal asked.

"Tell me," Antoine said. "Stop wasting time."

In short order, he had Sal disclosing that fetching mystery notes and cash from under a rock near Polk Realty & Storage was a system that he and Gerald had adhered to over a long period. When pressed to identify the instigator behind the notes Sal appeared to have some guesses in mind, but he refused to disclose any names. When prompted to say where Gerald might be, he waffled between looking miserable and hopeful. Not wanting anyone to see his truck near the house, he'd parked on a logging trail and walked in to scope things out. As to why the furnace needed to be removed, he professed to have no idea in the world.

"Period," Sal added for emphasis.

"Come," Antoine said. "On your feet."

With a squelching sound, the wet ground released Sal's lower half, and then he tripped his way through the weeds and briars, stinking of booze. We paused briefly to find my missing shoe. Antoine held it out for me, dripping and smelling of mud.

"Perhaps a pair in the house will fit you," he said.

"Shoes that belonged to a deceased woman," I pointed out.

"Suit yourself," Antoine said.

One painful step on a rock convinced me to secure the dripping shoe onto my foot. I continued onward, aware that Nicole would never end up making squashing sounds with every other step.

First, Antoine led us through the back door and down a short flight of broken concrete stairs. Seeing signs of significant leaks in the basement and major insect damage in the ceiling beams, I felt a stab of sorrow for the elderly couple who'd lived there and breathed their last breaths amidst poverty and cramped quarters. As Antoine set his flashlight ablaze and studied the walls, his murmurs suggested that he was surprised to see a home resting on an iffy foundation of loose stones and weak concrete. He crossed to the ancient furnace, and instead of using the illumination to point out details, he aimed the beam at us.

Squinting, unable to see, I gave up trying to reason with the man.

"This, Monsieur Hall," Antoine said, slapping his hand on the top of the furnace. "Has a cast iron interior that weighs two hundred and twenty-six kilograms. It would take several reasonably fit men to haul it out of the basement. In your inebriated condition, it would take ten."

"How was I to know that?" Sal complained.

"Bon, you're unaware that the kerosene *heater* was removed long ago," Antoine said. "It malfunctioned. The owners died from the fumes."

"Bastard sent me for no reason," Sal grumbled.

"*Who* sent you?" Antoine prompted.

"Nobody," Sal said. "People are out of town. That's why I came alone. I got down here, tried to budge it, and said holy crap."

"Hence, you turned to drink," Antoine said.

"Yeah, I got wasted and passed out," Sal said. "End of story."

Squinting, I said, "If the police collected the portable kerosene heater as evidence during the investigation, we're out of luck. It would be the only means of proving that Bud and Birdie were murdered."

"Murdered?" Sal said. "Wait a minute—"

"You understand the stakes?" Antoine asked. "Someone is implicating you in a cold case. I'm highly trained. I can protect you."

"I don't *know* who does the note writing," Sal said.

"What other errands have they arranged?" Antoine asked.

"This and that," Sal said. "Errands is the right word."

"Why not just tell you in the open?" Antoine asked.

"They're weird, maybe," Sal said. "You know how people can be."

"This is your choice? To throw your chances to the wind?"

"It's gotten me this far in life," Sal said. "I'm done talking."

Sal pursed his lips for emphasis. I used the pause to take a few photos of the furnace since it seemed an important element.

Antoine sighed. "Bon. On to next steps."

With his flashlight guiding the way, he ushered us up a flight of iffy stairs that led to the kitchen of the one-story house. He stopped abruptly, transfixed by a large black feather on the countertop.

"Merde," he said softly.

"Maybe it's a hawk feather," I said. "They molt in the fall."

"Hopefully, it was from a molt, not a death." As I started to reach for the feather, Antoine stopped me. "Let it rest in peace."

"You really get dark sometimes," I said.

"Follow me," he said. "Watch your step."

The appliances were ancient, the air musty. The floor creaked as we crossed to the living room, where cobwebs hung from the ceiling like torn rags. Sal flopped down on the sagging couch and slid his work boots across the floor to nudge a bottle of whiskey closer. His hands were bound in front, so it was no trouble for him to grip the neck.

I snatched the bottle away before he could take a swig.

"Stop that," I said. "Show some sense."

"I'm being held for no reason," Sal complained.

"I apologize for restraining you out of caution," Antoine said, cutting the plastic ties. "Trespassing is a minor offense."

"I'm free to go?" Sal asked.

"I can't let you drive drunk," Antoine said. "And you should be sober when it's time to … affronter les terribles fantômes."

"Wait, the terrible *what?*" Sal said, looking blanched.

"You don't speak French?" Antoine asked.

Sal snorted. "Where the heck would I learn a new language?"

"Forgive me," Antoine said. "Once sober, you can leave alone if you wish, but it seems you felt the terrible spirits out there, as I did. Like wind clawing at my skin, beseeching me to right a past wrong. Palpable, malevolent." Antoine shuddered, then he showed Sal the thin slice of tourmaline. "It helped me to clutch this in my hand."

"You don't believe in magical powers, a tough guy like you?" Sal said.

"It is a sought-after gem," Antoine said.

"You've landed on a passion of mine," Sal said, hitching up his pants with an authoritative air. "Gerald and me hope to find an open cavern with primo tourmaline one day. Never say never."

"Maybe a geologist could help with the search," Antoine said.

"We exchanged leads with a professor one time, but he tragically died a few years ago," Sal said. "Talk about the dangers of getting drunk. It was a slip-and-fall situation out on the coast."

"That must have come as a shock," Antoine said.

"He was way too young to meet an awful end," Sal agreed, now looking wise. "Hard luck can hit even the brightest of people."

"Bon." Antoine slipped the gem into his pocket. "Au revoir, Monsieur Hall. May you live a long and happy life."

"You're staying here, not heading out?" Sal asked.

"Just for a bit," Antoine said. "Don't let it concern you."

"I'm still woozy," Sal said. "I'm against drunk driving, so I'll hang back while you're doing whatever. I'll walk you out."

"You're very kind." Antoine snapped latex gloves onto his hands and offered me a pair. "I doubt we'll find anything."

"Papers, maybe?" I asked. "Records?"

"Whatever you think is best," Antoine said.

I gripped his arm and whispered, "None of that back-and-forth was lost on me. Thank you for staying. For caring."

"Focus your mind," he said. "Be alert."

I paused and watched Antoine prowl away on an intense search that might amount to a false front. In one minute, he'd excluded Sal from the French-speaking crew, nudged out his passion for tourmaline, and set the stage for Sal to deliver a philosophical, non-guilty view on the geologist's death. Antoine's talk of ghosts had me wondering if he'd heard the story about Sal getting bullied by Paul Polk and Isaac Munroe in the woods long ago, to the point where the poor kid had peed his pants.

Nervous jitters settled in my stomach as I stepped into one of the two cramped bedrooms. In the closet, a file box sat amidst orthopedic shoes designed for aching, arthritic feet. After my experience in Aaron's house, I nixed the idea of sorting through the paperwork. I wasn't an undercover operative. I was a photographer who hoped to carve out a lasting existence in the community. Scattered here and there were overdue electric and oil bills that were plainly visible without invasive prying.

Come winter, I make the rounds amongst seniors too stubborn to move in with relatives, Raymond wrote during an icy stretch. *I don't blame people for wanting the comforts of home. I'm that way myself. My memories are here in this house. Ella smiling, sewing her pillows. The rain on the roof, and the sheep peacefully grazing. This is where I'll lay my bones to rest.*

With a sigh, I checked under the twin bed, where dust bunnies the size of grapefruits roamed undisturbed. Seeing a photo album on a shelf, I tucked it under my arm and shined the beam of my flashlight on messy piles of books about birds, reptiles, and mammals.

"All I saw were a lot of overdue bills," I reported as I rejoined Antoine in the living room. "Did you find anything?"

"This." Antoine held up a tiny spy camera. "It hasn't been charged in a long time, but I think I can revive it."

As he stepped out and headed to his car, I sat on the couch and opened the ancient photo album. The spine crackled in protest, stiff and prone to splitting from years of neglect. The first photos showed the couple, Bud and Birdie, in wedding clothes, hand in hand as they stood amidst family and friends. Carefully unsticking the next brittle pages, I caught a sheaf of stapled papers that started to slip to the floor.

"It's a list of names, weights, and dates," I said.

"That's their list of turtles," Sal said. "They put special notches on the shells to tell one from the other over time."

"There's a photo of a baby," I said. "It died at a year old."

"Broke their hearts," Sal said, looking over my shoulder. "They wanted to ensure the tradition of protecting critters into future generations, but it wasn't in the cards for them, I guess. Your Dad used to visit Bud a lot. They had like minds in terms of wildlife."

Studying the turtle photos, I said, "This huge snapper looks fierce, but beautiful in a way. That's Bud holding it?"

"Notice his hands are way back on the sides of the shell. Bud was an expert handler," Sal added. "He knew exactly how far a snapping turtle's neck could swivel around. Never got bit. Not once."

"This photo is of a box turtle that was injured on the New Hampshire border," I said. "They're rare. Listed as endangered."

"When Bud and Birdie died, that critter and rescues like it went to a nature center," Sal said. "The wild ones are on their own."

Shining the light on a succession of photos, and finding Raymond in a few shots, I used my phone's flash to copy them, but given the darkness of the room, the results were blurry.

"I've heard you're getting Aaron's house ready for the market," Sal said. "It's Mrs. Pierce whose aunt died in here."

I hesitated. "Aaron's mother, you mean?"

"Yeah, she's Peg Pierce now, but she's Birdie's niece," Sal said. "You met Peg's husband. Kevin is a workaholic. He took one look at this place, the awful condition and unpaid bills Bud left behind, and was like, thanks a lot, God. One more giant lift to carry around."

"Who bought the land?" I asked. "Do you know?"

"My boss, Paul Polk, came in lickety-split and got a buyer lined up." Sal paused, looking worried. "Bud and Birdie died from an accident after having a drink or two. It's official, end of story, right? That guy you came with tossed murder into the mix to rattle me."

"At this point, the murder angle is unclear," I said.

"Don't tell Paul I was here. I'm not sure I trust your friend," Sal added. "This morning, he acted like he was from the south."

"He's from Canada," I said.

"Canada?" Sal asked. "Maybe he knows the guys who …"

As his voice trailed off, I shined the light closer to his face.

"The guys who *what?*" I prompted.

"They asked Paul about lakefront land. Sailboat people. Quit shining the light on me," Sal complained. "My head hurts."

"Sorry." I eased the beam away. "I was asking because of the burglary at Dan Bolton's house. The culprits spoke French."

"Maybe somebody he put away got mad," Sal said.

The story about "sailboat people" struck me as a lie, but I didn't want to rattle Sal. I gently prodded for insights on Gerald.

"People are wrong to think he's in league with his cousins again," Sal insisted. "He'll check in soon. We're a team."

I looked away and let a silence play out.

"Say a guy gets saddled with a health situation," Sal carefully ventured. "He's ended up with lung issues from his job. Cancer. Heath care is a maze if you need more than aspirin." Sal paused. "I'm told there's special clinics here and there. Charity doctors who lend a hand."

"Sal, is this your own experience?" I said softly.

"I'm talking about Gerald," Sal whispered. "He was checking around for that sort of thing, getting specialized help somewhere."

"Was it a definite diagnosis?" I asked.

"Through x-rays," Sal said. "Gerald is weighing his options. Doesn't want to end up an invalid. Paul didn't offer health insurance."

"Did they argue about it?" I asked.

"Pretty bad," Sal said. "Gerald felt cheated and angry."

"When did he get the diagnosis?" I asked.

"Maybe a month ago." Abruptly, Sal pointed to a spot across the room. "Grab that, would you? The rusted ice block tongs."

I crossed the room and shined my light on a heavy metal contraption that was about fifteen inches long, with wide loops for handles, a pin that allowed the two halves to work like scissors, and inward-pointing spikes for grabbing a huge ice block back in the day.

"Hand it here," Sal prompted, and then he reached for my flashlight. "Picture it, Isaac, Paul, and me sneaking onto the property way back when.

Hearing rumors of giant snapping turtles, kids come up with dares around whether one could be ridden around."

"Why are boys like that?" I asked.

"It was them more than me," Sal said. "We were tripping over sticks, lost and confused, when Bud popped out of nowhere. Isaac and Paul took off. They left me to meet a terrible fate alone. Bud shined his light like this." Sal held the beam under his chin so his eyes were hollowed out. "Just then, this awful moan was on the wind."

"Maybe Birdie was adding to the effect?" I asked.

"Yeah, they got me good," Sal said. "Bud told me it was a trained, awful spirit that he'd conjured up through magic. He held up these tongs." Sal demonstrated. "He said the moan was from a guy his granddad caught in the woods years ago. Pinned him by the ears with these things and hung him from a tree until he bled to death."

"He *really* wanted to scare you," I said.

"It worked," Sal agreed. "So bad I wet my pants."

"I heard Isaac and Paul were behind the scare," I said.

"Well, they were in a sense, leaving me out there. The funny thing is, Bud took pity on me," Sal added. "He was a good guy at heart, just set on people behaving themselves. Can I tell you a secret?"

"Absolutely," I said.

"The story about my name didn't come from family," Sal said. "It was Bud's attempt to ease how dumb I felt. He loaned me a clean pair of pants so I didn't feel ashamed, and drove me to the home."

I paused. "By 'the' home, you mean …"

"I was an orphan," Sal said. "Same as Gerald."

"So, lesson learned?" I managed.

"Afterward, Gerald took charge of my comings and goings," Sal said. "And I had his back in return. Regular kids like Isaac and Paul didn't see us as equals. It's been that way ever since."

"Sal, you can trust me with your other secrets," I said.

"You don't know what you're asking," he whispered. "Trooper Bolton has been digging into cold cases, stirring things up. All of a sudden, his house is attacked and Gerald is running scared."

"That's the point," I said softly. "Please tell me what's eating at you."

"If I say, he'll get run over," Sal said.

I hesitated. "Dan?"

"No, Gerald," Sal said. "Our system is tight. Unbroken."

"Not anymore," I said. "Maybe something went wrong."

"I can't risk it. He's in hiding, but fine. I know it."

In frustration, I rubbed my brow, desperate to arrive at the right thing to say, and during the pause, a barred owl hooted in the distance, somewhere out in the forest. Beautiful and mellow, it sounded as if the bird was purring, "Who cooks for you? Who cooks for you?"

"It's a sign," Sal said. "To leave it alone."

"Owls are beautiful and wise," I said. "Please talk to me."

"No," Sal said. "Do you hear me? *No.*"

"Ok, I won't push," I said.

"Let me rest a minute," he said. "I'm still half drunk."

With Sal looking spent and pale on the couch, I returned the photo album to the bedroom shelf where I'd found it. Next, I stepped into the kitchen and shined my light on the black feather that had stopped Antoine in his tracks. The night we'd met, he'd responded to my questions about Nicole with a story about a half-tamed hawk. Leaning closer, I saw a thick layer of dust on the soft webbing that enabled flight. In one of his journals, Raymond had described how the thousands of hooked barbules acted like zippers, allowing the bird to smooth them flat with its beak.

Antoine's reaction needed further explanation, so I brought the feather with me as I returned to the living room and set it aside on an end table, abruptly aware that Sal had fled into the night.

"Where is Monsieur Hall?" Antoine asked, coming in.

"He heard an owl," I said. "It freaked him out."

"I'll see if I can catch up," Antoine said. "In the meantime, the videos from the camera are on my laptop. You need to see them."

Antoine slipped from the silent house into the night.

With his computer balanced on my lap, I perched on the couch and clicked on a video of the room where I sat. Trapezoids of light falling across the couch and back wall told me the footage had been triggered in daylight. I choked with emotion as the audio track added realism to the moment in time: framed by angled daylight, my father stepped into view and studied the living room with a concerned frown, in uniform with his thumbs looped on his service belt, and the floor creaking underfoot as he moved. The back of Detective Allen's shirt obscured the view for a second, and then he crossed the room to join Raymond.

"Satisfied?" Roy Allen asked.

"Remnants of lobster take-out," Raymond said in a soft, resonant voice that was so real, it had my heart in a vice.

"There's open whiskey," Roy said. "That's the story."

"Bud and Birdie protected this land with zeal," Raymond said. "They had enemies. Neighbors and so-called pillars of the community."

"Your favorite theme of late," Roy said.

"It's a valid point," Raymond insisted. "Bud was sober for a decade. A binge happened, but why? It can't hurt to ask around."

"It'll lay waste to my ulcer," Roy said, "Our efforts are strapped enough in resolving clear cases of sudden deaths. We don't have the resources to chase shadows. The coroner said Bud and Birdie had a high blood-alcohol content. Leading up to that moment, Bud brought in a kerosene heater to keep warm. That was how the two of them lived. Patch this. Patch that. Never fix anything. I mean, look at this place."

"I know," Raymond said. "I see it."

"Then we're done. Come on."

Roy continued onward toward the front door, and then his footfalls faded to nothing as he left the house. My father remained there, rubbing his jaw as he pondered the contents of the room. I roiled with frustration, wishing I could reach through time and nudge him into saying more. With folded arms, Raymond was so still that the camera's sensor shut off, leaving him standing there, for all time to come, staring to one side.

I opened the next video.

In low light, possibly around dusk, a man in his late twenties stepped into view, looking so much like Isaac Munroe that I figured it was his son, Kick. Frowning as he looked around, he studied items on a shelf and paused with a troubled air. In the Corner Pocket, Thomas had said that Kick aspired to be a private investigator. Maybe Raymond's inquiries had prompted him to take a "fresh pair of eyes" approach to the scene. His visit was short. He took nothing from the house.

I clicked the next video.

Triggered by a blur of activity, the camera focused on a man whose face caused my heart to skip a beat: it was Aaron Pierce, Dan's best friend, looking alive and well as he crossed in front of the couch in the room, my first glimpse of him that wasn't a still shot.

"Unbelievable," Aaron muttered. "Crazy old man."

"Don't talk about your uncle that way," Peg Pierce said, arriving with Kevin. "I should have come here more often. Helped them clean up. Did you know their furnace broke down?"

"Of course not," Kevin said.

"Sorry I'm late," Paul Polk said, shaking hands all around with a toothy smile, and then settling to rest with an appropriately somber expression. "What a tragedy. I'm sorry for your loss."

"I'm getting calls from people Bud owed," Kevin said.

"You mentioned being willing to sell?" Paul said.

"The hell you did," Aaron said. "I thought there'd be more time to plan for the scenario I had in mind, but we talked about maintaining the Orland legacy of keeping the land safe. There are fewer and fewer tracks this big, and even fewer that are still pristine."

"That was a pipe dream from a bygone era," Kevin said. "This is reality. You've got a house, a wife, and a tight schedule."

"I was thinking we could launch a nonprofit," Aaron said. "If the land goes to a developer, it'll be spoiled before you can blink."

"Excuse us for a second, Paul?" Kevin said.

"Absolutely. Take your time."

Once the realtor was away, Aaron gripped his father's arm.

"Most people don't know there's a spring out there," he said. "Water means money these days. Tapping it would involve trucks, infrastructure, and damage for all time to come. Mom, tell him."

"I hate it when you two argue," Peg said. "The last I heard you were saving up for children. Isn't that the priority?"

"We're having trouble on that front," Aaron said tightly.

Peg touched his arm. "Why didn't you say so?"

"The doctor says IVF might work," Aaron said.

"In vitro?" Peg asked. "Will your insurance cover that?"

"I'm late for work," Kevin cut in, nudging Peg to the door. "Wait with Paul, ok? Aaron and I will talk it through."

"Spare me your version of a talk," Aaron snapped once they were alone. "The bills have piled up in recent months, but there has to be a way to keep this property in the family. There's more to life than the mill we're in, ushering criminals in and out of jail."

"*Enough*," Kevin hissed. "Your wife came to me in tears the other day. She's on the pill, so the story you told your mother is a giant coverup. You're refusing to get the proper help."

"Go ahead, rub it in," Aaron said miserably.

"You think I enjoy having to address the obvious?" Kevin said. "You're out of control with online gambling. Ever since you lost that scholarship in college, you've been chasing the highs of sports in all the wrong ways. It's over, son. Even Dan is fed up with you."

"He's in my corner," Aaron said hotly.

"Of course he is," Kevin said. "I spoke out of turn."

"You know what? Never mind, I see you checking your watch," Aaron said, heading for the door. "Work is your priority."

"*Aaron*," Kevin said, and then he followed his son out.

Once I recovered from seeing the wrenching personal details, my mind raced down other paths. Earlier in the day, I'd wondered if an illegal drug operation was the context behind Raymond's death.

"What if it's not?" I murmured. "What if it's about water?"

9

Hearing a rustle of footfalls, I looked up from the laptop as Antoine rejoined me, pulling wafts of chilly air into the dark room.

"Sal gave you the slip?" I asked.

"He was less drunk than he claimed," Antoine grumbled.

"These video clips are numbered," I said. "The one of Raymond is 15, the next is 21, then 29. Where are the rest?"

"In a separate folder." Leaning close as he joined me on the couch, Antoine clicked through multiple videos. "A moth. A sunbeam. A mouse. Another mouse, and so on. None of the clips show the owners, Bud and Birdie. Perhaps someone else left the camera."

"I assume you listened in on what Sal said to me?" I asked.

"Don't be downcast that he didn't budge," Antoine said. "It's early in the hunt. We regroup, and devise another plan."

Antoine leaned back with his hands laced behind his head and his sneakers crossed on the coffee table, pondering the next steps to consider with his molars working on a fresh wad of gum.

"So, two locations link the geologist, Vivian, and Dr. Clark," I said. "Paul, Gerald, and Sal have ties to this place. Nothing we did today was random. You had it all worked out."

In the darkness, Antoine focused on me. "Hmm?"

"You lured Sal here with a note about the furnace," I said.

"I left a note about fetching the heater," Antoine specified. "It took two minutes to uncover the note-under-the-rock system. Yesterday, as I watched, he crossed to the rock many times in hopes of finding a message from Gerald. Animals behave that way in zoos, following illogical impulses again and again. It was sad to observe."

"Your inquiries made him mistrust you," I said.

"Bad cop, good cop is a standard technique," Antoine said.

Frustrated and full of regrets, I was tempted to plunge outside, cup my hands to my mouth, and holler that Gerald had been murdered. If Sal was nearby, would he rush back and confess his secrets? All I knew for certain was that Raymond had stood in that same living room, just a few feet away, expressing concerns that might have led to Gerald's death.

"You seem troubled," Antoine said.

"I'm fighting unhelpful thoughts," I said.

"Hence," he said. "The tough choice we need to make."

I turned, abruptly aware of how alone we were in the dark room, with moonlight silvering the windows and touching the side of Antoine's face and soulful eyes. I'd braced myself for him to make a pass at some point, but he looked concerned rather than playful.

"What choice is that?" I asked.

"The 'Sonny effect' that you spoke of is very real," Antoine said softly. "I've come to see that it's a fast-moving, unpredictable element that could land you in harm's way. You did well today, but from now on it is best if you step back and let me handle the work."

I lurched to my feet. "You're not serious."

"I will be in touch now and then," he said.

"Gosh, *that's* a relief, given how you dodge your way along even during a candid moment," I said. "Come to think of it, you assured me that Nicole isn't the instigator who targeted Dan's house, yet you looked shocked and concerned when you clapped eyes on this."

As I held the feather in front of him, I watched his expression switch rails from a note of apology to full-blown alarm.

"Qu'avez-vous fait?" he demanded. "I told you not to touch it."

"I'm right, then," I said. "It's a message from Nicole."

Looking baffled, Antoine said, "How did you make that leap?"

"You described her as a wounded hawk," I said.

"One, that is a vulture feather. Two—" Antoine clamped down on his anger and escorted me back to the kitchen to study the dust on the countertop more closely than he'd done earlier. "The shape in the dust confirms that it sat here untouched for some time. It fits with Birdie's name. Match it to the dust pattern. Return it to its place."

I did so, having intended to leave the feather anyway.

"You have to admit, that was weird," I said.

"It is not 'weird' to show restraint and respect," he said.

I folded my arms. "For months on end, guilty parties have been drawing me into their worlds in the interests of damage control, so I've learned to pay attention to sudden changes of behavior. You were a pillar of calm until this business with the feather. If Nicole didn't leave it, who did you picture? What in the hell is going on?"

"Hell is the correct word to use," Antoine said. "You survive through hopes and superstitions, hunches and irrational associations."

"Is that what your reaction boils down to?" I asked.

He spread his hands. "Is that so difficult to accept?"

"Not at all," I said. "I'm trying to understand."

"It's been a long day," he said. "We're both tired."

I shook my head. "You're still being evasive."

"Pourquoi suis-je surpris?" Antoine directed into the darkness, chiding himself for being surprised. "J'aurais dû prédire cela."

"Here we go again," I said. "Ever since we met in Dan's house, you've used bursts of French and flirting and other means of throwing me off so I'm too distracted to look at the origins of this mess. I don't think Dan was the one who was careless in the wake of the job up north. I think it was either you or Nicole. I can see you tighten down, so I'll take that as a yes. You're not likely to break cover in that high-stakes realm, but you *will* start being straight with me about Raymond's death."

"Your behavior is why I tap the brake on sharing," Antoine said with ire. "You're reckless, hasty, overconfident—"

"This is not helpful," I said. "We need to head back."

"*And* you rudely interrupt," he added.

"Get moving." When Antoine stood there, looking stunned, I made a round-up motion with one hand. "Read the room. You're done."

"Vous êtes impossible," he said.

"Yup, I'm impossible, and it's time to fill in the blanks you dropped on my head today." As he doubled down on looking furious eye-to-eye, I used both hands to bulldoze him toward the door. "Why is Paul Polk tolerating a pot operation on his land? Why do you seem to be at odds with Nicole? Why the sudden switch to not wanting me to focus on the case? And *where* is the manuscript that you filched from Dan's safe?"

"I have kept it from prying eyes," Antoine said.

"I'm on the case," I said. "Cough it up."

Agog as I poked his back and snapped my fingers when he dawdled, Antoine spit his gum into the night, jammed a fresh piece into his mouth, and furiously chewed as he wrenched open the car door and plunged into the driver's seat. Without further prompting, he reached into the side pocket, plucked out a thick folder, and handed it over.

"*Thank* you," I said.

As I started leafing through the spiralbound copy of "A Tale of Local Intrepid Explorers" by Dr. Bertrand Clark, former archaeology professor at Westdale College, my smile turned to a glare.

"It's redacted like a secret document, with half the text blacked out," I said. "You broke protocol and ruined evidence."

"The text was redacted when I found it." Steering onto the road with the headlights illuminating the way, Antoine tapped his watch. "It's a forty-five-minute drive. As a link to multiple crimes, the manuscript must stay in my possession. Read while you can."

"It belonged to my father," I pointed out.

"Chain of custody is an important factor in law enforcement." Antoine pulled a thermos from the side pocket. "Coffee?"

"You had some all day?" I poured myself a cup, bolstered by the aroma, and discovered it was laced with brandy. "This would be great as a dessert option after dinner. Right now, I need to be alert."

Antoine tapped his watch. "Forty-two minutes."

"I'm sorry for snapping at you," I said. "Let's turn the corner and work in harmony again. I can see it's about a married couple from the 1800s, with citations about the archaeological digs. Cookware was found at a few sites. There's mention of some sort of treasure. The black marks make this *very* challenging. Tell me their names, at least."

"We will refer to them as, 'the missing couple.'"

"As in, they were murdered?" I asked.

"I would be grateful if you could answer that question." He tapped his watch again. "Thirty-eight minutes."

"Antoine, come on."

"I need to focus," he said. "You don't want the car to roll."

"Fine," I said. "Prepare to be impressed."

Braced for the next zero-gravity dip under the stars, I held the manuscript to the light of the dashboard and glimpsed descriptions of the couple who'd left the conveniences of city life behind to travel from place to place in the state of Maine with a pack mule. One line of text said it was their version of the "Grand Tour" that was popular during the 1800s. They'd counted on the goodwill of locals who loved reading about their adventures in newspapers across the land. Flipping pages, I fumed at the black lines, then I saw the words, "tourmaline gems."

"Maybe they paid their way with that sort of find," I said. "This looks like one of the articles about them. I can't read the date, but it's clearly from a later time. It's about treasure hunters."

"Here." Antoine turned on the overhead light.

"There's a glare," I said. "I'm not sure it helps."

"J'attends vos retours," he purred. "Continuer à lire."

"You're saying, 'I await your feedback,'" I translated. "Read on?"

"Bon." Antoine smiled. "Your French is excellent."

* * *

"Ugh," I moaned, squinting in pain as the lights of an oncoming car in the opposite lane split the darkness and stabbed my eyes for the umpteenth time. "There's a lot more brandy in that thermos than coffee. I can't focus anymore. Am I right about this?"

"Are you right about what?" Antoine asked.

"*This.*" With my spinning gaze averted, my finger stabbed at a page in the manuscript that looked blank except for smudges and specks. "There's a faint ghost image of a map of Maine."

"How could that be?" he asked.

"Ink can transfer in a book," I said. "The page with the map was ripped out, and the ghost image doesn't show details."

"If you say so," Antoine said. "I am driving."

Pitched to the right by a sharp turn, I used my arm to block the sight of trees swishing by beyond the windows. Lesson learned. When Antoine sought revenge, he didn't mess around. He destroyed opponents with their own foibles, and my foibles included guzzling coffee without an accurate sense of the booze-beverage ratio, and an inability to read text in a moving vehicle, even on a good day. In the dark of night, at top speed on a winding country road with dips and sharp turns, I was ready to be tossed onto an ER gurney, hooked up to an IV, and sedated into oblivion.

My cell phone dinged, causing me to groan.

"Look." Antoine nudged my arm. "An emergency."

"Oh no … what is it?"

Squinting at my phone sideways, I saw a colorful scene that blurred into a nauseating twist, as if the depicted reality had been whirled in a blender. Glimpsing it sent stabbing pains through my head and increased my nausea and vertigo by a thousand percent.

"What happened?" I asked. "Is someone dead?"

"It is a happy scene," he said. "Your mother is shopping in Paris."

"How is that an *emergency?*" I demanded.

"You wish to be with her, non?" he asked.

"You're a monster," I said. "I hate you."

"Gather yourself, Berrichon. We are here."

Pressed backward by a swift turn, then jerked forward like a rag doll, I slumped in a miserable heap, disoriented by the sudden lack of movement, except for what was happening inside my skull.

"What's going on …?"

"We're at the Corner Pocket, where we began this morning," Antoine said. "Here is your roommate outside the door, eager to help. I texted him to convey that you would need a ride."

I sagged, aware of the door opening and a cold rush of air on my right. Moaning, I reached into empty space and felt my body pour limply onto the pavement outside the sedan.

"What happened?" Jeremy asked, looming over me.

"She foolishly read while we were driving," Antoine said.

"That's crazy," Jeremy said.

"She is stubborn and impetuous."

"Monster," I moaned. "I'll *get* you for this."

Hauled upward by strong arms, I glimpsed Mrs. Brooks shaking her head as she beheld the spectacle of me being bum-rushed to Jeremy's truck with the toes of my shoes dragging across the parking lot. The door swung open. My top half was planted face down on the seat, and then with Jeremy gritting his teeth and hauling on my arms from the driver's side, Antoine's hands gripped my butt and shoved me into the cab. With faux attentiveness he secured my seatbelt and tucked the strap into place.

"My head is in a blender," I moaned.

"Are you sure she's not drunk?" Jeremy asked.

"She did drink a lot of brandy on an empty stomach."

"No way," Jeremy said. "I thought she had more sense."

"Give her raw eggs when you get home."

"Uhhh …" I almost fell from the seat as my stomach heaved, though nothing came out, since I'd been starved by my sadistic captor.

"Au revoir, chérie."

Smiling, Antoine closed the door.

* * *

My father's plaid couch was not the most attractive piece of furniture in the world, but I'd discovered it was a good place to curl up and die. Having no luck getting me up the stairs, Jeremy had veered to the right and dumped me onto the old cushions. All the while, the inside of my head performed pirouettes. Jeremy fetched a bowl of ice cubes and laid out a plate of crackers on the coffee table. Luke added his biscuit breath to my misery, licking my face in response to my moans.

"Leave her be," Jeremy said.

A half-hour later, all was quiet.

With grit and determination, I forced my eyes to focus on single points in the dark room. The trophy buck on the wall. The wood stove that I would most likely never use for fear of tending the embers incorrectly, and having the house go up in smoke and flames. I hauled myself upright, reached for the melting ice, and centered myself around the thunderous crunch of my molars reducing the cubes to bits.

I tempted fate by eating a cracker. It stayed down. I ate another.

My head still throbbed, but I found that walking to the kitchen sink and splashing cold water on my face helped by leaps and bounds. I pulled the rest of the lasagna from the refrigerator and felt an instant positive response from my body, which had earlier received the confusing message that the shop was shutting down without notice.

Before I headed upstairs, I attended to the demands of supporting my mother and my friends by endorsing the latest photos in their social media feed from their vacations in Paris, China, and St. Thomas. *Like. Like. Like. Like. Like. Like. Like. Like. Like.* I paused and decided an unhappy emoji was the correct response to my neighbor's news that things were not going well in South Carolina. Divorce was in the wings.

Yearning to ditch my muddy clothes and take a hot shower, I climbed the stairs and pulled up short on the landing, struck dumb to see Jeremy in my bathroom, buck naked as he scoured his teeth with my pink toothbrush. He paused. I paused. He stared. I stared.

"What the …?" Covering my eyes with one hand, I waved my other hand to prompt swift action. "Why would you stand there like that with the door open? Using *my* toothbrush, of all things!"

"You came up like a cat," he said. "I didn't hear you."

"Use a towel, for God's sake!" I hollered.

"I've got it on, now," he said.

I peeked between my fingers. "Oh my God, you've got it sideways, and there's still *way* too much information going on!"

"The mirror was fogged," he said. "I couldn't see my face."

"Nobody is this clueless about being naked," I said. "I'm canceling our little 'arrangement,' which I stupidly didn't question. Take my toothbrush. It's ruined, now. Then you need to leave."

I crossed to my bedroom and slammed the door.

Once I'd swapped my clothes for sweatpants and a cotton sweater, I sat on the edge of my bed and confronted the swirling emotions behind my blow-up. Not just Antoine's abrupt dismissal of my further involvement in the search for answers, though that definitely stung after feeling valued and appreciated for the first time during a case. Twenty-four hours had ticked by since Dan's team had made an arrest that must have some relevance, even if the crew remained at large. Dan had explained the need for secrecy and a tight workflow, so his silence wasn't a surprise. What I'd snagged on was the eagerness I'd seen in his eyes the other night, as if a hidden part of him had been yearning to get back into high-stakes under-cover action after months of tackling homegrown crimes.

Torn and uncertain, I opened my phone to the photos I'd taken during a canoe trip with Dan, his paddle poised with droplets flashing along the edge, and his brown eyes catching the sunlight as he smiled. We'd camped in a tent under the stars, despite the forty-degree temperature at night, keeping warm by snuggling together in a sleeping bag. We'd talked for hours, pausing now and then to listen to the same night sounds that my father had described in his journals. A great horned owl had impressed us with its resonant call, and every now and then a flock of ducks in the nearby river stirred with quacks and splashing sounds.

"Sonny?" Jeremy softly knocked on the door. "I'm heading out, but I wanted to say I'm sorry you saw me naked. It was me being dumb. Don't worry about running into me at the Corner Pocket because I got fired from that job, too. It's like I'm cursed."

"Wait," I said. "Hang on."

I opened the door and found Jeremy standing there, looking dejected with his duffle bag in hand, in jeans, a T-shirt, and sneakers that weren't sensible winter footwear. With a rueful twist of eyebrows, I apologized for letting the awkward interlude get to me.

"You don't need to leave," I added. "But let's promise to avoid a repeat moment. I'll stomp up the stairs, and you'll make sure to cover up."

"I can stay?" Jeremy asked.

"Yes. Now, tell me what happened at the store."

"First, let's check how mad you'll be about this." Jeremy handed over a mangled card with a heart entwined with flowers. "Luke attacked it for some reason. I found it on the floor near the couch all chewed up. I tried to fix it last night, but then forgot all about it."

Jeremy had used tape to attach the torn sections, which made Dan's handwritten note as frustrating to read as the redacted manuscript.

Sonny,

A colleague is checking your property ... gave him a key ... to leave this on the couch, knowing you sleep there during times of ... not fair to saddle you with ... every time my heart beats, there you'll be ... keep the faith ...

"He must have written this the night his house was attacked," I said. "I've been worried about his silence. He knew that in advance."

"Why does Luke seem to hate him?" Jeremy asked.

"It's the opposite," I said.

I explained how Luke had sulked all the way home after his hope of seeing Dan had gotten punted to the wayside. Even dogs, with their mostly innocent minds, were capable of using vandalism to convey their stung feelings. I further noted that instead of following me to my room as usual, Luke had curled up on his pillow in the living room.

As I headed downstairs with the card in hand, Luke's brow furrowed, as if he was thinking, *Crap, I knew I would get busted.*

"You're quite the outlaw," I said, kneeling to scratch his ears.

Luke's tail timidly stirred, his gaze hopeful.

"Come on," I said. "You're overdue for some love."

With hugs and a moment of tossing his rope toy, I apologized for being too distracted to address his stung feelings.

"Stop looking worried," I said to Jeremy. "We're good."

"Plus, your car is still at the Corner Pocket," he pointed out.

"All the better," I said. "I'll need a ride."

"I've got one other story to relate," he said. "Mrs. Brooks asked me and Thomas to study the comings and goings of the racoons that raided the garbage bins. As we checked the security footage, we saw a female cop in plain clothes step out of the shadows and startle Mr. Polk as he was leaving. He was flustered and insisted he didn't have the answers she was looking for. She's pretty and has a French accent."

"Her name is Nicole," I said. "Did you hear specifics?"

"Mostly, she spoke in a whisper, but your name came through during their exchange," Jeremy said. "The way you're frowning, she's out to get you for some reason. What's the extent of it?"

"It's not a problem for you to worry about," I said.

"I'm here to protect you," Jeremy insisted.

"I think you got your signals crossed when Antoine suggested you provide support while you're here," I said. "You're Brumby's brother, so that's how I'm seeing you. You're sweet, Jeremy. A great guy, but cheating is not in my wheelhouse. You need to know I'm loyal to Dan."

He paused. "You see me as a brother?"

"It's good to be honest, isn't it?" I asked.

"I've started seeing you as a sister," Jeremy said. "There's a big hole in my life. My mom died last year from a heart attack."

"I'm sorry to hear it," I said softly.

"It felt awful to be cast adrift," Jeremy said, candid and vulnerable as he glanced at me. "It's why I started looking for kin. I don't blame Brumby for seeing me as an unwanted mouth to feed."

"He'll come around," I said. "Give him time."

"I wanted to impress him with a stretch of success."

"Well, Jeremy." I patted his back. "By noon tomorrow, you'll have your job at the store, and a raise to boot. I'll handle everything."

"You're serious?" he asked.

"You've picked well in the sister lane. Watch and learn."

10

Leaning back in one of the chairs in the Corner Pocket's office, I fell into silence as Thomas mumbled his way through his attempt to find the security video of Nicole questioning Paul Polk outside the store. At dawn, Antoine had texted me a sad face emoji that I took to be an apology for our rough parting, even though I'd been foolish, stubborn, and impetuous, guilty as charged. I marveled that Antoine felt regret around it.

"You'll face this one day," Thomas said. "Once you reach your sixties, you'll be hard-pressed to recall … wait, here it is!"

I leaned forward and studied the footage of Nicole's hissed exchange with Paul Polk, including her efforts to learn more about me. Paul had little to share since we'd never met. Grudgingly, I admitted that Nicole's questions were not beyond the bounds of a normal police inquiry. Her presence in town was my main concern. Was the rest of Dan's team working close by as well? If so, why hadn't he gotten in touch?

"I mentioned this video to Detective Allen," Thomas said. "I was tied up at the register. He's stopping in for a copy later on."

Once Thomas prepared a travel drive, I asked him to stay and weigh in on Dr. Bertrand Clark's research and fall from grace.

For background, I used a search engine to pull up newspaper clippings from the 1800s featuring the couple who'd devoted their lives to exploring Maine with a pack mule and high spirits. Photographs showed them in stiff poses, in keeping with the need to stand still during the long exposures involved with capturing images on film with a bellows-style camera. One means of funding their adventure was to stage poker games with locals and politicians who wanted to boost their profiles by rubbing elbows with celebrities. There were reports that "somehow," the couple won most of the games. One reporter speculated that they were millionaires, with gold coins tucked here and there, and professed to have been shown how the wife carried a Derringer tucked into her bodice.

"They were bound to attract thieves," I said.

"Indeed, they were naïve," Thomas said, adjusting his glasses as he studied the succession of old articles I'd found.

"What was your sense of Dr. Clark?" I asked.

"He often had multiple digs going on at the same time," Thomas said. "He was quite secretive about how he knew where they'd camped. Perhaps he'd found a map they'd left behind. The digs were extremely popular with students and volunteers. I was tempted to join the fun, but my arthritis doesn't allow for kneeling and hard work."

"It was a known thing for people to launch a 'Grand Tour' of Europe," I said. "This couple stayed close to home."

One article covered their mule being found without its pack, wandering in the woods, and reduced to skin and bones.

"Ever since then, the legend has sparked treasure hunts from time to time," I said. "Townsfolk upending rocks, digging holes, and checking old barns and sheds where the couple might have camped. People lost their minds with it, vandalizing places without a thought."

"Dr. Clark himself was accused of taking things too far," Thomas said. "He alienated landowners with his test digs. Your father was a rare supporter. Raymond was like that. Unafraid to buck the norm if criticism seemed unjust. You realize we've blown a bit past our five-minute break," Thomas said. "Don't let my wife catch you in here."

"I need another minute to make a phone call."

"I'll cover for you as best I can," Thomas said.

I prepared myself to gently press Dr. Clark's wife for a fresh copy of the manuscript, and any details she wanted to share. Once she answered my call and I introduced myself, she seemed eager to talk.

"Your father was a key ally for Bertrand," she said.

"Can you fill in some of the history?" I asked.

"It's not breaking news that companies can fire people 'at will' without reasonable cause," Mrs. Clark said as if picking up from a previous conversation. "I was naive to imagine it wouldn't exist in higher education, but it's going on at every college where Bertrand's peers work. We reached out to a lawyer. He said bullying isn't against the law. Lives can be upended with a stroke of a pen. I know I sound bitter. It's too much."

"Did the college cite a specific reason?" I asked.

"Vivian Vandorne bought into the lie that Bertrand had misused college funds," Mrs. Clark said. "At functions and parties, she's all smiles with benefactors like Isaac Munroe and Paul Polk, saying, 'Call me Vivee!' It's not nice to say this, but I've heard she sleeps around to get ahead."

"Including the geologist who died?" I ventured.

"When the police questioned Ms. Vandorne about it, she complained nonstop that it was a miscarriage of justice to have her reputation sullied with a scurrilous accusation, and then she turned around and tossed Bertrand under the bus in the same breath."

"Your husband was exonerated?" I asked.

"Thanks to Raymond," she agreed. "He sorted it out when the police took their time crosschecking facts. As you can imagine, Raymond's death came as a terrible blow. A cruel twist of fate."

I paused. "Did I meet you at his memorial service?"

"We decided to reverse course in the parking lot," she said. "Bertrand was afraid his presence would strain the occasion."

"It got strained anyway," I managed.

"People stared and whispered?" she asked. "Made you feel unwelcome? If so, you got a taste of how Bertrand was treated by a community that he cherished. Even his friends doubted him."

While we talked, I looked up Bertrand's photo and found him to be a round-faced fiftyish man in wire-rimmed glasses.

"People will tell you that Bertrand and Raymond had a falling out after the geologist died," Mrs. Clark said. "That wasn't the case at all. Bertrand was terrified that his research was to blame. He was convinced someone was following him. From an open, honest man, he even stopped confiding in me. In hindsight, I think he was protecting me and our boys at his own expense. One has to be upfront with the police. It played into them thinking he'd had a mental breakdown or staged his disappearance."

"This is distressing," I said. "I'm so sorry."

"Our children are in their teens," she said. "They need their father, but after this much time, I can't help but think the worst."

"I'd like to follow through on this," I said. "I can't make sense of his manuscript because most of the text is redacted."

"Bertrand is the one who did that when the trouble first began," she said. "I fished it out of the trash and brought it to Raymond. Bertrand was furious. He rarely ever hollered. It was painful to watch. The work that had brought him joy was suddenly a source of paranoia. I've moved to my hometown to spare my boys from gossip and bullying. It was wrenching. If Bertrand comes back, he'll find our house empty."

"Paul Polk is your realtor?" I asked.

"I'm deciding whether I should end our contract," she said. "An early bid that he lined up shook me to the core. A detestable planned community. My husband's students protested and made a fuss. Hence the deal fell through. Anyway, Bertrand destroyed all of his work, except for a couple of historic photos. I can send them if you want."

"I would appreciate that," I said.

To keep afloat financially, she'd been forced to begin the process of declaring that her husband was dead. Far from getting answers that firmed up the picture, I'd expanded the list of unknowns.

My ten-minute break had extended to fifteen. Riddled with guilt for not providing the proper level of service, I slipped from the office to wipe down the coffee bar countertop, clean crumbs from the tables, and restock the napkins, sugar, and cups. In the crafts aisle, I carefully dusted off Sue's handmade baskets. Each was a marvel of artistry and precise rows that contained the fresh scents of sweet grass and willow wood.

While I paused, I overheard a man's voice in the next aisle.

"Chill, Nicole. You made the mess. Live with it."

I put down the basket and crossed to the end of the aisle to look up at the half-dome security mirror that offered a distorted glimpse of the man as he tucked his phone into his pocket. As he stepped toward the mirror and out of view, I heard a sniff and approaching footfalls.

I turned, but there was nowhere to hide.

"Hey, Miss?" he prompted.

"Um, yes?" I said to the thirtyish guy.

"The store used to stock …" Faltering as our eyes met, he looked away. "Umm, praline candy, from down south."

"I'm new here," I said, recognizing his dark crew cut, high cheekbones, and notched chin. "You're Isaac's son, Kick, right?"

His sighed. "Yeah, that's me."

"Your father talked about having you stop by Aaron's house to shred financial documents," I said. "Is that still in the works?"

"Here's the deal," Kick said. "My schedule is tight, but he's always signing me up for surprise ventures. I can't do it today."

"That's fine," I said. "I'm not pushing for it."

"Oh," Kick said, relaxing a little. "He made it sound urgent."

"Thomas would be the one to ask," I said.

Kick paused. "About?"

"The pralines," I said.

Nodding, he said, "Got it. Thanks."

With a quick smile, he continued onward without further interest in the pralines, returning a box of crackers to the shelf as he made a beeline for the exit. The bell jingled, and then his athletic build slipped into the driver's seat of an expensive-looking car.

"You come on too strong," Mrs. Brooks said behind me.

"We spoke for less than a minute," I said.

"It's the blue eyes," Mrs. Brooks said. "For young men, it's flustering when a woman is attractive and intense in equal amounts."

I focused on her rosy cheeks and piercing eyes, which were magnified by the glasses perched on the bridge of her nose.

"I appreciate your advice," I said. "I'll try to do better."

With pursed lips, she set about polishing her glasses, and then she snugged them on again, stalling and dawdling.

"I suppose you heard about the incident," Mrs. Brooks said.

"Spills are the worst, aren't they? A jar of spaghetti sauce, of all things." I blew out a weary breath and shook my head. "Sauce and glass everywhere. I can't imagine how Jeremy could be so clumsy."

"Your cousin, Charlotte, marched up and startled him," Mrs. Brooks said. "In her narrow mind, anyone connected to you is her enemy."

"It's shocking, isn't it?" I asked. "How people behave."

"In all the confusion, I think Jeremy got the wrong message," she said. "I heard he's pitching in at the Pierce residence."

"Jeremy is painting there right now," I agreed.

"I see." Mrs. Brooks looked downcast. "He's all set, then?"

"Do you want me to talk to him?" I asked. "See if he'll come back?"

"Only if it works for you," she said.

"I'll swing it, but honestly," I said, "this business of catching raccoons might be a sticking point. It's extra work."

"I'm happy to sweeten the pot," she said. "It's only fair."

I smiled. "With my female friends out of town, I'm having an odd man-centric week. It's been nice spending time with you."

"I suppose this is a bid for a raise?" Mrs. Brooks asked.

"You seem to forget that I'm here on a volunteer basis," I said. "I'm saying thank you. I've learned a lot from you."

"Apparently, you haven't learned to tidy the floor," she said, pointing at a footprint. "Get to it. No dawdling."

Once she was bustling away, I called Jeremy.

"You're all set," I whispered. "Act like nothing happened when you arrive at noon. Just come in and put on your apron."

"Got it," he said. "Umm, Luke has some paint on his fur."

I closed my eyes. "No worries. I'll handle it."

I fetched the microfiber mop and started my methodical march up and down the aisles with the soft pad collecting hair, dust, crumbs, and other unwanted elements. I found it meditative, a chance to ponder the latest developments. All I'd learned from the redacted manuscript was that some of the locations Dr. Clark had cited were circled on my father's map of crime locations, including the former home address of Dr. Bertrand Clark, who'd gone missing shortly after my father's death. I'd heard of people retreating from the world after a hard blow. Maybe the professor was out there somewhere, tattered and unkempt. Any image was better than concluding that he was buried in a shallow grave.

Hearing a man asking where I might be, I reversed course with my head tucked down and the mop whispering along the floor on my way to the office, where I could check the camera feed to plan a stress-free escape. Footfalls in the adjacent aisle had me taking a zigzag path through the gourmet food and wine section to reach my goal. Abruptly, a pair of dark, official-looking shoes rounded a corner up ahead.

"Sorry," I murmured.

As I tried to reverse away, the polished toe of one of the shoes pinned my mop to the tiled floor. I tugged on the handle. It didn't budge. With an apprehensive grimace, I looked up.

"We need to talk," Detective Allen said.

As always, Roy was an implacable rock, his hair cropped over a stern gaze that had a way of collapsing my spirits without words.

"I'm working," I said. "It'll have to wait."

"I heard Haydn Pike has surfaced," he persisted.

In a hushed tone, I encapsulated the gist of my encounters with Pike in the past few days: annoying, rather than threatening.

"You parked here yesterday, but were nowhere to be found," Roy said.

"Antoine asked me to join him on a drive," I said.

I recapped the previous day's journey, avoiding specifics and squinting my way through attempts to recall the names of roads. I was particularly leery of telling him about our encounter with Sal since it would open the door to an extensive conversation, and land Mr. Hall in trouble.

"I heard you returned to the store in rough shape," Roy said.

"Antoine's coffee had a touch of brandy," I said. "It went to my head."

"Why take you along for the ride?" Roy asked.

"While assessing my father's map of crimes," I said, "I provided some context, given Dan's focus in recent months."

"Yeah, about that." With a grimace, Roy rubbed his brow. "The alternate theory on Raymond's death has become a pain point."

I hesitated. "In what regard?"

"Per the latest thinking," Roy said, "a roof leak that ended fast would explain the lack of stains on the ceiling. As for the pan of water, I've sat by a bedside to soak my aching feet more than once."

"All of which means …?"

"There's no justifiable reason to change the cause of death and expand the matter into a cold case," Roy said. "Murder pulls an extra level of stress into the process. I can tell you care about Dan. If you keep the pressure up, it'll add unwarranted friction to your lives."

"If anything," I said, "I've urged him not to ruin himself on it."

"The door isn't entirely closed," Roy said. "We'll keep it in mind, but for now please dial back on your theorizing."

"Of course," I said. "Thank you for telling me."

My nod conveyed acceptance, but I felt shocked to the core by a turn of perception that felt premature and baseless. I put it aside as Roy asked to see the video of Nicole's conversation with Paul Polk. In the office, I stood nearby with my arms folded while Detective Allen sat at the computer and reversed the clip a few times in an attempt to hear the exchange, exactly as Thomas and I had done a few hours ago.

"Who is she?" Roy prompted.

I conveyed her name and what little I knew.

"I'm shocked that you don't know already," I added. "She was there the night Dan's house was targeted, but I've been alone in my concerns. I know about the micro detonator, by the way."

"How do you end up with insider tips?" Roy demanded.

"People come at me," I said. "I'm doing my best."

"Where is the rest of Dan's team?" Roy asked.

Sadly, I had to confess, "Your guess is as good as mine."

11

"Yoo-hoo! Sonny!"

On my way to my car, I paused in front of the Corner Pocket's front windows, startled to see Vivian Vandorne closing in on me with her high heels clicking on the pavement and her smile suggesting we were long-lost friends. She added a burst of finger wiggling to catch my attention, which had several rings winking at me in the sunlight.

"Umm, hi," I managed.

"I'm so glad I caught you!" Vivian said.

I gulped as she enveloped me in a perfumed hug that gave me a close glimpse of her red lipstick and doctored eyelashes.

"Never mind the fuss I made the other day," she quietly urged. "My special someone has sorted it out."

"How?" I asked. "And, umm, how?"

"By using logic," she said. "The past is the past. Things were settled, so why waste energy spinning my wheels? He's very protective."

"Is he anyone I know, or …?"

"None of that," Vivian said coyly. "I've worked too hard to land Mr. Right to let a man-magnet like you in on the secret. Though he seems to know quite a bit about you," she added with a worried frown. "Anyway, I can't linger. Meetings await."

"You didn't explain your worries," I said.

"Now there's no need," Vivian said. "We'll catch up later."

Left to stare after her smart-looking pinstriped jacket and skirt as she entered the store, I wondered what I'd just experienced.

Thinking I was looking toward him as he stacked items on a shelf, Jeremy smiled and waved, and then he conducted a pantomime indicating that he'd left Luke in his pen, per my instructions, lest my ambitious canine further his growing notion that he was the boss of me. Keeping the men in my life from spinning off the rails was starting to be a full-time job. Dan was the only outlier who was beyond control.

Fifteen minutes later, as I stepped into Aaron's house, I congratulated myself for entrusting Jeremy with a project on the to-do list. The scent of fresh paint hung in the air as I arrived in the guest bedroom and beheld a vision of glistening floor-to-ceiling success. Drop cloths were arrayed across the carpet, and all edges between the walls and the molding were crisp, with zero signs of drips and sloppy mistakes.

He'd finished that room and had started the base coat in the office.

"There you go," I said. "I'm a genius."

I closed the door because my next chore was going to raise dust.

As I pulled the stepladder from place to place with a cloth in hand, I thanked my mother's cleaning staff for teaching me the basics during my childhood. No doubt they'd felt uncomfortable when I'd confided my reasons for learning the ropes: their employer, Mr. Littlefield, was so vexed by my poor performance as a child that I was doomed to be cast out into the cold. By eight years old, I'd learned how to trim shrubs, disassemble a pool filter, and walk to school if I missed the bus.

Once the musty odor of neglected corners was replaced by the scent of lemon cleaner, I became a whirling menace to dust bunnies and cobwebs, hauling the vacuum over the carpets as I scoured the fibers into neat rows. I tackled the hardwood flooring with more care.

I hit the off button in the master bedroom, the last stop at the far end of the house, and stripped the bedding that showed a dent in Aaron's pillow with his wife's pillow untouched; one of those details that was better left to me to erase, since his parents might find it tough.

On my way out, I stared at a four-foot object that I'd taken to be a Medieval shield that Aaron had picked up at a flea market. Now I saw that it was a turtle shell mounted so that it could be hung on the wall. Below the polished scales was a plate inscribed with a caption: "Maximilian, 92 years old, 66 pounds, August 15, 1912, RIP."

The shell was all that remained of the ancient reptile that had inspired the Orland family to protect other turtles on their land from succumbing to the same fate of being "murdered" by hooligans.

I wondered if Aaron's wife had embraced the memorial, or if it was one of the things the couple had argued over. With that in mind, I frowned as I pondered Vivian's news that she'd found "Mr. Right." Everyone tended to brighten up at the first blush of a new romance, but her giddy demeanor troubled me. The other day, she'd struck me as businesslike and austere, not prone to embracing and confiding in near-strangers in public, and her makeup had been amplified to a noticeable degree. Then again, what did I know? We'd met for a grand total of five minutes.

Closing in on two o'clock, I discovered that the vacuum had tripped the circuit. Midway down the basement stairs, I saw games, hockey gear, and other items stacked along the walls on wire shelves. I frowned, puzzling over the patio pillows at the bottom of the steps, and yelped as my ankle snagged on a hook that appeared out of nowhere.

Pitched forward, with the concrete wall ahead, I curled inward to take the impact on my shoulder and mostly spared my head from a hard hit. As a figure loomed close, blocking the ceiling lights, terror rushed through me, visions of monsters coming to haul me into a grave.

"Goodness, talk about clumsy," a voice purred.

Moaning in pain, I gripped my bumped forehead and struggled to sit upright. The monster was female. It was Nicole.

"You tripped me," I managed.

"You tripped yourself," she said. "Thankfully, you fell onto pillows."

Under the basement lights, her face was in partial shadow, her eyes neither green nor gray. She'd pulled her hair back into a clip as if she'd come in expecting some hair-pulling. My waves and curls were spilling all over the place, bedraggled from hard work and dust. I reached for an office chair that smelled of mildew and used it to haul myself upward. Wobbling slightly, I plunged onto the seat and gripped my head.

"You could have killed me," I managed.

"Ah yes, the look of wide-eyed suffering that's alluring to men. I'm not fooled. I know who you really are. For *instance*—" Nicole leaned close with sudden intensity. "You gave a video of me to Detective Allen? You don't see that kind of shit will endanger Dan?"

"Thomas gave Roy the video," I said. "If your goal is to stay in the shadows, don't threaten people under a security camera."

Nicole's sour look acknowledged the mistake, and then she swung another office chair toward me, sat down, and leaned in.

"How was your day with Antoine?" she asked.

Her jeans were tight, her boots stylish, and her blouse was unbuttoned to show cleavage and a lace bra. She'd taken the time to apply mascara and perfume but hadn't thought to wear nitrile gloves.

"This is totally off," I said. "Get out."

"Fine, I'll share a story from my recent past," she said. "There I was, getting all kinds of close to a Maine state trooper who was new to undercover work. Handsome, and smart. We connected in a *big* way."

"This is not going to work," I said.

"One day, he didn't check in on schedule," Nicole said. "Then he sent a sweet message saying a family issue had come up."

"Get out of my face," I said.

"I'm glad to see this piece of the puzzle," she said. "Dan was distraught and messed up. You added to that burden."

With my head still swirling, I shoved her away and focused on the everyday items on the shelves in order to ground myself. Puzzles and board games. Jumper cables, climbing ropes, and books that would not come out of that basement without signs of mold.

"You *added* to his burden," Nicole shouted in my face.

"I told Dan not to risk his job," I said.

"Your actions say otherwise," Nicole hollered. "Pushing your way into private business, tripping over clues. Here we are again. Dan asked for *one* thing this week. Stay out of a high-level case that involved an attack on his house. What do you do? You put a picnic lunch together and jeopardize our whole team in a matter of hours."

"You're the one who's endangering the team," I countered. "Tripping me on the stairs and coming at me in a fit of jealousy."

"Did you see me here before this week?" Nicole hollered. "I don't get jealous. There's no need for it because Dan is seeing that with you, he'll be pressing repeat over and over again."

"You're lying," I said, pulling Dan's card from my pocket. "He left this for me to find because … hey, don't you *dare*," I seethed, as she snatched the note and tore it apart. "Stop it!"

"You stepped into *my* dance, not the other way around," Nicole said, scattering the pieces. "You caught on that Dan was committed to covert border work. You didn't respect the risk."

"I assumed he had it covered," I insisted.

"That was the past. This is now. *Stop* blundering into matters where you don't belong," she yelled in my face.

"I'm trying to help," I said.

"By endangering me?" she demanded. "Endangering him?"

"Back up," I said. "I need space."

Nicole gripped the handles of my chair.

"From here on out, *stay* in your own lane," she hollered at point-blank range. "Get it through your head that you're not a cop. I didn't upend your life. You're the one who upended mine."

"Dan loves me," I whispered.

"How stupid can you be? You're a disgrace to your father's legacy. He's rolling in his grave, not cheering you on."

"I need space," I said. "I can't breathe."

"You're a waste of Dan's time. He deserves better."

Her torrent continued, blurring into a roaring noise.

Human anger could be like that. Palpable. Visceral. An unchecked force that filled the air. The only thing I could liken it to was the thunder of a raging river flood that I'd survived with my best friend. One minute Arlene and I were asleep under a shelter in Costa Rica, with the drumming rhythm of a downpour lulling us to sleep. The next minute there was a din of trees splitting and boulders tumbling and the hollering of fellow hikers fleeing toward high ground. Arlene laced her fingers around mine as we clambered after them, and then the churning river struck us from the side. Milling, clutching at branches, and feeling the leaves strip off in my hands, I held fast when Arlene slipped and nearly went under.

Shouting encouragement to each other above the din, we caught hold of a vine that we lashed around ourselves as we climbed a narrow tree. The bark was loose, the trunk slick. We rested our toes on holds we couldn't see, our socks torn off, and finally came to rest with the torrent raging a foot below us, wet, gasping, exhausted, and terrified.

"If we survive this, we'll get giardia!" Arlene hollered above the din.

I'd tearfully laughed. "Vomiting and diarrhea."

"I'll still love you! I *do* love you," Arlene sobbed.

"We'll make it," I hollered.

"Your idea of a bridal shower!" she said.

"I strived for a special moment!"

"I think I'm pregnant," Arlene hollered.

I'd focused on her wet, blinking face and the increasingly bedraggled state of her Afro-Caribbean curls. "You're *pregnant?* Since when?"

"Last week," she said. "Lance begged me not to come."

Tearful and terrified to have two precious lives at risk, I'd gripped her arm and urged her higher up the tree to a safer branch.

Shouting over and over again above the din.

"Keep going. I'm here. I'll protect you."

Slowly, the memory of the roaring noise receded, just as the river had done, allowing the stillness of the basement to settle around me. When I opened my eyes, I felt calm, having drawn strength from the memory of surviving the impossible with my best friend.

Frowning, Nicole stared at me.

"You were whispering," she said. "Babbling, like you'd lost your mind. Now this moment. How did you go from shaking to calm?"

"My guess is, you don't have a best friend," I said.

"So, you did lose your mind," Nicole said.

"If that's what you need to hear," I said.

Wobbly, still aching from the fall, I pushed upward and limped to the nearest shelving unit. In her eyes, I was an amateur. Maybe so, but either she hadn't heard my entire story, or she didn't imagine that getting tossed around by murderers would inspire some high-level strength training, which by the way included pole dancing.

I gripped the shelving unit, assessing the puzzles and cables, and then my gaze fixed on a hockey stick that was within reach.

"Quite the actress," Nicole said.

Keen-eyed. Fair enough. I turned to face her.

"I'm not outside of my lane by choice," I said. "Somebody targeted the man I love, and will continue to love—"

"Prepare for heartbreak," Nicole said.

"I'm prepared all day every day," I said. "One thing I'll never do is trip a rival on the stairs and holler in her face."

"You tripped yourself," she said.

"You put the pillows there because you have just enough sense to not break my neck in Dan's best friend's house," I said. "And by the way, the case in May was linked to Aaron's death. Dan is *proud* of the role he played in getting answers and justice. It was a healing moment. A first step in climbing back from the worst shock of his life."

"You think I don't know that?" Nicole asked.

"You're too self-involved to notice suffering," I said. "If you're good at your job, you can handle the sparks from my wheels. I'm not looking to get involved, but here you are in my face."

"You outed me to be spiteful," she said. "A fit of jealousy."

"Enough with the bullshit," I said. "There's the exit."

"Why hasn't Antoine checked in?" Nicole asked.

"Maybe you've lost his trust. If I were you—*hey*," I said, shrinking away as she gripped my arm. "Stop. My shoulder hurts."

"I won't leave until you back down," Nicole said.

"If I don't agree, what then?" I asked.

"We sit down and start over," she said.

"Stop hurting me," I said. "I need water."

Using a technique Dan had taught me, I sagged for a split second, and then I unleashed enough fury to spin Nicole into an armlock. Shoving her forward until her face met the concrete wall, I applied pressure on her arm so she'd stop struggling. Breathing hard, she whispered curses in French, invoking Dan's name to provoke me.

"You wouldn't quit," I said. "This is the result."

"I'm an officer of the law!" she sputtered.

"The stick you used to trip me is over there," I said. "You weren't smart enough to wear nitrile gloves, so if I have to hold you here until morning when Jeremy arrives, that's what I'll do. I will pee on the floor. Go without food. How about you? Are we good?"

"What do you want?" Nicole growled.

"I want you to listen up," I said.

"My arm is breaking!"

"Don't care," I said. "Used to care. Not anymore."

"*Uhhh* ..."

"Guess what defined the monsters I faced this past year?" I seethed in her ear. "Unlike you, they were impossible to read. If there's a titanium form of ice on the planet, that's what ran in their veins. Right now, it runs in *my* veins because I'm sick and tired of cheats and liars. You call me an amateur. You don't have the sense to keep your pants zipped up and leave your stung feelings where they belong. In the past. You're an infant who refuses to grow up. Now, get your skinny ass out of this house of sorrow, and if I so much as *smell* your cheap perfume in the air, I will call 911 and out you for real. Are we clear?"

Nicole choked out one word. We were clear.

I spun her out of the hold and reached for a hockey stick in case she tried to come at me. Rubbing her wrenched arm, she backed away with off-color eyes that said I'd made an enemy for life.

Come what may, so had she.

12

Across the road from my neighbors' yellow house and landscaped yard, which beamed encouragement toward my entrance of overgrown weeds on the opposite side of the wooded lane, I skipped checking my mailbox, not caring in the least if a logging truck thundered by and scattered the next round of bills to the four winds. After Nicole had skulked away in dark sunglasses, I'd tried to mend Dan's card and smooth sections she'd crumpled in her fist. The result was truly sad, leaving me with a love note that looked like it had been collected from a crime scene.

It *was* evidence from a crime scene.

Now it was me with sunglasses on, hiding within the dark lenses, half wishing I hadn't put Nicole into an armlock, and half wishing I'd pushed her to admit why she'd confronted Paul Polk, and if she'd been the woman that Kick Munroe had been talking to on the phone in the Corner Pocket: "Chill, Nicole. You made the mess. Live with it."

The bottom of my driveway cut through a stretch of tall pines, white paper birches, and lichen-speckled boulders. I drove onward through the shade, then sunshine claimed my car as I nosed upward toward the house and barn at the top of the hill. From my first days on the farm, the property had seemed so round and well-proportioned that I felt as if I'd entered a snow globe, an effect that would be amplified in a few months when deep snow would be draped from evergreen boughs and rest in dollops on every fence post. Just then, the sky was a wide expanse of New England blue above the tree-strewn greenness of an early winter afternoon. The house, alas, was green as well: a vibrant shade that my mother had tartly rejected, adding that she would never set foot in the place until I hired professionals to repaint the exterior with a "dignified" shade.

"Then it'll be green forever," I'd replied under my breath.

On my right, the golden paths of the strawberry field curved around the slope in neat rows. On my left, Dodge lifted his head with sprigs of grass in his muzzle, bellowed a resonant hello, and then flanked me up the hill on the opposite side of the fence with a dramatic thud of hooves, with his neck arched and his mane aglow with sunlight.

After I parked, I crossed to the pasture fence to reward Dodge for his heartwarming welcome, which he delivered through thick and thin. His whiskers tickled my cheek, and his eyes reflected knowledge of my suffering. I patted his neck and crossed to Luke, whose nose was wet and chilly as he took his turn sniffing my face. As always, he presented a toy as the go-to method for righting the wrongs of the day.

After Bubbah's death, my flock was twenty-five strong, and every one of them wanted to know if I had treats in my pockets as I climbed through the fence rails and headed for the stream at the bottom of the pasture. With Dodge adding the thud of his plate-sized hooves to my walk, and Luke bounding ahead of me, squeaking his toy, I thanked Raymond for giving me pets with trusting eyes and pure spirits.

The closer I got to the stream, the cooler the air felt, stirring my hair with the breezes that temperature changes brought to the landscape. Flickering in the angled light, the water gurgled and splashed, beckoning me onward to a boulder that held the warmth of the sunny day. I sat down with Nicole's voice hollering things in random order.

You outed me to be spiteful.

Wrong through and through.

Dan asked for one thing this week. Stay out of this high-level case.

Then why seek me out? Why grill me?

Dan was distraught and messed up. You added to that burden.

I'd begged him to not take risks many times.

You stepped into my dance, not the other way around.

My heart slammed over this claim, but I hoped it was a lie she'd tossed out to break me down. If anything, I'd said no to Dan's interest multiple times. He'd persisted until I'd simplified the matter by seeing how I felt after diving in for a heated kiss. That leap led to a blur of further kissing and a sense of fitting together that took us by surprise.

I remembered a particular afternoon at a nearby lake, turning amidst the flickering light with his arms around me and my hands exploring his back. I'd felt unraveled and locked in. He'd reflected the same level of heat, with no hint of the scenario that Nicole had put forth.

From the beginning, Dan had seemed an unlikely fit for the dark immersion that was necessary for undercover work. He'd signed on in a moment of turmoil after Aaron's death. Even on a tough day, his easygoing side was quick to surface. If there had been a time when he'd responded to Nicole, surely it would have made him feel more alone and desolate. It would weigh on him as a mistake. A sign of how far he'd fallen.

I turned toward a peace-spoiling honk that echoed from the direction of the house. Luke bounded from my side, planted his paws on the bank, and barked at a man at the top of the hill on the far side of the fence, waving his hand and hollering a hello. It was Paul Polk.

"It's as if he read my mind," I said to Luke.

I brushed off my pants and rushed up the slope, determined to get a clear sense of Paul's conversation with Nicole. I would start slow, and ramp up the questions until I was satisfied that the realtor hadn't launched an attack on Dan's house, or murdered Raymond.

On the way, I refreshed my sense of Gerald Leblanc's employer: midfifties, combover, large glasses over which his forehead showed signs of Botox numbness, and a smile that would photograph well in any light, and fit Sal's description of "a flash of teeth."

"Hello," I said, breathless as I arrived from the awkward business of crawling through the fence rails. "I bet you're here about the video we gave to the police this morning. Come to find out Nicole is a police officer herself. Did you know that?"

"My goodness, you get straight to a point," Paul said.

"Sorry, it seems a matter of concern."

"This was tangled in the weeds near your mailbox," he said, handing me an overnight envelope. "I was afraid it would blow away."

I nodded. "Thank you."

"I noticed it's from Dr. Clark's wife," Paul said.

"It's a personal matter," I said. "Back to Nicole …"

"Well, she showed her badge, and then it was off to the races, starting with questions that put you in a poor light," Paul said. "My name reached her ears thanks to the uproar your cousins caused after not inheriting Raymond's farm. As you may recall, they had plans of their own regarding the property. They turned to me for advice."

I was aware that my cousins had talked about dividing the land into lots and building fast-construction homes perched on bare dirt where fields and forests had existed for over a century. They'd gone so far as to pitch their plans to my father when he reached his late forties, insisting that he would be happier in a smaller home in town.

"I stressed that your involvement in recent crimes stemmed from your father's work," Paul went on. "The osmosis effect."

"That's a good way to put it," I said.

"Your devotion to Dan seems sincere," Paul said. "You're not trying to capitalize on the situation in terms of using police resources."

"Of course not," I insisted, struggling to stay on point. "Did you see Nicole's last name when she flashed her badge?"

"I think her thumb was in the way of the information." Paul motioned for a slow-down. "I don't mean to imply that she deliberately obscured her badge. Her tough talk didn't seem unusual if you compare it to the sort of grilling you see in true crime shows."

"If you get a repeat visit, let me know because she's working outside the sphere of the local police. She's actually—"

My mouth clamped shut lest I blurt the undercover element.

"Actually what?" Paul prompted.

"She's mostly an unknown," I said.

"Look, I can see that you're overwhelmed by recent events," Paul said carefully. "I don't mean to put you on the spot, but as Gerald Leblanc's employer in recent years, I've had to conduct a careful audit to make sure that he didn't abscond with customer data and cash."

I paused. "Did he?"

"Not that I can tell, but here's the latest shocker."

Paul pulled out his phone and played a voicemail:

Umm, it's Sal here. I'm under the weather. It's a stomach bug. Plus, maybe a fever. Real bad. I'll keep you posted. Sorry for the late notice.

"What do you make of it?" Paul asked.

"Sall has a stomach bug," I said. "It's very clear."

"Nothing is clear with those two anymore," Paul said. "Be straight with me. You saw Gerald the night he disappeared."

I paused. "Who is saying that?"

"Everyone," Paul said. "It's all over town."

I fumed at the smirking image of Haydn Pike in my mind, though it was just as likely that an onlooker could have overheard some mention of me *seeing* Gerald in the van, so technically, it was the truth.

"I never met Gerald," I said. "But I heard a rumor that he's turned his life around, and might be facing some health concerns."

"I can't disclose private details about an employee," Paul said. "I can see I got my signals crossed about your involvement. Speaking of which, I heard you had a tough moment with a visitor."

I frowned. "Nicole?"

"No, I felt we were finished talking about her," Paul said.

I closed my eyes and regrouped.

"Right, Isaac stopped in. Yes, that was a tough moment."

"You argued with Isaac?" Paul asked. "About what?"

"You were talking about Haydn Pike? Roy Allen? Mrs. Brooks? My cousin? My other cousin? Then, I'm sort of lost …"

"I was talking about Vivian," Paul said.

I nodded. "Of course. That was weird more than tough."

"Oh?" he said. "In what regard?"

"You know, I can't remember," I said. "All is well."

Offering a bright smile that signaled insanity, for all I knew, I admitted defeat in my attempt to steer the conversation. As always, I had an audience of sheep, a Belgian draft horse, and a King Shepherd watching my efforts with expressions that said I must have skipped some stops on the reincarnation loop. Instead of reaching human status from life as a dolphin, I'd jumped the line after a stint as an earthworm, or a gelatinous form of life that drifted through the ocean's depths.

"Clearly, your rough start in Maine has taken a toll," Paul said gravely. "Don't add to that by letting Isaac Munroe sway you into thinking he's a better prospect than Dan. I'll be stunned if Isaac doesn't make a play for you, given your family ties in Boston."

"Isaac is not my type," I assured him.

"He and Vivian made a go of it for a while," Paul said. "Like minds in terms of priorities in life. Things were bound to fall apart."

"Why, in their case?" I asked.

"The usual problems," Paul said. "People imagine Vivian and I were involved, but that was to lend comfort when her geologist friend died. I heard Dan has been looking into that. What's the latest?"

"He doesn't discuss work with me," I said. "If you heard otherwise, it's off base. You'll know more about it than me."

"It happened so long ago I can't recall specifics," Paul said. "Bertrand Clark murdered him. I'm not sure why."

"I thought Dr. Clark was never charged," I said.

"But then he disappeared, so it's obvious his colleague didn't fall to his death by accident," Paul said in a confiding air. "I volunteered at Bertrand's archaeological site, the one that was on my forested land. We worked with tiny trowels and soft brushes much of the time."

"I know it's painstaking work," I said.

"Well, this has been a marvelous first chat," Paul said, studying me shrewdly as he dropped the news that it was only a first volley. "I expect we'll be working together once Dan puts Aaron's house on the market. I'll stop by and take a look, how about that?"

"Please wait until Dan gets in touch," I said. "It's way too soon."

"Understood," Paul said. "Keep me in the loop."

As his car pulled away, I remembered what Antoine had said of his tough arc as a cop: "Give me a supernatural foe."

I didn't want my foe to be a pushy realtor. I didn't want it to be an undercover cop, or a drug smuggler, or anyone who had a heart and should know better. As for having a supernatural foe, I'd felt dogged and harried by Donald Littlefield's ghost for eighteen years. I could still hear him chiding my mother for the secret origins of my blue eyes and curly hair. *It's intolerable. I feel cheated. It's her. Where she came from.*

All the same, I could see what Antoine was talking about. Aside from exceptions like Donald, a supernatural foe would have one burning goal. To have a second shot. To live again. Human foes were shifty and tough to fathom, with tricks up their sleeves. A glaring example was Haydn Pike, who refused to accept that his own bad behavior ended his career as a cop. There was a stigma around "ratting" on a police officer. If I pressed repeat with Nicole, the headwinds against me would increase.

More than likely, she expected me to fling myself at Dan in the wake of her attack, wailing about being mistreated, a needy burden who didn't match his future plans. Getting put into an armlock was lesson number one for Nicole. Lesson two was yet to come.

* * *

With Luke diverted by a toy, I crossed to my stereo system and launched my yoga playlist, starting with a Tibetan singing bowl track of echoing tones made as the musician tapped a brass vessel. Singular and resonant, the notes hovered in the air before fading into vibrations.

In my one-piece leotard, I fell into a rhythm of easy stretches, reaching each arm straight up to feel the positive effect in my ribs. Next, I reached back, grasped my ankle, and felt an immediate stab in my shoulder joint from the injury Nicole had delivered. Wincing, I rubbed out the ache, but even my basic yoga poses brought stabs of pain.

On my back, I stared at the ceiling and wondered what Nicole would have done if tripping me on the stairs had resulted in my death. It seemed doubtful that she would call 911. More likely, she would wipe the place down on her way out, and proceed with a solution based on Maine's 17.5 million acres of forests. There were 6,000 lakes and ponds in which to hide a body, and 5,100 rivers and streams to dump remains.

I wouldn't just be gone. I would be *long* gone.

With a sigh, I gave up trying to stretch my troubles away and used the index for my father's journals to hunt down Paul Polk's name.

If ever there was a man with jackal DNA, it's our local 'friendly' realtor, Raymond had written. *After Ella died, most folks knew to give me space. Paul Polk came straight to the farm with hints about whether or not I was willing to sell. Thankfully Joan from across the road sped up the hill like she saw flames coming from the house. She took him by the arm, talking under her breath as she led him to his car. It's why he's still in one piece.*

"Was that the end of it?" I wondered.

I climbed the stairs to wrestle with Roy Allen's jarring reversal on the circumstances of my father's death. In my bedroom, I sat on the edge of my bed and rekindled the scene I'd encountered on my first visit to the farm in the wake of a blizzard that had left two feet of snow and ice across the hill and on the roof. The pan of water had been close to the window, not close to the bed where I sat. Even a ten-foot giant couldn't have soaked his feet in that pan. The ladder had been visible through the window, propped against the house to indicate a roof leak. Every element had been staged to make Raymond's death look like an accident.

Even with basic logic, I could unravel that treacherous lie.

"Hey," Jeremy said, arriving in my doorway and taking up a whole lot of space as he leaned his shoulder against the jam. "I called out multiple times. Talk about being deep in thought."

"Sorry," I said. "I didn't hear you come in."

"Yeah, the music is kind of loud." Jeremy paused with a worried frown. "Is that a bruise on your shoulder?"

I grabbed a shirt to slip on over my spaghetti straps.

"I lost my balance on the stepladder," I said. "In Aaron's basement. Hence, there's a scrape from the concrete."

"It looks bad," he said. "How high did you climb?"

"I was a klutz," I said. "Let's not dwell on it."

"I played football in high school and had to learn about concussions and stuff," Jeremy said. "I know how to check bones."

The pain was worrisome, but a trip to the ER, with its antiseptic smells and unnerving bright light, was out of the question.

"Ok, but not in my bedroom," I said.

With the air of an official medic, Jeremy sat me down in a kitchen chair and began rotating my shoulder with one hand applying pressure.

From behind me, he gently pulled my arm forward in front of my torso, which stretched the joint and the back of my bicep. Satisfied with that result, he took on an assessing frown as he felt the bones.

"I think it's just a bruise," he said.

"You're really good at this," I said. "Did you get training?"

"From our coach." Jeremy eyed me carefully. "You got weird when I asked about the bruise, like there's more behind it."

"I'm embarrassed," I said. "A total klutz."

To redirect his focus, I stepped away to retrieve the documents that Mrs. Clark had sent in an overnight envelope.

"Look at this photograph," I said, pulling out a sepia print of the 1800s couple in the city clothes they'd once worn. "The husband was a physician. Hardworking, middle class. In other words, the couple wasn't filthy rich as the legends claim. Mrs. Clark included copies of their train tickets and receipts from a hardware store. Bertrand was a meticulous researcher. It's tough to picture him committing crimes."

"Did you hear from Antoine today?" Jeremy asked.

"No," I said. "I think he's done with me."

"You didn't mess up that bad, Sonny," Jeremy said.

"I don't suppose you've brought dinner?" I asked.

"I'll get the burgers going," he said, heading to the stove. "If you wash up, remember the rules. Close the darned door."

My eyes filled with tears a little as I cracked up for the first time in a long stretch of days. From a mystifying comment that had put my guard up when Antoine had agreed to help my cause, I could now tell him that the "first ghost" was turning out to be a godsend.

13

"Luckily, I'm used to being treated like a yo-yo," I said to a photo of Aaron on the kitchen counter. "I can get a lot done here."

Big news had arrived at the Corner Pocket: the owners, Sue Black and Kate McKenna would be heading home a day early thanks to a tropical storm heading toward St. Thomas, where they'd been enjoying a delayed honeymoon for over a week. Further, the clerk who had ducked out for a stay at the casino had come back "worse than broke." Mrs. Brooks had informed me that since Jeremy had proven to be "immune from having his head in the clouds," he was in, and I was out.

I'd put my morning to good use by applying the last coat of paint in the guest bedroom, and then I'd spruced up the bathroom walls with the same misty bluish-green color Aaron had used.

Now I was taking a break to revisit a screenshot I'd taken of an entry in Raymond's journal, where he'd mentioned Dr. Clark.

Raymond wrote, *Bertrand's account meshes with facts and timelines. I'm concerned by the mob mentality unfolding in town. People want simple answers and someone to blame. He was overzealous in finding sites where the 1800s couple camped. We all get carried away. I think somebody out there is using the momentum against him to cover a string of acts that are starting to feel like a land grab. Maine has resources. That spells money.*

I resumed my inspection of my father's map with a magnifying glass. The folds had erased some of the lettering, making his notes difficult to decipher. The properties I'd visited with Antoine fell on a diagonal line across the map, forming a swath of ridges and low spots from southwest to northeast. Otherwise, my inquiries had led nowhere.

No matter. When it came to learning a thing or two in the state of Maine, one method outperformed all others: ask the neighbors. Using my father's map as a guideline, I made note of any farms on the list of participants for the winter "Farm Crawl" that would bring visitors to my trails for sleigh rides in February. First thing tomorrow, I would head out with my cameras and offer to help some of the farmers with their social media presence, and spread the news that the editors of *Coast & Candle* magazine had agreed to devote at least one article to the event.

While I was at it, I would pose questions about what might be going on with the neighbors next door. Had anyone met the new owners of the turtle sanctuary? Were they locals, or from out of state? Were there signs of pot growers or other drug operations in the woods? Since the magazine would pay me for my efforts, my plan amounted to a win, win, win.

A flash of reflected light alerted me to Kevin Pierce's arrival in his pickup truck, right on time. I folded the map and set it aside, a little on edge from the impending task of collecting paperwork.

"You got my text?" Kevin asked, stepping in with his brisk demeanor of needing to be ten places at the same time.

"Yes," I said. "But I didn't know where to look."

"In the office, for the most part," he said.

Midway across the living room, Kevin stopped short with a look of surprise as his gaze swept from the vacuumed floor to the far end of the hallway, where sunlight was spilling from the bedrooms.

"How did you get all this done so fast?" he asked. "It was dusty and dark in here. I pictured you dabbling at the work, but this … it's like how it was when Aaron was alive. The good times."

"I'm sorry if it's tough to see," I said.

"It's tough," he agreed. "But it's what's needed."

Kevin fell into a moment of silent anguish, despite his effort to make light of it, and then he focused on the task at hand.

I followed along as he snagged a couple of the boxes that Dan had left with the paint cans. In the office, I helped Kevin stow folders and loose paperwork that included bills, tax returns, and other documents, including a large, legal-sized envelope marked "Divorce Agreement." I averted my gaze throughout and helped seal the boxes with tape.

Once we carried the paperwork to the living room, Kevin glanced out the window and saw that Kick was running late.

"You're ok with Isaac and his son handling the shredding process?" I asked. "Clearly you are. I only just met them."

"I get it," Kevin said. "You're from away, not sure who to trust."

"Do you want me to make some coffee?" I asked.

"No, I've got a twenty-ounce travel mug of it in my truck," Kevin said, pausing near the kitchen to study me gravely. "I'm late in learning that Dan raised concerns over your father's cause of death. As a probation officer, I'm at the other end of the chain. Not privy to cases underway, so what I'm hearing is the final score. The matter is closed."

"According to Detective Allen," I said carefully. "You know Dan's meticulous nature. He wanted to verify the chain of events."

"I can guess what it was like for you to have doubts," Kevin said. "Dan is a good kid. We love him to pieces, but I'm disappointed that he didn't do more to shelter you from the heartache."

"He did try to shelter me," I said. "But at one point his concerns were obvious. I've been worried that Dan's inquiries led to the burglary, but that was more likely to have stemmed from—"

As I stopped short with wide eyes, Kevin chuckled.

"Dan's stint up north is less and less under wraps," he said. "I agree it's the likely reason behind the burglary. I could have told him that sort of endeavor would go wrong in a big way."

"Hopefully, it'll be sorted out soon," I said.

Kevin turned as a truck eased to a stop along the curb.

"Why is Haydn visiting?" he asked, looking surprised as an attractive woman in a flower-patterned dress emerged from the passenger seat and headed toward us, pale but determined.

"It's Peg, isn't it?" I asked.

"I told her to hold off," Kevin said. "It's the first time she's been here since Aaron died. Give us a minute, ok?"

"Of course," I said. "I understand."

"Honey, I had the paperwork situation covered," Kevin said, devolving out of tough-guy mode as he greeted Peg with a sweet kiss on her cheek. "Are you sure you're up for this?"

"I won't be if you make a fuss," Peg said.

"There's a strong paint smell," Kevin said.

"Five minutes won't bother my allergies," Peg said, heading toward me. "Sonny, if you remember, we met at the Fall Fest."

"I do remember," I said. "How are you?"

As Peg hugged me, I was immersed in her soft perfume, reminiscent of lilies or some other light floral scent. In a knee-length dress and cotton sweater, she exuded an air of delicacy and fragility, from her pale complexion to her soft voice and shy smile. I remembered Dan saying that she had a "deer-caught-in-the-headlights" vibe at times, even before the shock of losing her son, but she wasn't a basket case by any stretch.

"You pulled Haydn from work?" Kevin asked.

"He needs my help picking out a tie for his cousin's christening," Peg said. "On the way, I wanted to thank Sonny."

"I need to head back to work," Kevin said, hovering and looking torn. "I wish you'd told me you were ready for this."

"Go on, if you have a meeting," Peg insisted.

"No, it's fine," Kevin said. "I'll make some calls."

As she led the way down the hall, Peg tossed me a quick smile that reflected patience and understanding over Kevin's worries.

"You do take after Raymond," she said. "Especially your blue eyes. I'm so sorry you never got to know him."

"I'm sorry for your loss, too," I said. "I truly am."

"You're a darling," Peg said, blinking as her eyes filled, and then she sat us down on a wicker couch in the guest bedroom. "The truth is, I've been here several times," she whispered. "To fetch items and sit amongst Aaron's possessions. It helps me feel close to him if that makes sense. I won't sugarcoat my situation. I'm still crushed from losing him, but Kevin is the one who hasn't faced reality. It's often harder for men."

"They tend to clamp down on their feelings," I agreed.

"Haydn has been a huge support for us," she said. "Nobody can replace a child, but he lost his parents when he was young. Kevin and I lost Aaron, and Dan as well, in a sense. He left shortly after Aaron's death."

"I think Dan regrets that," I said.

"As long as healing happens, we can't fault each other for the path we choose," Peg said. "If it's helpful to know, I chided Haydn for the way he treated you when that awful case landed on your doorstep. It's not always easy for him to see both sides. He's getting there."

"I'm glad if he's a comfort for you and Kevin," I said.

"Well." Peg smiled and grasped my hands. "The paint fumes are an issue. I'm prone to headaches, and my live wire is fretting nonstop about it, judging from his pacing in the kitchen. Kevin is not an easy man to love. I do love him, of course," Peg quickly added. "You know what I mean. His toughness is exhausting at times. Dan seems to have escaped that side of male DNA. I hope he's supportive and caring."

"He's been good to me," I said. "Very caring."

"He's got business smarts and musical talent," Peg said. "If you can, press him in that direction. Police work will destroy his spirit."

"I've had the same concern," I said. "Dan doesn't have time for music lately. He's caught up with rebuilding his house."

"I heard your neighbor, Joan, is getting a divorce," Peg said with a worried frown. "They've been together for years."

"Her husband's work was an issue," I said. "He was always out to sea."

"I'll reach out to Joan to make sure she's ok," Peg said.

"She would appreciate that," I said.

As I followed Peg down the hallway, I was heartened by her shared view that Dan might get shredded by law enforcement. He'd expressed his own concerns about that possibility, but I couldn't shake seeing his look of eagerness in joining his covert team to solve the case.

As efficiently as she'd arrived, Peg kissed Kevin's cheek, promised to have a roast ready when he got home and stepped out.

"She's lovely," I said, watching her cross to Haydn's truck.

"That was bravery right there," Kevin said. "Not to fault Dan, but he didn't let us weigh in on the timing in getting Aaron's house ready for the market. Peg dotes on him. Won't hear a cross word."

"Her affection for him came through," I said.

"If you want my advice around supporting Dan's work, Peg is the ideal to look toward," Kevin said. "She's active in church and lends a hand to charities. I had concerns about your recent history, but this is a fine thing you're doing," he added, indicating the cleaning and painting. "I'm taking it as a good sign. You're calming the noise."

"Less noise is a cherished goal," I said carefully.

"You tangled with Haydn," Kevin said. "What's your sense of him?"

"All that matters is your sense of him," I said.

"Once again, Peg won't hear a cross word, even when he's banged up from a bar fight," Kevin said. "You can see her effect, how she brightens a room. Her doting sets up the enabler dynamic shrinks talk about. She buys all his favorite cookies and snacks. My son was solid gold. Same with Dan. Pike is a wooden nickel. Keep an eye on it for me, ok?"

"I'll tuck it away for future reference," I said.

"Thank you, Sonny. You're an ace." Kevin checked his watch. "I'm sorry to rush off, but I've been asked to be present at Polk Realty & Storage in time for Gerald Leblanc's fall from grace."

I paused. "Umm, in what sense?"

"His friend Sal left a message yesterday saying there was an emergency he wanted me to weigh in on," Kevin said. "It'll be about Gerald's cousins. Some vigilante caught them dismantling their mini pot farm. The deputy let them off the hook. The pot was long gone."

"They didn't end up in jail?" I asked.

"If you knew the reality we're facing in terms of stopping crime, you'd understand. We're lucky to get the big fish. My money is on Sal being in a panic over the cousins hiding their stash in Gerald's storage bay. Detective Allen is heading there with a warrant."

"At this very minute?" I asked.

"Hence, I'll be tasked with re-explaining the hard facts to Gerald if his bay is a drug depot. And surprise-surprise, Isaac Junior is out there along the curb yakking on his phone instead of coming to pick up the boxes," Kevin said. "Grab this one for me, would you?"

"Can I join you in going to Polk Realty & Storage?" I asked.

"Of course not," Kevin said. "That would be nuts."

With the weight of the box in my hands, I followed him out to Isaac Junior's luxury car with robotic moves. With apologies that he was running late, Kevin made quick work of loading Aaron's paperwork into the open trunk of Isaac Junior's car and then slammed the lid.

"Thanks a million," Kevin said. "Sorry to rush off."

As his pickup truck headed away, I stared after his tail lights, bogged down by the mental demands of the past half hour, from Peg's sweet, but misguided faith in Haydn Pike to Kevin's opinion that if I stuck to cleaning, painting, and "calming the noise," I might be a suitable match for Dan's high-stress job. Most gear-grinding of all was Kevin's anticipation of being on hand to arrest Gerald, who had been dead for days.

"They *still* don't believe me," I murmured.

"Sonny?" Kick prompted.

I turned to Isaac Junior standing nearby in dress slacks, a drycleaned shirt, smartly-cut hair, and every other element signaling that he was a chip off the old block, but possibly less intense.

"It's great, how you're helping the Pierces with a painful chapter," he said, automatically shaking my hand. "Don't let Kevin's focus on heading to work fool you. He's trashed from losing Aaron."

"Remind me," I said. "Isaac Junior, or Kick?"

"Kick is fine," he said. "A soccer reference, but when I wasn't pro-level in talent, my father switched gears and started calling me his 'sidekick.'" He smiled with a good-humored roll of eyes. "Listen, you'll have noticed my weird reaction in the store, ducking out when we crossed paths. A minute before I rounded the corner, I got a call from a troublemaker who'd reached out to me previously. She wanted dirt on you."

I paused. "Oh?"

"Apparently, she's a cop," Kick said. "Super-hot. I'm guilty of letting that sway me for a minute, though it seemed odd that she'd come to a non-professional. My work at the bank led to a side hustle where I help people with Wi-Fi setup and tips on avoiding scams. Her reasoning had to do with not landing you in the crosshairs of local police unfairly, so I pulled together the basics on you. She wanted more."

"Is her name Nicole?" I asked.

"Yeah," he said. "That's her."

"And?" I prompted.

"I told her it was a bridge too far," he said. "She showed her true colors, spelling out the confidential nature of her inquiry on you."

"When was this?" I asked.

"Back in May," Kick said.

I stared at him in shock. "Not recently?"

"She got in touch again this week," Kick said. "After her call, I blocked her number. What did you do to land in her crosshairs?"

"It's a long story," I said. "While we're here, it's come up that after Bud and Birdie died, you visited their house."

"Nicole is doing a double-play, asking about me?" he asked.

"Umm, well …"

"No worries," Kick said. "After Bud and Birdie died, your father and others had some concerns that kids might go after the turtles and vandalize the property. I found the door open more than once, maybe from the wind. I never saw anything amiss, but it did seem odd."

"Thanks for explaining it," I said.

"My turn," Kick said quietly. "Are you dating a crooked cop?"

I stared at him. "You can't be serious."

"Dan got secretive last year," Kick said. "Police work can test a person. You're known to be intolerant of lying and wrongdoing. If you see him as a good guy, I'll take your word for it."

"Absolutely," I said.

"Excuse me, I've got a thing going on," Kick said, turning away as his phone rang. "What's the latest?" he said to the caller. "If I'm not mistaken, Paul is the one to ask. Why does it feel off base to you, not the flu or a stomach bug?" Kick listened for a moment, and then with a pained groan, he said, "All right, I'll let you know."

"It sounds like a complexity arose," I said.

"Yeah," he said. "A friend is off the rails a little."

After we promised to catch up later, I was still within earshot when I heard him leaving a voicemail for Vivian Vandorne.

"Vivee, it's not fair to put me in this position—"

As he shut his car door, cutting off the rest of his message, I crossed around his fender and signaled that I needed another word. Kick multitasked, completing his message and putting his phone aside as he started the engine and opened the window.

"I'm running on the late side," he said.

"If I'm right that you called Vivian," I said, "she stopped by the other day, upset about Dan's inquiry into a cold case."

"The geologist's death?" Kick asked.

"Possibly," I said. "I don't know."

"That explains things," Kick said, looking bogged down by conflicted feelings. "I'm sorry to rush off. We'll catch up later."

Left to stare after his departing tail lights, I resolved to focus on my chores. I'd no sooner reached the sidewalk when Kick's sedan halted and quickly reversed. As the tires chirped to a stop next to the curb, he opened the window and leaned across the cup holder to see me.

"My brain just connected the dots," he said. "Do you have ten minutes to spare? You're the perfect person to talk to Vivian."

"Sure," I said.

"Can you follow me in your car?" he asked. "I'm due at work."

Nodding, I said, "I'll get my bag."

It was amazing how fast I could regroup when a mystery-related task was tossed in front of me. I was like Luke with his lobster toy.

I dashed to the house to grab my bag and lock the door. Fold by fold, wrinkle by wrinkle, the fallout from Dan's inquiries into Raymond's death demanded my direct involvement. As I followed Kick's car without regard for the speed limit, I realized I should have paid attention to Antoine's driving methods. After six or eight winces, averting disaster at the last second, I swung into a curbside spot directly behind Kick. On our right, a flagstone walkway led to a cottage-style burgundy house that looked well maintained, fronted by trimmed shrubs and areas where perennials had died back from the frosts of October and early November. Vivian's hybrid car took up the entire short, cramped driveway.

Kick was on the phone as he climbed out, conveying a message for someone to tell his father he might be late.

"Between this and helping at Aaron's house, you'll be due for sainthood," Kick said as we met under a leafless tree along the sidewalk. "Before we stop in, you'll understand this is a sensitive matter. What was your drug of choice? Back in September," Kick prompted when I looked blank. "I heard you got high and passed out on your driveway."

"I was drugged by one of the bad guys in that case," I said.

Kick gaped at me. "Seriously? That's messed up."

"You're afraid that Vivian takes drugs?" I asked.

"It's a crutch she turns to instead of hauling her life on track, and her assistant hinted at it," Kick said. "Look, I brought you here thinking you had a similar experience. If you want to bail …"

"No, I'm happy to help," I said. "In fact, she seemed overly giddy the second time we met. Does that sound like her?"

"When she's high," Kick said. "Hang back at first, ok?"

Kick rang the doorbell and leaned to one side to peer through the expansive front window, looking worried when she didn't respond. Kneeling on the doormat, he flipped open the mail slot and peered into the interior of the house as he called out Vivian's name.

"I see her on the couch," he said. "She's fast asleep."

"Do you have a key?" I asked.

"Yeah," he said. "We should check her."

With his hands shaking, Kick opened the door and used his foot to discourage an ice-eyed, Persian cat from bolting out. I did the same as I followed him into the house, where the lights were off.

Gripped by dread, I hovered next to an unlit lamp as Kick crossed the room and knelt in front of the couch, where Vivian was curled up as if to protect herself from a chill in the air, clad in silky, flowered pajamas. Her feet were bare, and there was an appalling lack of activity in her limbs as Kick shook her with increasing intensity.

"Vivian?" he prompted. "Vivee!"

Seeing her street address on her mail, I called 911 and reported that an unresponsive woman had been found, while Kick made desperate attempts to rub life into Vivian's hands and smooth her hair. Abruptly, he staggered past me, colliding with the fluffy cat, then he lurched through the doorway and heaved out his lunch on the side lawn.

Prompted by the dispatcher, I drew strength from nowhere as I knelt next to Vivian to provide an accurate assessment of her condition. I rested my fingers on her neck in several places, desperate to feel signs of a pulse, but her skin was chilled and lifeless. She'd been gone for hours.

I stood and swayed, staring at her silent face.

"Ma'am?" the dispatcher said.

"She's wearing, umm … diamond earrings," I said.

"Police and EMTs are on their way," she said.

I nodded, feeling sick and dizzy. The strong smell of bleach in the air drew me to the bathroom, where the harsh scent was coming from. Silver wrapping paper and a matching bow were crumpled in the waste basket. I turned to the bedroom, where sheets and blankets suggested a wild night. A velvet-covered jewelry box was open on the vanity. I pictured Vivian smiling as she watched the diamonds sparkle on her earlobes. I touched nothing, so I couldn't confirm what the box had held.

"Ma'am?" the dispatcher prompted.

"There's a strong bleach smell," I said.

"It's best if you wait outside," she said.

I nodded. "Of course."

As I crossed to the door Vivian's cat orbited my legs with every step, swirling its fluffy tail. I stroked its head and whispered that help was on the way. Again and again, its mouth opened with silent pleas. The cat had been crying for hours, begging for attention until it was hoarse.

14

My statement was the briefest I had ever delivered at an "incident" scene. Isaac Junior and I had been present for two minutes, possibly less, when I'd called 911. A nosy neighbor across the quiet street corroborated our account and disclosed that Vivian had been all smiles lately, which the busybody took to mean that she'd finally found the right man.

EMTs had sat Kick and me side by side with blankets draped over our shoulders until the color returned to our faces.

"Do you want to talk about it?" I said softly.

"If I'd come first thing instead of delaying ..."

"They're saying she passed away overnight," I said.

"How is that possible?" Kick asked. "She called in sick."

"According to the officers," I said, "Vivian made the call at two o'clock in the morning. You dated her at some point?"

"In hindsight, I'm not sure what to call it," Kick said. "I'm not saying she wasn't brilliant and attractive, but she, umm ..."

Based on his dismay, I grasped that Vivian had been trading favors to get ahead. In Boston, I'd known a few colleagues who thought nothing of using all assets in their corporate climb. I could still hear them saying, "Sure, I've heard how it can backfire. That won't apply to me."

"I met Vivee at a round-robin squash event at Westdale College," Kick said. "The geologist who died, the cold case you mentioned? He was totally smitten, but she found that annoying. She doesn't respond to weakness. I know it was wrong to dive in when she came onto me. Her interest was in picking my brain. My knowledge of finance."

"She wasn't broken up by the geologist's death?" I asked.

"In the same timeframe, she was in the midst of carrying out a bold idea initiative for the college. Instead of mourning his death, she was like, 'I'm trying to land a deal. I refuse to let a putz like him ruin my life.'" Kick rubbed his face. "Sorry for oversharing. As far as I know, the geologist was drunk. That's why he fell from the cliff."

"How long were you and Vivian together?" I asked.

"A few months," Kick said. "We had some fun. Dinner and movies, then I caught onto this aspect of her life," Kick added, motioning toward her house. "Pills to take the edge off. It's a shock when that happens, somebody putting it on par with a glass of wine."

"That's what ended things for you?" I asked.

"I didn't want to be hauled to the curb buck naked after a neighbor tipped off the police," he said quietly. "Speaking of which, she got out of a few parking tickets through her cop connections. You might want to ask Dan if he's on her go-to list." Seeing me stare in alarm, Kick motioned the comment away. "I'm sorry. Shock is messing me up."

I stuffed the notion under the rock where Nicole was buried.

"Earlier, you mentioned Paul Polk," I prodded.

"Yeah, he was in the picture now and then," Kick said. "The thought of being a follow-up to him … you get my drift."

"Any other names you care to share?" I asked.

Kick's look of conflict and distress as his gaze flicked toward his father arriving down the block answered my question without words. I endeavored to not react, but my shock was obvious.

"It was after I ended things," Kick said. "Vivian gave me an eye roll when I shared my view of sleeping around, but if a person is truly ok with their choices, they don't need drugs to get by."

Just then, his father stepped up, looking pale and unsettled.

"I heard the news," Isaac said. "Are you ok?"

"I know what a dead body feels like now, so that ought to be a gauge," Kick said, shedding the blanket and flushed in the face as he stood. "I need a hot shower and some alone time. Can I leave?"

"Yeah, I've got it settled," Isaac said.

"I'm sorry I dragged you here, Sonny," Kick managed.

"No need to apologize," I said.

As Kick headed away to his car, Isaac looked poised to prod me with questions, but an EMT intervened, checking my pulse until the banker gave up and swung away in pursuit of his son.

"Thank you," I said.

"Just doing my job," the EMT said with a friendly wink.

"Did I hear Polk Realty & Storage on the radio chatter?" I asked.

"The police searched Gerald Leblanc's storage bay, but it didn't go as expected," he said. "It was a waste of time. A non-starter."

"There's no sign of drugs?" I asked.

"No sign of Gerald. No sign of Sal. Detective Allen grilled Mr. Polk on their possible whereabouts." The EMT shook his head. "The trail is cold. Neither one is in their usual haunts."

I closed my eyes, gripped by the fear that Salvatore Hall would never joke about his name again, or confess what he knew.

"He's hiding, but fine," I whispered, as Sal had said of Gerald.

* * *

Wrapped in a thermal quilt, and sitting on a couple of all-weather cushions that protected me from getting chilled by the damp grass, I felt the warmth of the day slowly leave the boulders against my back as twilight settled over my pasture. If I ever needed to hide on my farm, I was a goner. Whether out of curiosity or concern, my animals always hovered nearby when I came to rest in one spot or another, forming a knot around me that had brought Jeremy straight to me when he'd pulled up the driveway. I'd explained that I needed to be alone, and then I'd had to sharply double down when he'd persisted in trying to urge me into the house.

The chilly air sparked thoughts of Vivian curling up on her couch for the last time in her flowered pajamas. She was the first female victim that

I'd had the misfortune to encounter after all hope was gone, killed in her diamond earrings. Gerald's neck had been stubbled, with creases alluding to his age. Vivian's neck had felt delicate and still.

Sensing my somber mood, Luke nuzzled my hand. I stroked his soft fur and took comfort in the quiet sounds of the sheep nibbling the early winter grass with sideways nips, blowing out dust or some other irritant through their soft nostrils. Having grazed for a moment, Dodge thudded toward me and tugged at my hair with his lips.

"You're a softie," I said, cupping his velvet nose, partly to draw on his warmth, and partly to offer the sugar cube I'd brought.

Hearing footfalls approaching, I gathered myself to chide Jeremy for not giving me space, then I frowned in puzzlement to see the outline of a man's suit against the backdrop of darkness and stars, complete with dress shoes polished to the point where they reflected glints from the rising moon. It was Antoine with his hair tightly braided along the curve of his head: a vastly different look from his usual ponytail.

As Luke greeted him, Antoine held out a treat and uttered a command in French, which sent Luke racing away toward my house.

"It was my luck to adopt a dog who worships men," I said.

"May I join you?" Antoine said, and then with a tired groan, he knelt and settled into place by my side, casting warmth and the crisp scent of drycleaned wool as he adjusted his jacket and stretched out his legs. With his watch and cufflinks casting glints, he tucked the quilt around us and secured my chilled fingers in his warm hand.

Looking grave and troubled, Antoine gave every indication of sharing my sense of having failed to stave off disaster. We'd assumed that reaching out to Vivian could be put on hold for a day or two.

"Once again, fentanyl is to blame," he finally said. "Fifty times more potent than morphine. People don't know that, or in hearing it, they think they can handle it. There's talk of her having a secret lover. Someone with ice in his veins. He wiped the place down."

"You're the only one I can talk to about Gerald," I managed. "How he looked in his last moment. Anguished, and robbed of hope. Vivian had a similar expression, like she knew the next shiny thing in her life was a lie. No wonder she numbed herself with drugs."

"I hope I'm not hearing temptation along those lines," he said.

"No," I said. "Drugs won't be the slip-up that tanks me."

Antoine studied me with a worried frown.

"How is your shoulder?" he asked. "Your roommate is concerned that you've been tangling with foes and not telling anyone about it."

"Like the person who left the feather?" I asked.

"Birdie is deceased," Antoine said. "A ghost can't inflict damage."

I snorted, unable to suppress a humorless laugh.

"I've been in the crosshairs of a ghost since I was ten," I said. "Physical damage is possible. It's the norm. He hates that I'm alive. Lashes me with misfortune. He took Raymond during a blizzard and sent murderers after me. You shouldn't be here. It's not safe."

"Berrichon," he said softly. "What are you talking about?"

"Donald Littlefield knew I wasn't his daughter, and he was not a man who liked to be duped," I said. "You're in an uphill war against crime. I've been at war with a vengeful spirit who killed Vivian because she dared to talk to me. The Sonny effect has a dark side."

"Je suis vraiment désolé," Antoine said with anguish.

"Sure, throw some French at it," I said. "That'll help."

Struggling upward, I fought Antoine's efforts to console me, and then I collapsed into tears, sobbing over the aches of the week, from the shock of Vivian's death to the awful conviction that Dan was out there at that moment rekindling the flame with Nicole.

"Just leave," I managed. "You fired me, after all."

"I regret how I behaved the other day," Antoine said. "The feather was a trigger for me. I didn't handle it well."

"I wasn't voicing a complaint," I managed, wiping my eyes with the remaining tissues I'd brought. "It was a wry effort to say that I agree. You prefer to work alone. That's how I roll."

"I felt it was *necessary* to work alone," Antoine said softly. "In less than twenty-four hours, you had persons of interest tumbling over themselves to get in front of you. During our drive, a sedan attempted to follow us. The license plate was obscured. I couldn't confront the occupant with you in the car, so I relied on evasive techniques."

"That's why you drove so fast?" I asked.

"It's a necessary breach of rules during this kind of stretch. I train for it," Antoine added. "I think you picked up on that."

"Back to the feather …"

With a groan and roll of eyes, Antoine relented. "In one of life's twists, my sister collected feathers of all kinds," he said. "The one in Birdie's house looked like a vulture feather. I can't explain further why it's an issue. You're not the only one afflicted by shadows."

"You use contractions when you let your guard down," I said.

"I suppose I did just now," he said. "Can't, it's, and you're."

"That's almost a meaningful sentence," I said.

"And now she smiles, a burst of light out of nowhere," Antoine said, brushing a curl from my face. "I talked about this the night we met, how the swirling chaos of investigations tests even the strongest of us. Hearts race and certain notions come to mind."

"Antoine …"

"I know you're devoted to Dan," he said.

"Plus," I said, "you might be sitting on sheep droppings."

"Voilà," he said, instantly cured. "Well done."

"Let's talk about crime," I said.

"Another excellent segue."

I began with my encounter with Vivian outside the store.

"Looking back on her behavior, I think she was high," I added. "Is her secret new lover the only suspect in her death?"

"There is talk of Dr. Clark having a motive to kill her," Antoine said. "Vivian was involved with his exit from the college, but there appears to be a pile-on effect where Bertrand is blamed for every event that hits the fan, from vandalism to cold-blooded murder."

I tugged the silk tie Antoine had loosened near his collar.

"What's with your high-end suit?" I asked.

"I spent the day in Portland posing as an investor interested in buying land," Antoine said. "Starting in the city is what a real investor might do, and it's best not to approach persons of interest directly. I see you eagerly awaiting news of connection points. It's still early days."

"I got a major news flash from Detective Allen," I said. "He's decided that Raymond's death was an accident, and my quest for justice is stressful on Dan. Basically, he ordered me to back off."

Antoine massaged his brow with a tired sigh.

"Think of law enforcement as a large touring bus," he said. "Sturdy and well-oiled, outfitted with state-of-the-art tools, but it can't navigate a rock-strewn hillside. That takes a fast, determined person who can jump from a horse to a bike, whatever it takes."

"The bus has run me over more than once," I said.

"Come," Antoine said. "Rest your mind."

For days, I'd sensed that he was shored up with titanium structuring that enabled him to crush down ideals like true love and commitment. He was a flirt, and possibly a player, but after a jarring day, it felt ok to let him slip his arms around me and settle my face against his chest, where I was soothed by his warmth and steady heartbeats. Far from secretive and aloof, he was snuggly to lean against. It threw me for a loop.

"You've been a puzzle to sort out from the first moment," I murmured. "Like the straitjacket hold you used on me in Dan's house. It felt oddly relaxed, considering you expected to be stabbed."

"It was surprising for me as well," Antoine said. "Early in my career, I theorized that it was a fast way to secure an opponent, especially a woman, without a painful armlock. In practice, I was flipped or slammed against a wall. Other times, I got a split lip, a bloody nose, a black eye, or stomped toes. With you, it was like watching a sunset."

I cracked up, and he did too, grinning and squeezing me for emphasis, like we were best friends, or something more. I found myself looking from his eyes to his lips, and Antoine followed suit.

"We're in danger of crossing the line," I said, pushing away from the warmth zone over his look of protest. "Dan is the one who should be here. It's messing with my head. I can't let it take over."

"I was lending support, not making a pass," Antoine said.

"What about five minutes ago?" I asked. "I feel the tug. We're built to seek love, but it's like diamonds and gold. I have to guard against robbers and thieves because that's what I've experienced." I sighed. "I don't want to end up like Vivian. That's what I'm trying to say."

Antoine frowned for a second, and then he closed his eyes.

"Remind me to get my wiring adjusted," he said tiredly. "The other night, I promised to dissuade Nicole from indulging any whims with Dan. The truth is, it's not a valid reason to break silence. Personal matters are their own realm. It's out of the norm to take sides."

"I didn't expect you to intervene," I said.

With a sigh, Antoine shook his head. "Here you are again, doubling down on being selfless. We're past the point of no return."

"I'm not sure where this is going …"

"If Dan betrays your faith in him, I will drop him out of a plane over wild Mongolia. With a parachute," Antoine added. "I found the experience to be jarring, but after a week or two of honing my survival skills with nothing more than my wits, a hatchet, and a fishing line, I began to understand that misguided habits had not served me well."

"That literally happened to you?" I asked.

"Once in Mongolia, and once on a Pacific atoll."

"You didn't learn the first time?" I asked.

"As a fellow stubborn person, you cannot be surprised." He rubbed my shoulders. "You're shivering. Let's get you inside."

"I don't suppose …"

I paused, waffling over which question to indulge.

I don't suppose you've talked to Dan? Know why Nicole returned to town? Can assure me that Sal is alive and well? Have the bandwidth to stand guard in my house so I can fall asleep?

In his damp, ruined business attire, Antoine let all questions fall away as we led a procession of sheep and a draft horse up the slope. Once he delivered me to Jeremy, who had cocoa and lasagna warming on the stove, Antoine told us he had a few calls to make. When I turned to thank him, he was a subtle shadow slipping into the night.

15

At last, I was able to nose my car into a parking space outside the yellow façade of the Corner Pocket not as a clerk, but as a customer at 8:15 a.m. Behind me, past the grassy common and small pavilion that hosted local bands during the summer months, people were chatting outside the brick post office, a volunteer firefighter was hosing off one of the trucks, and the heady aroma of bacon was drifting from the bed and breakfast.

Beyond the windows, I saw Jeremy at work, stacking fresh bread on a shelf in the aisle of baked goods. Sue Black and Kate McKenna were near the register, looking tanned and rested after their stay in St. Thomas. They were among my best friends in town, offering support and sage advice when I'd gotten caught up in the maelstrom of capital crimes. Once again, my life's implosions were many and extreme, with bouts of seeing Vivian's ashen face all over again, but I was determined to not lean on Sue and Kate this time around. I didn't want to ruin their vacation buzz.

I took a deep breath and then stepped in.

Turning as the bell jingled above the door, Sue and Kate headed over without delay, beaming at the sight of me.

"You're an angel for filling in," Sue said, hugging me as her glossy hair spilled toward me around her shoulders. Tall and dark-eyed, with features that reflected the Passamaquoddy side of her ancestry, she held me at arm's length and studied me for a moment. "Talk about a wild week. You're still standing, but I'll open the brandy if it'll help."

"I'm fine," I said. "How was your trip?"

"Perfect," Sue said. "Our long-awaited honeymoon."

"I loved the photos you sent," I said.

"My turn." Kate was a blur of sunburned freckles and red hair as she hugged me. "Thank you for helping out."

"Any time," I said. "It was a lesson on how hard you work."

"Come sit with us," Sue said. "We've got fresh brownies."

"I'll swing back later," I said. "I've got a full day ahead."

"Aaron's house," Kate said somberly. "How is that going?"

"I've made fast progress," I said. "Thanks to Jeremy."

"Finding Vivian had to be a shock," Sue said with concern. "Not to mention the awful burglary. Dan is away again?"

"It's necessary," I said. "He's with a team."

I'd steeled myself before stepping in, fully aware that their combined minds were like a supercomputer as they processed all the gossip that unfolded in the store from dawn to dusk. After considering all the facts and theories, their guesses tended to be on the money more than not, so I had to proceed with the utmost care. Even from thousands of miles away on a Caribbean island, they would have stayed up to date.

Now their keen gazes were trained on me.

"You don't need a brownie break?" Kate asked.

"Maybe later," I said. "I'm sorry to rush off."

Frowning, Sue said, "What's going on?"

"Nothing." I beamed. "I've reached out to folks who plan to participate in the Farm Crawl. I'll be on the road all day."

"What's your connection to Antoine?" Kate asked.

"He's a friend of Dan's," I said. "A colleague, rather. I was surprised you gave him the security code. Then it made sense."

"The Prime Minister endorsed him," Sue confided.

I paused. "The Prime Minister of …?"

"Canada," Kate said.

"Right," I said. "Of course."

My eyebrows hurt from being hoisted to my hairline and then abruptly wrenched down again. I smiled and fashioned an exit strategy.

Then my butt started ringing. Blinking in confusion, I looked to one side, certain that Dan's instructions had only covered the need to make outgoing calls. This was a curveball.

"Your butt is ringing," Sue pointed out.

"Yes," I said. "I'm aware of that."

"It's a flip phone," Kate said, circling me.

"Yes, it's a flip phone," I agreed, backing toward the door. "An added option. You know how I roll. Always prepared."

"Why a flip phone?" Kate asked. "That's an odd choice."

"I love retro options, don't you?" I asked.

"I love advanced technology," Kate countered.

"Let her go," Sue said. "This is painful to watch."

"Thank you. I'll catch up later."

Outside the store, I pulled the flip phone from my pocket and gathered my wits in case it was Dan checking in.

"Hello?" I prompted.

"This is Liam down at the Box & Bag. The wet-dry vacuum that you ordered is ready for pickup. What's a convenient time?"

"I didn't, umm …"

"Because of tight inventory, it's best that you come to the store today," he said. "Morning? Afternoon? What's best?"

"Sort of … morning, I guess," I said.

"Excellent," he said. "We'll see you soon."

Click.

* * *

From a tight, strategic plan, my next move for getting answers had skidded off the rails in record time, but if Dan's team wanted to loop me in on their investigation, I was ready, willing, and able.

In the parking lot of the Box & Bag, I didn't see any sign of a tactical vehicle, and nobody with a law enforcement vibe was signaling to me. I proceeded into the store's brisk air currents, high ceiling, and vast aisles of home improvement products. At first, it seemed a mad idea to stage a meeting there, though the security cameras in strategic points would spark panic in criminals, followed by a swift retreat.

The only person looking my way was a fiftyish man behind the customer service counter. Wearing the store's green apron, he signaled for me to step forward. Perhaps he'd been inducted into the job of watching out for me and getting me to the right location.

"I'm Sonny Littlefield," I said softly.

He looked at me sideways. "And ...?"

"I'm here to buy ... rather, to *secure* a wet-dry vacuum," I said. "I think a special model was put aside for me. Maybe out back?"

"Let me check." The man grabbed a microphone from the desk and sent his voice booming across the store. "There's a customer up front who put a wet-dry vacuum on layaway or something! I'm new in customer service, so I don't know where to send her!"

"Can you please just direct me to the right aisle?" I hissed.

"Hang on," he said. "They're checking in."

"We don't *do* layaways," a voice tersely boomed.

"Are you sure?" he hollered into the mic. "She seems fixed on it."

There was no reply, thank heaven.

"Thank you, I'll shop on my own," I said.

"I won't leave you hanging," he said. "Let's have a look."

With a groan, I glanced in all directions as I trailed behind him down a succession of aisles, no idea who Dan's team had sent.

"Here we are," the man said, stopping next to a surprising array of choices on the shelves, from small wet-dry vacuums to ones that wouldn't fit inside a cart. "I've done a bit of cleaning after burst pipes. Don't just buy for today. It's important to prepare for future events. Let's start with the basics. How much water are you dealing with?"

"I'm not dealing with water," I said.

"If you *did* need to remove water, how much are we talking about?"

"It's not a water situation," I said.

"But if you *did* need to remove water ..."

"How could I possibly—?" I closed my eyes and lifted my hands. "You know what? I'll give it some thought and come back later."

I headed away, scanning every person in sight to the point where several men thought it was their lucky day. Their smiles died when I blew past them in frustration, grabbing an empty cart that rattled in front of me as I cut an erratic path from the plumbing section, through the nuts-and-bolts section, to the paint section where I felt at home, given all the work I'd been doing in Aaron's house. I paused to catch my breath.

"*Sonny,*" Dan said, slightly out of breath as he donned a green apron and joined me in the aisle. "You didn't wait for two hours."

"We didn't plan for an incoming call," I said.

"Never mind, we're here. No, don't hug me," he whispered, turning me toward the paint cans. "Outdoor paint, right?"

"Yes! Outdoor paint is what I need!"

"Normal tone," Dan said.

With a glance around us, he confirmed that for the moment, we were alone in the sheltering quiet of the aisle. Aside from his alert gaze, the green store apron, and the baseball cap tucked over his brow, he was the man I'd fallen in love with, dressed in jeans and a gray jersey shirt that set off his muscles, tanned face, and trimmed beard.

"I haven't seen you in a beard since May," I whispered.

"Sonny, I'm just a guy," Dan said. "Calm down."

"Right." My love-starved smile died. "What now?"

"Where do I begin?" Dan whispered. "Somehow, you were on hand to alert 911 when Vivian Vandorne's body was found, and it's come to light that you spent a day with Antoine exploring locations on Raymond's map. What did that involve?"

Picturing Nicole listening in, I pointed to the radio on his shoulder and used American Sign Language to say, *Turn it off.*

Once Dan complied, I stressed that I'd spent time with Antoine after seeing the bust up north and taking it as good news.

"The crew of three is still at large," he said. "The arrest you saw online was a former contact. Nicole tracked him down."

"So, you've gotten nowhere?" I asked.

"Where did Antoine take you?" Dan prompted.

"The coast, Dr. Clark's property, then some woods," I said. "Mostly, he drove past places at top speed. Normal fieldwork."

"Antoine told you to park at the Corner Pocket?" When I nodded, Dan fumed. "He knew I'd arranged for colleagues to make sure you were safe and sound. They saw your car, and figured all was well."

"Hence, you're late in knowing I met with him?" I asked.

"Exactly," Dan said. "Antoine has never dropped off the radar to this extent. Did you get a bead on his mindset?"

"There are signs that he doesn't trust Nicole, which resonates with my gut feeling," I said. "I've had concerns from the start."

"That's no reason to put her in an armlock," Dan said.

I hesitated. "What …?'

"She's on the job," Dan said. "You assaulted a cop."

"Where would that have happened?" I demanded, fully prepared to upend Nicole's false narrative with logic.

"Your farm, I assume," Dan said.

"You bought her story without question?" I asked.

"She admitted that she took you off guard," Dan said. "But it sounded like you had a personal bone to pick."

"That's not who I am," I said. "Not in the *least*."

"It did sound off the mark," Dan admitted.

"What other crap has she flung my way?" I asked.

"Nothing," Dan said. "Just, she's worried about your history."

"Solving cases, you mean," I said. "Instead of meeting me, maybe it's time to check in with Roy and see what he thinks."

"Apparently, you've already done that," Dan whispered.

"Thomas is the one who flagged the video of Nicole questioning Paul Polk," I said. "Roy needed my input on who she was. *That's* the shock, but hey, I'm just a civilian. I bet Nicole put a nice spin on Brumby's brother staying at my farm. I can't wait until you meet him and see he's a vulnerable kid who's paying me back by helping in Aaron's house."

"I figured that out," Dan said. "There's a bigger concern I need to raise. Apparently, you ripped up the card I left for you to find."

Choking and tearful, I walked away a few steps, pacing to weather the shock of how successfully Nicole had deployed her string of lies. Dan had listened to her awful whispers. He'd believed every twisted, concocted story that had dropped from Nicole's pretty mouth.

"Sonny, I'm sorry," Dan said, risking a hug that didn't look too inappropriate. "I know that night was tough."

"*This* moment is tough," I said, wrenching the tattered card from my pocket. "What's your sense of it, detective?"

"This is what Nicole described, so …" Inspecting the ruined message of love, Dan frowned. "Are these teeth marks?"

"Luke destroyed the card," I managed, bringing my tears under control as customers drifted into the aisle. "His feelings were hurt when you didn't take a minute to see him the other night. But golly, super job of seeing me through Nicole's skewed lens in record time."

"I'm here to clear it up," Dan said. "Put this in your pocket."

"No, it's better off with you," I said, pulling away when Dan tried to return the card. "Ripped up with teeth marks and missing words. It's the perfect symbol for how I'm feeling right now."

"I didn't doubt you," Dan said. "I heard this, I heard that. It piled up, hence the need to meet. We're good, now, ok?"

"Until Nicole hits the reset button," I said.

"Did you tell her that Luke ripped up the card?" Dan said.

I closed my eyes. "No."

"I'll stop the pattern," Dan assured me. "No more letting her opinions run loose, but on the work front, she's a team player. Antoine is acting on his own. How can you not see that he's the odd one out?"

"Because he *believes* in me," I said. "He values my input, and was there for me after I found a dead woman on her couch."

"I didn't know about that until today," Dan said, pulling me close and hugging me, steamed up from emotion.

"Come home with me," I whispered. "Exit the madness."

"I can't until we have answers," he said. "It needs to be resolved."

"With Nicole pulling the strings," I said. "Best of luck."

Restraint was suddenly out the window. Dan kissed me right there in the paint aisle, crushing me against him as if reviving my faith in him was the most desperate challenge he'd faced in his life.

"*Ahem*," a voice prompted.

We broke apart under the glare of a stout woman standing nearby with a large purse suspended on one arm, tapping her foot impatiently.

"I have been waiting for help for five minutes," she said. "If your little matinee is over, I have questions about what to buy."

"There's a button over there," Dan said tightly.

"It's not working," she said. "If you're busy, call someone on your walkie-talkie thing, but I have a mind to speak to the manager."

Dan's walkie-talkie was not connected to the store's staff.

"Follow me," he prompted, ushering us to the adjacent aisle, where he snagged two cans of latex paint and stowed them in an empty cart. Rolling forward, he grabbed brushes, rollers, and a pan.

"I didn't tell you what I need," the woman said.

"You brought a list," he said. "It's in your hand."

"I wanted *eggshell* finish," she specified. "Bone white."

"That's what I grabbed," Dan said.

"Why is that brush angled?" she asked.

"To keep edges clean." Tossing tape and other supplies into her cart, Dan turned to her. "Is that it? Anything else?"

Captivated by how fast his mind worked when tasked with a targeted plan, I lamented the glaring areas where a fuse blew and everything stalled. He was supposed to be tucked away in a safe location, not making a scene in public. I took the pause as my cue to head for the exit.

"Sonny," Dan prompted. "*Sonny*."

Turning to face him, I walked backward a few steps with my hands joined in a heart shape, and then I continued onward, more determined than ever to pitch in and get answers.

"Antoine, you had better not be a crook," I said under my breath.

16

With my heart half broken, I was bound to feel vulnerable in the company of a dark-eyed, incorrigible flirt who gazed at me with adoring eyes. Even worse, my suitor had a twin brother who followed my every move on the sunny hillside, seeking my hand and refusing to let me focus on posing careful questions about Dr. Bertrand Clark.

"They've taken a shine to you," the farmer said.

"They're this way with everyone, surely," I said.

"Nope," he said. "It's a match made in heaven."

With a groan, I looked down at the fuzzy faces and bright eyes of the cutest miniature sheep that had ever roamed the earth. The farmer had disclosed that when they reached adulthood, Olde English Babydoll Southdown sheep typically reached a height of 18-22 inches at the shoulder, roughly 16 inches shorter than my flock at home.

Above us, the sky was a shining expanse of blue, with fluffy clouds that further enhanced the scene as I set about the work of fending off the twins long enough to kneel and capture them standing next to the farmer's jeans, which told the story of their diminutive height.

In the distance, silver silos could be seen here and there next to red barns and pastures dotted with Holsteins. Patches of tilled earth alternated with drying cornfields awaiting a harvester. I posed the mini sheep with their curly backs aglow and their ears facing the view as if they'd paused to admire it. The editor of *Coast & Candle* magazine had asked me to capture humorous shots that might serve as greeting cards.

"Adorable, aren't they?" the farmer asked. "An ancient breed with fine, springy wool. Best temperament under the sun."

"It's not practical for me to buy more sheep," I said.

"They'll fit right into your car," he said.

"Please don't bring that picture to mind," I said. "Back in September, it landed me in the worst trouble imaginable."

"It all but broke the gossip mill, how you found that poor fella in his last moments on Miller Road or thereabouts."

I closed my eyes. "Back to Dr. Clark …"

"Sure, we got to know him a bit," the farmer said. "Keen on history. Affable early on. Claimed his hard luck was a set-up. That's what you're after, isn't it? You've got a taste for solving crimes."

I winced. "It's that obvious?"

"He fell off a cliff, maybe," the farmer said.

"Unless you've heard something specific …"

"I'm passing the time until you buy these sheep," he said.

I frowned. "You said Dr. Clark was affable 'early on.' Did that change at some point? His wife hinted at a period of paranoia."

"Maybe," he said. "Maybe not."

"I'm asking out of concern," I said. "It's not to get gossip."

"I'll relax my guard in thanks for your picture taking," the farmer said. "You're right, it's fair to say Dr. Clark got paranoid at one point, according to this and that source in our farm district. You know he was obsessed with that married couple back in the 1800s who ditched city life to explore full-time. Bertrand welcomed everyone to work at the digging sites, though folks came away disappointed by and large."

"That's a shock," I said. "I would have found it exciting."

"Folks pictured finding piles of loot," he said. "For the most part, they unearthed everyday items like pottery and cookware."

"Did Raymond volunteer at any of the digs?" I asked.

"Sure did," he said. "The spot the marijuana gang took over."

From the pocket of his overalls, the farmer pulled out a battered phone that fit other devices I'd seen in the hands of Mainers with hard jobs, with a cracked screen and smudges that alluded to bouts of use during engine repairs and other chores like changing blown tires.

Despite the cracks, I recognized Raymond in one photo as he stood near a dug area marked off by strings. The next image showed a sepia print of the 1800s couple who'd become Dr. Clark's obsession. The husband wore a fringed buckskin jacket and baggy pants with a length of rope for a belt. The woman's full skirt and long-sleeved jacket looked hand-sewn, with signs of mending over a long period.

"You can see the handle of her Derringer," I said.

"Check out the sack by their feet," the farmer said. "I bet it's a money bag from a bank. Stuffed with coins, maybe."

"I'm pretty sure it's a burlap bag of potatoes," I said, sending the photos to myself before handing his phone back.

"After Dr. Clark vanished without a trace, his wife had no choice but to sell their house," the farmer said. "Folks want a home that's free of a sorry past, but one guy was keen on buying it for a bit. We worried what it would be like to have a banker for a neighbor."

I hesitated. "Not Isaac Munroe?"

"Mr. Moneybag is how we see him. We've got old tractors and manure in use. Having him pinching his nose and complaining nonstop seemed a done deal, but *then* …" The farmer paused with a self-deprecating roll of eyes. "You've got me gossiping to no end, but there's no stopping me now. Guess who else was on the paperwork?"

"His son, maybe?" I asked.

"No, it was Vivian Vandorne," the farmer said gravely. "Her role in the purchase was kept hush-hush at first, but when Raymond got wind of it from Paul Polk, he made a beeline for the bank and confronted Isaac on his own turf. Folks who were on scene at the time said it was like a theater event, echoes flying every which way. Isaac tried to have Raymond tossed out, but not before your father drilled down on the wrongness of Vivian's involvement. It was thanks to her firing Bertrand that the family's house had to be sold. It was wrong through and through."

"Totally corrupt," I agreed.

"By some accounts, your father got right up in Isaac's face," the farmer continued. "Raymond said to him, 'Be aware, I have looked into your past,

Mr. Munroe. Come to find out you've got a history of bad moves and poor judgment. You haven't learned from your mistakes.'"

"How did Isaac respond?" I breathed.

"He threatened to sue. Your father had decency on his side. The way he scoffed at Isaac had the county talking for days."

"Why didn't anyone tell me about this?" I asked.

The farmer shrugged. "My guess is his friends figured why bring it up to you if the matter was over and resolved."

"Not for Dr. Clark," I said. "He went missing."

"That was another strange chapter," the farmer confided. "The search dog ran in *circles* as if Dr. Clark had vanished into thin air. Don't get me started on the tales of the woods being haunted by the 1800s couple. The boring version of the story is that he was picked up by somebody after he left his car near his property."

"Isaac backed out of buying the property?" I asked.

"To ease the scandal element, he made noises around Vivian and Paul Polk not informing him about Dr. Clark's troubles with the college," the farmer said. "Isaac set up a charity fund for the family and offered a reward for tips on Dr. Clark's whereabouts. It's a stunt to convince people to bank with him, but it's a helping hand all the same."

"If you had to guess what happened to Dr. Clark …?"

"If Raymond was right that Bertrand was a victim, rather than a guilty culprit in all regards," the farmer said, "maybe Bertrand decided not to take it lying down. He confronted whoever set him up, and it went wrong. He's in a shallow grave out there in the woods."

"That's a dismal thought," I said.

"My goodness, if you don't look like Raymond, frowning at signs of wrongdoing," he said. "It's awful the two of you never met."

His gaze said his moment as a gossip had come to an end. In parting, I promised to send the photos I'd taken that day, and explained all over again that it wasn't practical for me to buy more sheep.

"I understand," the farmer said with a wave of hands. "You've got lots of pictures to look at if you find yourself missing them."

"True," I said. "Pictures will suffice."

"I hear you. Come on, boys, it's lunchtime."

With a stream of excited bleating, the Babydoll twins trotted after the farmer on impossibly small hooves, like fuzzy couch pillows with ears and soft noses. What was it about mini animals that tugged at the heart? They were custom-built for those who needed a hug.

With firm resolve, I crossed to my car.

* * *

A short detour brought me to the gravel driveway of the charred remains of a house and old barn that were being consumed by weeds. Antoine had excluded it from the locations to visit the other day, but I wanted to study the farm that I'd dashed toward in September when I'd discovered that my vindictive cousin had brought two of my lambs to a butcher. A man with a fatal gunshot wound had upended my rescue attempt. When Dan arrived on the scene and took a look at the map, he'd explained that Raymond had circled the butcher's *former* address. Now all that remained was linking the unsolved arson case with the other locations on the map.

I consulted my father's notes on the farm in front of me.

Fifty acres of woods and fields, he'd written. *Gravel pit next door. Problem neighbors; ties to check washing and drug smuggling. PP wanted the listing, but owner needs fields for crop rotation and won't sell. DC thought 1800s couple camped nearby. Bertrand assured me he didn't dig test holes, but an "unknown source" claimed to have seen him the night of the fire.*

"Here's Paul Polk in the mix again," I murmured, recalling Antoine's remark that a pile-on effect was taking place where Dr. Clark was blamed for every event that hit the fan, from the geologist's death to the burned farm. Maybe the disgraced professor was guilty, but in my mind, a credible tip required an eyewitness who was willing to step forward.

I put the notes on the passenger seat and stepped out to another clear, surprisingly warm day for early November. The closer I got to the torched ruins, the more I inhaled the scent of the charred boards and beams. Stray bits of charcoal were brittle underfoot, and the ash smelled a little sour as I skirted the perimeter of the ruined house.

It was a close match for how I felt after refusing to return Dan's card to my pocket. I wanted it back, taped and torn or not.

With an effort, I focused on the scene in front of me. Paul Polk had struck me as a machine when it came to real estate, so it was no surprise that he'd wanted the property's owner to sell. I chided myself for letting Paul steer the conversation when he'd stopped by my farm. In order to know if he had the kind of cutthroat mentality it would take to set a farmer's home ablaze, I needed a better sense of him.

The guilty party was not likely to absorb the level of inflicted harm. I saw pain everywhere my gaze landed, especially the charred bookcases where photo albums and precious mementos would have been featured in proud display. I saw the dark, gutted hulk of a couch. Nothing but rusted springs were left. Next to the wall was a melted TV.

Hearing a car slow down on the road, I turned and groaned as I recognized Detective Roy Allen's unmarked cruiser. He stepped out into the sunny day, hitched his belt over his extra pounds, and skirted past the weeds to join me, working a toothpick in his mouth.

"You're on minimal rations again?" I said, recalling how he'd ordered a fruit plate during our lunch meeting a few months ago.

"Want a toothpick?" he asked. "It helps with stress."

I shook my head. "No, thanks."

"I read your statement from yesterday," Roy said. "It's not clear why you went to Vivian's house with Isaac Junior in tow."

"That's confusing. It's written in plain English." Ignoring his scowl, I added, "I don't suppose there are any arrests?"

"You know the ropes," he said. "It takes a village, and it takes a while."

"Her neighbor mentioned a new love interest," I said.

"What did you make of the description she offered?" Roy asked.

"The neighbor shared some telling details," I managed. "I spoke with Dan this morning. You can imagine what *he* made of it."

"Yeah, it looks like Vivian might have been harboring one of the crew who burglarized Dan's house," Roy confided. "He came and went in the dark of night. Fit and agile. A different vibe from the dates Vivian entertained in past months. Keep it in mind."

"It's tucked away right here." I tapped my forehead.

Roy studied me. "Jeremy Jones is occupying your couch?"

"Yup."

"What, no defensive outburst?" Roy asked.

"Nope."

At last, Roy shifted his position until he was obstructing my view of the burned homestead and barn, head tilted slightly, with folded arms. He'd tried to glare me into submission in the past, but there I was, unscathed and unmoved. When would he learn?

"You're wondering why I'm here?" I prompted.

"Given your recent digging around, it's fairly obvious," Roy said. "To be honest, I'm impressed that you arrived at the same notion we did early on, that Bertrand Clark torched this farm."

I nodded gravely, feigning full knowledge of the matter.

"But he was elsewhere the night this incident took place," Roy said, indicating the charred ruins. "It's awful when a grown man lets a hobby pitch him off the rails. Raymond defended Bertrand. Insisted he wasn't the sort to dig holes without permission or break into sheds. All the same, this landowner got fed up with the nightly raids."

"Hence, this arson case is still unsolved," I said.

"Never say never," Roy said.

"Then there's the *other* matter," I tossed out.

"Right again, an early theory connected to Dr. Clark." Roy narrowed his eyes. "Say the one person who supported Bertrand changed his mind. He'd be angry, maybe fume about it. An effort to regain Raymond's trust could have gone sideways. I went so far as to verify that Bertrand did not attend Raymond's memorial service."

"Telling," I said. "Very telling."

"Remember, we're back to seeing Raymond's death as an accident," Roy pointed out. "If Dr. Bertrand Clark shows up, we'll have a proper sit-down with him, but people picture him finding the long-lost treasure. He's on a sunny beach, without a care for his family."

"A shocking prospect." After a pause, I added, "For a *minute*, I thought you were talking about the time Raymond hollered at Isaac Munroe for joining Vivian, of all people, in buying Dr. Clark's property. If not for my father's protests, they would have secured a tract of valuable land. Paul Polk was involved as well, from what I heard."

"They called it the 'Westdale Circle' concept," Roy said. "Townhouses perched around shops to gratify professors and bigwigs. The price tags made it a haven for the elite. I have to say Dr. Clark was popular with his students. Hearing how his land would be misused, they vandalized Paul Polk's sign, painting 'thief' on it and such. You get my drift. The purchase was poised to fold even without Raymond's hollering."

"Your standpoint is clear," I said.

"Any new insights from your day with Antoine?" he asked.

"We drove around," I said. "Had some laughs. I came home."

Roy glanced at me, and then frowned at a metal object amidst the ash. "I'm surprised the techs missed that."

"What?" I asked, kneeling to study the rectangle.

"Give it here," Roy said.

"Without proper gloves?" I asked.

"Doesn't matter after all this time," he said.

At Roy's prompting, I brushed soot and black grime from the object's surface. It looked to be an ordinary hinge.

"Oops, I guess I was wrong," Roy said.

I glared at him. "Thanks. My hands are filthy."

"Exactly. The boss walks away, clean as a whistle." Roy signaled for me to toss the hinge. "Does anybody fit the bill?"

"You want me to point to Antoine," I said.

"You're still a fan?" Roy asked.

"Nicole, the woman in the video, is the bigger wildcard because she's arrogant," I said. "Her methods are a poor fit for Dan's team. A poor fit for law enforcement, if anyone wants to know."

"It's my opinion as well," Roy said.

"That's good to hear," I said.

"Look, when it comes to drug smuggling and human trafficking, I've seen the benefits of having 'specialists' who muddy the waters a bit. But this is my patch. Those above me in the chain have dictated that I refrain from overt steps that would get in Antoine's way."

"It galls you?" I asked.

"Explain why you're not bothered," Roy said.

"He respects the rule of law, but he talked about the limitations you face within so-called 'normal' law enforcement," I said. "He's frustrated when criminals are helped by loopholes, like Gerald's cousins who were guilty of trespassing at the very least."

"Paul didn't want to press charges," Roy said. "The fact that Gerald's cousins were involved caught my attention. We figured they'd stashed the pot in Gerald's storage bay, but that idea didn't pan out." Detective Allen spread his hands, looking discouraged. "So ends the hope of a tie-in on the burglary at Dan's house. Back to Antoine …"

I frowned. "What is it that you're asking?"

"I want to meet him face to face," Roy said.

"If he reaches out, I'll pass your message to him."

"By what means?" Roy asked. "He gave you his phone number?"

"No, it's unlisted," I said. "He uses a hyperspace portal to get around."

"Other than that, don't poke around," Roy said.

"Today is about helping participants prepare for the Farm Crawl," I said with a smile. "I'm in my own lane."

"No more playing with fire," Roy said as I headed away. "Raymond would chide you for repeating past mistakes."

I nodded. "You're probably right."

* * *

"You have *got* to be kidding me," I said.

"He's taken a shine to you."

"The farmer down the road called you," I said. "This is a prank."

The apple grower scrunched his face. "Which farmer is this?"

"I'm a single woman, trying to make ends meet," I said, indicating the blue-eyed waif looking up at me. "This isn't fair."

Below me, scarcely even knee-high, was a coffee-colored mini horse attached to a tiny red wagon, upon which even a monkey wouldn't fit. Ensconced in a polished leather harness with reins at the ready, the pint-sized gelding shook his combed mane, blew out with his tiny nostrils, just like a "real" horse, pawed with a hoof that scarcely dimpled the ground, and then he looked up at me to see if I was impressed.

"He'll fit right into your car," the farmer said. "Wagon and all."

"Ok, that's enough," I said. "You've had your laugh."

Beyond his red barn, the hill swept downward into a vista of countless apple trees planted in precise rows, with gnarled, downward-reaching branches that were trimmed to allowed easy access to the fruit. Just then, the last of their fallen leaves were being raked up by workers and dropped into a barrel that cast deliciously sweet smoke into the air. I photographed the scene with the distant hills reduced to a bluish haze and then sensed that the apple grower was eager to talk.

"I heard you were on hand when Vivian Vandorne was found," he said. "After that kind of shock, I'd be hiding under my sofa."

"It's better to keep busy," I said.

"I also heard you're curious about a certain story," he said.

I hesitated. "Which story is that?"

"I'm the one who saw Sal and Gerald washing up in a stream," he said. "I was hunting some time ago and heard a burst of hollering. I was shocked to see the two of them in their skivvies."

"Washing off some kind of powder?"

"They were covered in the stuff," the apple grower agreed. "You don't come across naked men in the woods every day. Sal was saying things like, 'What are the symptoms to worry about? I can't feel my feet.' Then Gerald hollered back, 'That's from the cold, dummy.'"

"They were good friends?" I asked.

"Best buddies," he said. "It was like they were commuting to whatever job they had going on, complete with lunch pails. A few times, they walked under the hunting blind where I was situated. Months after the incident at the stream, they were still going on about the drug's side effects. Gerald was real concerned about a cough he couldn't shake."

"No wonder," I said. "If contact with a drug was a regular thing."

"They were obsessed about getting it off their clothes," he said. "All the while, it was caked in their hair and eyebrows. Even their ears were packed to the gills, the poor darned dummies."

"It's sad if they kept at it," I said.

"Later on, they shifted gears with the glamping idea," he said. "Not my cup of tea, but it's a heck of an upgrade from handling drugs. I got curious the last time I was hunting out there and jumped on the platforms, thinking they might be flimsy. Heck no. From insurance concerns, maybe, they're built to sustain a tank blast."

"Did you ever see Raymond in those woods?" I asked.

"His job as a game warden kept him out and about all year," he agreed. "My permits are always up to snuff."

"Of course, it's a question I ask just about everyone," I said, smiling to ease out of my intense mindset. "This sure is a nice view."

"Similar to your place," he said. "My wife has picked berries there."

"Given that I live on a hill," I said, "I've been wondering if I need to worry about my well running dry during a drought."

"Underground reserves are under pressure," he said. "With the right terrain, it can press uphill. The higher ground you're seeing yonder is taller than ours. We've got a good flow."

"You hear about companies tapping aquifers …"

"Now, Miss Littlefield, how about you get to the point?" he said. "I've got hay to stack and a batch of cider to press."

"I've heard the turtle sanctuary has a valuable spring," I said. "An outfit called Pintail Holdings bought the land."

"That's a telling word," he said. "They'll 'hold' this and that, then all of a sudden, they're taking over and running the town."

"Whoever owns it now is veiled in secrecy," I said.

"Maybe the new owner died. I don't need to tell you that people are kicking the bucket left and right, like that geologist from the college. He and Dr. Clark walked these woods a time or two, excited about the papers they were writing. One paper was focused on geology, the other on history. You'd never imagine that one would kill the other."

"Murder is always a shock," I agreed.

The farmer massaged his chin as he studied me.

"Something I *may* have heard means you'll want to talk with the cheese people," he said. "But it's best to wait until tomorrow."

"Why not today?" I asked.

"Mainers are welcoming folks by and large, but there are those who like advance notice on visits. I'll pave the way for you."

"Thank you," I said. "I'm tied up for the afternoon anyway."

"I heard you're fixing up Aaron Pierce's place. It's a fine thing you're doing, tackling work that would be tough for his folks. His friend as well. Trooper Bolton is a fine young man. Rock solid."

"I've always felt that way," I said.

"Brumby Jones is a friend as well?" the apple grower inquired.

"We're strictly friends," I said. "I'm immune to his charms."

"He's in a pickle over in Vermont. Sparked a divorce. A big show barn in the horse world. One of his top clients. With the husband out of the picture, it's fallen to Brumby to lend a hand."

"I've wondered why he's been in Vermont so long," I said.

"Well, I've got chores, so I'd best get on with it." The farmer looked down at the mini horse. "Sorry, bud. I tried my best."

"I can't afford more animals," I said.

"Same with us," he said. "Too many mouths to feed before winter sets in, but don't you worry about it. We'll find a way."

With a gloomy parting glance, the knee-high, coffee-colored steed allowed himself to be led away toward the barn with a soft peppering of tiny footfalls, the red cart too ridiculous to believe, its wooden wheels squeaking pathetically. Without uttering a word, the tiny horse had let me know that in turning my back on his necessary sale before winter set in, I'd wounded his pride and stripped him of his sense of self-worth.

"Come on," I begged. "Show some mercy."

"Don't fret. His heart will mend."

What about *my* heart? Who was in charge of mending that?

17

At four o'clock, close to dusk, I stopped by my farm to take a hot, reviving shower and change out of the jeans and sweater that had taken a beating as I'd crawled over fences to photograph mini animals. In a fresh change of clothes, I was ready to tackle the rest of the nonstop action that I'd instructed myself to carry out by the end of the day.

Dodge and my sheep were peacefully nibbling on the cropped clover and grass near the lush border between the pasture and the stream. Seeing their backs aglow with angled November light, I reminded myself that at some point I needed to create some captivating photos that advertised my own participation in the Farm Crawl.

Twenty minutes later, I turned into Aaron's driveway, surprised to see Kevin's truck parked there at such a late hour, especially with all the lights off. I kept Luke on his leash as we stepped into the house.

"Kevin?" I called out.

Greeted by silence, I calmed my thudding heart as I walked down the hallway past the dark bedrooms, and paused near the garage entrance. My stomach clenched, knotted with pain as I remembered Dan's description of coming into Aaron's house and being greeted by that same kind of awful silence, and the shock that quickly followed. Instructing Luke to sit and stay in the hallway, I carefully opened the door to the garage.

"Kevin?" I said with a quavering voice.

Confronted by darkness, I stepped across the threshold and paused again, inhaling the heavy odors of motor oil, garden fertilizer, insecticides, and related industrial scents in the two-bay garage.

"You found me," Kevin murmured.

Outlined by moonlight, he was sitting in a lawn chair, holding a bottle of whiskey in front of the tragic area where his son had died. I crossed through the darkness, found a second folding chair, and opened it so I could sit with Kevin and see him eye to eye.

"This is your boyfriend's chair," he said in greeting.

I paused. "How so?"

"Dan didn't mention it?" Slightly drunk, but mercifully not plastered, Kevin made a rolling motion with one hand. "In the days afterward. I'm told he sat here and talked to Aaron. Begged to know why he did it." Kevin rubbed his eyes. "It kills me that it's too late to make amends for riding Aaron's case. It was from worry, not a lack of caring."

"I don't think he would fault you."

"Part of what piled up was Aaron's job," he said. "High stress with low pay and minimal thanks. It's not fair. It's not right."

"I know," I said.

"You recall my rush the other day?" Kevin said. "No sign of drugs in Gerald's storage bay, so I raised the alarm for nothing. It's egg on my face. Meanwhile, Vivian Vandorne is stone-cold dead in her nightclothes. Slept around with Isaac Junior, his father, Paul Polk, and who knows how many others. Ambition led her down the wrong path. For what?" Kevin said with disdain. "A circle of ugly townhouses and shops nobody can afford to visit. The guys are calling it Snooty-ville."

"The plan was abandoned, from what I heard," I said.

Kevin snorted. "Then why was she a pill-popping Jezebel?"

"It's not helpful to talk that way," I murmured.

"Fast forward, I got home tired and beat a few hours ago," Kevin said. "There's Haydn having dinner at my table while I was fighting the crime of the world. Holding Peg's hand and offering tissues like he's the man of the house. It was too much. I spoke my mind."

"How did that go?" I asked.

"I'm here on my own, aren't I?" Kevin moaned. "Peg is as mild as a spring day until I snap from the pressures of my job. She'd met Vivian at church or whatever, so of course it would be a tough passage for her once the awful news of how Vivian died got out." Kevin paused, looking pale and haggard as he sat forward. "Shit, I might vomit."

"Then this isn't the right move," I said, securing the bottle and setting it aside. "Drinking makes things worse, not better."

"You've had experience with it?" Kevin asked.

"Not directly," I said. "Raymond went through a bad patch."

"Yeah, I know," Kevin murmured. "I'd do anything to have him here. You can't imagine how much. Raymond knew how to handle things."

"I've heard that many times," I said.

"I failed him at Ella's service," Kevin said. "Raymond was glassy-eyed, wanting to crawl into the grave. I just stood there, tongue-tied."

"It's in the past," I said. "Don't kick yourself."

"What would Raymond say to me now, do you think?" Kevin asked.

"He'd tell you that grief unfolds in stages," I said. "No two experiences are alike. Activity can help. Hobbies and talking with friends."

"Friends and hobbies didn't help my son," Kevin said. "Aaron wanted to keep the property Peg inherited from her aunt a few years ago. With the state of his marriage, it wasn't practical. It wasn't feasible. Those were the words I used. Killing his dream killed him."

"It's never just one reason," I said softly. "There are a lot of bright vibes here in Aaron's house, once the dust is cleared away."

"It went downhill fast," Kevin said.

Nodding, I said, "That's my sense of it."

"Who can this be?" he said as the headlights of a truck pulling into the driveway washed over us. "Maybe it's Dan checking in."

"No, it's Brumby's half-brother," I said. "He's had some hard luck. In exchange for a roof over his head, he's been helping out here."

"Then I'd best get on with thanking him," Kevin said, swaying slightly as he stood. "I owe you thanks as well."

"There's an exuberant dog to contend with," I cautioned as he headed for the door. "I hope you're not allergic."

"Not in the least," Kevin said.

I was worried to see Kevin locking his feelings away so fast, but maybe it was best if he tackled the battle in small doses.

"What a fine animal," he said, ruffling Luke's head as he stepped into the hallway where Jeremy had flipped on the lights. "I can see he's part shepherd, but I've never seen the likes of his coloring."

"He's a King Shepherd cross," I said.

"Fit for a king," Kevin joked. "Perfect for Dan."

"Sonny, there you are," Jeremy said, looking worried as he caught onto Kevin's glassy eyes and inebriated gait.

"Jeremy Jones," Kevin said, clapping his shoulder. "Sonny tells me you're helping out. You've done some fine work."

"I'm happy to help, Sir," Jeremy said.

"I'll make some coffee," I said, slipping past them and heading for the kitchen. "Does anybody want a granola bar?"

"I am starving," Kevin admitted.

I made quick work of brewing a pot of coffee, drawing a glass of ice water, and returning to Kevin with the snack.

"There's a job on the list I can't tackle," I said. "According to Dan, we need to install a railing on the basement stairs."

"It's regulation these days," Kevin agreed.

"Can you mark out the placement?" I prompted, desperate to keep him occupied so he didn't attempt to drive home drunk.

"Let's take a look," Kevin said, getting steadier after wolfing down the granola bar. "Why not tackle it tonight?"

"I'm up for it if you are," Jeremy said.

Soon, I delivered a second cup of coffee to Kevin as he assessed the supplies Dan had stowed in the basement.

"It's a heaped-up mess," he said. "That boy needs a talking to."

"I'll be upstairs," I said.

"What planet did she come from?" Kevin asked Jeremy.

"If you figure it out, let me know," Jeremy said.

"You're all right, kid," Kevin said. "I like you."

With the beginnings of a smile, I grabbed one of the pastries Jeremy had brought from the Corner Pocket and headed for the guest bedroom, which looked bright and welcoming with a fresh coat of paint. The closet was another matter entirely. I assembled a few boxes Dan had dropped off with the paint some weeks ago, gathered old games, jigsaw puzzles, and other obvious choices to donate or toss out, and then I tackled the dust and cobwebs in the closets with a wet cloth.

On my way back to the kitchen, I paused near the basement doorway, transfixed by the bursts of deep-throated, male laughing unfolding down there. Outside my childhood home, where laughing was frowned upon, I'd always enjoyed seeing how men loved to joke around with each other, to bring down the house with their boisterous high spirits. Jeremy and Kevin were discussing a moment in football history that struck them as nonsense. Why had coach So & So made such a bad call?

Luke bounded toward me up the stairs, paused to lick my hand, and then shot straight past me to the kitchen to slurp water. I shook my head as he returned to the basement for more male bonding.

Perched on one of the stools next to the kitchen island, I opened my laptop to conduct some research on Paul Polk and Isaac Munroe, using different words in the search field like "dispute" and "land development." Aside from news articles about their financial support for local causes, I didn't see any signs of trouble. With their history with Vivian in mind, I wasn't about to give either one of them a pass just yet.

I typed in "Antoine Chamailard" to see if my high-octane tour guide of local crime scenes could be understood through an online search, and wasn't surprised to not find any indication of a social media presence. He'd mentioned that his sister had died from an overdose at a young age. I tried different queries that combined their last name with the sorrowful subject and landed on a memorial page for Chloé Chamailard.

With a leaden heart, I read the brief account of her death from a heroin overdose in an off-campus apartment. Seeing a photo of the burial service, I zoomed in and held my breath as I recognized Antoine looking boyish and gutted as he stood there, poised to toss flowers onto the coffin. It was moving to see a younger, less contained version of the sharp-eyed, enigmatic undercover cop that he'd become.

It had me wanting to talk to him. Where was his hub for dialing down after his nomadic inquiries? Hotels were the best bet, clean and efficient with the added value of offering food, but they were miles away. I pictured him securing private lodgings on the local front.

"Holy moly, I'm an idiot," I murmured.

"Can I get that in writing?" Jeremy asked as he arrived in the kitchen to fetch a pastry to wolf down. "What's up?"

"Who is renting Brumby's apartment?" I asked.

Jeremy paused, slowly chewing. "Why?"

"I think it's Antoine," I said.

"It's tourists, as far as I know," he said. "They paid online, so I've left it to the pizza guys to alert me if they're throwing parties."

"They've been quiet?" I asked. "Almost invisible?"

"I'll call," he said. "Let me check it out."

"If the pizza guys alert Antoine, it'll spook him into finding another crash pad. Bring Luke home for me, ok?"

"Sonny, hang on," Jeremy said. "He's still an unknown."

That was the point. Antoine left more questions than answers in his wake, and in showing up unannounced, turnabout was fair play.

18

At 6:30 p.m., well after dark, I parked along the street near Brumby's studio apartment, which occupied the entire floor above a small pizza shop. An exterior staircase flanked the building's side wall and led to the apartment's small landing and door.

Tucked here and there alongside the quiet street of fenced-in yards were small businesses, including a thrift store and a beauty salon. With clients in the far reaches of Maine and other states, Brumby had embraced the trend of pulling in extra cash by offering up his digs to strangers. During the current stretch, he'd been in Vermont so long that I might need to find a new farrier to trim Dodge's hooves. I didn't dare tell Brumby how much I missed his easy grin and the way he strode about like he owned the world. Jeremy could learn good and bad habits from him.

Not long ago, his efficiency apartment was a messy space where he'd slept among farrier supplies, saddles, and an array of colorful shirts. With a mind toward repaying his help around my farm, I'd helped turn his space into a reflection of his origins as an Aussie cowboy. There were matching lamps made from hand-tooled boots, photos I'd taken of him working with horses, and blankets with vivid Southwest themes.

It was close to freezing, which had scattered damp patches along the sidewalk frosting over or turning to ice. The dark of a winter night had set in, the stars glittering beyond the bare branches of maples and other trees.

In his journals, Raymond had likened the feel of early winter to an animal curled up in the forest, fast asleep. Alive, but still.

The pizza restaurant beamed light in all directions, showing scattered patrons eating at tables. In the floor above, a lamp was on in Brumby's apartment, and a shadow was on the move. I paused as a woman slipped from the side door and started down the staircase in a baseball cap with the collar of her jacket turned up. I shrank down as she walked toward me along the sidewalk not more than five feet from my car.

It was Nicole.

Once she was past my rear bumper, I swiveled and watched her cross the street to a sedan that looked a lot like the one Antoine had used during our day together. Maybe they'd been in touch all along. The headlights flared on. She gunned the engine and sped away.

I slipped out into the chilly night, expelling puffs of vapor into the air as I crossed to the pizza shop. With the shades drawn, Antoine's silhouette indicated he was toweling off his hair, and then his shadow crossed out of view. My heart thudded as I reached the stairs.

Wincing as every other step creaked, I continued onward and reached the landing. I hesitated, scarcely breathing as I saw that the apartment lights had shut off. I lifted my arm, poised to knock, and then yelped as the door abruptly opened. A hand snagged my arm and swung me inside with a deft move that only Antoine could pull off.

Except it was Dan.

"You're here alone?" he asked.

"It's you up here?" I asked. "I don't understand …"

"Hang on."

In the darkness, he spoke into a radio, shut it off, and then he switched on a lamp with a hand-tooled cowboy boot for a base.

Shocked and numb, I staggered a little as he steered me to a chair. His questions were lost in a haze as he knelt in front of me, dressed in a T-shirt, with droplets in his hair and trimmed beard from his shower, his face tanned, and his pulse thrumming near his clavicle.

"Sonny?" Dan prompted.

"How could you?" I managed. "Stringing me along for days on end while you decide which way you want to go."

"You're scaring me," Dan said. "What is going on?"

"I saw Nicole leave just now, so—" I closed my eyes. "You know what? Talking is pointless. I'm done with you."

"Hey … *hey*." When I tried to stand, Dan held me in place. "I was in the shower. If Nicole was here in the apartment—"

"Stop it," I said. "I deserve better."

"Wait, hang on." Dan grabbed the radio and hit a button. "Liam? Did Nicole stop in without alerting me?"

There was a crackle, then, "Umm …"

"Spit it out," Dan said.

"She left her extra phone there. In and out, two minutes."

Dan delivered a terse reminder of the need for proper notice, ditched the radio, and turned to me with raised eyebrows.

"Satisfied?" he asked.

"Actually, I'm still processing the shocks from this morning," I said. "Is there a reason you let Nicole twist your head around?"

"We're flying from place to place, on each other's nerves," Dan said. "There's a protocol with teams. No blurring of the lines."

"Was blurring ok up north?" I asked.

"One, it's not what you think. Two, you have yet to explain—" Dan's eyes narrowed. "You expected to see Antoine."

"That's … sort of true," I admitted.

"Here you are giving *me* a hard time," Dan said.

"I didn't think to check the tenant until now," I said. "It's frustrating to be left in the dark. I wanted some answers."

"Join the club," Dan said. "He left gear here and a note saying hi, but clearly has some other place to crash. It's classic Antoine. So, we've set up a makeshift headquarters nearby, and figured why not enjoy some shuteye at his expense." Dan paused and glared at me. "What were you thinking, heading here to meet him alone in the dark of night?"

"I trust him," I said. "I've explained why."

Dan's hands indicated an explosion was happening in his head.

"In May, you didn't trust me for days," he said. "Somehow, it's lost on you that Antoine might have a hidden agenda in play."

"You're the one with a blind spot, and I'm not alone in seeing signs of trouble in your 'specialized' team," I said. "Roy is concerned that Vivian's new lover was one of the three burglars who targeted your house. If so, the guy has been hiding right here in town."

Dan flipped his hands. "And?"

"For *some* reason, you're still at square one," I said.

"Allow me to enlighten you." Dan opened a briefcase, plucked out a handful of mug shots, and tossed them on the table, one by one. "We got this guy off the streets. This guy off the streets. This guy off the streets, and so on. How was your week, honey?"

With annoyance, I pulled out my phone and started scrolling through my photos. "Farm Crawl, Farm Crawl, Farm Crawl."

"All right, I get it," Dan said. "Let's calm down."

"We've both had a tough week," I said, "starting with me saving your mother's life, which nobody seems to appreciate anymore."

"It's appreciated every second of every day," Dan said.

With a look of apology, he pulled me to my feet, extracted me from my jacket, and engulfed me in his arms. I hugged him tightly, sinking into his warmth, and then I sighed and looked at him.

"Your week started with active shooter training," I said softly. "Then the attack on your house. Now nonstop arrests. When you get locked into your work, I liken it to times when my cell phone's operating system is updating. Technically, it's awake, but wound up in its private inner workings to the point where I can't get in."

"That's what it's like trying to get through to you sometimes," Dan said. "For instance, today in the store."

We leaned against each other and kissed, soulful and intense, with a shared goal of melting each other's arguments away with our hands. As always, Dan had size and strength on his side, employing muscle power to the point where I needed to be heard again.

"You wore a beard back in May," I said, touching his whiskers. "I love it, but there's an element of déjà vu. I'm worried that if we keep cycling backward, it won't stop until we're strangers again."

"We're not cycling backward," Dan said. "I'm trying to get to where we were last week. Pure good vibes and hope."

"Even in saying that, you look troubled," I said.

"It's come to my attention that you've pitched yourself into doing the work in Aaron's house," Dan said. "Painting and cleaning, pushing the darkness away. It put a weight in my chest today, knowing how you've stepped up for me despite the turmoil going on."

"How can helping you be a weight?" I asked.

"Because in the process, you'll get a handle on Kevin, how opinionated and difficult he can be," Dan said. "I strive to be the opposite in all regards, but Sonny, it's tough when you're in harm's way. I keep not getting it right. It came through loud and clear in the store."

Dan's eyes glistened with tears that hovered along his lashes but didn't spill over because men had superpowers along those lines, dropping their guard but not to the point where they completely unraveled. He rested his forehead against mine as if to transfer what he wanted to say directly, but it didn't work. Words were necessary.

"It gutted me to hear you talk about Antoine the way you're supposed to talk about me," Dan managed. "He was the one who supported you last night, and I'm forced to feel grateful about it."

"Twenty-four hours ago," I pointed out.

"I felt too upset to make amends tonight," Dan said. "It's why I needed downtime, but even that's gone sideways. I'm sorry if I say and do things that make you doubt me. It's this aftermath situation, not knowing how or why the gig up north followed me home."

I hugged him with my eyes shut and my soul in tatters from the anguish of having secrets take hold between us. I would keep digging into Raymond's death. I would question Antoine if I got the chance, and Dan would fight my risk-taking with every step.

"Sonny," he whispered. "Don't lose faith in me."

"Come home," I said. "Let others handle the mess."

"I can't," Dan said. "My choices sparked the trouble somehow, so it's my duty to stem the threat. It would help to know you're safe."

"I am safe," I said. "It's been quiet for days."

"Except for finding Vivian," Dan said.

"At least you know about it," I said. "As opposed to your secret work up north. I picture dark alleys, seedy bars, and sitting in icy vans listening to wiretaps. Did you have an apartment, or what?"

Instead of answering me straight away, Dan used a remote control to launch a playlist over the speakers in the room, adjusting the controls until a proper level of drums and bass and the purr of a soul-bending electric guitar thrummed through the air and across the floor.

Once that was settled, he secured me in his arms.

"Let's fill in some of the gaps," Dan said, smoothing a curl from my brow. "Seedy is the right term for my living space. The Canadian border didn't feel far enough from the rough chapter, so I streamed Nordic crime dramas when I had a minute to wolf down food. Finland looked viable at one point. I liked hearing the language. The words are round and complex as if there's a dimension to them. So, I downloaded an app, and tried to compete with Antoine's multilingual chops."

"You're going to drop Finnish on me now?" I asked.

"Nope," he said. "It bounced off my head."

I cracked up, grateful for his ability to make me laugh. "What changed your mind about leaving Maine?"

"Well, there's you," Dan said, dropping a kiss on my lips, "and there's you, and you, and … let's see … there's you."

His lips rejoined mine, sexy and playful, and then his muscles flexed as he steered me around chairs and end tables, kissing me and unwrapping my clothes as we neared the bed. My shirt flew to the left, then my bra, and then he was making fast progress with my jeans.

"What's this?" Dan asked of my bruised shoulder.

"Nothing," I said. "I fell."

"How?" Dan asked. "It looks bad."

I slipped my hands under his T-shirt and wrenched it upward, losing myself in the heat of his naked chest. Neither of us was going to change. Neither of us was going to stop asking for adjustments from each other. As always, we agreed to disagree, except for this one glorious connection point where we dissolved together in delicious heat.

We pitched onto the mattress, side by side, kissing and exploring. I shivered as his lips moved to my neck, igniting ripples of pleasure across my skin, and then he went on an exploratory mission, adding a light nibble on my ear as if to make sure it was working. His caress was asking things, conveying what he loved and needed and wanted without words, switching positions with ease, and taking command of my hips when my fluttering eyes and heated-up core reached the molten zone.

And then I heard a noise. Abruptly self-conscious, I pulled the sheet in front of myself as I gazed toward the door, flustered by the prospect of tossing half-baked excuses at Antoine if he walked in expecting peace and quiet. Dan gently turned my face toward him.

"Nobody is about to walk in," he said.

"What if the bad guys are outside listening in?" I asked.

"The music is sufficiently loud," he said.

"I'm sorry," I said. "I'm new on the undercover front."

"Then let's ditch the covers entirely," Dan said, tugging the sheet from my hands so it slipped off the side of the bed.

It was a dizzy, confusing moment, with my mind torn between guilt and the warm submersion Dan brought about with his kiss, in synch with the music, as if the thrumming guitar notes were sinking into me through his skin. In no time, I was lost in the heat of his caress, and pleasure took charge, building fast. He sought ways to elicit moans, seeking my ear with his teeth, very gently, and discovering what kind of pleasure his beard would stir on my neck. I moaned in breathy gasps, savoring the feel of his muscles flexing under my hands, and the delicious heat hit the molten zone for both of us. I flexed, twisting from the power of it, gripped by ecstasy, and then all I could do was breathe in tiny gasps.

I lost track of the room, except for Dan's murmurs in my ear.

"Stubborn beyond belief," he gasped.

"You win," I breathed.

"If only," he murmured.

We settled in side by side, kissing, exploring each other with caresses, and studying each other's faces. My pleading gaze begged him to accept me as he found me. His twist of eyebrows begged me to show some sense. Tomorrow would test us all over again. For now, we drifted to sleep in each other's arms, breathing slowly in unison, able to rest for the first time in days, at peace with each other's steady heartbeats close at hand.

* * *

At two a.m., I parked in front of my house under the stars, still shimmer-ing from head to toe after hours of reconnecting with Dan. I saw that the living room lamp near the couch was on, confirming my worry that Jeremy had spent the night worrying, even though I'd texted him that all was well, and I would be home later than I'd figured. Through the window, I saw him cross into the kitchen and open the door. Luke bounded toward me as I reached the porch, licked my hand, and then headed to the yard to conduct a round of sniffing and complete his business.

"I was about to come find you," Jeremy said.

"I was right that Antoine is renting Brumby's apartment, but he must be elsewhere tonight," I said. "I fell asleep."

In catching up with Dan, I'd learned that his frustration had reached the point where he was tempted to use himself as bait to draw the crew of three out of hiding. I'd put my foot down. It was too early to change tac-tics. Hopefully, his team wouldn't outvote me.

"Antoine never showed up?" Jeremy asked.

"No," I said. "I'll try again some other time."

As Luke returned to the porch and wagged his tail, I led the way into the warmth of the house, where the baseboard heat was faintly ticking. I dropped my bag on the kitchen table and sat down, wishing there was a way to contact Antoine to get an update. Was he still posing as a wealthy investor, or was he concocting another plan?

"What's in your pocket?" Jeremy asked.

Swiveling in the chair, and seeing that Dan had tucked his card there, I slowly smiled, thankful to have it back.

"You look surprised to see it," Jeremy said.

"I forgot that I had it," I said.

"How did it get more torn?" he asked.

I flipped my hands. "What's with the third degree?"

"You worried the heck out of me," Jeremy said, and then he wrestled his features into a look of apology. "Working with Kevin was a mixed bag tonight. I think he's mostly a fan, but he's concerned about your habit of taking risks. Law enforcement is a tough job. He's worried that all the trouble you've gotten up to will be taxing on Dan."

"Yes, Kevin made his feelings known," I admitted. "His wife, Peg, is shut down and unhappy, partly because of his job. As a further ironic note, Peg's top supporter is a guy who harassed me back in May."

"Thomas told me all about it," Jeremy said. "Haydn Pike and Aaron were bad influences on each other. Drinking and gambling, the antics that led to Aaron's divorce. According to Thomas, your father faulted Haydn's performance as a deputy. Accused him of favoritism, and didn't think he was fit to wear a badge. Kevin's review on Haydn is mixed. There's potential in him, but he needs to curb his lazy ways."

"That's quite an update," I said.

"I don't agree with the notion that you're taxing on Dan," Jeremy said. "It's the opposite. I'm worried about you, Sonny."

"I've had my eyes open from the start, so you can put that worry aside," I said. "How did things go with the railing?"

"It's the most secure railing on the planet," Jeremy said. "Plus, we got lots of the sports equipment and other items sorted into bins so they're ready to roll. With the last coat of paint finished in the guest room, we're ninety percent done with the to-do list."

"I'm glad Kevin pulled out of his funk," I said.

"For now, anyway. A son's death is a lot to absorb."

I looked up at Brumby's brother standing there with his hands in his front pockets, frowning at the array of crazy events to ponder. Tomorrow or the next day, we would need to have a tough talk. With Vivian added to the casualty list and Salvatore Hall missing without a trace, it wasn't safe for an innocent like Jeremy to stay. Not one bit.

19

"Yes, Cheeseman is my actual last name," the farmer said, dressed in bib overalls with a notepad and pencil tucked into his chest pocket. "It's thanks to an ancestor who wanted his next in line to stick to making cheese. A cooper down the way was named Cooper, so it made sense to him to organize his family that way. Got legal papers drawn up."

"You've been the Cheeseman family ever since?" I asked.

"Exactly," he said.

"That's a great story," I said. "You should put it on your website."

"You like it, eh? That's very supportive."

With that, he pulled the spiral pad from his pocket, and with the sharp scratch of his pencil on the paper, he wrote himself a note.

"You're taking the tip to heart," I said.

"I sure am," he said. "I appreciate it."

He'd greeted me in front of his red barn, beyond which the hillside swept upward to a stand of trees. All around us to the east was a view that rivaled the sprawling scene of distant forests and fields outside my door, minus the weeds. His secret in keeping the place in immaculate shape strode by now and then: guys ranging from late teens to mid-thirties, and youngsters amiably chatting as they attended to chores. I'd arrived in time to see a school bus stop at the bottom of the driveway. Once the door swung open, eight or ten children poured out, flushed with health and giggling as they raced each other up the hill.

"I bet this is a fun place to grow up," I said.

"What about Raymond's farm?" he asked. "You weren't keen on it?"

"I would have loved growing up there," I said. "My mother kept her affair with Raymond a secret, so it was a shock when I inherited his farm last February. I wish I'd known him. I truly do."

"What do you admire in him?" Mr. Cheeseman said.

"It's a long list," I said. "He was strong and principled. Generous with friends and strangers. A pillar of the community."

"I'm told you share his sharp mind," he said.

"I like to imagine so," I said. "I'm an artist, and he was in law enforcement. I'm sure we would have had differing opinions, but I think he would have been a loving father. I've certainly come to love him."

With a smile, I turned away to hide the inevitable brimming eyes that arrived when Raymond's absence in my life confronted me. When I turned back to Mr. Cheeseman, his pencil was in motion again, scratching another note on his pad. A keen-eyed man, he seemed amiable in nature, yet with an air of watchfulness that brought me back to the need for an advance invitation from a fellow farmer.

While I waited for him to finish his apparent means of keeping track of himself, I noticed a hawk flying low in the sky. It blocked the sun for a second, and then its shadow combed over the yard in a circular pattern that put the farmer and me in its bullseye. I smiled, recalling Raymond writing about shadows in his journals. When tramping through the woods, it was important to take note of sudden shifts of light.

"All right, let's go," Mr. Cheeseman said.

As I turned to him a luffing sound came from above, a sharp snap of wings, and then the hawk's shadow was increasing in size.

Squinting, I looked up in time to see the giant bird of prey streaking toward me from above, its yellow eyes ablaze over its sharp beak and its wings tucked close to gain speed as it dove downward, a feathered bullet in front of the rushing clouds. Its talons were up front and extended as if it meant to haul me away and eat me for lunch.

"*Woah*," I yelped, cringing as I ducked, assailed by the downbeat of the hawk's wings as its beak snapped an inch from my head. Its talons snatched up a stray curl, ripping it painfully from my scalp.

"Nice reflexes," the farmer said.

I gaped at him. "What *was* that? Is it rabid?"

"No, it's a situation we've been dealing with for a while," the farmer said. "We get wind storms up here on the hill, and chicks falling out of nests. With that one there, a red-tailed hawk, I thought I might try my hand at falconry, and he ended up with an attitude."

"Raymond relocated bears and other animals now and then," I said. "The hawk would thrive in a wilder area."

"We like him as a watch animal," Mr. Cheeseman said.

"I see." Aware that I was his guest and needed to be patient, I added, "You could come up with a funny sign for the yard."

"Want me to make him dive again?" he asked.

I hesitated. "You can *make* him dive?"

"He's flown off, so I guess it's a moot point."

"What, umm, do you want me to focus on for photos?" I asked.

On our way to the goat pens, Mr. Cheeseman lagged behind, entrusting another note to his pad. I puzzled over the strange back-and-forth and scanned the sky for signs of the hawk. Looking behind me as I stepped forward, I felt my right foot connect with a strange, unstable object. There was a whooshing sound as if a long, thin pole was moving fast through the cool air, then a rake handle struck my temple hard.

"*No*," I hollered, seeing stars and clutching my brow. "Not again."

"Not again?" the farmer prompted. "It happens a lot?"

"Several times in recent months," I said.

"Hmm."

With a look of concern, Mr. Cheeseman appeared to be adding this disclosure to his notepad as a worthy element. If I didn't know better, I'd been drafted into an interview process that I hadn't signed onto, and heaven only knew the consequences of a failing grade.

"On we go," he said. "Let's look at the goats."

"Listen, I don't mean to sound paranoid …"

"Uh-oh." He studied my face. "You experience that sort of episode?"

"No, I'm razor sharp," I assured him. "I'm asking out of concern that maybe you weren't keen on me visiting after all."

His eyebrows twisted. "That's *classic* paranoia."

"Never mind." I smiled. "Let's see the goats."

Soon, I relaxed into the routine of choosing the right lens for capturing close-ups of the goats. They were handsome animals with rich reddish-brown hair and mischievous, intelligent eyes. I was intrigued to learn that the milk from their particular breed was ideal for creating hard cheese and soap. When prompted to climb over the fence to get to know them, I studied their backward-curving thirty-inch horns.

"They're very polished," I noted. "And quite pointy."

"These critters are loved and pampered, that's for sure," he said.

"This seems like a small herd," I said.

"You're right, it takes more animals than this to keep us afloat," Mr. Cheeseman said. "My brother has the livestock end of the operation covered at a neighboring farm. What you're seeing here are pets, basically. My grandkids show them at local fairs."

"They're beautiful," I said. "I bet they win lots of ribbons."

"Climb in, they're real friendly," he prompted.

The next half hour was a nightmare of swerving at the last second lest I get snagged by the seat of my pants, and leaping onto the fence rail to capture shots of the fast-moving pranksters when they loomed close. In an adjacent pen where long-eared multi-colored Nubian goats were housed, I was spared the prospect of getting gored, but nearly got butted into a puddle, and with a quick, one-handed move, I performed an Olympic-level leap over the top fence rail to escape an aggressive buck.

Normal animal antics, nothing to be paranoid about. I focused on the good news that none of the goats on the property was a mini in need of a new home before winter set in.

Captivated by a ginger cat in the doorway of the red barn, licking its paw after a snack of goat's milk, I knelt to photograph it, especially as two handsome buff hens clucked past the cat, nearly the same color, but different creatures in every other respect. With its feline eyes shining in the afternoon light, the cat seemed to say, *You do realize I could go for the chickens and have a nice dinner, but I'm civilized. A good sport.*

We continued to the cheese-making building, where I enjoyed the yeasty humidity of the air, and marveled over the complex array of vats and presses, above which family members toiled. In clean white coats and hair-nets, they symbolized the professionalism of the farm. Walking forward, framing them with my eye poised against my camera's viewfinder, I saw a quick flash of orange on my right and leaped away in time to avoid being tripped by an extension cord that Mr. Cheeseman appeared to have sent into a snakelike flip as I passed by.

"Thank heaven I got it out of your way," he said.

"Yeah, that was great," I said slowly. "Thank you."

Increasingly wary, I reached out in time to stop an empty six-foot rack from crashing onto my head and took shelter in a quiet corner to assess what in the heck might be going on. Mr. Cheeseman was amiable with kindly eyes and a humble vibe. He wasn't a hired assassin.

Turning back to him, I gulped to find my wide eyes reflected in the glistening blade of a chef's knife just inches away from my nose.

"Want to try some cheese?" the farmer prompted.

Carefully, slowly, I secured the blade that he was holding up, and with a deft, one-handed move I turned it so the handle was aimed toward the ceiling and the lethal point aimed at my foot which, on second thought, wasn't much of an improvement.

"I think I'd like to call it a day," I managed.

"Come on," he said. "You can't leave without trying our cheese."

"Really, it's getting late," I said.

"I've got information to convey," he whispered.

I paused. "About …?"

"Raymond," he said. "You need to hear me out."

Shepherded forward with his hand on my back, I shortened my steps until I was forced to put on the brakes and skid the rest of the way toward a giant refrigerator door that looked like it could sustain a tank blast, should my day end with a rescue operation.

"Welcome to our cheese cave," he said.

"Cheese *cave?*" I asked.

"Humidity and temperature are essential," he said.

"I'm not ok with this anymore."

"I'll explain once we're in there," he whispered.

Reaching around me, he opened the door and ushered me into a dim, cavernous space where racks of semi-hard cheese cast an intoxicating aroma into the air, and the thick walls promised to block even a flicker of cell service. The door shut with a resonant *thunk* that spoke of its weight, plunging me into yeast-smelling darkness.

"Umm, hello?"

I reached out and felt a source of warmth covered by overalls, with a small notepad tucked into a pocket. There was a sharp click, and then I saw that my hand had found Mr. Cheeseman as he'd reached for a thin chain to turn on the light.

"Now for the real reason you came," he said, looking more than a little worrisome with the light bulb carving out hollows under his weathered eyes. "Nobody can eavesdrop on us in here."

"So, even yelling wouldn't be heard from the outside …?"

"To be honest, I've been tempted to reach out for months. Raymond's death was a shock. I didn't know where to turn."

I hesitated. "Oh?"

"I'll start from the beginning," he said.

"That would be nice," I said. "Really good."

"I got word that you're investigating Dr. Clark's disappearance," he said. "There's a concern that you don't know the stakes. Even I don't know the stakes," he added. "You've heard he was obsessed with the story of the married couple who disappeared in the 1800s. Bertrand never lost hope of finding their remains in a shallow grave or at the bottom of one of the low cliffs in the county. He heard about Raymond's keen alertness in unraveling puzzles. The next thing we knew, Raymond brought in a dog handler who specialized in unearthing remains."

"That signaled quite a commitment," I said.

"After Ella died, Raymond spent all hours pursuing his job," he said. "Helping Bertrand was a hobby, but you get my drift. They searched the forest day and night, then the visits faded to a halt."

"Were there hints that they made any progress?" I asked.

"No, I'm sure I would have heard," Mr. Cheeseman said. "Next thing I knew, Dr. Clark was accused of wrongdoing and fired. You couldn't ask for a more upstanding man. You listen to the stuffed shirts spouting high ideals about tolerance, but there they are treating a man like rubbish after years of service. Makes me glad to be a farmer."

"Back to Raymond helping him …"

"I'm getting to that," he said. "Dr. Clark came up the hill one day, looking like ghosts were on his tail. Downright paranoid, which is why I made a note of you possibly inclining that way. I wondered if you'd gotten bitten by his madness, though it sounds like you never met him."

"No," I said. "All this happened before I moved to Maine."

"It's no wonder he was rattled, given how he was accused of pushing the geologist to his death over on the coast," Mr. Cheeseman said. "Other accusations piled up, like his habit of trespassing, and talk of him misusing college funds. Anyway, he comes up the hill, looking this way and that, all sweaty, and drags me in here for a chat."

"He knew it would be soundproof?" I asked.

"Exactly," he said. "Once we were in here, Dr. Clark gave me one of those letter-sized envelopes you can't tear. Made of special material. It was sealed tight. He pressed it into my hands and asked me to hang onto it for a bit. Maybe a month. In the event that something 'unexpected' happened, he told me the only one to contact was Raymond."

"You're making my hairs stand on end," I said.

"He was specific. *Only* tell Raymond, no one else. I balked at first. I'm not cut out to be a middleman, but he said he felt the weight of burdening Raymond. The envelope had to do with a whole new problem. He hoped to leave your father out of it. You'll hear tales of them having an argument. A falling out. I don't believe that for a minute."

"So, you let Dr. Clark leave the envelope," I said.

"Yup, I agreed to the arrangement," he said "When *more* than a month went by without word from Bertrand, it was a curve ball. There was talk of him needing to settle his mind and secure a new job at a distant college. It seemed premature to reach out to your father."

"I would probably have waited a bit as well," I said.

"I've got a complex farm to run," he said with a note of self-reproach. "I lost track of time, and then your father died."

"You never told Raymond about the envelope?" I asked.

"Believe me, it's a pain point." With a look of worry, Mr. Cheeseman glanced toward the door. "We had a burglar in our house last month. Brazen, considering we're here day in and day out. Somebody made a science of our comings and goings. Slipped in and took a look around. We're a messy lot, I'll freely admit it, but there's a method to where we put things. Not just that. My wife and I *smelled* a stranger's presence."

"I know the sensation," I said. "I've been there."

"Of course you have. It's why I hung back instead of handing 'it' over to you," Mr. Cheeseman whispered.

I held my breath. "By 'it' you mean …?"

"*Shhh*, even in this cave I get worried about some special device that can hear us through the walls," he said, gripping my arm. "There's been glints in the forest up there that can't be explained, quiet footfalls in the night, and dogs barking down the lane."

"You're giving me goosebumps," I said.

"Sniffs that can't be the wind," he softly added, "My wife has keener ears than I do. Just last week she said a man was prowling under our bedroom window at midnight."

"Have you told the police?" I asked.

"I made mention of it, sort of in passing, to a deputy who stopped in to buy cheese," he said. "I couldn't convey my *real* concerns. He chalked it up to kids playing pranks, or maybe an escaped goat."

"It's a difficult situation if there's no evidence," I said.

"All we've got is a mounting sense of dread," he said.

He paused with an air of having even worse things to share.

"Raymond was about as tough as a man can be," Mr. Cheeseman said. "Skilled with tools, and knowhow to beat the band. When we heard he'd passed away from a so-called accident, it gave us pause. Your father would know better than to clear ice dams during a storm."

The hairs on my arms lifted all the more, straight on end, and the nape of my neck felt a whisper of chilly air, as if from a ghost's breath. For the first time, someone other than Dan had put two and two together on the confusing facts around my father's death.

"I'm right, aren't I?" Mr. Cheeseman asked gravely.

"The police aren't being clear about it," I said.

"They're a part of the system," he said. "That's why me and my fellow farmers in this neck of the woods like to handle matters on our own. One careless move, and the next thing you know, a politician is seeing potential in the land and taking control in a bad way. The eminent domain situation makes landowners vulnerable. It's happened lots of times."

"I know," I said. "I'm a landowner myself."

"This leaves me with a dilemma," Mr. Cheeseman whispered. "I can't hand 'it' over to a wide-eyed little thing like you, even after seeing you pass all the tests that I devised to assess your character, strength, and agility under pressure. It's best to keep 'it' locked down."

"I did pass your tests," I insisted. "Plus, I'm dating a police officer, and I'm friends with Sue and Kate. They're strong allies."

"Hmm," the farmer deliberated. "That's some pretty fierce back-up, but Raymond had all that and more. He carried a gun, was smart as a whip, and had fists of steel. He got cut down all the same, and I'm more and more convinced his death has to do with 'it.'"

"I'm Raymond's heir," I whispered. "I appreciate your concern on my behalf, but if Dr. Clark left something of importance here—"

"Look at the time," he said, reverting to his jovial persona as the door swung open and a man strode in with a round of cheese.

"Sorry, gramps," the worker said as he caught sight of us.

"No worries, Miss Littlefield is taking pictures."

Once we were alone again, Mr. Cheeseman studied me.

"I can see you're determined, and I have to admit, an alternate option never came along," he said. "Don't you *dare* end up dead."

"You know my story," I said. "I'm tougher than I look."

"I'm sorry the handoff will involve you buying some cheese," he said. "Midway through, factor in a visit to the restroom."

"Ok, what then?" I asked.

"You'll find a T-shirt folded in the cabinet," Mr. Cheeseman said. "Put it on. My wife sewed a special pouch for 'it.' With the worry that bad guys are watching to see if I hand a certain envelope over to someone else, I can't think of any other way to hide 'it.'"

"That's a great idea," I said. "I'll wear 'it' out."

"Exactly," he said. "Are you ready?"

"Thank you so much," I said.

"You can thank me by staying in one piece," he said.

"Well, that's the gist of the grand tour, Miss Littlefield," the farmer said, ushering me out of the cheese cave. "It's a fine thing you're doing, helping us advertise for the Farm Crawl."

"I'm glad to help," I said. "Is your shop still open?"

"You've caught us just before closing time," he said loudly in case a mystery stalker was observing us. "Soft cheese, or semi-hard?"

"I'd love to try both," I said.

The cheese shop was small, geared for the convenience of local clients who stopped in now and then. For the most part, the farm's profits came from sales to restaurants across the state and stores like the Corner Pocket. In front of the refrigerated glass case that also served as a countertop, I sampled the honey-flavored soft cheese with a smile.

"What do you think of our T-shirts?" the farmer asked.

"I love them," I said. "I'd like to buy three."

"That's kind of you," he said. "What size?"

"Medium. Look at the time," I added. "It's a long drive to my house. Is there a restroom I can duck into before I head out?"

"Right over there," Mr. Cheeseman said.

Smiling, I said, "I'll be back in a minute."

In truth, there would have been a need to ask anyway, given how long I'd been holding my bladder in check. Once the bathroom door was closed, my heart thudded as I opened the cabinet and pulled out a folded T-shirt with a secret envelope sewn into a back compartment. Cleverly designed, the rectangular pocket took up the exact dimensions of the farm's logo so the stitching was too subtle to see unless closely studied. I wrenched off my button-up shirt, yanked the T-shirt over my head, and then fastened my overshirt as I answered the call of nature. Sweating, worried that I'd taken too long, I finished up and washed my hands.

"Thank you for your hospitality," I said as I rejoined the farmer.

"Here's your cheese," the clerk said, handing me a small paper bag. "Do you want a bag for the T-shirts?"

"No need," I said. "I'll carry them out."

"Drive safely," she said. "It's getting dark."

"I'll be in touch," I said. "Thank you again."

Amidst an array of children with rosy cheeks playing catch in the yard, I endeavored to make it clear that I was exiting with a small bag of cheese, my camera on its strap, and extra T-shirts draped over my arm. On the fly, I'd figured out that there would be no safe place to store the envelope, or even *look* at the contents until I was certain the transfer had gone unnoticed. I planned to replicate the pouch on the extra T-shirts so I could change them out, maybe once a day. Breathless from knowing that a highly dangerous document was pressing against my shoulder blades, I climbed into my car and tossed Mr. Cheeseman a parting wave. He didn't quite nail the job of looking nonchalant. His worry that he'd done the wrong thing was obvious, but it was too late to turn back.

20

As if he'd said the words to me directly, I found myself recalling one of Raymond's journal entries as I headed for home.

Again and again, he'd written. *I've seen people get talked into trouble of every sort. They get talked into a doomed romance. Talked into making a quick buck or ignoring their instincts. Even without anyone in the room, they can talk themselves into trouble. A jealous rage. Phobias and paranoia. It's a wonder our brains can function smoothly. I'm as guilty of it as anyone. For me, the tried-and-true fix for the nonsense is to sit still and breathe.*

I couldn't sit still and breathe my way to calm just then. I was driving a car, but Raymond's point about people talking themselves into trouble had a clarifying effect. Mr. Cheeseman was a new acquaintance, entirely unknown to me until that afternoon. It was smart and reasonable for me to err on the side of caution in case his sense of the situation was correct, but it was just as likely that whatever fumes were involved with making cheese had warped his thinking a little bit.

And yet, he'd not only accepted the notion that my father had been murdered, he'd seen it that way from the start.

For the second time in days, the sun shimmered like an orange cat eye above the black fringe of trees on the horizon, casting its fiery glow into a sky that promised to be clear, spangled by the Milky Way and studded with countless stars. Hungry and chilled as I aimed my car down the winding, narrow road, I reached for a granola bar I'd left in the cup holder and bit off a chunk, casting crumbs onto my lap. By the time I finished the snack, my mouth was all the more parched. My skin felt aflame from worry, and my efforts to take deep breaths made me feel light-headed. I opened the window a crack to let in a current of bracing air and told myself to stop being a paranoid nut. I would get home safe and sound.

What then? Who could I confide in? Not Jeremy. I was certain he would blurt the secret. I had half a mind to swing by Brumby's apartment to see if Dan was there, but he would share the envelope's contents with his team, including Nicole. More than likely, he would push me out of the loop straight away, which would be *so* unfair.

Under the night sky, with my headlights carving a narrow path in the darkness, I flicked from high beams to low as a car approached in the opposite lane. Once it swept past me with a bluster of wind and bits of gravel, I'd no sooner breathed a sigh of relief when a sport utility vehicle peeled out from a turnout up ahead, causing me to yelp and slam on my brakes. Behind me, the sedan swung in a sharp circle, with its tires squealing, and gunned toward me in an effort to block me in.

Seeing two shadows in balaclavas emerge from the utility vehicle, with their eyes visible in my headlights, I felt my skin ice over. Were they the crew from Dan's house? I hit the gas and aimed for the narrow gravel shoulder to the right of their back bumper, wincing as my car tipped precariously on the rim of the roadside ditch. My rear fender nicked a part of their vehicle with a shriek of metal on metal, and then I was free and clear. My heart pounded as I hit the gas. Behind me, the sedan's headlights swerved as the driver followed my path, fishtailed, and then its front grill got closer and closer in my rear-view mirror.

Desperate to escape, I dove down a fork, nearly airborne as I sailed over a bump, and then I surged onward down the winding, country road. The sedan's high beams closed in again, and on my right, I saw the utility vehicle plunging over the bumps and ruts of a field, casting light skyward as it lurched and swerved, and then it steadily closed in.

"This can *not* be happening!" I hollered.

Grasping their intent, I opened my window to the fullest extent, sending a blustering gale of cold air through the car, and reached for some mail I'd fetched from my box days ago. Swerving as I switched the envelopes to my left hand, I focused on the lane ahead, still with my foot on the gas, and waved the mail outside the window for a second.

The sedan fell back. I flung the letters into the air and saw them scatter upward, tumbling in the glare of the pursuer's headlights.

The driver bought my ruse, slowing to a halt in case I'd given up the documents the crew was seeking. With the utility vehicle closing in on my right, I slowed a little, and then with a Hail Mary move, I hit the brake hard as I hauled the steering wheel into a counterclockwise turn, hollering and gritting my teeth as the back end swerved precariously toward the ditch with an ungodly shriek of tires burning to nothing on the road. My car rocked into position, and then all was quiet except for the plumes of gravel dust and burned rubber smoke I'd cast into the night air. With my car's front end now aimed down the opposite lane, I hammered the gas, fishtailed, and then spun forward into the night.

The sedan driver had fetched the envelopes and grasped that I'd tossed junk mail into the air. A dark, hooded blur on my left, with his teeth bared and his eyes flashing as I rocketed by, his dark silhouette was soon behind me, and his sedan was a blur of red tail lights.

"Don't panic," I managed. "What next?"

Reaching for my phone, I prepared to call 911, no idea what road I'd landed on, and felt the device drop from my hand into the dark void of the floor. The utility vehicle had rejoined the road and was closing in from behind. Within seconds, its headlights were an angry menace in my rearview mirror, a forewarning that they were about to stop playing nice. I yelped, gripping the steering wheel as my car lurched from his test impact. I no sooner recovered from the jarring feel of it when the driver corrected his aim and smoothly pushed on my left rear fender.

In a split-second din of tires howling on the pavement, I ducked and winced, expecting my car to flip and roll, but the skidding, sideways momentum slowed as my foot missed the gas pedal, ending the chase with a slow-motion slide into the roadside ditch.

As I hit the gas pedal, the tires spun, sliding me further into the ditch. The chase was over. I lurched for my bag and secured my canister of pepper spray into the cuff of my long-sleeved shirt, and then I hit the emergency beacon Dan had secured to my dashboard after I'd managed to get kidnapped two times. A repeating siren blared from under the front hood just as two masked men neared my car from behind.

I opened the door and lurched out, desperate to reach the shelter of the drying cornfield beyond the opposite lane. A rush of boots rasping on the pavement forewarned a hard shove from behind, sending me into a painful, tumbling heap along the roadside. Cursing under his breath, the man who'd landed the blow frisked me to see if I was armed. He wrenched the flip phone from my pocket and then held me down with his hand between my shoulder blades and his shin on my thighs.

"I don't have anything," I said.

"*Shh.*" He shoved me for emphasis. "Boss, I've got her under control," he hollered to the men who were searching my car. "The siren will attract attention. Do you need help with it?"

Aside from whispered curses, the boss was silent.

"I found folders with paperwork," the third guy said.

"Viens," the boss growled. "Dépêchez-vous."

As they approached, I railed at myself for leaving my father's notes in my car. I was not likely to see them ever again.

Roughly, my captor rolled me onto my back and shined a flashlight into my face, blinding me and causing me to blink and squint. A yard or so away, a silhouette with an air of swagger knelt with one knee resting on the pavement. He studied the flip phone his subordinate had taken from my pocket, then he handed it back to his underling.

"Now, what about you?" he whispered.

Squinting against the light in my eyes, I tried to get a sense of his face beneath his balaclava, but the tilt of his head kept his eyes mostly in shadow. Subtle changes in what little skin I could see told me that he was smiling, and camouflaged with face paint. As the third guy paced a little, the boss snapped his fingers to stop the activity.

"Who are you?" he softly asked.

"I'm a photographer," I managed.

"Driving like that?" he asked. "All the moves the other night?"

"My father had enemies," I said. "I learned self-defense."

"Did you read the documents?" the boss asked. "See the map?"

"There wasn't time," I said. "I drove straight out."

"What does the cheese farmer know?" he asked.

"Nothing," I insisted. "He wants no part of it."

"No part of what?" he asked.

"Please, just let me go," I said.

I curled in a ball, a false front of terror, and eased the pepper spray from its hidden spot under my cuff. Blinded by the light in my face, I used my knowledge of the device to aim it the right way.

"Let's go," the third man said. "The siren is a problem."

His worry sparked an idea that would land an extra punch.

"Please leave the flip phone," I implored. "It belonged to that guy who disappeared. I promised to mail it to his wife."

"It belonged to Monsieur Clark?" the boss prompted.

"Yes, the archaeology professor," I said.

Just then, a zipping sound sliced the air and thwapped against the third man's chest. He staggered and yelped in pain as the report of a gunshot echoed in the night from a distant spot. A repeating string of sounds had the boss rolling away and lying flat to avoid further hits.

"It was a plastic bullet," the stricken man said.

As the man holding me awaited instructions, I tapped his arm to draw his gaze and doused his eyes with pepper spray. With a guttural shriek he lurched back with his hands clutching his face.

For the second time that week, the crew was forced to haul a wounded comrade from the business of menacing me, which would nix me forever from their holiday card list. I yearned to spray the other two, but Dan's training echoed in my head: "If you can run for cover, run for cover, understand? No theatrics. Run—for—cover!"

Yes, Sir.

Scrambling forward and diving into the rustling embrace of the cornfield, I didn't turn to ensure the crew was leaving. I focused on forging ahead, slipping now and then on a thin layer of mud that promised to ruin my favorite shoes. Once I was twenty feet from the road, I carefully pushed my way through the stalks to hide my location, and then I crouched and paused for a second, casting puffs of vapor into the night air under the stars. Shivering, but pumped to the hilt, I listened to their tires squealing, and then their vehicles gunned away down the road.

In the distance, police vehicles were hurtling toward me on winding roads, adding to the blaring siren still issuing from under the front hood of my car. I was poised to head from my hiding place and shut it off, but an approaching rush of tires on the pavement caused me to stop and hold my breath. Two vehicles skidded to a halt.

Multiple doors banged open. The siren halted, except for a faint echo that bounced against the dark hills. Only one person knew how to shut off the warning signal. I paused another second to be sure.

"Sonny!" Dan hollered. "Shit, they took her."

Trembling, on stress-weakened legs, I stood up.

"No, I'm over here," I called out.

"Thank God," Dan said, crashing toward me through the winter cornfield, shoving stalks away and making quite a mess, and then he gripped my arms as we met halfway.

"I'm fine," I assured him. "I ran for cover."

"How?" he asked.

"This helped."

As I lifted the pepper spray, Dan gently secured my arm and aimed the canister in the opposite direction. Once he'd led me from the cornfield back to the road, he began examining me for injuries.

"What happened?" Dan asked.

"It's confusing," I said. "They came out of nowhere."

Nicole pushed in, glaring at me with her cold, calculating eyes.

"Bullshit," she said. "What did you do to spark this?"

"I was at a farm taking photographs," I said.

"Back off, Nicole," Dan warned.

"You're blind when it comes to her," she snapped.

"You'd give anyone else a break," Dan countered.

"*Hey*," I hollered, pushing them apart. "Stop arguing and go after the crew. It was three French-speaking men, like the night of the burglary. They're in two vehicles, a utility truck and a sedan."

"We can't leave your car in the ditch," Dan said.

"There's no time for arguing." I gripped his tactical vest and drew his gaze to my face. "I faked them out so they'd think the flip phone is a key element. They've got it. You can track them."

Dan paused. "They have the flip phone?"

"Yes, and listen," I said. "The police are on the way."

"In force," Liam agreed, working the controls of a drone he'd sent into the air. "Civilians as well. Firefighters, maybe. Who in the hell are you dating, Bolton? She's former CIA?"

"Is your neck injured from the PIT?" Dan persisted.

"*Go,*" I said. "I really am fine."

Dan pulled me into a fierce hug, and then as fast as Liam snagged the grounded drone from the pavement, they jogged to their respective vehicles. With a chirp of tires, they hit the gas and sped away.

Crossing to my car, I paused as Antoine emerged from the darkness with a rifle slung over his shoulder. Wearing threadbare jeans, sneakers, and a tight button-up shirt, he was breathing hard from his fast dash across the field, with his rare, captivating grin intact.

"Berrichon," he said. "Well done."

"You were the one shooting plastic bullets?" I asked.

"From a high spot," he said. "Lucky hits."

"How did this happen?" I asked. "Do you know?"

"Earlier today, one farmer whispered to another that it was time to honor a promise that had been made to Dr. Clark," Antoine said. "There was mention of giving you an envelope they referred to as 'it.'"

"Unfortunately, Mr. Cheeseman's behavior rattled me," I said. "It felt like a setup, so I ended up leaving without the envelope."

Antoine stepped closer, chewing mint gum, and studied me with his keen eyes, so close that wafts of his signature clean scent stirred across my face. With twisted eyebrows, I folded my arms and squarely met his gaze, asking if he could please stop doubting me.

"If that's the case, what did the crew take?" Antoine asked.

"My father's notes," I said. "My car was unlocked during my visit at the farm. Maybe somebody hid the documents in there."

Without question, Antoine crossed to my car to search the interior. I looked at my muddy sneakers, hating the need to dupe him, but I had no choice until I understood the nature of the secret.

"Are you all right?" Antoine called over.

"Yeah, I'm just tired," I said. "I wouldn't mind knowing what the fuss is about. The lengths they've gone to are off the charts."

"You heard the men," he said. "Documents and a map."

"A map to what?" I asked.

Antoine leaned into my car and emerged with the bag of cheese. He bit off a chunk and tossed me the main piece.

"Thank you," I said. "I'm starving."

While I paced to keep warm, savoring the creamy, nutty flavor of the cheese, Antoine's gaze lifted to me now and then as he continued his quick search of the interior. After each area was checked, he closed the doors, one by one, and then he rejoined me in the darkness.

"I found nothing," he said. "That leaves only one place."

With an eye roll, I pulled out my jean's pockets, kicked off my muddy sneakers, and unbuttoned my overshirt with an air of impatience to convey that we had more important things to discuss. In the midst of turning in a circle, I pointed to my back pocket, which did the trick of keeping his gaze on my butt, and not on my new T-shirt.

"Notice the flip phone isn't there," I said, shivering as I buttoned my shirt. "I convinced the crew that it belonged to Dr. Clark. They have it with them right now. I told Dan."

Antoine smiled. "At last, he will nab them."

"Why stay in the shadows instead of working with his team?"

"In this phase, I prefer to work alone," he said.

Shivering from anxiety and actual cold, I knelt to put my shoes back on. Antoine returned to my car to fetch my jacket and found me fumbling with the laces. He helped tighten them, and then he hauled me to my feet, which landed me in front of his chest as he snugged my jacket around my shoulders. I backed up and brushed grit from my pants.

"What are you not telling me?" Antoine asked.

"For one thing," I said, "an imbalance has formed, with you lending support and then disappearing into the night. Before you dash away, thank you for helping me get through this awful week. It has me wanting to help you if I can. I found the online page for Chloé's funeral."

Antoine held his breath, taken off guard.

"On the surface, we're a world apart," I continued. "You're a cop, I'm an artist, but we've both ended up trashed by hard luck and loss. What's important right now is that Dan started out with trust in you. Your silence is making him wonder whose side you're on."

"You're doubting me as well?" Antoine said softly.

"I've been blindsided enough times to hold back. You're philosophical and jaded in equal amounts. You've wrestled with demons, the same as I've done. My stubborn side wants to be right about you."

Antoine studied the distant hills, where the drone of truck engines and police sirens were getting closer by the second.

"It's like chasing a comet," he murmured. "Fast-moving and unpredictable, but so far so good. I can't unravel your doubts."

I shrugged. "What do you mean?"

With a wry smile, Antoine smoothed my cheek with his palm, and then he rested his fingers under my chin. The next thing I knew, I was stepping closer. A strange, almost mystical tug had been performed, a subliminal command. Muscular, manly, a supreme example of power held in check, Antoine rested his shaved jaw against my cheek.

"Your eyes give you away more than you know," he whispered.

"Stop being a lone wolf," I managed. "Work with Dan."

"Not quite yet, Berrichon," he said.

With his rifle strap in place, Antoine jogged across the road, leaped over the ditch, and vanished into the night with a whisper of threadbare jeans swishing through dry winter grass.

And just in time.

I squinted as the glare of approaching headlights stabbed my eyes. Along with police vehicles I glimpsed rusted fenders and heard growling old engines that told me the farmers had heard the commotion, and were coming to the rescue. I stood there with an ache in my heart, dizzied by the knowledge that my father's friends and supporters would dive into the unknown in the dark of night to save his daughter.

With a tumult of wind, trucks with gun racks and cars without mufflers spun out of the darkness to surround me with startling precision, engines roaring, tires squealing. The silhouettes of men and women leaped down, even before their trucks stopped moving. Plumes of exhaust filled the air, and weeds rattled in protest here and there.

"Honey," Mr. Cheeseman said as he hugged me. "I heard the awful crunch of you getting hit and thought the worst."

"I'm ok," I said. "Thank you for coming."

"What the heck are you thinking?" a sheriff's deputy hollered. "If this was an accident, you're mucking up the evidence!"

"We're volunteer firefighters, son," Mr. Cheeseman said.

"Head down the road and stop cars from coming through, and stay on the lanes! You've mucked up the fields."

Mr. Cheeseman raised his eyebrows, asking if I was up to the demands of facing the complexities without his assistance.

"I'll be ok," I said softly.

"It would take two seconds to sneak you out of here," he said.

"The bad guys are nowhere to be seen, and one is blind from pepper spray," I said. "I know my rights. I'll be home by ten."

Offering fist bumps and smiles, the farmers headed to their vehicles to get on with their lives. I promised to be in touch.

* * *

It was not lost on me that my life had devolved into disturbing patterns. Not every element was the same. Detective Allen was a model of neatness, in a state police jacket, but instead of glaring me into a cinder, he greeted my theories with appreciative nods: maybe the crew attacked me out of revenge, or figured my father's notes held clues.

Prompted by a burst of radio chatter, Roy stepped away for a moment, and then he returned with the great news that Dan's team had nabbed two of the crew, though the third man had escaped the net.

"Dan tracked them with the flip phone," Roy said.

"Because I duped them with it," I pointed out.

"We're still assessing your car," Roy said. "Thanks to tonight's events, you'll grasp that its serviceability is compromised. Expect to hear a scraping sound indicating iffy wheel bearings, busted CV joints, stripped tires, any number of things gone wrong in the undercarriage."

"I think most people would try to escape," I said.

No more than a few ounces in weight, the secret envelope helped block the chilly breeze from my back, with a hard spot that had me thinking a flash drive was included in the panel. Most of the police cars had retreated, leaving a few troopers, the EMT van, and evidence technicians who were shaking their heads over the compromised skid marks.

I held my breath as a barred owl hooted in the distance, drawing my gaze to the surrounding dark hills. Beautiful and mellow, it sounded as if the bird was purring, "Who cooks for you? Who cooks for you?"

I had a feeling it wasn't an owl. It was Antoine saying he wasn't fooled. One quick move would have secured the envelope, but maybe he figured I'd done a good job of hiding it, so why not stick with that?

"Ok, let's get your neck looked at," Roy said.

"My car didn't flip," I insisted. "I'm fine."

"It's the procedure after a PIT," Roy said. "Come this way."

With a roll of eyes, I followed him to the EMT truck and allowed him to give me a hand up into the bright, rectangular interior: a scary place of medicinal smells, defibrillators, tubing, syringes, oxygen bags, and other life-saving supplies. As if following instructions to ignore my protests, two medics "assisted" me onto my back on a gurney.

"What's going on?" I managed.

"*Shh*, calm yourself," Detective Allen whispered.

Handed a note, I focused on the words he'd written down.

Given tonight's events, we need to meet in a secure location. I know you have a phobia of hospitals. This isn't about needles and scans. If you're willing to be straight with me for once, I'll return the favor and fill in some answers that will knock your muddy socks off. For instance, the man in your house is not Brumby's brother. He's an undercover cop from up north.

"Whiplash is a serious injury," Roy said as my eyes flew open all the more. "I'm urging you to get X-rays."

"Umm, I guess my neck does hurt a little ..."

"That settles the situation right there," Roy said. "It'll take a few hours to get you properly checked. Your car will be processed by then. I'll tag along to keep you company," Roy added. "As a friend of your father's, I have a protective side when it comes to you."

"That's very kind," I managed.

"Lights and sirens, boys," Roy called out.

The doors slammed, cutting off my view of the snowflakes drifting down from the cloudless sky of infinity and stars.

It's not really snow, Raymond said. *Sometimes, on cold nights after a warm day in early winter, vapor turns to ice and drifts back down to the forests and fields where it came from. The flakes melt on impact.*

The same could be said of my best hopes in life.

With my eyes closed, drawing on yoga breathing to fight the medicinal smells that threatened to pitch me into a panic, I refused all questions on the high-speed, blaring ride to the secret meeting, shoring up my strength by reminding myself that I'd survived being kidnapped by the worst of the worst. If Roy thought I would buckle and tell him everything without a foundation of assurances and ironclad rules of engagement, he had a lot to learn when it came to dealing with a spaniel who could plunge down a rock-strewn hillside, and possibly even survive a surprise trip to Mongolia with nothing more than a hatchet and a fishing line.

"Why is she smiling?" the EMT whispered.

"You don't recall how Raymond switched gears?" Roy asked.

"Yeah, but the two of them never met."

"It's DNA at work, son," Roy said. "Watch and learn."

Perfect. My favorite go-to phrase.

21

Having secured a tucked-away conference room in the hospital's upstairs office area, Roy's team had gotten me there via the radiology department, where my neck was checked for injury. Safely delivered, I lurched out of the mandatory wheelchair and confronted Roy.

"A car would be preferable for the ride back," I said, unnerved by the medicinal smells on my clothes. "This had better be worth it."

Roy motioned toward the conference table in the center of the room, where crime scene technicians and a few troopers in plain clothes took up positions around the table, with laptops and notepads.

"Take a seat," Roy prompted. "I'll talk first."

With folded arms, I listened with rapt attention as Roy confessed that he'd entertained doubts about Jeremy from the start.

"So, I got the notion to call Brumby," he said. "No surprise your blacksmith friend didn't respond to my voicemail straight away, but yesterday he called and told me where to stick my inquiries on his family. The tables turned when I texted him a photo of Jeremy."

"Brumby went ballistic?" I asked.

"He was set to 'tune the guy up,' as he put it," Roy said. "I explained our preference for letting the situation stand. I'll ask the same of you. We can turn the tables to our advantage." Roy studied me. "I figured your impression of Antoine would change, but I'm not seeing outrage."

"It's a well-known fact that I'm independent," I said. "I wouldn't have accepted him as a bodyguard. He's been an asset, helping me swing a tough schedule, and he played a role in outing Nicole's chat with Paul. I'm taking that to mean he wanted me to keep my guard up."

There was embarrassment in not seeing the obvious, and I didn't know if it was fair to fault Jeremy more than Antoine. Just then, all that mattered was navigating the current test of my grit and endurance.

Next, Roy disclosed that the allegations against Dr. Clark were falling apart. Vivian's diary chronicled her guilt in concocting a false paper trail that made it look as if Bertrand had misused college funds. Roy showed a copied page that was tough to read at a glance, except for the exclamation points Vivian had added in her vexed summary of the professor's refusal to grasp how a certain proposal would "set him up for life."

"Maybe she was pressing him to sell his land," Roy said. "It would fit her ambitions around the Westdale Circle concept. Scott Butler seems to have been involved to one degree or another."

"Remind me who that is?" I prompted.

"The geology professor who died from a fall," Roy said.

"A little over two years ago?" I asked.

"Yes, give or take," Roy said. "She didn't express much sorrow when he died. A list of love interests is coming to light, but there was an abrupt change in her entries. No more names, as if one of them demanded secrecy. That leaves us in a jam. It's imperative that we identify the lover that Vivian's neighbor saw. What's your best guess?"

I froze as the officers sat forward in their chairs, as if awaiting my answer with keen interest. Nothing in my recent experience had forewarned the surprise of having the police look to me for insights.

"All I could provide is hearsay and gossip," I said. "With that in mind, you should verify that Vivian's neighbor can be trusted."

"We'll cover that base," one of the officers said.

"We had a chat with Gerald's cousins," Roy continued. "They painted a picture of Gerald and Sal using drills and other equipment in their quest to find tourmaline on Paul's land. With nagging rumors of the two of them processing drugs a year or more ago, we took a close look at the tent platforms they built. Instead of signs of a heroin depot we were perplexed to find a ton of rubble tucked underneath."

"I heard about that," I said. "An effort to make them sturdy?"

"Gerald and Sal are a goofball team," Roy said. "Hearing mention of insurance concerns, they might have addressed the problem to an extreme. Did anyone check for links with the geologist?"

"They didn't travel in the same circles," an officer said. "I wondered if they were washing off rock dust when they were seen in their skivvies, but their fear was around the effects of a drug."

"Sonny, did the perps make mention of drugs?" Roy asked.

"No," I said. "All they took were my father's notes."

"It's not adding up," Roy said. "The trio successfully laid low for days. Tonight's attack is puzzling. A substantial risk."

I couldn't refute that notion, since Dan's team had captured two of the crew after a chase through the countryside. I'd faced the worst of the worst more times than I could count, so I had little doubt that the boss was still at large. If I was right, he'd hidden in town, cold as ice, pulling the strings and killing anyone who posed a threat to his plans.

"Sonny, you're quiet all of a sudden," Roy said.

"My feet are damp and chilled," I said. "Is it possible to get fresh socks? A quick break will help me focus and think."

Once the requested pair was secured from the nursing staff, I stepped into the nearest restroom, savored the warmth of the dry socks as I slipped them on, and then I stared at my ashen face in the mirror.

I'd dealt with Roy enough times to know that he'd relied on one major disclosure to get the ball rolling, and was now poised to switch gears and dig for answers. Mere hours into wearing the secret envelope, I was spent and exhausted. It wasn't a practical option. In a cabinet, I found a box of nitrile gloves. I snugged a pair onto my hands, stripped off my top layers, extracted the envelope from the pouch, and removed the contents: a sheet of cryptic test results, an ancient map, and a travel drive.

Wincing as the map crackled during the unfolding process, I put my phone on silent mode and photographed the topography in overlapping grids. The light in the bathroom was perfect for getting sharp, clear images. I photographed the test results, initiated the process of uploading the images to my cloud account, and returned the items to the T-shirt pouch. With the gloves still intact, I shrugged my way into my button-up shirt and smoothed the front. With my eyes closed I paused for a moment, and then I stepped out with the folded T-shirt in my hands.

"This is why the crew of three targeted me," I said.

With grins and high-fives, the team celebrated their crafty means of outmaneuvering the bad guys *and* the undercover cops. With nitrile gloves in place, one of the techs cleared space on the table to spread out the faded, hand-drawn map of Maine with an 1885 date. Along with notations and symbols marking the locations the couple had visited during their travels, drawings of trees, figures, and animals appeared to be a means of keeping track of special details they'd wanted to remember. For the moment, I stifled the urge to point out that many of the locations mirrored the places my father had circled on his map of crime locations.

"What's this?" Roy said of the sheet of test results.

"Check the letterhead," the tech sitting next to me said. "It's from the geology department at Westdale College."

After a quick online search of the symbols, the findings were discussed in whispers amongst the officers and technicians.

"Tell me," I demanded.

The guy on my right slid the sheet toward me.

"Pegmatite is a coarse-grained igneous rock. Maine is a rare source of a kind of pegmatite that contains spodumene." Prompting a colleague to hand him a remote control, he extracted the batteries and set them on the table. "These are regular, but you'll be familiar with the rechargeable kind. Spodumene is a lithium aluminum silicate mineral."

"Lithium?" I prompted.

"Yeah, it's a major element in all kinds of industrial applications," he said. "For making glass, steel, medicine—"

"Oh my God!" I blurted. "If Gerald and Sal were mining this stuff on Paul's land it would explain their fear during their notorious washing effort at the stream. Lithium is a powerful drug."

"Bingo, that's it," the tech said.

"What if the rubble that supports the tent platforms isn't worthless?" I continued. "Maine adopted strict mining laws after some toxic spills, but

I think the restrictions are easing up. Raymond wrote about it in his journals. If I'm right, it would make sense to act in secret and hide the lithium-bearing stone until it could be sold without breaking the law or attracting attention. It's probably worth thousands."

"Billions," the tech said. "It's like a stolen bank bag. Tricky in terms of capitalizing on the loot. The mine itself could be hidden by tree branches, or maybe it's another reason the platforms were built. It's all neatly tucked away until the culprits in charge think the coast is clear."

Roy narrowed his eyes. "Raymond kept journals?"

"Records," I said. "Farm notes. Minor scribblings."

"Maybe Dr. Clark's flash drive has more details," the tech said.

One file was on the device: a video the tech launched on a widescreen monitor fastened to the wall. Bertrand Clark looked haggard as he sat at a desk in front of an antique world map, his brow furrowed and tanned from outdoor pursuits, and his hair turning gray around the temples. He adjusted his wire-rimmed glasses, blinking back tears.

"Hello, my friend," he began. "I was in the Corner Pocket when you came in with a colleague. I heard him admonishing you to get a grip and stop buying my 'flimsy stories,'" Dr. Clark said with air quotes. "I can't tell you how much your support has meant to me, but I saw in that moment that it's come at a cost. We've assumed my troubles stem from all the talk of 1800s treasure. I don't want to burden you with a false lead, but I'm pursuing another angle that I didn't see at first. If you receive my package, my attempt to get answers has gone awry. I've been naïve, I suppose, seeing tales of prejudice and blindness on the news and thinking it would never happen to me. I've given up hope of reclaiming my life, but I can't leave my wife and children to suffer the weight of being connected to me. If it's too big a risk, leave it alone. *Please* be careful. Farewell."

As I turned from the screen and glanced around the table, even Detective Allen looked thrown and unsettled as he massaged his brow. If he thought his headache would be brief, he was wrong.

"Dr. Clark started the video with, 'Hello, my friend,'" I said. "The map, the test results, and the flash drive were meant for my father's eyes alone. I'm sorry to jump in and direct things, but I think we should put what we know on a timeline. A bird's-eye view will help."

With a nod, the tech linked his laptop to the widescreen monitor and created a timeline that spanned multiple years.

"Ok this marker reflects the date Gerald and Sal were washing in the stream," he said. "Assuming they'd been at it for a while, we'll color this section of time with a bar spanning to last week."

"The geologist's death is a critical element," I prompted.

"Yeah, that happened back here," the tech said, adding a marker two years ago. "Dr. Clark's troubles began a bit later. This marker is the date he was fired from the college for misconduct."

"Vivian's diary reflects anger at Bertrand for not playing along with a proposal," I said. "We need to fill in the blanks. If the geologist was in love with her, he might have shared the find to secure their bond. But he didn't have business chops. Something went wrong and he ended up dead. Vivian moved on. She cultivated a new partner."

"Isaac Munroe," the tech said. "Or his son."

"Or any number of guys we don't know about," I said. "Her new secret lover, for instance, if that rumor proves out. We need to be clear on facts so we don't turn anyone into a wrongly accused victim."

"True enough," Roy said. "For all we know Bertrand is alive and well and running the show. This video might be a false front."

I paused in the interests of remaining civil.

"What else goes on the timeline?" the tech asked.

"Add the date that Bud and Birdie died," I said. "Plus, the date when the farm in Little Edge was torched, and the other crimes on my father's map. The instances of scams, for instance. Victims of that kind of crime are too bogged down to care if anyone is trespassing on their land. Look what's forming. A cluster." I lurched from my chair and pointed at the timeline. "If the pegmatite on Paul's land started to diminish, whoever hired Gerald and Sal would be driven to find a new source."

"Why add Bud and Birdie's death?" Roy prompted.

"Bud fell off the wagon after ten years of sobriety because someone tempted him with a bottle of whiskey," I said. "All of a sudden, he was too drunk to chase trespassers away. It fits the pattern."

Vibrating with excitement, I returned to the table to study the sheet of test results, which had been enclosed in an evidence bag. Squinting to see through the plastic, I pointed to the letterhead.

"This sheet is dated a little over two years ago," I said. "According to the initials the rock sample was obtained from Dr. Clark. It makes sense. It's probably a known practice to create profiles of the geology at different sites. There will be other test sheets, but *this* sample of pegmatite stood out. I've heard Bertrand had a secretive side when it came to the 1800s couple. If asked for specifics, he might even lie about the source. If that was the case, the geologist was left to guess at the exact location."

"The vein on Paul's land seems an easy find," Roy countered.

"Maybe logic was applied," I said. "At that time, Dr. Clark had a major dig underway on Paul's land. Gerald and Sal were directed to check the rock formations and ledges. They discovered a vein. The trouble began when the vein ran dry. Greed took over. Why dig test holes when it was easier to pressure Bertrand?" I motioned toward the timeline. "Only one man was committed to connecting the pattern of crimes. My father's death ended the quest for answers. Surely you see that now?"

"I have a further thought," the tech ventured, seeming wary of Roy's scowl. "The pegmatite would range in value depending on the richness of the source. It's possible the vein on Paul's land was low quality. Maybe Dr. Clark's rock sample was extremely high end."

"I guess we'll need to take a fresh look at the Pierces," Roy said. "They benefited when Bud and Birdie died. This is what happens when you open a can of worms. We'll be delicate about it, of course."

I glared at him, aware that he was using the circumstances to school me on the harsh ins and outs of law enforcement.

"All right, I'm out of line with that thread," Roy admitted in a softer tone. "The verdict was absolute. Accidental death. But I'm seeing the need to put two more markers on the timeline. Dan's house was burglarized, and Gerald Leblanc, according to Sonny, is dead."

The tech cleared his throat. "Sir—"

"Yes, I know the trace evidence backs it up," Roy said. "My delay was partly from not knowing why they'd take his body."

"Gerald had cancer," I said. "An autopsy might include traces of the rock dust. I doubt his body will ever be found."

Warmth drifted around me from the ceiling ducts amidst the rustle of officers and technicians exchanging glances that reflected a recalibration of how they'd perceived Dr. Clark, and possibly me.

With a sigh, Detective Allen cast me a glance that said he would know better than to trick me into a conference room ever again.

"We're all in agreement?" Roy said. "We'll let it sink in overnight, but as of now, I'm adding a new case to the mix."

Roy swiveled his laptop so the screen showed a photo of my father in his uniform: the image from Maine's official website.

"Check the facts," he said. "Dig deep. If Raymond's death wasn't an accident, we need to move heaven and earth to sort it out."

Handed a tissue, I wiped my brimming eyes and attempted to collect myself, gripped by a mix of anguish and relief. The grave silence in the room assured me that I wouldn't be alone in the search for answers anymore, but it was a cold case with slim chances.

Roy patted my arm. "Let's get you home."

* * *

As I steered what remained of my car along the lightless, wooded road that led to my farm, I missed the lulling drone of well-balanced wheels carrying me forward. The damage that Detective Allen had alluded to was audible, from iffy wheel bearings to "busted CV joints" and other issues. With an undercurrent of rattles, a circular rasp, and other ominous noises engulfing me, it felt as if the car was a living thing groaning in pain.

A mechanically inclined crime scene technician had gotten my car into a borderline roadworthy condition under the proviso that I would seek alternate transportation in the days to come. Above me, a police drone followed my progress in the night sky to see if anyone followed me, but even the criminals were apparently getting some rest.

At last, my driveway was up ahead. In parting, Roy had doubled down on asking me to turn the tables on "Jeremy" to see if anything of interest might be learned. In place of Dr. Clark's documents was a phony map and a sheet of cryptic notes in Navajo, which had formed the basis for an unbreakable code that American marines had used in World War II.

I would never forget the sight of grown police techs and plainclothes officers giggling as they used a language app to translate locations in Maine into Navajo: a source of headaches instead of clues.

"And that's just for starters," I said, backing into a space next to my berry field, where my car could begin its retirement.

Light spilled from my kitchen doorway as Jeremy emerged in time to greet me on the porch. Luke bounded out and softly whined as he sniffed my clothes, telling me that he'd honed in on Jeremy's concern after my jarring experience had become breaking news.

"What in the heck happened?" Jeremy demanded.

In the bright glare of my kitchen, I launched into a description of getting knocked from the road and hauled to the ER.

"It was awful," I said. "They took a sample of blood."

I showed a bandage that covered a cotton ball on my inner elbow, with a red pen dot on my skin for a note of realism.

"The police wondered if I landed in the ditch because I was high," I added. "It's sorted out. They were apologetic in the end, but this is a turning point. It's not safe for you to be here."

"Nonsense," he said. "I'm not leaving you on your own."

"You're *so* good to me," I said.

Abruptly, I dove against the mole's broad chest, allowing him to hug my troubles away, which had his hands pausing over the strange pouch on my T-shirt, and then I peeled away with a frown.

"You're sweaty," I said. "You need a shower."

"I was too worried for normal activities," he said.

"I need to be alone so I can come up with a plan," I said. "Go ahead and take your shower. Seriously, that's the best way to help."

"If you're sure you're ok …"

"Totally," I said. "I'm strong."

Once he was upstairs, I waited until I heard him ditch his clothes and adjust the squeaky old knob in the tub. In my father's room, I made a racket of pulling away the floorboard where he'd kept secrets and installed the envelope with the phony map and bogus codes.

I returned to my kitchen and paced. My practical side was still inclined to assume the best of the secret arrangement. The rest of me was fuming over Jeremy's ability to dupe me with a phony identity. I had a soft heart for sob stories. He'd played it to the hilt, and I was back to questioning his "dumb" move of leaving open the bathroom door.

He deserved at least some measure of payback. I grabbed a wad of steel wool from a kitchen drawer, dashed up the stairs, tapped on the door a few times, and stepped into the steamy bathroom.

"*Hey,*" Jeremy said. "You're breaking the rules."

"My eyes are properly averted," I said, arriving at the sink where he'd left his shaving kit. "I need some dental floss."

Having caught onto his habit of shaving twice a day, most likely to keep himself looking youthful and innocent, I used the steel wool to take the sharp edge from his razor, and then I secured the dental floss from a drawer and apologized for the intrusion.

I grabbed his duffle bag of underwear, snagged a red tablecloth from the closet, dumped the items into the washing machine in the first-floor bathroom, engaged the hot setting, and hit the "on" button.

With my eyes closed, I savored Jeremy's bellow as the water turned to ice. The upstairs knobs squeaked as he attempted to counteract the change. I switched the wash cycle to the cold setting.

"Jesus Christ!" he yelled. "What's going on?"

"I'm doing laundry," I conveyed, silently adding with a dark smile, *prepare to wear shrunken pink undies and T-shirts for a while.*

"I'd think you would want to rest!" he hollered.

"I'm full of jitters," I said.

"I get it," he called out. "I'm done."

In a whisper, I said, "Oh, yeah. You're *done.*"

* * *

"Sonny, wake up. I need to make sure you're ok."

Hearing Dan's whisper, and feeling his kiss on my cheek as he knelt next to my bed in the darkness, I emerged from a dream and drifted into an alternate reality where he'd just returned from ice hockey practice. Then my eyes fluttered and I saw his fatigued expression.

I sleepily allowed myself to be engulfed in his arms. We kissed for a moment, relaxing into the spell that was cast by physical contact. All the while, his hands assessed me for signs of injuries.

"You assured me that you were ok," Dan said.

"The trip to the ER wasn't because I was injured," I murmured. "They needed to process my car and Roy wanted to talk to me. I'm too tired to explain. I heard you caught the bad guys."

"Only two of the crew," Dan said. "The interrogation is still in progress, but I couldn't focus. I can't believe you've gotten pulled into the thick of things, despite my best efforts to keep you safe."

As he'd done the other night in Brumby's apartment, Dan closed his eyes and rested his forehead against mine, as if to transfer his thoughts and whirling feelings directly into my head. As before, words were necessary. Dan sighed in the near darkness and looked at me.

"There's a passage in one of Raymond's journals," he said, smoothing a curl from my sleepy eyes. "He was in the yard when a monarch butterfly settled onto a purple aster. It was migrating. Heading for Mexico. He was transfixed by how miraculous they are, with markings that look like eyes, and digitalis in their bodies to foil predators, but with wings that are more delicate than paper. It crossed his mind to bring it to Mexico to spare it from the wind and driving rain it would face. No surprise he didn't bring it to Mexico," Dan added. "On the road earlier, the passage was a part of how I managed the feat of hearing your assurance and heading away. Don't tell my team I was thinking about butterflies."

"Wrong vibe?" I asked.

"And potentially a new nickname," Dan agreed. "I'm not as agile as you on the emotional front, but I made a breakthrough tonight. I left you stranded in a ditch. It's romantic beyond words."

I cracked up. "One for the record books."

"My work introduces conflict," he said. "It's a part of the problem, but I can't dial down until I get this situation resolved."

"In the meantime, embrace your epiphany about the monarch," I said. "See all the strengths that keep her airborne."

"Sadly, the monarch's ride is totaled," Dan said. "I've had a fix in the works. A new set of wheels. No arguments," Dan pressed on as I started to protest. "It's my work that landed you in the crosshairs."

"I'll catch a ride with dumb-dumb," I said.

Smiling, Dan said, "Jeremy is on your nerves already?"

"I'll explain later," I said. "What's the latest on the notion that Vivian was involved with one of the bad guys?"

"We're checking that possibility," Dan said. "Her assortment of local love interests claim she cut them out of the picture lately."

"Please stay safe," I said. "You need rest."

"Ditto."

With a quick final kiss, Dan slipped away. Luke trotted after him with a din of clicking toenails. I crossed to the window to watch Dan exit and slip into the driver's seat of a police vehicle. He'd come alone.

Downstairs, I heard Luke softly whining from Dan's exit, and Jeremy stirring and sitting up. Earlier, I'd heard the covert operative slip into my father's room to fetch the documents from under the floorboard. I made a quick trip to the bathroom and loudly splashed water.

"Is everything all right?" Jeremy called up the stairs.

"Yeah," I said, yawning. "Dan wanted to make sure I'm ok. Sorry if he woke you. I'm groggy from a sleeping pill."

"I might step out for some fresh air," he said.

"Whatever," I said. "I'm not your keeper."

With that, I closed my door and hovered instead of returning to bed. A moment later, Jeremy stepped outside and crossed to the barn, where a figure emerged from the shadows. I'd left my bedroom window open a crack in case a rendezvous took place.

"The farmer gave her this," Jeremy said quietly.

With a tiny flashlight in hand, Antoine paused and swept the beam over Jeremy's pink T-shirt, and the bits of tissue stuck to an array of shaving nicks on his face and neck.

"I've had a rough night," Jeremy explained.

Without comment, Antoine shined the beam on the phony map, and then he consulted the array of bogus codes the techs had devised. After a long pause, during which I held my breath, Antoine cracked up to the point where he doubled over and looked to be in pain.

"*Shh*, you'll wake Sonny," Jeremy hissed.

With a choked-off noise, Antoine shined the beam on Jeremy's nicked face and laughed all the harder. Staggering to a bale of straw I'd left outside the moonlit barn, he collapsed to one knee, and then he crawled onto the perch as if he'd been wounded in action.

"What the hell?" Jeremy whispered.

"I haven't laughed in a decade," Antoine said. "My gut hurts."

"You can read that code?" Jeremy asked.

"It's written in Navajo." Wiping away tears, Antoine tapped his own face to stop his body from releasing tension through laughing.

"It's a bogus lead?" Jeremy asked. "Something the farmers cooked up to throw us off? Why would they go to that length?"

"Stop, get away," Antoine begged, motioning toward Jeremy's pink shrunken T-shirt and the bits of tissue on his face. "The sight of you is making it worse."

"Your mind has finally snapped. This is nuts."

Choking again, Antoine cast a look toward my bedroom window and devolved into a staggering exit past the barn, not even dimly trying to travel in stealth. With his laughing echoing toward me as he descended the logging trail, I frowned in the darkness.

"That is *not* the reaction I expected," I said.

22

In the hay-smelling center aisle of the barn, where I'd curried and brushed Dodge's chestnut coat, I held the bridle in front of his long, handsome face and slipped the snaffle bit into his mouth. As always, he started playing with it, making silly sounds, his eyes a deep brown with complex flecks, and rimmed by ridiculously long, curved lashes. I slipped the crown piece over his ears, settled his blond forelock over the browband, and buckled the throat latch. The reins had a supple feel and smelled of saddle soap from my efforts to keep them flexible after every use. I patted Dodge's neck, climbed onto a blanket chest, and swung onto his back.

My ankles tapped his sides, sending him thumping forward across the thick, ancient floorboards, and then his hooves touched down on the dirt and grass outside the barn. With the reins shifted to the left, I guided him to the logging trail that wound through the forested acres of my father's land. Dodge's haunches and broad shoulders created a wonderful rocking motion that could put me to sleep if I wasn't careful.

Just then, I was on high alert, even with Luke bounding ahead along the trail once he'd caught onto my trajectory into the forest. My heart thudded as I rode through the shadows under the trees, with the golden light of dawn behind me on the horizon. I'd dug a fleece vest out of my closet to keep warm in the chilly air, but the day promised to warm up fast. Dodge began blowing and snorting, catching the scent of two overnight guests on the wind, thanks to Detective Allen's multi-phase plan to ensure my safety, with one of the crew of three still at large. Feeling Dodge rock back onto his haunches, a signal that he wanted to wheel and flee, I patted his neck to settle him before I nudged him onward.

"It's all right, big guy," one of the officers said, dressed in camouflage gear that made him look like an upright pile of leaves. "No need for theatrics. We're friends, not bad guys."

As if in agreement, Luke sat nearby, panting and excited, with a gaze that said, "Look what I found! Tactical guys like Dan!"

"Yes, you are a marvel," I assured my dog.

"What's got you out so early?" the officer asked.

I slid from Dodge's back, shrugged off my knapsack, and handed him a thermos of hot coffee with a bag of delicious cheese Danish pastries that Jeremy had intended to serve as his breakfast.

"I hope you weren't too cold last night," I said.

"Naw, we're used to it," the officer said around a mouthful of pastry. "Just past midnight, your houseguest met with Antoine. We were geared for trouble, but Antoine came down the trail laughing his head off. He knew we were here, somehow. He prompted us to come out, shook our hands, and thanked us for keeping an eye on the place."

"Like he's your boss," I said.

"Maybe he is for all we know. Roy's instructions were to let him come and go without interference. Maybe the drone alerted him."

"Yes, Antoine would have noticed that," I said.

"Sounds like you're in for a payday," the other guy said. "Mr. Munroe over at the bank put up a reward for whoever helped nab the crew. You gave them a trick phone. Played a key role."

"I won't take the reward," I said. "It wouldn't feel right."

"Use the money for a new car," he said with a merry smile as he wolfed down another pastry. "I heard your ride is a lost cause. Shot wheel bearings, all kinds of shit gone wrong, and tires close to bald. That, my friend, is a totaled car."

"My wife is a horse nut," the other guy said.

I hesitated. "Oh …?"

"Yeah, she's got three," he said. "It's breaking the bank."

"I bet *lots* of state troopers own horses," I said.

"No, it's a money drain. Most cops are smarter than me."

"Nonsense," I said. "You're as sharp as a tack."

"I'm smarter than the undercover guy," he said, pointing to my house. "My wife says the ruse might have worked. There's little or no contact in the Jones family, but with you involved, Mr. Mole needs to be long gone before Brumby gets back. He's a passionate guy."

"Yes," I said. "That is Brumby in a nutshell."

Looking skyward, I asked heaven why it was necessary to disclose the identity of the man whose wife had been conducting an affair with Brumby Jones as recently as two months ago in September.

"She's my soon-to-be *ex*-wife," he added. "Dan picked up on your hints about Brumby's affair with a cop's spouse."

"I'm really sorry," I said.

"You live and learn," he said. "I'm bouncing back."

I was bouncing back as well after sitting bolt upright in bed, wrenched out of sleep by an epiphany. Antoine's covert skills would have enabled him to hack my cloud account and grab the photos I'd taken of the 1800s map, which would have put him ahead of Roy's team after all. No wonder he'd laughed when Jeremy showed him the fake documents. For all I knew they'd met every night all week as I'd slept the hours away.

Once the troopers secured their gear and headed down the trail to be picked up along the road, I turned Dodge's nose homeward and clicked him forward up the slope, with Luke racing ahead to find Jeremy, in case I couldn't tackle the heavy lift on my own.

Below me, Dodge's hooves thumped on the forested trail and stirred fallen leaves that were still burnished with touches of autumn gold, a rustle of sound that was contained by the tall pines and bare branches of maple and birch trees. After a stressful day and jarring night, I'd emerged from the chaos with a sense of satisfaction that was not likely to last.

I embraced it while I could. Kevin had sent word that he'd arranged for people to stop by Aaron's house to pick up the last of the furniture and possessions that were sorted into boxes and tubs.

I'd hoped to give Dan a chance to check the house for items he might want to keep, but Kevin was a "get-the-job-finished" sort of man, jamming the cleanout into a short-notice event that was bound to be painful for Peg. Instead of politely asking if I was free to help, Kevin had tasked me with opening the door and supervising the process.

I resolved to pitch in, as requested. On the silver lining side, once the day was over, the work in Aaron's house would be finished.

* * *

"May I help you, Miss?" Thomas said with a grin. "I've been pressed into action again, since Jeremy is helping at Aaron's house."

"It's why I'm getting an array of snacks," I said, indicating the crackers, cheese, and cookies in my basket. "I figure if people pause to reminisce about Aaron, it'll lessen the feel of a rushed event."

"In case you haven't heard," he said. "We're adopting Vivian's cat."

Wincing, I said, "I've heard it's quite a handful …"

"Mrs. Brooks thinks she can offer the right balance of care and structure." With an eye on an influx of customers, Thomas added, "We do miss you. Stop in when you have more time."

While Jeremy waited for me near the cash register, where he would be pressed into paying for every last item in my shopping basket, I took my time sorting through bottles of hot sauce, ranging from three-chili-pepper warnings to twenty. Was I evil enough to spice up his favorite tacos to the point where he needed medical assistance?

Just then, Sue and Kate closed in on me from opposite directions, the sort of trick people used when cornering an escaped puppy. They came to rest on either side of me with arched eyebrows.

"Never mind this." Kate snatched the hot sauce from my hand and returned it to the shelf. "We have some questions. Such as, why is Jeremy's face riddled with shaving nicks, and what's with the tight look about him today, as if his undies are suddenly too small?"

"You look rested and serene this morning," Sue added, "but Jeremy is a tough read. I can't put my finger on it …"

"It's like he's a *different* man," Kate mused.

"You know he's not Brumby's brother?" I whispered.

"Antoine tipped us off this morning in the spirit of explaining things in person," Sue said. "I think he was disappointed in us for not figuring it out. He's charming, I have to say. Smitten with you, it seems."

"He's a player," I said. "What else did he say?"

"Uh-uh, you first," Kate said.

"I don't want to ruin your vacation buzz," I said.

"Sonny, most of what we hear day in and day out are tired rumors and half-baked theories," Sue said. "You come in with facts and riveting questions. Sure, you need sorting out now and then. You get lost in the weeds, but we've *missed* your version of insane."

With a sigh, I gave a quick recap of every insider element of the past week, to the point where their eyes were wide from shock. That was before I told them the current murder spree might stem from a local source of lithium-rich igneous rock that was worth billions.

"You never disappoint," Kate declared.

"Buckle up, ladies," I said. "It's far from over."

* * *

In Aaron Pierce's living room, I greeted people when they stopped by to take the items they'd signed up to own. Kevin had brought rolls of paper to keep the carpet clean against the foot traffic. With somber expressions, the friends, neighbors, and colleagues reflected a comforting frame of mind: they were embracing Aaron's things.

As always, the exceptions made themselves known.

Paul Polk dispensed with hellos as he arrived, securing my elbow and leading me to a quiet corner of the living room.

"This is a somber occasion," I reminded him.

"Hence, pulling you to one side," he whispered. "You will have heard that I dated Vivian for a short while. She's active in local matchmaking events ... *was* active, I should say. The police are demanding answers from me when it should be the other way around. Why would a refined woman like Vivian become the victim of foul play?"

"Please lower your voice," I urged. "But to be clear, when you stopped by my farm, you professed to have *not* dated her."

Paul waved off his earlier lie as inconsequential.

"I think Gerald and Sal have been up to no good behind my back," he said. "When they asked permission to conduct business on my property, perhaps I didn't grasp that they were speaking in slang. You're street-smart. Is 'tourmaline' a new kind of drug?"

"No, Paul," I said. "It's a kind of gem."

"You can't blame me for going down the rabbit hole," he said. "One hears about smack, crack, Ganja, oxy, meth, blow—"

"*Stop,*" I said. "This is a solemn setting."

"I'm trying to make sense of Vivian dying from an overdose," Paul said. "As a realtor, I need to protect my reputation. Isaac is implying that I was using expensive gifts to buy favor with her. He's the one with flashy taste. I saw it in play before and after that debacle with Dr. Clark's land. I have a mind to break the confidentiality clause."

"That's a wonderful idea, and look," I said, motioning toward the door. "Here comes Detective Allen. If you have tips to share, conduct the conversation in the yard, not here in Aaron's house."

When I turned, Isaac Munroe was waiting to have a word.

"Let me guess," he said. "Paul is throwing me under the bus."

I sighed. "Are you here to pick anything up?"

"No, I'm paying my respects," he said. "Is Dan coming?"

"It's not likely," I said. "He's out of town."

"Clearly, you're not up to speed," Isaac said. "He stopped by the bank to conduct a closed-door meeting with an internal auditor from our home office. I'm shocked that he didn't alert me."

"Excuse me," I said. "I need to focus on this event."

"Darn it, I'm off on the wrong foot again," Isaac said, motioning with both hands. "You were kind to my son during a tough moment. I'd like to return the favor when you get a free minute. Lunch. Drinks after work. My treat. I'm intrigued to know your plans for your farm."

"Well," I said. "I'm living there, for instance."

"You're not selling the property?" Isaac asked.

"Absolutely not," I said.

"I heard Paul has a high-level buyer in the wings," Isaac said. "Your thirty acres have potential, so that's where my thoughts went. Back to my son, I think I saw sparks the other day," Isaac added with a cagy look. "Dan is the target of criminals. It's ok to say enough is enough. You're from a high-end family," Isaac pressed on. "It's ok to rebel, but you're not making smart choices. You could be a philanthropist."

"Gosh, you've given me a lot to think about," I said.

"With my backing … my son's backing, rather, you could grow your operation by leaps and bounds. Food for thought." Smiling, Isaac shook my hand. "I'll send some dates."

"Sadly, I will be tied up for weeks," I said.

"Whenever," he said. "Keep in touch."

Watching him walk away, I agreed with his self-assessment that he was "emotionally unaware." He'd donned a friendly vibe the way he would switch up his shirt to head from his office to the gym. Now that I knew the stakes that might be in play in his mind, I realized it would be smart to start painting my farm as a wasteland of briars and boulders and un-workable clay soil: the opposite of a pegmatite paradise.

"I can't believe my eyes," Peg said, pulling me into a hug, and then holding me at arm's length to study me with her pretty gray eyes. "You were in an accident last night."

"A fender-bender," I assured her.

"Kevin heard it was a bit worse than that," she whispered. "The fact that you came to help anyway shows strength I can't begin to understand. I know it's for us as much as for Dan."

"Do you need a tissue?" I asked, offering one.

"Turns out I do," Peg said. "Thank you."

Peg smoothed her pink sweater, looking pale and drawn, though her underlying grit showed through when she lifted her chin and smiled at people who glanced her way. Kevin had described her as an ideal to strive toward. Just then, I saw the loneliness of Peg's existence. Her presence was meaningful and pivotal. She was Aaron's mother, yet the officers and other colleagues offered nods instead of heartfelt support.

"Let's not get run over," I said, gently steering her to a quiet corner near the front window. "Can I get you anything?"

"No, I'm just passing the time while Kevin makes sure everything is all set. That's one of Raymond's colleagues," Peg added, pointing to a man in a game warden's uniform. "Shall I introduce you?"

"Maybe some other time," I said.

As if I was the one to be comforted, Peg rubbed my arm.

"I know you've faced some headwinds," she said. "In my eyes, the bond you've formed with Raymond is natural, but men get fixed ideas in their heads. Some men, at any rate. Give them time to trust that your intentions aren't some cooked-up effort to get attention."

"I'll keep that in mind," I managed.

"When I'm at the cemetery visiting Aaron, I make sure to put flowers on Raymond's grave," she said. "I hope you don't mind."

"Of course not," I said. "It's kind of you."

"You know, I'm kicking myself for not securing Aaron's blueberry bowls and plates," Peg said distractedly. "Thick earthenware, kiln fired. I made them myself years ago. He loved blueberries."

"I'll track down the set for you," I said.

"Thank heaven, look who's here." Peg motioned toward Haydn Pike as he arrived, prompting him to cross directly to us. Peg tucked her hand under his elbow and beamed at him before she turned back to me. "If not for his support, we would have gone under."

"How are you holding up, Mrs. Pierce?" Haydn said, dressed in a New England sports team T-shirt that showed off his muscles, though he'd arrived too late to help out.

"I'm fine, dear," Peg said. "Stop looking sour to see me with Sonny. For Aaron's sake, be kind, tenderhearted, and forgiving."

"Ephesians something-or-other," Haydn said dryly.

"Don't make fun of my favorite bible verse," Peg said.

"Kevin is talking shop instead of paying attention," Haydn said with a worried frown. "How about if I give you a ride home?"

"Nonsense, you just arrived." Peg dug through her purse for her keys, betraying a small bottle of vodka amidst her things. "What am I thinking? I came with Kevin, and it's time he headed to work."

"Stay here, I'll handle it," Haydn said softly.

"It's fine, I'll fetch him," she said.

As she headed away, Haydn turned to me with a baleful expression. "I know you saw that, but you did *not* see that, understand?"

"She drinks?" I whispered.

"Only during tough stretches, so don't think the worst," he said. "It's not all day every day. If you stir up gossip along those lines—"

"I wouldn't dream of it," I said.

"I'm late in getting here because I got questioned about my whereabouts last night," Haydn said. "It's a trip down memory lane, you landing in trouble and me getting blamed for it."

"I didn't look to you for blame," I said. "But you're not helping matters by approaching me with an attitude in the aftermath."

"It's just like you to say, 'Gosh, I would never,' and then imply the opposite idea in the next second." With narrowed eyes aimed at a distant point, Haydn added, "'Stare down the sun, and your eyes will boil.' Guess who I'm quoting?"

"Umm, Genghis Kahn?" I ventured.

"I'm quoting your father, more or less," Haydn said. "He'd tell you to not see people with blinders on forever and always."

I sighed. "Point taken. I'll try to do better."

In the kitchen, I was relieved to discover that nobody had taken the blueberry earthenware that I'd tucked into boxes on an earlier visit. I signaled to Kevin when I caught his eye, then I sank into gloom to see him coming toward me with a tight expression that must have been cosmically transmitted from one law enforcement professional to the next in recent months. In short, my conduct needed to improve.

All the worse, I'd worried that Kevin would feel embarrassed and confused after I'd found him in the garage in a drunken, emotional state. In my experience, proud men often doubled down on strict ways as a means of erasing a moment of revealing they were human.

"Umm, Peg wanted the blueberry bowls," I said.

"I know," Kevin said. "Grab the other box, would you?"

"I should stay in case there are questions ..."

"Out you go," he said. "I'd like a word."

Aware that Haydn might have conveyed that I'd seen the vodka bottle, I would assure Kevin the secret was safe with me, express my heartfelt condolences, resume my work, and then head home to conduct another round of examining my life while I stared at the ceiling.

Kevin made quick work of stowing the boxes in the cargo bed of his pickup truck, and then he faced me with folded arms.

"Look," he said. "I'm thankful for your help, so this is an awkward moment for me. What did you do to land in trouble?"

"It can wait," I said. "Let's focus on finishing up."

"Dan is in law enforcement, the same as I am," Kevin pressed on. "It's a tough haul even on a good day. The last thing he needs is to come home to a boiling pot on the stove. What's needed to balance it out is stability and calm. We talked about this the other day."

"This week's chaos was sparked by Dan's work," I said.

"Maybe so," he said. "But it was *your* car in the ditch."

"Kevin," Peg said sharply, looking appalled as she closed in on us. "Can I speak to you in private for a moment?"

"She doesn't see that we're protective of Dan like he's our own," Kevin said. "In Raymond's memory, I've endeavored to be patient, but this week has been an education on who Sonny is deep down. Instead of helping at the Corner Pocket, she ended up at the—"

As Kevin stopped short, Peg folded her arms and glared at him, as if he'd hit a subject that had sparked arguments in the past.

"It was the *other* clerk who went to the casino," Peg said.

Kevin frowned. "What other clerk?"

"The one with the purple hair that you think is 'too much.'"

"Fine," he said. "I stand corrected on that point."

"This is Raymond's daughter you're growling at," Peg added. "If he was here, he would punch you in the nose."

Flushed in the face, Kevin devolved into the look of a man who'd just been planted into his body after a ride in outer space. I'd seen the same wide stare in grieving people more times than I could count. Huge emotion had a strong, sideways pull.

"I suppose you're right," Kevin managed.

Peg rubbed his arm and urged him to wait in his truck.

"Let me apologize on his behalf," Peg said urgently. "He did this to himself, alerting people to stop by at the last minute, and then coming to help, though he knew it would be hard. What you witnessed just now is healing in me, by the way. Haydn is flawed. I'm not blind to it, but he's immune to Kevin's crabby spells. His way of delivering wry humor and standing up to criticism has rubbed off on me."

"I'll be wishing the best for you," I said.

"Same here, Sonny," Peg said.

With a quick hug, she crossed to Kevin's truck. When I turned back to the house, Jeremy was hovering nearby.

"Are you ok?" he asked.

"I won't find fault with a man in grief," I said. "It looks like we're pretty much done. Hopefully, nobody took the vacuum."

"Antoine lets me use my judgment on protection details," he said with a sorrowful twist of eyebrows. "It's hard to know a person's inclinations in advance. With you, I got it wrong."

"Jere—" I closed my eyes. "What is your real name?"

"I'm sticking with how you've seen me," he said. "My family situation is as messed up as I told you. The brother angle felt real to me."

"Family is the point," I said hotly. "If what Antoine told me about his early life is the truth, he experienced turmoil and loss. For him to not grasp that I'm especially sensitive about getting duped—"

"It was my call, and the dynamic worked so well that I didn't confess the truth," Jeremy said. "Please understand it wasn't about spying. Unlike a number of local cops, we've seen your intuitive side as an asset. You need allies with a similar approach. That's why I'm here with your things when your phone starts ringing," he added, offering my bag.

"What is your real name?" I demanded.

"Ancient history," he said. "I'm sticking with Jeremy."

I sighed. "Stay put. No eavesdropping."

Casting dark glances at the puppy hunk as I stepped out of earshot, I was relieved to see that Sue Black was calling me.

"This is fate," I said. "I need your advice."

"Sonny, it's time for a deep dive," Sue said with her usual calm tone. "You need to trust Jeremy. He'll bring you to me."

"Are you being held captive?" I asked.

"Like anybody could take me by surprise," Sue said with amusement. "Antoine has asked if I can help with your request. It's different from the work you and I did in September, but I'm intrigued by the idea. More than intrigued. I'm stoked."

"Umm, it's great that you're excited …"

"Perfect," Sue said. "I'll meet you there."

Click.

When I turned to Jeremy, torn between bafflement and bewilderment, he opened his phone and launched one of my videos from my website.

"Listen to what you said," he prompted.

As a female hummingbird that I'd filmed sipped nectar from a native honeysuckle vine, her wings blurred at a staggering rate of 50-75 beats per second. Narrating events, I'd slowed the speed to marvel over her nimble ability to twist in midair as she slipped her beak into the flowers. I'd mused about my mind's lack of a slow-motion feature that would enable me to relive fleeting moments and see details I'd missed.

"It's not good for this week to be a blur," Jeremy said. "With the high stakes involved, we think it's time to pause the feed."

"Sue used hypnosis to help me retrieve a night I'd blocked," I said. "Apparently, I'm geared for taking deep internal dives."

"I know you're steamed at me," Jeremy said. "But if I'm on hand during the session, I can answer questions that come up, pull pieces together, and bring a law enforcement perspective to the process. Let's make sure you're not playing into the hands of a murderer."

I had to admit, that would be a refreshing change.

23

The forest was awash with echoes, from the rippling splashes of a nearby stream to the whispers of sixty-foot pines that seemed to be reaching their fragrant needles toward the afternoon sky. With every step, my footfalls were softened by a thick layer of damp leaves that had piled up over the course of eons. Up ahead, Sue Black was waiting for us in the cleared area where Gerald's cousins had dismantled their pot operation.

As always, Sue's hug was lengthy, heartfelt, and warm, instilling calm as her silky hair cascaded around my face and shoulders. She led me to the center of the twenty-foot square that had been dug to a depth of two feet as part of Bertrand Clark's archaeological efforts.

"This is a place of spiritual power," Sue said. "It's a unifying point for past and present lives. The 1800s couple camped here. Dr. Clark walked this stretch of woods. So did the geologist who died, plus Gerald and Sal and countless others, including Raymond. A tent platform is a better place for our session, but I wanted you to pause here and feel the aura of interlacing forms of life. Think of the thread-thin roots under our feet, reaching from tree to tree, whispering riddles and secrets."

I sensed it so strongly that I felt a little dizzy.

Sue clasped my hand. "Let's get started."

After ten minutes of hiking, we reached the tent platforms that Gerald and Sal had constructed to hide their mining efforts. Built on the ledge I'd seen in the glamping brochure, each one offered a view of the forest, with supporting rubble that might include spodumene pegmatite.

"This stuff has *amazing* channeling properties," Sue said, pointing to the hidden rocks under the boards. "Prepare yourself."

Metal bowls filled with kindling occupied the four corners of the platform. Jeremy helped Sue light the piles, sending sweet wood smoke into the air. Over each bowl, they added a domed screen that sheltered the low flames and kept sparks at bay.

"Did anything specific bring this notion to mind?" I asked.

Jeremy nodded. "With one of the crew at large, it's a good idea to see if you get an ah-ha moment as you look inward. Plus, it was a shock when you found Chloé's funeral page online. You can imagine it was erased from the web when Antoine got into undercover work."

"Who would have re-launched the site?" I asked.

"For all we know it's thanks to an error during a program update," he said. "That kind of thing happens from time to time. For this exercise, it's best not to cloud your mind with hypotheticals."

"Should I lie down on the platform?" I asked.

"It's best if you're on your feet," Sue said, gathering us together so that we formed a triangle. "Close your eyes."

As we joined hands in the flickering light, Sue slipped my father's slice of pink tourmaline into my palm. I remembered Antoine telling me that the watermelon-tinted form of the gem was seen as a means of restoring inner balance and melding a person's conflicted selves.

"Focus on the crystal," Sue murmured. "Feel it warming between our palms, drawing strength from those who join us here in the forest. Those who've left us, and those who remain. Squirrels and foxes and owls and salamanders and the roots of a thousand trees …"

As she spoke, a subtle weight drifted downward through my mind, like a drop of warm rain sliding over my forehead and settling into a shimmering light. I watched it intently, feeling a sense of peace, my conflicted selves united into a single radiant point.

"What do you see?" Sue's voice whispered from a distance.

In a murmur, I described seeing myself crouched next to June Bolton in Dan's garage with a staple gun in my hand. I watched myself use the tool to injure the masked man, and then I turned as the crew's boss arrived in response to his comrade's screams of pain.

"What is your impression of the boss?" Sue asked.

"He's cursing in French, and seems perplexed," I murmured. "He's shocked that things have gone awry. The man I injured needs help. That's the focus. The boss helps him get away."

"Watch how he carries himself," Sue whispered. "His vibe, his gaze, and his voice. Is he familiar in any way?"

I crossed around the hooded man, stopping him in mid-motion to study him as he carried his comrade out of the garage.

"I'm certain that he's not familiar," I murmured.

"You met him another time?" Sue asked.

"Yes," I said. "His crew ruined my car."

"Tell me what you see," she said.

My recollections were crisp and clear. Two of the men were beta in nature, worried about the siren on my car attracting trouble. The third man, the boss, was the same as before, puzzling over me, not sure how to view me, easily duped into taking my flip phone.

"I see why he's a shadow," I murmured. "His eyes are rimmed by tricks. Paint, I think. Marbled swirls. Beautiful, in a way."

"Does his gaze unsettle you?" Sue asked. "Trigger terror?"

"I'm looking elsewhere," I said in frustration. "I'm focused on holding the pepper spray so I don't blind myself."

The rest drifted from my mind in murmurs. The sharp sound in the air, plastic bullets hitting the men. How I'd tapped the closest man's arm and sprayed his eyes. He was blinded and hollering.

"They're in a rush to get away," I said. "Then Dan arrives with his team. Nicole is awful, no remorse for the way she came at me. Once they leave to chase the crew, I'm surprised to see Antoine," I said, watching him emerge from the darkness alongside the road. "He's smiling. Pleased to see I'm still standing. He is an owl in the night, a lynx amidst the leaves. I think I can trust him, but I hesitate. At the turtle sanctuary, there was a moment when he lost his temper. He wasn't calm."

"What was it about?" Sue whispered.

"I thought it was about Nicole. Look," I said, crossing to a countertop once we entered a dark kitchen, where spiderwebs hung from the ceiling. "There's a lot of dust. It makes sense that Birdie was the one who put it there, but Antoine's reaction was strange."

"What are you pointing at?" Sue asked.

"It's right there on the countertop," I said. "A black feather."

"Holy shit, a *what?*" a man hollered.

Startled and confused, I stumbled into a flailing arc with a basement wall dead ahead. I curled inward to take the impact on my shoulder and felt hands gripping my arms, locking me in place.

"Horrid monster!" I hollered. "Let go!"

"Sonny, wake up," Sue's voice echoed.

By degrees, I emerged from the memory and found that Jeremy had caught me before I'd staggered off the tent platform. Sue rested her hands on my face to draw my gaze to her concerned eyes.

"I'm sorry I startled you," Jeremy said. "But I think the next moment you relived had to do with your bruise. You talked about Nicole not having any remorse. You can trust us with the truth."

I closed my eyes and nodded in agreement.

As they sat me down near the warmth of one of the fire bowls to clear my head, I described how Nicole had tripped me on the stairs in Aaron's house and hollered at me until I'd nearly blacked out.

"I figured she would lie to Dan about it," I said. "She told him that I'd put her in an armlock for no reason. He bought it without question. It's painful to see her ability to twist him around."

"You're the woman he loves," Sue assured me.

"Their history is part of his locked-down undercover work," I said. "Dan needs to sort out his feelings about her on his own and I have some soul-searching to do as well. In the meantime, you are both honor-bound to keep the story under wraps if that's what I want."

"Of course," Sue said. "Why was the black feather a trigger?"

"Ask Antoine," I said. "He was weird about it."

"Jeremy?" Sue prompted.

Having trained his frown on the forest as he'd knelt next to us in the afternoon light, Jeremy shifted his dark eyes from Sue to me, intensifying a stretch of silence that had my hairs standing on end.

"What kind of feather was it?" he ventured.

"Antoine thought it was a vulture feather," I said, all the more alarmed when Jeremy grimaced. "What does it mean?"

"In our line of work, it's sort of a death threat," Jeremy said. "If that was the case he would have told me. Explain the context."

"Antoine went from calm to angry when he saw that I'd picked it up," I said. "But seeing the dust pattern, he decided Birdie, the house's owner, had left the feather on the counter years ago."

"Makes sense," Jeremy said. "Problem solved."

Sue and I folded our arms and glared at him, a forceful show of female unity, which had a shrinking effect on Jeremy.

"You're asking me to break a code," he whispered. "Antoine's instincts are not to be ignored, and his superstitions stem from real events. Right now, his voice is hollering in my head about making shit happen by just talking about it. It is my informed opinion that we should forget this entire thread, and leave well enough alone."

Sue and I continued glaring at him with folded arms.

Jeremy sighed. "Antoine's parents were lowlifes. When they died, he and Chloé got sucked into the boss's family, who saw stray kids as recruits. Antoine went into silent mode, recording calls, copying data files, keeping track of who did what. Picture him sitting down at a lunch counter next to a detective when he was ten, cool as ice. The police stopped chuckling when he delivered wins. He spent time in a juvenile facility so the players wouldn't suspect his covert role. Then Chloé's death was tied to a guy from the crime family who saw himself as a half-brother. Antoine came out of the shadows at that point, pissed as hell to only get the guy for distributing. A short sentence. You can imagine the dealer would want revenge, but not the quick variety. It's been a hellish ride ever since."

"I need to see his photo," I said.

"I can't break that rule," Jeremy said. "For one thing, the guy changes his appearance, his name, whatever it takes to stay in the game. If you did recognize him and react, he'd embrace you like you were friends. You'd feel a jab, drop to the ground, and wake up not knowing your name. He's on the loose because he's fast, and always prepared."

"You're afraid he's the crew boss?" Sue asked.

"The sloppy elements don't fit," Jeremy said. "He's built a fortune from the fentanyl trade and high-stakes global stuff."

"*Hello*," I said. "Vivian died from a fentanyl overdose."

"According to the lab work, her stash was the commercial form, not the cooked-up batches this guy is known to distribute," Jeremy said. "He wouldn't help a wounded comrade or let a witness walk away. Every now and then, he'll decide to test himself against Antoine. It often ends with a gladiator-style battle." Jeremy spread his hands. "Now you know one of the reasons Antoine is a complicated, solitary dude."

"He should have told me," I said.

"Need to know is a critical concept," Jeremy said. "It's not fair to make you jump at shadows. You need to focus on known threats."

"So, the nemesis is the only threat to worry about?" I asked.

"Well," Jeremy said, searching his mind. "There might be a few other possibilities to check." When I signaled for him to share, he consulted a list on his phone. "Was he wearing a rat skull on a choker?"

"Umm, no," I said.

"Was he missing a ring finger?" Jeremy asked.

"No," I said. "I would have noticed."

As his list continued, Sue and I grimaced. Did he have a hatchet scar between his eyes? A ragged ear? Gold teeth? Gold fingernails?

"This is quite a list," I said.

"A few are guys who vowed to kill Dan when he threw them out of the bar where he worked," Jeremy said. "So, no rat skull on a choker?"

Once again, I let a glare convey my thoughts.

"That leaves us with a garden-variety culprit from here in town or up on the border," Jeremy said. "After this deep dive into your recollections, we're at the ninety-nine percent mark."

Sue rubbed my shoulder with a look of sympathy. Ninety-nine percent odds might sound great to the rest of the world. When it came to landing in trouble, I fell into the one percent groove.

* * *

Trashed after a stretch of hard days, I slumped against the passenger door of Jeremy's truck on the drive to my farm, dimly aware of stops and turns. My eyes fluttered as the tires rumbled over the familiar gullies along the bottom of my driveway. Squinting against the afternoon light, I lurched awake as I clapped eyes on Dan's extended-cab truck parked midway up the hill next to a much smaller dark blue truck.

"It's Dan," I said. "Hurry up."

Once Jeremy's truck emerged from the pines that flanked the road, I had my hand on the door handle before the truck stopped. I burst out and dashed toward Dan, who was coming down my porch steps, wearing jeans and a white shirt that amplified his tan and turned his quarterback physique into a magnet for my eyes as he walked toward me.

From a foot away, I dove forward and allowed myself to be gathered into his arms and swept in a circle. Tearfully grinning, I snuggled my face against his neck and savored his warmth, his freshly shaved face brushing against my cheek as he took a deep sniff of my ear, and then he settled my feet on the ground and delivered a quick kiss.

"It's only been a few days," Dan said.

"It feels like a century," I said.

"I know," he said. "It's the same for me."

"You shaved off your beard," I managed.

"Yup, undercover Dan is retired," he said.

"For real?" I asked. "Don't mess with me."

"It's for real," he said softly. "Two of the perps are in custody. It's good to have played a role in that part, but I can't stay in if it's taking chunks out of your life. Even your car became a casualty of the chaos." Dan steered me around to face the small blue truck. "This was meant to be an add-on vehicle to help around the farm. Given recent events, I fast-forwarded the updates." Dan jangled a set of keys in front of me. "It's used, so don't start hollering that I'm not allowed to buy it for you."

"I can't accept a gift of this magnitude," I said.

Dan sighed. "It's a smaller model, per the views you've shared. I had a welder create a custom rack to cover the cargo cap."

"For lumber?" I asked.

"Sure, but it can also serve as a rollbar, should you get chased through the countryside and land in a ditch again," Dan said dryly. "Take the keys, and admire the heart-shaped fob."

"Thank you," I said, kissing his cheek. "The thought behind it is wonderful, but I insist on paying you back."

"I will draw up a pathetic bill of sale," Dan said. "As you can see, it's basically a toy truck. Set me back a hundred bucks."

"The bigger the fib," I said, "the more your eyebrows twist."

"Talk sense into her," Dan instructed my dog.

Luke wagged his tail, seeing great possibilities in the new set of wheels, since it offered a front seat for him to ride shotgun, and a cargo area for times when I would normally leave him in his pen. As he bounded toward Jeremy to include him in the celebratory moment, Dan's sudden scowl told me that Roy had updated him on my housemate's identity.

In turn, Jeremy said goodbye to his demeanor of being an innocent who felt out of his depth in a harsh world. As he stepped up to Dan, his face was the picture of a man who grasped the power play that was about to unfold and had zero impulse to back down.

"Sonny, can you give us a minute?" Dan asked.

"I think I should stay put," I said. "Let's shake hands and join forces in solving the crimes, shall we? Let's have a beer."

Jeremy raised his eyebrows. "How about it? Shake hands?"

"That says a lot, launching in as a smartass," Dan said. "You think it's ok to con Sonny into seeing you as friend material?"

"I was here in case shit hit the fan," Jeremy said.

"Deception is not the way to get it done," Dan said.

"Get back on the bus, schoolboy," Jeremy growled. "You're pissed off because Antoine had to step in after you dropped the ball."

"That's enough," I said, pushing in front of Jeremy. "A short while ago you apologized for getting it wrong, and I witnessed your mole activity from my window last night. You don't think your shrunken clothes and shaving nicks were random bolts out of the blue?"

"Yeah, I'm up to speed on it now," Jeremy said tightly.

"I'm willing to believe you had good intentions, but when I'm blind-sided, trust is lost," I said. "It's time to call it quits."

"The brother angle felt real to me," he said. "That's where I'm coming from. This morning Kevin hollered at you, saying your choices are hard on Dan. Talk about a cockeyed load of crap. I've kept my mouth shut, but after the story that Sue and I just heard—"

"Don't you dare," I said sharply.

"What's this about Kevin?" Dan prompted me.

"It was a hard day," I said. "He's still in grief."

"I regret all the lies," Jeremy pressed on, "There's no going back, but listen up. Brumby does have brothers. This right here is Journey Jones." He held up his phone for Dan to see. "Upstanding. Built and handsome. Sonny's heart is set on you right now, but if you don't smarten up, I will bring Journey into the picture and see if it's a match."

I reached out. "Can I see his photo?"

"*No*, you cannot," Dan said, shoving Jeremy away from me and indicating the duffle bag next to the driveway. "I left your gear over there so you can hit the road. Tell Antoine to get in touch."

Jeremy shouldered his bag, patted Luke in parting, climbed into his truck, and gunned the engine. Dan watched him reverse quickly down the driveway, then turned to me with a torn gaze.

"I hate to admit it, but he's right," Dan said. "I had guys checking your farm and keeping track, but they missed signals all over the place. Jeremy is an example. He walked in under their noses."

"We're here," I said. "Let's move on."

Dan had tossed hay to my sheep and played with Luke to make up for his absence during the past week. In the kitchen, Luke slurped water from his bowl and collapsed into a contented heap at our feet as Dan joined me at the kitchen table. With his usual air of intense thought, he listened as I filled in the details and elements that he might not have heard from Detective Allen, starting with my encounters with Haydn Pike.

"Peg says he's reformed," I added.

"Some colleagues think that as well," Dan said. "There's a tendency to blame the pressures of the job. I was on my way to help at Aaron's house when I saw Pike's truck there. He's extra steamed from being questioned about his whereabouts. It's a tough enough chapter for Kevin and Peg to see the house go up for sale, so I peeled away."

"I think that was a smart call," I said.

"Where did you go afterward?" Dan asked.

"I spent some time with Sue," I said, determined to remain silent about Nicole's attack, at least at that delicate stage. "In all honesty, Jeremy was a help this week. He cooked and offered support."

"Did he ply you with moves?" Dan growled.

I sighed and described the time I'd seen him naked.

"I wish you'd conveyed that part before he stepped away," Dan said tightly. "What about Antoine? Did he make a pass?"

"He sort of … he exchanged our wads of gum," I said.

Dan closed his eyes. "He did *what?*"

I explained the gist of Antoine's surprise first visit.

"He caught me off guard," I said. "I pushed him back. End of story."

Dan's gaze lingered on infinity for a second, and then he sighed with an air of apology as he reached for my hand.

"You were thrown into the deep end," he said. "There's no room for anything but appreciation for how you've coped."

"It was tough when Roy flip-flopped on Raymond's suspicious death," I said. "What's your take on how Bud and Birdie died?"

Dan paused. "Why are you honing in on that?"

"An outfit called Pintail Holdings bought the property," I said. "The secrecy element might point to a land grab."

"Not in this case." Dan spread his hands. "I'm Pintail Holdings."

I paused. "You jumped in to help Aaron?"

"Financially, it was out of his reach," Dan said.

"Why do you look calm?" I demanded. "If Dr. Clark's sample of rock came from your property, it's a motive to get rid of you."

"Land isn't like cash," Dan assured me. "Nobody can grab it up without a complex interaction involving signoffs, but now that we know what's at stake, we will take a close look at the terrain."

"You're informed about the billion-dollar motive?" I whispered. "The spudla-stuff from whatchamacallit rock?"

"Spodumene that's found in pegmatite," Dan said.

"I want to be a part of checking the terrain," I said.

"Hence," Dan said, "my use of the word 'we.'"

"Back to Aaron," I said. "In the midst of cleaning his kitchen, I found a worrisome pile of online betting receipts."

"Yeah," Dan said. "That's part of what went wrong."

I held my breath as he shored up his strength in order to delve into a painful time he'd skirted around until then.

"You've met Peg," he managed. "She's a gentle soul who isn't cut out to be married to a tough guy like Kevin. She and a few friends cut loose at a casino. The family budget was tight to begin with, so it put them into a bind. I don't know if it was genetics, but Aaron leaned into gambling when turmoil hit the fan. It started with poker games."

"You had a tough talk?" I asked.

"Yeah," Dan said. "I stuck my oar in a few times."

"You were trying to help," I said softly.

"Tell that to Aaron's ghost," Dan said. "He had dreams about keeping Birdie's land in the family, but the bank turned him down for a loan. He had alimony payments in the wings, so I ran the numbers to see if I could swing the purchase before a developer scooped it up."

"How did Aaron receive the idea?" I asked.

"He was pumped," Dan said. "Then reality set in. His name couldn't be on the paperwork. Not with a divorce in the wings. Properties with old deeds involve complexities. The process dragged on. Aaron was impatient to get access to the property, and so on. The way forward was for me to be his landlord. In no time at all, I was saying it would come with the need for him to have a business plan, lest he screw it up."

"You had good intentions," I said.

"Aaron was like a kid brother, so I delivered a lecture," Dan said. "Quit the gambling. Stop the drinking, especially if you're on antidepressants. Cop talk." Dan rubbed his face. "Buying the land was an outlay of cash. An act of friendship. His attitude pissed me off. So, it's my fault. Talking shit, and then not checking in for weeks."

"I'm so sorry," I said, rubbing his shoulder.

"Kevin and I are good now, but it was a rough time," Dan said. "After a shock like that, he needed someone to blame. It's why I took the gig up north, the horror of how I'd misjudged Aaron's mindset. You know I'm the one who found him. I'm surprised to still be standing."

"Sweetie," I said. "Honey …"

I tried to soothe him as he rested his elbows on his knees and gripped his head with his hands, and then he sat back with an air of wanting to get on with being a wall of strength, poised and unflappable.

"So, there you have it," Dan managed. "The whole story."

"People fall out," I said. "You can't blame yourself."

"It feels strange to tell someone. It's lived here for so long." Dan indicated his ribcage. "It's probably why I make you feel like I'm hot and cold."

"You're never cold," I said. "Just …"

"Remote, like this week," Dan said.

"Your job involves stress," I said. "I get it."

With emotion in his eyes, Dan reached for my hand and steered me into sitting sideways on his lap, where he could see me up close and encircle me with his arms. I hugged him, kissed him softly, and smiled as I smoothed my hand over his shaved jawline, studied his soulful brown eyes, and felt the warmth of his steady heartbeats.

"Things got tense between us at the Box & Bag and in Brumby's apartment when you first arrived," Dan said. "If you're upset because of the way I've handled this week, I need to hear it."

"I'd rather focus on the recent wins," I said.

"That's another thing," Dan said. "The flip phone was meant to alert me if a threat like Pike showed up. You used it to nab the crew."

"Right now, all I can think about is the aroma of pizza in the air," I said, preferring to dwell in the present. "I'm seeing it as a pivotal moment. Your fate hinges on the toppings you picked."

"Fortunately," he said. "I'm a crack detective who knows you love Greek topping on one half and spicy chicken on the other with a second pizza devoted to the traditional fare of sausage and peppers."

I smiled. "I'll get the plates."

"I'll pour your favorite red wine," he said.

For a half hour, we devoted ourselves to lifting wedges of pizza from the warming stone with gooey strings of cheese still attached, and rolling our eyes at the perfection of the flavors, the heated thickness of the puffed crust, and the delicious spots where the toppings had browned. In between, we cleaned our palates with the mellow richness of merlot. For dessert, Dan had bought chocolate ice cream, which melted into a yummy blur after I took strawberries from the freezer and quickly heated them into a sweet, tangy sauce.

Leaving the dishes for later on, Dan pulled his chair closer, showing again how well his white shirt defined his muscles. Awash in the evening light coming in through the windows overlooking the paddock, he leaned forward and studied me with an arched eyebrow.

"Back to the gum-swapping moment," he said. "It sounds like the kind of maneuver that would take a coordinated effort."

"I shut it down," I said. "That's what counts."

"That's all you have to say on it, huh?" Dan said.

"Yup."

"All right …"

After a trip to the countertop, he sat down, secured my butt with both hands and stirred instant warmth by arranging my thighs so I was facing him and straddling his lap. He brought further rockets to the situation by delivering a long, delicious, kiss, and then he broke away and held up two pieces of gum: one for me, and one for him.

I cracked up. "This is nutty."

"Start chewing," Dan said.

"Have you ever done a swap before?" I asked.

"No," he said. "But how hard can it be?"

Three seconds into joining our mouths together, we were not swapping our respective wads of gum. We were laughing so hard that my piece landed on my shirt.

"Here." Dan retrieved it. "Try again."

"It's impossible when I'm laughing," I said.

"Focus," he said. "I'll do the heavy lifting."

I cracked up after two seconds. "You made me drop my piece again."

"You were fibbing," Dan said. "It didn't happen."

I shrugged. "If that makes you feel better."

"I will not be outdone," he said. "Ready?"

Minutes later, after ditching our gum, the chair creaked ominously as I kissed him, snuggling closer and unbuttoning his shirt.

"Upstairs?" he murmured.

"As fast as possible," I said.

Dan obliged me with kisses all the way up the stairs to a soft landing on my bed. Soon his warm skin was next to mine. I explored his shoulders and chest, unraveled by the way his hands unlocked every inch of my spine, and then he slowed down as if there was something on his mind.

"What's going on?" I murmured.

Dan brushed my hair from my face with a look of worry. "Where did you go after you left Aaron's house?"

"I already told you. I went to meet Sue." Grasping that he'd sensed my dodge, I added, "We had a hypnosis session."

Dan frowned. "Similar to back in September?"

"Sort of," I said. "It's nothing to worry about."

"Sonny, I've learned to pay attention when you start a sentence with 'sort of,'" Dan said. "Why was it necessary this time?"

"This week has been a blur," I said. "I wanted a closer look."

"And?" Dan prompted.

"I honed in on my sense of the crew," I said. "That was the gist of the session, reconstructing my run-ins with them to see if they were familiar. Jeremy added to the situation by describing a few guys who vowed to kill you during your stint up north."

"None of the descriptions rang true?" Dan asked.

"Not even close," I said.

"It feels like you're leaving things out," Dan said.

I gaped from the irony of his words, complete with eyebrow maneuvers so extreme that I worried they'd become permanent.

"Police work involves a tight approach," he protested.

"And when will you be calling it quits?" I asked.

Dan closed his eyes. "Sonny …"

"I'm not pressuring you," I said. "Think how well it would go if you asked me to give up photography. But if you stay in the game, there are some issues that will need to be addressed and sorted out. I'm not going to be a Peg. We have to be equals in all regards."

"Trust me, I don't want their dynamic," Dan said.

"Then get on with kissing me," I said.

With a conflicted twist of eyebrows, and then a wry smile, Dan resumed his explorations, but the pause had left its mark, the way rain would dampen a campfire. Some element of overthinking was bound to happen in the wake of his revelations about his best friend, so I pushed onward with my eyes closed, sinking into the feel of our full-length caresses, our bodies in sync with constant, delicious motion.

I let him kiss me and take me, but found it impossible not to dwell on his knowledge of which angles made my eyes roll, and how he timed moments of growling in my ear, sending the deep rumble of his voice through my skin all the way down to my erogenous zones. Despite my worries, the fear that we'd plunged into the iffy realm of routine, a tremor of pleasure sent stars shooting through my head, and then his deep, ecstatic growl furthered my shivers. We lay in each other's arms, exchanging soft kisses and smiles assuring each other that all was well.

As always, Dan drifted to sleep before I did. Wide awake from the whirlwind day, I frowned in the darkness and hoped that tomorrow would feel more normal, though I couldn't fathom what was needed to pull it off. Of course, I did. The missing element was trust.

"Are you ok?" Dan murmured.

"I'm perfect," I said.

"Full of yourself, as always," he said.

With a groggy smile, he resumed catching up on his sleep.

24

At 6:30 a.m., Dan and I were awash in the rays of dawn coming in through my bedroom windows. Listening to his steady heartbeats, I smoothed my hand over his chest, submerging myself in worries as he stared at the ceiling, submerging himself in his worries. Absently, he played with my curls, then as Luke yawned on the floor, Dan kissed my cheek.

"Sorry for the alerts on my phone," he said.

"You're taking long overdue personal time," I said.

"With the caveat that I'd stay in the loop," he said.

As he listened to a voicemail that Roy Allen had left, I overheard the Detective's sorry excuse for involving Dan in some inquiries. That fast, my blissful awakening to a new day in the state of Maine was plunged back to the same old same old of staying in my own lane.

While Dan showered and shaved, I slipped on my spaghetti strap leotard, in need of an extra-long yoga routine to keep my mind from slipping into the dark corners of all the unknowns confronting me.

Scrubbing pizza from last night's plates, I decided it wasn't fair to reach out to Dr. Clark's wife. She'd suffered enough heartache, and the police were already pressing her for specifics on where her husband might have found the rock he'd given to his colleague.

I heard Dan's keys land on the table, and then he was kissing my neck and slipping his warm palms under my spaghetti straps.

"I will make it up to you," he murmured in my ear.

"Hopefully, by the time we reach old age," I said.

Dan turned me in place to regard me from inches away with a look of apology that involved a twist of eyebrows and dimples, which gave him an unfair advantage during arguments, big and small.

"We haven't sat near the ocean for ages," I said, tugging his plaid collar to straighten it. "We need to dial down and catch up."

"I'll start with an ah-ha moment," he said. "I was conflicted about you helping with Aaron's house. I've avoided the history for a reason, but when the subject came up yesterday, it felt natural, telling you the story. There's nothing but love in how you've tackled the work in his house. I don't know why I got twisted around about it."

"Because you're human," I said. "Specifically, you're a man."

"The next phase is hiring a realtor. Paul Polk is not on the list."

"I can line up some options," I said.

"Hey …" Catching onto my unconvincing smile, Dan studied me with a worried frown. "You seem quiet. Are you ok?"

I hugged him. "I'm fine. I'm good."

Except that as he'd checked his phone messages, I'd seen a dozen texts from Nicole that had come in overnight. She didn't care about his need for personal time off if it involved him being with me.

* * *

For the second time in a week, a noodle of mist had gathered above the stream. With my eye on my camera's viewfinder, I framed a succession of shots. The light changed rapidly, casting a palpable warmth across the horizon, then the mist flattened as it drifted toward me as if the sleepy pasture was drawing a blanket over itself in the last moments of slumber. With my breath held, I let my camera's weight settle onto the strap around my neck and reached out to pet the phenomena, and found that I could feel its whisper of moisture and cool air, leaving my hand damp. Within a matter of seconds, the low blanket of fog lifted upward and dissipated into curling streamers and scattered puffs of vapor.

I led Luke into the house, checked my phone, and found that Dan had left a voicemail saying a new development demanded his involvement. He dropped some French on me, and then the recording ended.

"Well, that didn't last long," I said of my high note.

Events had shot along so fast that I'd failed to assess Dr. Clark's map on my own. With the coffee maker gurgling on the countertop, I sat at my laptop at the kitchen table and assessed the photos I'd captured in the restroom before giving the envelope to the police. I cropped and tweaked the images as I pulled them into a document until the result was a good likeness of the original map, and then I printed the file on 13" x 19" paper: a handy size for folding and hiding in a magazine.

Back at the kitchen table, I studied the relic from the 1800s. Though not drawn to scale, the locations correlated with my father's map of crime scenes. On the right, beyond the coastline, were curled shapes indicating ocean waves. A hand-drawn campfire symbol told me the couple had camped near the ledge where the geologist was murdered.

The heck with not delving into his life. Turning to my laptop, I found news items on Scott Butler's death over two years earlier. He was single, in his mid-thirties, with no siblings, and worked at Westdale College at the time of his death. The further I delved into the incident, the more scattered and unhelpful the results. The world had moved on, leaving him in the broad and soulless category of "unsolved death."

I pushed my laptop aside and returned to the map. Campfire symbols alluded to locations where the couple had set up their tent. In a few of those places, Dr. Clark had launched archaeological digs. I honed in on the cleared area where Gerald's cousins had set up their pot operation. Some miles away, two narrow lines formed a winding noodle in a forested area. I took it to be a trail or a stream where the couple might have fished on the land that would become a turtle sanctuary.

With elaborate loops, the names *Roderick and Edwina Galbraith* were written in ink on the bottom edge. Here and there were symbols of their daily lives: a horseshoe indicating a blacksmith who could trim their mule's hooves; chickens indicating a farm where they could buy meat and eggs; a pair of boots indicating a cobbler who could keep their footwear in top condition, and so on. The simplicity of the diagram was a stark contrast to the crew's violent attempts to fetch it. Nowhere on the map were symbols indicating places where the couple stashed loot.

With folded arms, I pictured Dr. Clark laying the map across a table and puzzling over the symbols, and then dashing to a class with the map left in place. Either Vivian or someone else could have glimpsed it and not seen it as important. At some later date, after the first few mines dried up, the guilty party wondered if the old map could narrow down their search for the source of the spodumene sample. Now that I knew the significance, I regretted my role in bringing the map to the light of day. The need for new sources of lithium was a global issue. Like other resources, it would be pursued until the land was gutted and empty of worth.

Hearing a rumble of tires approaching up the driveway, I felt a ray of hope. One or more of the persons of interest was coming to confront me! However nutty it seemed to feel elated I embraced what I'd always known: I wasn't geared to be left out of the action.

Quickly, I hid my printout of the map on a bookshelf. As I opened the door, Kick Munroe paused before climbing the porch steps, worried to see my fierce dog bound out with his gaze on high alert.

"Luke," I prompted. "Settle. He's a friend."

"I guess I should have called first," Kick said.

"Nonsense. Come in, come in," I said, inviting him to sit at my kitchen table. "Do you want coffee? Tea? A pastry?"

"Some water, maybe." Looking exhausted, in khakis and a blue shirt, Isaac Junior stared at my yoga outfit. "Wow."

"Stretching is a daily routine," I said, tossing on a sweater and fetching a glass. "I've been meaning to ask how you're doing. Your father as well. I heard he and Vivian had a dream of building townhouses."

"Westdale Circle," Kick said. "Nobody listened when I predicted it wouldn't pan out. Off-campus enterprises aren't a big sell, so the funding wasn't there. It was a rare instance when my father got it wrong. His past is the reason I'm here. If it's a burden, just say so."

"Nonsense," I said. "I'm here for you."

"Gosh, I expected you might be sort of …"

"Start from the beginning," I said. "What's troubling you?"

"All right," Kick said. "Here we go."

Isaac Junior followed my invitation to the letter, describing his early years. How he'd idolized his father growing up, all the soccer trophies on the shelves. I nodded in sympathy as he described the turmoil of his parents' divorce: how he was torn between two households, per a custody arrangement. It wasn't a fun phrase for a child to hear. "Custody" related to people who landed in jail, and his father wasn't good at masking his irritation when the arrangement intruded on his golf outings and dates with a succession of women. Kick's drive to live up to his father's "awesomeness" went awry: an injury tanked his soccer dreams.

"It must have been very tough," I murmured.

"I can't believe how kind you're being," Kick said.

"Is there a more *recent* problem on your mind?" I asked.

"Actually, I'm late in processing the bruise on your shoulder," Kick said. "You were in an accident the other night."

"A fender bender," I said. "What's troubling you?"

"Here," he said. "This will bring you up to speed."

Handed his phone, I saw that the video he planned to show me had been recorded in a curved lecture hall.

"My dad had some success early on," Kick explained. "He used to give talks around becoming an entrepreneur."

Pulling the screen closer, seeing that Isaac was a younger, less intense version of his current self, I hit the play button.

"I know what you're thinking," Isaac said as he strolled. "All this talk of creating a detailed plan feels boring. Old school nonsense. The concept of being an entrepreneur can be traced to the Stone Age, so you're right in some regards. You're excited, driven by a fresh idea, but there's a reason it's become more of a science in the past few decades."

Isaac's pause as he glanced to his left had me leaning forward. Somebody in the audience had gotten under his skin.

"You'll face pitfalls. Critics with half-baked notions and zero facts." Isaac stretched his neck, and then went on, "You don't want to live in a flimsy building. So, don't build a flimsy business model. Create a detailed plan. Test it out. *Invite* critics to weigh in. How about that? Say, go ahead, bring it on, then leave them in the dust."

The video alternated between the view of Isaac and the room at large. Sitting apart from the rest of the crowd, a man sat with his arms draped across the adjoining seats as he stared at Isaac with a mix of condemnation and skepticism. His long-sleeved jacket was open, showing a bold T-shirt that said in large letters, "Justice for Chloé."

I leaned closer and gaped. It was Antoine.

"What the hell?" I whispered.

"Do you know that guy?" Kick asked. "My father dated his sister."

As he went on, his voice blurred into noise as a seemingly minor detail fell into place. The boyfriend Antoine had mentioned, the one who'd been dating Chloé before she'd died, was Isaac Munroe?

"Paul heard about a high-end developer who's looking for land," Kick was saying. "He got a photo of the guy from the meeting, and brought it to me as a part of his normal vetting process. The buyer is wearing a flashy suit nowadays, but it's this guy here in the video."

"I can see why you're concerned," I managed.

"You as well, apparently," Kick said.

"It's, umm, fatigue." Swaying as I stood, I grasped his arm and steered him to the door. "Thanks for the visit."

"Sonny, you've dropped into panic mode," Kick said softly. "You got evasive when I asked about the bruise. It's impossible not to link it to the concerns I've had about Dan for months. He's been a good guy for years, but was never the same after Aaron died."

"The bruise is from the accident," I insisted.

"It feels like you're leaning on that as an excuse," Kick said. "If Dan lost his cool with you once, it'll happen again."

I closed my eyes and centered myself.

"You're kind to worry about it," I said. "But the bruise is from the seat belt. The crew who targeted Dan's house came after me to get revenge. I'd injured one of them. That's why I'm hot and cold."

"You're prone to flashbacks?" Kick asked.

"Exactly," I said.

"I'm glad to know it wasn't Dan," Kick said. "You had me worried for a minute, especially after what happened to Vivian."

"I totally get it," I said.

"Maybe you can see what Dan makes of the video?" Kick asked.

"It's the absolute first thing I'll do," I assured him.

Once I succeeded in getting Isaac Junior out the door and heading to his car, I texted "SOS" to Dan, our agreed-upon code indicating an urgent circumstance that did not involve imminent bodily harm.

"Great timing," Dan said.

"Isaac Munroe dated Antoine's sister years ago," I said.

"I know," Dan said. "How did you find out?"

"I'm looking for shock," I said. "A huge reaction."

"We ironed it out ages ago," Dan said. "Antoine's change of heart, the whole story. Isaac is still a person of interest in this recent case. He can be a cold, ambitious guy. It's good to check in because I'll be out of cell service for a stretch. I'll check in later on tonight, ok?"

"Where are you?" I asked.

"With Antoine," Dan said. "I need to head back in."

It sounded like a meeting, nothing for me to worry about.

"I'm going to loop back to this topic later on," I said. "I'm not finished asking questions. In the meantime, stay alert."

After we hung up, I glared at Luke for wagging his tail and squeaking his lobster toy, though I knew it wasn't fair to vent my frustration by finding fault with his sweet nature and simple ways.

Within two seconds of playing fetch, I found myself squeezing the toy with a vengeance, causing its eye stems to pop out and its voice to shriek in an upper register. For days on end, I'd railed at Dan for trusting Nicole. Now I was railing at him for assuming the best of Antoine. He'd sounded pumped and confident, while I was stuck in limbo for the umpteenth time, stripped of importance, though I had proven myself again and again that week. In Dan's house. On the road. In the conference room amongst seasoned troopers and crime scene technicians.

It had me feeling crazed and tormented, beyond the reach of yoga. At times like that, I was driven to do the unthinkable.

I needed to put on my sneakers and take a run.

In jeans and a sweat-wicking shirt, I stretched out the lingering ache in my shoulder to prepare myself for getting peppered with gravel from passing cars, jumping into a ditch if a logging truck thundered by, and pausing to adjust my sports bra to curb jiggling.

I'd no sooner laced up my sneakers when Jeremy's truck pulled up the driveway. I'd given him a pass the other day. Now the fragile beginnings of trust in my heart had been blasted all to hell.

I signaled to my recumbent, yawning canine that he needed to sharpen up. His long-awaited game-time moment had arrived. Luke had come to see Jeremy as a friend, but Dan had trained him with French commands with that kind of confusing situation in mind. I led the way outside. As Jeremy climbed out of his truck, I signaled to Luke.

"Protège-moi," I said sharply.

Jeremy pulled up short as my dog's protection skills were unleashed. In a bristling stance, Luke bared his teeth and softly growled.

"Steady," Jeremy said. "Reste."

"Protège-moi," I countered.

"Reste."

"Protège-moi."

With a sigh, Luke sat down and stared heavenward.

"Jeremy, whoever you are, you're not welcome here," I said firmly. "I just found out that Isaac dated Antoine's sister."

"Think about it," Jeremy said. "If he'd disclosed the full history, your impression of Isaac would have been unfairly skewed."

"Like my impression of you right now?" I asked.

"I meant what I said about the brother angle," he said. "I've done some soul-searching on my path in life. As part of ditching unwanted baggage, I am legally changing my name to Jeremy."

"You're not serious," I said.

"I'm dead serious," he said, looking dead serious.

When my phone rang in my pocket, I hoped to heaven it was Dan calling to provide a further update. Before stepping away, I stood in the shadow of Jeremy's muscled physique and leveled my forefinger in front of his tousled hair, dark eyes, and country-style good looks.

"If either you or Antoine turn out to be the masterminds behind the current crime spree," I said. "I will hog tie the both of you in front of my barn, and let hungry coyotes teach you a lesson."

"Those are acceptable terms," Jeremy said.

Casting dark glances at him as I stepped away toward my porch, I was relieved to see that Sue Black was calling me.

"This is fate," I said. "I need your advice."

"*Major* déjà vu alert," Sue said. "Those were your exact words when I called you about setting up the hypnosis session. The air is crackling with energy today. You know our policy against spreading rumors and gossip, but after your rough couple of days, I'm coming to you with what Kate and I have witnessed in the store the past few hours."

Sue reported that after getting into a growling match with Haydn Pike earlier that morning, Dan had bought a six-pack of bottled water as if he was embarking on a hike. Sue and Kate wondered if it had to do with the police making repeat visits to the glamping tent platforms.

"No, that's been going on for days," I said.

"Hi Sue," Jeremy said, steering my forearm closer so he could be a part of the conversation. "What else did you alert on?"

"Paul came in and asked if we carry hiking shoes. Duh, of course not, but Isaac overheard him and turned it into a showdown. It sounded like a fight over a piece of land. Kick came in and calmed them down, saying it was high time they put their childish feud aside."

"Ok, I've heard enough," Jeremy said. "Sonny's input is needed in a complex matter. Can you babysit Luke tonight?"

"Sure, drop him off at the store," Sue said.

"Great, we'll be there in a half hour," Jeremy said.

Click.

"*Hey,*" I said. "That was totally rude."

"If Sue Black says the air is crackling with energy, it's time to switch gears," Jeremy said. "Stop looking outraged and listen up."

"I've fired you as a helper," I pointed out.

"You're dressed for taking a jog," Jeremy said.

I hesitated. "So?"

"You hate jogging," he said. "You're pacing and boiling over from getting hauled into action and then shoved to the wings. You met with the state police for two hours and advanced cases that have been on ice for two years. You deserve to be on hand during a critical moment." Jeremy strode to his truck and reached inside to secure a black duffle bag. "We need to gear up. Proper equipment is essential."

"What's going on?" I asked. "Why the big rush?"

"You're prone to blurting details and ruminating out loud," Jeremy said. "It's strictly need to know from here on out."

"I'm calling Dan to get his input," I said.

"He won't pick up," Jeremy said. "Instead of telling Dan how you got the bruise, you left him to judge Nicole with half the picture in place, and she's on the move. We can argue over this for a minute or an hour, but the outcome will be the same. You'd rather dive into the unknown a hundred times than cool your heels while others tackle the work."

Furious to be talked to like a toddler, I marched over and leveled my forefinger under his nose. "I *hate* that you are correct."

Jeremy shouldered the duffle bag through my kitchen doorway and set it down with a clank. From its contents, he pulled out black cargo pants, a matching shirt, a tactical belt with an array of tools and pouches, and black lace-up boots. He tossed the pile my way.

"The more you strive for a normal life, the further away it gets," Jeremy said, tossing his jeans aside, and then directing my gaze from his toned physique, per our agreement. "Crimes fall out of the trees as you pass by, causing Dan to have a coronary every other minute. Antoine as well. I'm not your squeeze or your boss. I'm in the brother lane, so I'm the one with the solution. To become a private investigator in the state of Maine, you'll need sixty hours of coursework and a thousand hours of training with a sponsor. I can serve in that capacity from this day onward."

"That's an intriguing idea," I murmured.

"Get in gear," Jeremy said. "Sharpen up."

I snapped out the folded cargo pants, only to discover that the label was still fastened to the back with a plastic loop.

"This is annoying," I said, cutting the tag. "Clearly, people had the time to shop for clothes. The helpful thing would have been to not lie to me for days on end and leave me in the dark."

Hopping my way into the cargo pants, I looked up and found that Jeremy was dressed and geared up, complete with laced boots.

"This is your fastest speed?" he asked.

I'd camped in jungles amidst mosquitoes and biting midges, and once during an invasion of army ants. Outside the military, no woman on earth could cover up bare skin at a faster pace. With my boots tied, I started to tuck my phone into my pocket. Jeremy snatched it away, opened it with my passcode, and shut off the Wi-Fi and cell service.

"Leave it in dark mode," he said, handing it back.

"You hacked my passcode?" I demanded.

"You used it in front of me a zillion times," he said.

Once he secured my tactical belt and buckled the clasp, I assessed what in the heck kind of equipment he'd stowed in the pouches.

"Flashlight, gloves," I said, looking down. "Water bottle, granola bars, sunglasses. It's a lot of weight, even without a sidearm." I hoisted the belt into place, the way I'd seen Dan do a hundred times. "You know what? This feels great. I love the boots as well," I said, striding around a bit. "If I'd been dressed like this in May and September, I wouldn't have needed a SWAT response. This is a game changer."

"Come on, Luke," Jeremy said. "Bring your toy."

"No need," I said. "Sue and Kate have replicas at their place."

"I was talking about you," Jeremy said.

I started to level my finger under his nose, caught onto his compressed lips and weighty glare, and then I headed for the door.

My first hour of PI training was about to unfold.

25

"So, by the time we left the Corner Pocket, Dan, Antoine, Isaac, Kick, and Paul Polk were trapped in a cave," I said crossly.

"Dan and Antoine weren't near the spot that collapsed," Jeremy said. "If you don't mind, I'll focus on driving for a minute."

"They have plenty of air?" I asked.

"Tons of air," Jeremy said. "Speaking of which, hang on."

Once again, I was treated to a zero-gravity ride on a wooded road, this time in the dark of night, with my hands braced on the seat as Jeremy's truck soared into space for whole seconds at a time and then landed on axles that should have been retired from service a decade or so ago. After a hard *whump* that made me six inches shorter, I was pulled upward into space again. Dizzied by pressure changes in my ears, I winced every time it seemed unlikely that we would remain upright.

"Ever been to Maui?" Jeremy asked, skidding to a halt at a crossroad, and then peeling out with a spray of gravel. "That's where Antoine trained me. The Road to Hana is sixty-four miles of one-lane bridges, straight up-and-down drops, and six hundred twisted, hairpin turns."

"Yes, I've taken that drive," I said.

"Antoine says to me, real calm as we're nearly dying from plunging off a cliff, 'If one bisects a series of turns with the straightest line possible, he will cut miles from the journey.'" Jeremy glanced at me. "Trust me, this road is a piece of cake compared to the island of Maui."

As the headlights offered glimpses of the curves ahead, I gripped an imaginary steering wheel and hauled left or right, depending on the maneuvers necessary to keep from plowing headlong into the trees. Every so often we crested a hill, and then the truck plunged straight down in a trajectory that released me from gravity and pitched my stomach into swirling confusion. My right foot pressed an imaginary brake.

"You're cracking me up," Jeremy said. "Antoine would say, 'You are helping, Berrichon. Our minds are acting as one.'"

"Hopefully not in real life," I said. "Smashed against the windshield."

"On the 1800s map, you may have noticed a drawing that looked like a stream with narrow ends," Jeremy said when a straight stretch allowed him to resume filling in the blanks. "That's the cave. It's on the turtle sanctuary that Dan bought after Bud and Birdie died. We need to hike to the cave in silent mode and be on the lookout for glowing red eyes."

I hesitated. "Animal kind of eyes?"

"Trail camera kind of eyes," Jeremy said. "Dan had no idea the cave existed until you found the map. Bud and Birdie kept it a secret, possibly for safety reasons. It's not clear who installed the cameras, but it's fair to guess it has to do with the quest for lithium deposits."

"To see if anyone else was digging test holes?" I asked.

"With extensive territory to cover it makes sense," Jeremy said. "Plus, if the culprits wanted to act in secret, they'd check the feed to make sure they could do it on the sly. That's our best guess."

With an expert flourish, Jeremy swerved into the entrance of a logging road, and then he gunned the engine to accomplish the feat of skipping lightly along the tops of bumps to keep from getting mired in the puddles and mud. My eyeballs vibrated from the rapid shocks, and then Jeremy slammed the brakes, bringing us to a skidding, leaf-strewn slow-down, and an eventual halt a mere ten feet from a sizeable boulder.

"Given that Dan didn't install the trail cameras," Jeremy went on, "we need to copy videos from the data cards, but leave the cameras in place as evidence. Antoine identified the model," Jeremy added, showing a product image on his phone. "See the data card release? Memorize the placement. We'll approach from the back so you're not filmed."

Jeremy handed me a hard drive for copying the data cards.

"Anything else?" I asked.

"Antoine set up a cell signal jammer," Jeremy said. "Nobody can come at us by tapping into the main grid, but our gear is linked through an encrypted networking device. Antoine, Dan, and the two of us are the only ones in the loop. Your phone is only useful as a camera."

"I guess that makes sense," I said.

"At some point, we'll split up so I can grill Nicole about why she's here uninvited," Jeremy said. "You can peel away to talk to Sal."

I hesitated. "Sal is alive and well?"

"We think the secret note system lured him here," Jeremy said. "The land is a hundred acres, more or less. Antoine sees your role as a critical element. You don't believe me?" Jeremy added, opening his phone and holding the screen for me to see. "Here's Antoine's text."

"It says, 'Bring the strudel,'" I said tiredly.

"SWAT is a full-course meal," Jeremy explained. "Antoine tried the contained approach first. Meat and potatoes, he and Dan."

"I'm the strudel?" I asked. "Really nice."

"Strudel is a delightful dessert option," Jeremy insisted. "The perfect complement for the heavy elements of meat and potatoes."

"Antoine sent this text five minutes ago," I said.

"The best agents predict events," he said. "Out you go."

In the darkness, I climbed out onto vibrating legs. Jeremy shrugged on a ballistic vest, then dropped a smaller vest over my head, indicating with quick tugs how to fasten it. He stepped away to return a call from the two guys I'd met from Dan's team. Still listening, Jeremy opened a long toolbox in the bed of his truck. Electronics glowed inside. I stepped forward and stared as Jeremy downloaded files to a computer and sent them to a tiny printer that shot out a succession of small sheets.

Without a word, he ended the call, shut the toolbox, rolled the papers, sealed them with a sticky tab, and tucked them into my vest.

"What was all that?" I asked.

"Need to know," Jeremy said. "Silent mode."

As we left his truck behind, I focused on not stumbling under the dark trees as we jogged forward under a sky of stars. Jeremy used his flashlight in quick bursts to indicate potential hazards: *watch the rock, don't step on the stick*. Mostly, we traveled in silence and near darkness.

Seeing a flash of red, I drew Jeremy's attention to a glow coming from a knothole eight feet up a tree trunk. Once we'd circled behind the tree, he laced his hands and prompted me to step into them and reach around the trunk to feel my way through my appointed task.

Swaying in the unstable perch, I downloaded the files to the hard drive in my gear and reinserted the data card. Jeremy turned my dismount into a smooth ride by lowering his hands while I stepped down.

I saw a second camera on the trail ahead. We crossed behind the tree and repeated the process of securing the footage.

"*Shh*, listen," Jeremy prompted.

As we stood there in the moon's glow, panting from our quick pace, a breath of air wended through the forest with a low moan, like the voice of a mythical animal, and then it faded into silence.

"It's from the cave," Jeremy whispered.

"It must be what Sal heard years ago," I said. "It wasn't Bud and Birdie trying to scare him, though I bet they took advantage of it."

Ahead, the trees thickened as we hiked up a gradual slope, sparing our boots from hidden puddles and the squelching grip of mud. It was chilly, around forty degrees, but I liked how the grip of cold kept me alert. I snugged on the gloves from my tactical belt and discovered they were similar to the ones I used for photography, offering coverage for my fingers up to the first knuckle, and leaving my fingertips free.

Seeing Nicole step from behind a boulder, I straightened my spine and focused on the all-consuming thought of saving Dan.

"How did you escape being trapped?" Jeremy asked.

"I'm fast and smart." Catching sight of me, Nicole went from cocky to outraged. "Are you crazy, bringing *her* to the scene?"

"Per Antoine's request," he said. "I can see you're injured."

"A shoulder hit from a ricochet. Salvatore Hall aimed at the ground, and somehow managed to miss." Nicole pulled the sleeve hole of her ballistic vest toward her other side to show blood in front of her shoulder tip.

"It missed hitting any bones. I'm limited in range, but I've put pressure on it with padding, so I'm good to go."

"Don't shoot, it's me," Sal said, emerging from the trees. "I can't tell you how sorry I am. I was aiming at the ground."

"You hit a rock," Nicole snarled. "Your aim sucks."

"*Quiet* mode," Jeremy hissed. "We're almost there."

Jeremy slowed our pace as we crested a hill. Based on my recollection of the map, I figured we were a quarter mile from Bud and Birdie's house. Using his flashlight, Jeremy combed the ground along the edge of the ridge, and then he halted in front of a cracked boulder.

"Sal, help with this stone," Jeremy said.

Kneeling to watch, I saw that the two halves of the boulder could be rocked apart: a means of hiding the entrance in plain sight. Unzipping his bag, Jeremy made fast work of securing a nylon rope to a tree with means of controlling the line as it descended downward.

"*Psst*, Antoine?" he called into the entrance.

"He's supposed to be waiting for us?" I asked.

"All I know is this appears to be a stable entrance. The cave extends that way," Jeremy said, indicating the downward slope of the low ridge. "It follows the land sideways, more or less. Nicole, I assume you've scouted out other possible places to get in and out?"

"The cave collapse happened at the far end," Nicole said.

"Bring me there," Jeremy said. "I want to check it out."

With a flick of eyes, Jeremy conveyed that I was to press Sal for answers while he pressed Nicole for her version of events.

As they headed away in the darkness, I asked Sal if he needed water or a granola bar, but he waved off the notion of eating as an impossible feat. I realized with a jolt of distress that he was wearing hunting camouflage like the kind Gerald had worn during his last moments of life. Seeing my sorrowful gaze, Sal looked all the more anguished.

"Even tonight, I expected Gerald to show up," he managed.

"My guess is, a secret note directed you to come here," I said. "Gerald would want you to trust me. Let's look at it together."

I traded my tactical gloves for nitrile gloves and asked Sal to hold the note still so I could photograph it with my phone, then I took it from him and illuminated the page with my flashlight.

Hello again, trusted comrade, I am concerned about Gerald. If he met with foul play, I know you will want to help get justice. I'll meet you in the spot where you heard the spirit sound years ago. I can't reveal my identity, so exercise care and restraint. Bring your rifle, but don't shoot directly at anyone! When I give the signal, holler and shoot the ground so the bullets don't hit rocks and go astray. I will handle the rest. You will be a hero, Mr. Hall.

AS ALWAYS, BURN THIS NOTE!

"Did you see who left this under the rock?" I asked.

"*This* note?" Sal specified. "No."

Seeing his level of nerves, I decided not to push too hard.

"Describe what happened today," I said.

"Dan Bolton arrived at the far entrance at maybe one o'clock," Sal said. "It was confusing, since I'd started to think Gerald's cousins were involved. Hours later, Paul and Isaac showed up. Then Kick showed up. They argued so bad it was tough to make sense of it. I got to wondering if they'd gotten notes as well. I sat there scratching my head."

"More likely, they got texts," I said.

"Paul saw me scratching my head and hollered," Sal went on. "I took it as the signal and shot a few rounds into the soil. There was a zipping sound and that crabby female cop caught the ricochet. I swear to God, I was *not* aiming at the group. There's no way any of my rounds caused the entrance to collapse. That was a shock."

"The group probably jarred some loose stones," I said.

"Yeah, they jammed in all at once, hollering and yelling and pushing past each other," Sal said. "Once it was dark, I noticed trail cameras. I'm sitting there thinking if there's a camera that can tell us who's coming and going, why am I shivering in the cold?"

"Exactly," I said. "We'll help you sort it out, ok?"

"Do you have a match?" Sal said. "I was supposed to burn the note, but I kept it intact to make sure I got things right."

"It's evidence," I said. "You can't burn it."

I signaled to Jeremy as he and Nicole returned from their survey of the ledge. After reading the note with a tight expression, despite my latest amazing win, Jeremy sealed it in a small evidence bag.

"You're a giant pain in the butt," he said.

I gaped. "*Excuse* me?"

"Sal, you seem remorseful," Jeremy said. "Can you be trusted to wait over there on that log?" Once the dejected vigilante was out of earshot, Jeremy whispered, "Step away like you're upset."

"Luckily, I *am*," I hissed.

I marched toward a tree, putting distance between myself and Nicole. Jeremy caught up and fell into hand motions suggesting he was criticizing my attitude, but his update had me staring in shock.

"Dr. Bertrand Clark is in the cave system," Jeremy whispered. "Gaunt and terrified, addled from hunger. Antoine has been trying to befriend him for days. He brought in Dan because he's got a calm vibe. Bertrand will peer at them and listen, but the second they try to head toward him to lead him out, he scrambles away. It's awful and sad."

"He's been hiding here for months?" I asked.

"Close to a year, maybe with help from the farmers," Jeremy said. "If any of the trapped people are behind the events that drove Bertrand into hiding, you can see the need to maintain secrecy."

"Absolutely," I said. "I get it."

"Antoine is totally pissed that Nicole followed him here, but it's best to let that stand," Jeremy whispered. "I'll keep an eye on her. Hence, I'm sending you in alone. I'm sorry if it's scary, but we've got a separate plan in motion that might startle Dr. Clark all the more. Antoine will meet up with you. *If* he gets a chance. That part is unclear."

"Let's get on with it," I said.

Jeremy showed me how to operate the bodycam on my vest, adding that I should keep it active unless Dan or Antoine asked for a private word. Once it was on, Jeremy continued in a normal tone as we crossed back to the entrance where the boulders had been pushed aside.

"We're clear on your role?" he asked. "If you don't see Antoine or Dan, stay put within twenty feet of this entrance to serve as a guide. If the need arises, you'll be poised to help get people out."

"I hear you," I said. "I understand."

Totally *not*. Was I to stay put or find Dr. Clark?

"In you go," Jeremy said, ushering me into a harness. "Remember the basics. Don't grab the rope. Let it play out nice and easy."

My tight smile reminded him that I had *not* gotten a lesson.

"It's a short drop," he whispered. "You'll be fine."

I stretched my neck on both sides, knelt next to the two halves of the boulder with the rope secured to my harness, slid my legs down into the opening, and endeavored to calm my racing heart.

"Here, this will help," Nicole said.

Leaning in, she blinded me with a bright light that changed in intensity through three white settings, and then a red glow. Holding the device on my forehead, she released the back band with a snap.

"You are *such* a jerk," I seethed.

With a pointed look, Jeremy conveyed the need to refrain from emotional outbursts that might frighten Dr. Clark. I nodded and dialed down immediately through deep, calming breaths.

"My eyes are still seeing spots," I whispered.

"Hence, the sunglasses in your tactical belt in case there's a situation where you need them," Jeremy said. "Once your eyes adjust to the darkness down there, bursts of light will be all the more blinding. Mostly, keep your headlamp on the red setting. It'll offer plenty of light."

"Any other tips?"

"Don't be spooked if you see a ghost," he whispered.

"How is that helpful?"

"Rely on instincts. That's your best bet."

I sighed. "Ok, here I go."

"Tell me if I'm feeding the rope too fast."

As my weight slid downward, leaving the bare trees and stars behind, I inhaled the stirring scents of damp earth and fallen leaves. I looked over my shoulder and nearly got my ear torn off by the jagged edge of a rock. Instead, I scissored my legs to gauge what kind of space I was entering. As

I left the upper world behind and entered a realm of dirt and rock ledges, the scraping sounds of my descent took on a splashing, echoing quality, tumbling downward into the underground cavern.

"How's it going?" Jeremy's voice echoed.

"It's a big space," I said. "Keep feeding the rope."

Dangling, I trained my headlamp's red light on the space below and saw a flat area where I could land and discard the rope. I cursed Nicole all over again, still plagued by spots in my field of vision, and then one of the spots morphed into a face-like shape with textured contours as if it was a wild animal with bristling hair and burning red eyes.

"Umm … there's something here!" I managed.

"What's that?" Jeremy's voice echoed.

I struggled to free myself as the creature gripped my harness, pulling me down until its bristled hairs touched my neck.

"Let go!" I hollered.

"Ok!" Jeremy hollered back.

The rope went slack, sending me into a painful, tumbling heap. The wild hair and beard resolved into a haggard human face. Even at a glance, I could tell that living in the cave had taken a terrible toll. Unraveling here and there, his filthy wool sweater revealed his frailty.

"Dr. Clark?" I whispered.

He cast a fearful glance toward the entrance. "Only you?"

"Yes," I said. "I have water."

Bertrand motioned away my offered bottle and thankfully didn't press me for food. In Raymond's journals, I'd read about the difficulties that faced lost hikers who hadn't eaten for a long while. "Refeeding" had to happen under medical supervision. If a starving survivor wolfed down food too fast, especially the wrong kind of food, it could kill them.

"How have you managed?" I said, making quick work of escaping the harness and coiling the rope so it was out of the way.

"A farmer sheltered me last winter," he whispered. "Months of feeling guilty, so I said goodbye. He still leaves cheese and eggs."

I pictured Mr. Cheeseman leaving out food without knowing if the donations were taken in the dark of night by raccoons or the archaeologist who'd turned to him for help months ago. I understood Mr. Cheeseman's decision not to admit that he'd sheltered the fugitive. Running a farm had shaped him into a kind-hearted, crafty strategist.

"Sonny?" Jeremy hollered, causing Dr. Clark to flinch.

"I'm good," I called up. "Silent mode, please."

Jeremy signaled agreement, then all was quiet.

Dr. Clark motioned for me to take a snapshot from his hand. Someone had printed my photo from my website.

"I'm Raymond's daughter," I whispered.

"Yes, I know," Bertrand said, gulping and blinking away tears. "I was poised to attend his memorial service. My wife and I had just pulled in and parked when you arrived. I saw your face. Pale and stricken. I didn't want to mar your first and last moment with Raymond. I'm *so* sorry for your loss," Bertrand added, clutching my hand. "It's my fault."

"That's not true," I said, hugging him. "We've unearthed the real story. You were set up. It's safe to head home."

"It's not safe," Bertrand whispered.

With his video in mind, I knew he was kicking himself for innocent mistakes. Holding him in the near darkness, feeling how frail he'd become, I tried to rub warmth into his chilled fingers.

"The envelope you left for my father is why I'm here," I whispered as his tears subsided. "Where did you get my photo?"

Dr. Clark donned a noble expression as he pointed to my tactical belt to indicate that the person wore similar gear.

"It's either Antoine or Dan," I whispered. "We're here to help you, but there's a complexity. A few people got trapped."

Dr. Clark nodded and motioned for me to follow him.

The ceiling of the cave ranged from three to five feet high, sparking the need to crawl on our hands and knees for short stretches. The soles of Dr. Clark's shoes were worn, his clothes threadbare. He traveled in silence as we climbed over boulders along the way, awash in the red glow of my headlamp. In wider areas where we could move forward in a crouch, my boots rasped on the stone floor and cast echoes every which way.

"*Shh,*" Dr. Clark prompted, pausing to listen.

Up ahead, Dan's voice echoed toward me as he urged Paul Polk to choose his footing carefully. Before I could stop him, Dr. Clark reversed direction, preferring to flee the approaching men.

A moment later, Dan said, "I heard a woman's voice up ahead. I think it's the colleague who followed me today. Nicole?"

"No, she's been demoted," I called out.

Dan paused. "*Sonny?*"

"The one and only," I said. "I'm here to save the day."

Soon, the shifting beam of a flashlight played over the walls, fractured by boulders and cracks and other complexities in the low cave. Appearing around the curve, out of breath, Dan was covered with dust, in the jeans and the plaid shirt that he'd worn in my house, but with the addition of a tactical vest and a bodycam unit similar to mine.

"What are you doing here?" he demanded.

"I am a volunteer in a rescue effort," I said to formally introduce the way things needed to unfold. "Is anyone injured?"

"Isaac wrenched his back," Dan said. "He's stabilized for now, but his wish is not to be treated like baggage. I wanted to test out using the upper entrance, but a stretcher would be a tight fit."

"Yes, he would be in for a rough ride," I agreed.

"Hello," Paul called out, hidden by the bend that Dan had navigated. "Is it ok for me to come through?"

"Yeah, take it slowly," Dan said.

He swiveled his knees and reached downward into the opening he'd come through, and helped pull Paul into the chamber. While the realtor brushed rock dust from his clothes, as if terrified of ending up with lung cancer like Gerald, I used American Sign Language to update Dan: I was there to help Dr. Clark, whom I'd already met; Sal was remorseful; Jeremy was poised outside the upper entrance.

"You two make a handsome couple," Paul said.

"I'm still not clear on how you got trapped," I said.

"Sal is to blame," Paul said with a disgusted tone. "The lower entrance got trashed when he fired a rifle out there. Dan was good enough to help me reach the exit in one piece. I'm claustrophobic, and there was an awful episode when I used the restroom. I can't speak of it."

My eyebrows twisted. "There's a restroom …?"

"In a manner of speaking," Dan said. "Watch for puddles."

"Got it," I said. "Thanks for the warning."

"Paul showed great interest in the geology down here," Dan said with a wry look. "His pockets are full of samples."

"I'm a *hopeless* rock hound," Paul said.

"Your depth amazes me," I said.

"Paul, can you give me a second with Sonny?" Dan asked.

"Absolutely."

Slowly, Paul pressed forward with the awkward, limping progress of a man whose only means of exercise was signing contracts. Dan shut off his bodycam and signaled for me to do the same. Once we were truly alone, he planted a quick, dusty kiss on my lips, and explained that Antoine had recognized the lines on the map as a cave. To check for signs of mining he came in not knowing the archaeologist was there.

"He didn't catch onto the trail cameras until it was too late," Dan said. "He brought me in to speed up the rescue, but our urgency had the wrong effect on Dr. Clark. So here we are, saddled with two operations to work through. So much for keeping you out of harm's way."

"I'm not leaving until everyone is out," I said.

"This isn't a normal rescue," Dan said. "It's not safe."

"Because of the lithium?" I asked.

"Because of the assholes," he whispered. "Antoine is investigating side passages to make sure we're not taken off-guard again."

"Did you know this cave was here?" I asked.

"Bud described it as an unstable ledge, off limits in terms of safety, so Aaron and I never explored this part of the property," Dan said. "Birdie's sister died when they were in grade school. A bad fall. My guess is it happened here. Hence, their efforts to keep people away."

"I took a photo of the note that brought Sal here," I said.

After studying the note, the sheets Jeremy had printed, and the trail camera footage, Dan retreated into the cave's downward bend to conduct a hissed exchange with Jeremy over his radio.

"This amounts to a *third* situation to handle when the cell signal is in dark mode," Dan whispered, apparently unaware that the cave acted like an amphitheater. "What happened to the contained approach?" Dan listened for a second, then sighed. "Yeah, I'll get it done."

As he returned to me, he donned an upbeat smile.

"Jeremy is on his own out there clearing the rubble," he said. "If you pitch in, think how fast it'll go. We'll be out in no time."

"What about the third situation?" I asked.

"So much for the concept of 'need to know,'" Dan said with air quotes. "I've got it covered, especially with—" He paused and narrowed his eyes. "You're playing me, trying to get me to disclose things."

"Isn't it best if I'm fully informed?" I asked.

"It's best if I know you're safe," Dan said, "and *yes*, I hear the double standard, no need to point it out." With an air of resignation, he continued, "If you can escort Paul to the exit, that would be great. Find Antoine, then focus on your task. I'll get the others out."

"Be careful," I said. "Stay safe."

After a quick kiss, we switched our bodycams to the 'on' setting, and then Dan headed away to rejoin Isaac and Kick.

I went in the opposite direction and took over guiding Paul through narrow passages, which stirred dust into the air. Paul was gasping and sniffling as we arrived at the spot where the rope and harness were dangling from the entrance. Taking a tissue that I offered, he blew his nose with a ridiculous, blustering level of snorts and related noise.

"You look worried," I said.

"One can't help but wonder what kind of dust it is," he said.

"Can I see the rock samples you collected?" I asked.

"Actually, I wanted to borrow your tactical belt to stow them in," Paul said. "There's another loose piece on the ground."

I reached down. "This one?"

"Yes," Paul said. "It's got signs of crystals."

"Why is that important?" I asked.

With a shrug, he said, "Perhaps it's tourmaline."

"That's fascinating," I said. "Show me."

Paul dug chunks from his pockets and dumped them into my cupped hands, thinking I was volunteering to carry them for him.

"Is this everything?" I asked.

Receiving a nod, I tossed the rocks away into a dark corner.

"Why would you do that?" Paul demanded.

"Because this cave doesn't belong to you," I said.

"Isaac and I each own fifteen percent," Paul said.

I paused. "What …?"

"Dan wasn't able to swing the full price, so we offered to help. Knowing Isaac, he added some sort of 'gotcha' clause that could push us to the curb," Paul added tiredly. "If I were you—"

"Jeremy!" I hollered. "Get ready to haul!"

Quickly, I shoved Paul into a sitting position, wrenched his legs into the harness, and instructed Jeremy to prepare for a lift.

"Who is coming up?" Jeremy's voice echoed.

"Paul Polk!" I hollered. "Tug hard!"

"Wait … *whoa*," Paul exclaimed as the harness became a vice around his crotch, and then he was a wild-eyed, dangling weight.

"Face the rock and climb," I growled. "Come *on*."

Following my orders about which rock projections to use to climb upward, Paul got to the point where Jeremy and Sal could join forces to haul him the rest of the way into the open air above.

"Sonny?" Jeremy asked. "Is anyone else coming up?"

"No," I said. "I'm heading back down."

"Good job! You're doing great!"

"She's barely done anything," Nicole's voice echoed.

"Yeah," I muttered, "Same to you."

26

I scrambled down the passageway, scraping my skull a few times and landing damage to my knees and elbows. Winded and shaking, wiping sweat from my brow, I accidentally flicked off my headlamp. My heart thudded as I ran my fingers over the oblong lens, remembering at the last moment to shut my eyes as I pressed the "on" button and cycled to the red light setting. Why didn't I hear voices? Had Jeremy cleared the rubble? If so, and a rockfall cut me off, I would be trapped in the cave all alone, covered with dust that might have ruined Dr. Clark's mind.

"Stay calm," I whispered.

Right on cue, a breath of air stirred through the cave with a mournful sound that had my hairs standing on end. I was about to use my radio when I heard the scrape of boots in the passageway.

"Dan?" I called out.

"No, it's not Dan," a man said.

As his hand appeared, gripping the wall to pull himself upward, his wristwatch gleamed in the red light of my headlamp. I was confused to see the distinctive uniform of a game warden, with a gold badge and a hat that shadowed his face and neck. My breath caught in my throat as I saw the bold lettering on his nametag: Raymond French.

I stared at him, unable to breathe.

"Uh-oh, Jeremy didn't warn you," he said.

Crouched under the low ceiling, he sidled closer and took off his hat. It wasn't my father waking from the grave. It was Antoine.

"I'm sorry," he said. "It was necessary to—*uuuf*…"

Antoine's eyes crossed as my fist hammered his bread basket, another first for the record books. My personality had swerved in recent months.

"That took me off guard," he wheezed.

"What kind of cruel bastard are you?" I demanded.

"It was to help Dr. Clark," he said. "To gain his trust."

I paused, recalling how frightened and addled the recluse had seemed, too wary to stay when Dan and Paul arrived.

"Oh," I said. "I guess that makes sense."

"I resorted to this trick to sort myself from foes in Bertrand's mind," Antoine managed. "We were *almost* there."

"Then Isaac, Paul, Kick, and Sal barged in," I said.

"I'd hoped to leave you out of harm's way, but your empathy is an undeniable asset," Antoine said. "The need for quick action is paramount, so I left a photo of you for Bertrand to find."

"I know," I said. "We've already spoken."

Antoine paused. "From a distance?"

"No, he was there when I came down," I said.

"How close did you get?" Antoine asked.

"We hugged and talked," I said. "He led me here."

"He was lucid and rational?" Antoine specified, reflecting wonder and relief when I nodded. "Well done, Berrichon. When time permits, I will chide myself for not bringing you in sooner."

Antoine leaned in the direction he'd come from, hauled a black duffle bag into view from around the bend, set it on the ground with a clank, and unzipped it from stem to stern. With telltale clicks and snaps, he loaded a firearm and secured it in a multifaceted tactical belt.

"Umm, what are you doing?" I asked as he unbuttoned his uniform and stripped off his T-shirt with an air of not planning to stop.

"Look away if you wish," he said. "I need my normal gear."

"I know about your history with Isaac," I said, looking on as layers of clothing peeled away until Antoine's toned physique was bare except for his boxers. Even in the shadowed red light of my headlamp, I could see scars on his ribcage, shoulders, and forearms from injuries that clearly hadn't occurred during mishaps on a basketball court. "Jeremy assures me that you're not out for revenge."

"That is correct," Antoine said. "This isn't your father's uniform, by the way. All I borrowed was his name tag."

"Can I have it back?" I asked.

"Of course," Antoine said, handing it over. "Make sure to speak softly. We can't lose ground with Dr. Clark."

"He's not here right now, so let's clear the air," I said. "How do you explain the common element of Isaac Munroe?"

"Shit happens," Antoine said. "Fate is a bitch."

"You can see where I might be concerned," I said.

"Help me with this," Antoine prompted, signaling that he wanted me to wrap his wrists with support tape.

"Why is this necessary?" I asked.

"Jamming the cell signal helps contain the rescue operation, but leaves us vulnerable in other regards," he said. "I'm forced to cover the SWAT angle on my own. *Not* too tight," Antoine added, and then he devolved into a quiet rant in French that cursed his bad luck that day.

"Cursing is alarming even in a whisper," I said.

Antoine closed his eyes to regain his composure and then calmly continued, "How did things go with Monsieur Polk?"

Watching with fascination as he donned elbow and knee protection that looked to be some form of lightweight body armor, I shared that the realtor was a bad liar who'd squirreled away a pound of rock samples that I'd confiscated and tossed into a corner.

"Excellent," Antoine said. "What else?"

"Paul warned that Isaac might have built a surprise element into the contract with Dan," I said. "He described it as a 'gotcha' clause."

"I would not be surprised," Antoine said.

Resorting to lying on his back, he wrenched on black military-style pants and shrugged his way into a matching shirt. Midway through his quick work of lacing up his boots, I stopped staring and wondered if he was using the shock value of stripping in front of me the way I'd kept him from finding the secret T-shirt pouch the other night.

"Is Dan up to speed on the implications?" I whispered.

"Everything is unfolding as planned," Antoine said.

"You're gearing up like it's a disaster." I closed my eyes. "You're stalling the minutes away. I'll loop back after I've updated Dan."

"Berrichon, *wait*," Antoine prompted.

Ignoring him, I ducked away around the next bend.

* * *

"How in the heck long *is* this cave?" I said, scraping my head on the ceiling for the third time, but pushing onward into the darkness.

Finally, Dan's voice was up ahead, relaxed and easygoing.

I took a calming breath, smoothed my hair, and continued onward. Faint light illuminated the opening for the lower chamber as I slipped into view, sparking looks of surprise in the three men. Isaac was sitting with his back against a section of the wall with his dress slacks and pricey shoes stretched in front of him, covered with dirt and dust.

My gaze landed on Dan, who was in the midst of handing a sidearm to Kick handle-first: proper form, but oh my *God*.

"What are you doing?" I demanded.

"I borrowed his sidearm to check for a prowler," Dan said. "Now I'm explaining why I ejected the magazine and put it in my pocket. There's a danger of ricochets and other issues." With that, he resumed handing the sidearm to Kick. "Here you go. We're all set."

"There were reports of a rabid raccoon in the area," Kick said when I continued to stare. "I saw a fox with the disease some years ago. It's something you don't soon forget. Scary beyond words."

"In Maine, there's leeway in carrying without a special permit," Dan said. "As for Paul's report of a prowler, I think the confined space got to him. He insisted that he saw Raymond's ghost."

"Yeah, it's spooky in the cave," I agreed.

"I'm glad you're here, Sonny," Kick said. "Maybe you can make sense of Dan's explanation for why the cell signal has gone haywire. For our phones, anyway. I've got a giant blank instead of bars, but the light on his bodycam says his equipment is getting a signal."

"It's connected to an encrypted networking device that's off the main grid," Dan said. "It's an experimental thing. To test it properly, I set up a jammer to cancel out the signal our phones use."

"Can't you unjam the signal?" Isaac asked.

"The device is in my truck," Dan said. "And I'm stuck in a cave."

"Why take that kind of measure?" Isaac asked.

Dan spread his hands. "Training exercise, an effort to stay on my toes. Your visit is an example of how the unexpected can hit the fan. You own a small share, but why come without telling me?"

"I was getting to that before Paul's claustrophobia fake-out," Kick said. "He's going behind our backs, trying to sell this land."

"Fine with me," Isaac said. "I officially hate this place."

"It's possible the Orland family came to see the cave that way," Dan said. "Birdie's sister might have died here during her youth. A decision was made to close the entrances and foil trespassers."

"The one we ducked into was wide open," Isaac said.

"That is a puzzle to sort out," Dan agreed. "You didn't see it when you were here with Paul and Sal years ago?"

"I don't know what part of the forest we stumbled into," Isaac said. "We figured Bud was behind the weird moaning sounds, but I've heard it a few times today. It's the wind pulling through."

"I think Sonny's father figured it out," Dan said. "If you recall, he had suspicions over the way Bud and Birdie died."

"They were careless drunks," Isaac said.

"New information has come in," Dan said. "A clerk at Golly's Liquor Haven got a bad feeling about a customer who'd bought whiskey a few days before Bud and Birdie died. It's a known problem, how people clamp down on a tip instead of stepping forward."

"The thing to be talking about is the buyer Paul is lining up for this land," Kick said. "Prepare to be shocked."

Kick handed his phone to his father and launched the clip of Antoine attending Isaac's lecture fifteen years ago. The soundtrack played against the cave walls, then Isaac frowned and pulled the phone closer as the frame froze on Antoine in his "Justice for Chloé" shirt.

"Say hello to Paul's high-end buyer," Kick said.

Isaac looked up. "The guy in the video? You're not serious."

"He met with Paul at a different bank from ours, and Dan appears to know him as well," Kick said handing his phone to Dan so he could study the video. "What's your connection to this guy?"

"He's a colleague," Dan said. "A good friend."

"Antoine was a pain in my ass at first," Isaac said. "Once he caught his sister's drug dealer, he apologized for stepping out of line. In other words, I've been twisted into a pain pretzel for no reason. The issue with Paul could have been ironed out in my office."

"I'm not sold," Kick said, "Why is your friend in town?"

Dan shrugged. "To help with the case."

"The attack on your house?" Kick asked.

"Yeah, it was a giant puzzle at first," Dan said. "Why was I a target, seemingly out of the blue? What could it be about? None of the parts seemed to fit, and then I did one of these." Dan bumped his head the way people do from an epiphany. "It's Sonny's fault."

I hesitated. "*What?*"

"Because of the case that unfolded in May," Dan explained. "There I was, committed to a high-stakes sting operation up north when you landed in front of me. Beautiful, talented, and in the crosshairs of a serial killer. I had to stay and help."

"I urged you not to risk your job," I said.

"The pull of not wanting to leave you in danger was too strong," Dan said. "Somebody caught onto my pattern of coming and going. That's my best guess. Hey, we're due for an update on clearing the rubble. Sonny, can you exit on the other end to see what's up?"

"I'm still resting," I said.

For a moment, we devolved into intense messaging with our eyes, and then Dan grasped the low odds of shooing me away.

Watching us, Isaac said, "Apparently, I'm the only one who's not losing their cool in being trapped. Kick is sweating. You two are directing barbs at one another. What in the hell is going on?"

"We're trapped because Dan's cop friend caused the rockslide," Kick said. "I don't know why he waited all these years to seek revenge, but that's the reality. I'm sweating because Dan disabled our only line of defense. If you mean well, give back my ammo."

"That's not going to happen," Dan said softly.

"Why is Antoine here?" Kick demanded.

"I told you," Dan said. "To help with the case."

"If that's true, how about a progress report?" Kick asked.

"Well—" Dan winced. "If you insist on delving into it now, why did you withdraw ten grand in cash last month?"

Kick stared in confusion. "What do you mean?"

"According to the paper trail we've unearthed, you had some sort of problem that couldn't be handled through normal channels," Dan said. "It's a simple question. Why did you need ten grand?"

"I went to the casino," Kick admitted.

"Great story, but the rest of these transactions were made out in your father's name. Diner, gas station, nightclub," Dan said, pulling the printed receipts from his pocket. "The two of you have the same first name. Kids do this, sometimes. Use a parent's credit card."

"You did *not* use my card on a gambling spree," Isaac said.

"No worries in that regard," Dan said. "None of these receipts are from a casino. They're from the location where I tackled the border work. Kick followed me there and made some new friends back in May. He thought about it for a while, then looped back to cut a deal."

"This is crazy," Kick said. "Antoine has gone rogue."

"I had that concern for a minute," Dan said, having closed in on Kick so slowly that I hadn't noticed it. "But Antoine didn't buy whiskey for Bud and Birdie. He didn't push a geologist to his death, or chase Dr. Clark for months on end, bent on knowing where a certain rock sample came from. He didn't head north to hire criminals to go after me. That was you. Your father's past troubles offered a shred of cover."

"Tell him he's *wrong*," Isaac hollered.

"I'm not wrong," Dan said. "Your son caught onto a resource that's worth a lot more than ten grand. Instead of pursuing it the standard way, he tried to eliminate the guy who started looking into some cold case crimes that made him nervous. A guy who also happens to own the majority share of this land. Sadly, this cave is not a source of the relevant kind of rock. If you thought that, you were wrong."

"Sonny," Kick said, motioning for me to weigh in. "I told you my concern that Dan is crooked. He got dark after Aaron died. He came and went in a troubling pattern, so yeah, I set out to see if my dad was in business with a shady cop. You're geared like I am, Sonny. To know the truth. The ten grand was a means of buying information."

"That lie is the worst of the worst," Dan growled. "Whoever you hired to take me down is the one who went rogue."

"Junior, tell him he's out of his mind," Isaac insisted.

"He *is* out of his mind," Kick said. "It's bullshit."

"You're the bullshit artist," Dan said. "Once you came up with a plan for laying blame elsewhere, you left gear in the cave that fits the description of the crew who hit my house. Plan C, D, or E, maybe. I bet you staged today's rockslide as well, and every step is captured on the trail cameras that you bought with your father's credit card."

"You were Vivian's secret lover," Kick said.

"She kept diaries," Dan said. "I'm not listed on a single page, but guess what she wrote about the geologist's death?"

"That was Vivian's fault," Kick said. "An accident."

"Were you a part of the crew who hit my house?" Dan asked.

"Of course not," Kick said.

"If that's the case, the guy you hired plied Vivian with gifts in exchange for a place to hide," Dan said. "How does that feel?"

"How do you think it feels?" Kick said. "Awful and messed up."

"*Who* did you hire?" Dan growled. "I need a name."

"He's like … I don't really know."

"Sure, you do," Dan said. "Out with it."

Wild-eyed and panic-stricken, Kick snatched a knife from an ankle holster and swept the blade so close to Dan's exposed neck that my heart stopped. With a swift turn, Dan caught his wrist.

"Drop the knife," he said. "Show some sense."

"You've got my intentions all wrong," Kick hollered. "The guy is a cop. He flashed a badge. I've been running scared for weeks."

"Drop—the—knife," Dan growled, finishing the takedown by pressuring Kick's arm until the blade clattered to the ground.

"Kick, what the hell?" Isaac hollered.

"You slept with Vivian when you knew we were together," Kick said tearfully. "Let's start with that."

"*Shh*, calm down," Isaac said.

"Take your father's advice," Dan said.

With a snap of handcuffs, he secured Kick's wrists and crossed the chamber to hug me. The intensity of his embrace conveyed conflict and turmoil that translated his thoughts without words.

I pulled away. "You read him his rights?"

"I did that with all of them when they first came in," Dan said.

Gripping his hand, I held his gaze. "You were awesome just now, but you can't leave the job half-finished. To close the chapter once and for all, you need to continue the questioning at the barracks, whatever is the norm in terms of keeping him engaged and talking. That means putting aside any impulse to stay on scene while I'm here."

"The thought of leaving you in the cave ..."

"I'm committed to my task," I said. "For our relationship to work, we need to accept each other's choices. *Both* of us." I motioned toward the glimpses of night sky where Jeremy was clearing the rubble. "Focus on getting personnel in and out fast to minimize the jarring vibe."

"I get it," Dan said. "You need calm to do your bit."

"Exactly," I said.

I sounded a lot more grounded than I felt, but I didn't want either of us to look back on the night as the time Dan put a moment of success aside to hold my hand. My lips were chilled and numb, not quite able to appreciate his quick kiss. I turned and retraced my journey.

27

On my own again, I had some dire news for the scientific community: an object in motion did *not* necessarily stay in motion.

Exhausted and sweating, chilled from head to toe, I gripped the cave wall and marveled over the way Dan had secured the scene and remained calm until Kick turned the discussion into a showdown. Meanwhile, I had failed to see the murderer in front of me. *Again.*

Just a few hours ago, I'd welcomed Kick into my house. I'd expressed sympathy as he'd described his troubles, and I'd misread his efforts to erode my trust in Dan. I'd thanked him for his caring spirit.

Discouraged and shivering, I wrenched off my tactical vest to mop the sweat that was chilling me to the bone. Paul had taken most of my tissues. I reached under my shirt and used the rest to dry my skin until they were a damp, unhelpful wad that shredded into bits.

"*Hey.*" Antoine was suddenly there, gripping my arms and looking me up and down to assess what had sparked my sudden halt. "Your vest has a fitness tracker. It looked like you died."

"It feels like I might have," I said with chattering teeth.

"Ok, shirt off," he said. "We need to act fast."

Looking grave and focused, Antoine wrenched a quick-dry cloth from his belt and rubbed me down with so much vigor that my eyeballs vibrated in my head. Once I was more or less dry, he snagged a thermal shirt from his bag of gear, shoved my arms into the sleeves, and wrenched the shirt over my head. There I sat, in an Antoine-sized tent, with way too much fabric going on. He stifled a laugh as he rolled up the sleeves and motioned for me to smooth the noodle of excess fabric tucked into my pants. Soon my overshirt was returned, and my vest was in place.

"Next phase." Unwrapping a granola bar, Antoine secured it in my chilled hand. "It's breezy in this spot. Eat as we climb, ok?"

In a seamless advance, Antoine gripped my hand, secured my elbow, and protected my head in low spots until we reached a sheltered chamber where we could rest. Leaning his back against the wall, Antoine slid me into place next to him and draped his arm around my shoulders to provide warmth. To give my brow a rest he slipped off my headlamp and set it aside to provide a soft glow instead of a glare in his face.

"Is there an awful mark?" I asked.

"A third eye effect," he said. "I rather like it."

While we waited out the noise of EMTs and officers arriving to help get Kick, Isaac, and Paul to their respective locations, Antoine described his shock at finding that Dr. Clark was in the cave. Not long afterward Kick had arrived, having caught onto activity in his camera feed.

"He assumed that I'd left," Antoine went on. "I doubt he ever realized that Dr. Clark was here. Stealth is not his strong suit. Later, I found that he'd stowed a weapon, clothing, and a balaclava that's identical to the gear used by the two fugitives Dan's team rounded up."

I frowned. "That will be tough for him to refute."

"I was poised to stop you from heading down there," Antoine said. "In seeing Kick's unraveling, you compromised your ability to identify him as the crew boss without bias. Your presence was a powerful influence. The more he sought your approval, the more he revealed."

"If Kick is the crew boss, he's a *really* good actor," I said. "I understand why you hung back. It set the stage for Isaac to insist that you'd buried the hatchet long ago." I paused, frowning. "Kick got rattled when Dan asked who he'd hired. You were on edge before I headed down. I think it's time for you to explain why you're wearing body armor."

Even in the dim light, Antoine could see from my raised eyebrows and uncompromising glare that his efforts to steer my mind into placid waters was not going to work. With a sigh, he rubbed his brow.

"The hypnosis session was supposed to clarify things," he said.

"What's your best guess on the crew boss?" I asked.

"I don't *have* a best guess," Antoine said. "That's unusual for this stage, so I'm sweating out a possibility I haven't faced in a long while. My parents were lowlifes. When they died, Chloé and I were sucked into a crime family. Foster kids of sorts. Jeremy told you I helped collapse their operation. I figured bringing them down would be the end of it."

"Amidst the chaos, how did you own a spaniel?" I asked.

Antoine smiled. "You would hone in on a stray element. In my teens I spent a few years with a cop's family. A glimpse of normal." Antoine spread his hands. "There's one remnant of my early days who sees me as a brother. It's not the truth, but what can I do? He's a deft crime boss, always on the move, but every now and then he involves himself with my life. It's been like learning a secret language, knowing the signs."

"Jeremy said the crew boss isn't the right fit."

"I'm working on an ulcer from the things that don't add up," Antoine said. "You're a rare person who can understand. The gut feeling that won't go away. You have a ghost. I have a living, breathing nightmare, and if it proves out, Isaac Junior might be off the hook."

"How?" I asked. "He's implicated every which way."

"Because my nemesis would have groomed him," Antoine said. "Bits and pieces that could sway a jury. On the side of logic, the nightmare is a high-stakes player who dabbles in arms dealing. This is Maine. He'd have no interest in pegmatite, even if it's worth billions. Not when tossing drugs onto the market earns riches with minimal effort."

"You didn't mention this possibility to Dan," I said, rubbing my aching eyes. "Because if he knew, he wouldn't have left."

"Dan is a meticulous strength in numbers kind of cop," Antoine said. "I've seen the best of the best, just like him, launch in with a tactical advantage, only to get speared through the gut or electrocuted by a booby trap. Now you'll ask why I brought you here."

"I'm safer with you," I said.

"Good God, you get that?" Antoine managed. "It's arrogant for me to think so, but I've worked every angle to its bitter end. I shepherd you away, you end up in the trunk of a car. I plan out a special operations response, the forest blows up. Telling you is giving me a pain akin to heart failure," he said, massaging his sternum. "Your skill and agile mindset are the counterbalance. Terror can take hold, then you regroup."

"So, your nemesis hits you hard, and then retreats," I said. "Children act out that way. It's tough to fathom in an adult."

Antoine shook his head. "Only a psychologist could explain where he's ended up in life. If I'm jumping at shadows, as often happens, we can laugh about it. If not, he's known about you since May." When I blanched and stared at him, Antoine touched my chin. "He would know about *all* of you. For him to carry out a slow burn that involved months of waiting, it would indicate elements I haven't dealt with before, like a setback he suffered, or an illness. Again, it's guesswork and shadows."

"Did Jeremy tell you about Nicole?" I asked.

"I think she left with the EMTs to get her injury checked," Antoine said. "Maybe you're asking if I knew she looked into you back in May. I'm not entirely satisfied with her reasoning, but you were new in Dan's life. A wild card. There were grounds for it."

Antoine's calm gaze told me that Jeremy had honored my wish to keep Nicole's attack a secret. I turned away and left it alone.

"I know it's tough, not knowing how your father's death might fit in," Antoine said softly. "That will take more time."

I nodded. "Can we proceed? The cave is getting to me."

"Let me check with Jeremy," he said.

With his finger pressed against a hidden earpiece, he revealed that he'd been multitasking by keeping track of events outside the cave. All the while, Antoine stared down the passageway, using his eyes and free ear to hone in on suspicious sounds or signs of unexpected trouble. I realized his jaw was flexed and silent: for the first time since we'd met, he wasn't chewing gum. Goosebumps rippled up and down my arms.

Antoine studied me in the dim light. "Dan cleared the scene in record time, so we're set to proceed. After your interaction with Dr. Clark, I made inroads, but I held off so you're not robbed of the win."

With a smile, Antoine reached back and rapped his knuckles on the section of the wall he'd been resting against. To my surprise, it was made of wood. Motioning me aside, he joined me in looking on as a shuffling sound beyond the wood preceded cracks around a hidden panel painted so cleverly that it meshed with the surrounding stone in color and texture. The panel slid backward, revealing a two-foot hole.

"I guess you did make inroads," I whispered.

With signals, Antoine urged speed in crawling through.

I slipped onto my belly and used my elbows to drag myself forward into the darkness. My red light illuminated an inner chamber that caused me to stop and hold my breath. From floor to ceiling, every wall was scored with pictograms showing figures and animals, moons and stars, hillside farms, and lapping waves that I took to be lakes or streams. Urged onward by Dr. Clark, I continued wriggling forward and crawled to the left. Antoine's shoulders were a snug fit in the opening, but soon he was shifting his tactical belt to get his sidearm through, followed by his duffle bag. Once inside, Antoine joined me in staring in wonder at the pictograms, and then he nudged me and gave me a fist bump.

"I'm shocked to be here," I whispered. "This is his safe place."

"Yes, it's an honor to be invited here," Antoine said as he rested a hand on Dr. Clark's frail shoulder. "Thank you for trusting us."

The recluse motioned. "Safety first."

Seeing that he wanted to close us in, I helped him with the door, tugging the inside loops that he'd created until the seal was tight. Dimly, it occurred to me that I should feel at least a little claustrophobic to be cut off from an escape route. The hopeless adventurer in me cast the worries aside the way I would brush confetti from my shoulders.

"Am I correct that this area is an old mine, maybe from the 1800s?" Antoine asked. "Mining was big back then."

Dr. Clark nodded. "Feldspar was found here."

"What are these?" I said of the drawings.

"To recall my troubles," Dr. Clark murmured.

Some of the sketches showed a figure being chased through the woods, chased down roads, chased along streams, and hiding in a ditch.

Bertrand described events in murmurs, staring vacantly as if reliving scenes in his head. After a friend asked him to identify a rock sample, he'd submitted it to Scott Butler in the college's geology department. Writing a personal check to cover the cost gave him latitude in not disclosing the source, who wanted to remain anonymous. Vivian flagged the transaction when Scott "lost" the check. Even though Bertrand's relationship with Scott became strained, Bertrand was stunned to be accused of pushing him to his death. They'd worked in harmony for years.

"It took a long while to understand the link," Bertrand said. "Vivian's obsession was in getting the map. She accused me of hiding a possible dig site on my property, and she was right. With treasure hunters in the picture, I kept that location a secret, even from Raymond, I'm ashamed to admit. I think the townhouse concept for my land was a false front. Vivian convinced herself that the rock sample came from there."

"Did it?" I asked.

"No, and I'm committed to keeping the source a secret," Bertrand said. "Scott, the geologist, tried to shame me, saying he needed to know the source for a paper he was writing. Love for Vivian drove him to act out of character. She's still out there vying to destroy me."

"Vivian died the other day," I said gently.

"Good heavens," Bertrand said with anguish. "How?"

"She had a pill habit," I said, clasping his hand. "This day marks a new chapter. The man who tormented you was arrested."

"Isaac Junior came in right after you did," Dr. Clark said to Antoine. "It's why I didn't trust you. I *couldn't* trust you."

"I understand," Antoine said softly.

"There's no need for you to hide anymore," I said. "Your drawings are important evidence. I need to photograph them."

Snugging on the sunglasses from my belt, I showed Dr. Clark that I wanted him to cover his eyes so the light didn't blind him, and then I began capturing the walls with a grid approach so I could join the photos with a program later on. Encountering, a void in the back wall, I shined my phone's light into another chamber and paused in shock.

I reached back and gripped Antoine's hand.

"It's the 1800s couple from Dr. Clark's research," I said, recognizing the wife's full skirt and the husband's fringed, buckskin jacket and pants draped around their skeletal remains.

"Merde," Antoine whispered, crossing himself.

"Bud Orland made the secret door," Dr. Clark said, motioning toward the sealed opening. "He preserved their resting place."

With a mix of astonishment and sadness, I pondered the tragic tableau not more than ten feet away. Nearby was the pack saddle their mule had carried during their travels, and a dusty carpet bag. The dry conditions in the cave must have helped keep the thick material in relatively good shape. Their bodies and possessions looked undisturbed, telling me that their remains had escaped the notice of fiendish treasure hunters.

"They died hand in hand," I said. "Were they trapped here?"

"No, they cherished love and peace," Dr. Clark said softly.

Looking grave, he wiped his hands on his sweater, and then he carefully unfolded a sheet of ancient paper that he'd left to one side. When Antoine reached for it, Dr. Clark signaled that it was too precious to be handed around. Once the relic was smoothed on the stone floor, Antoine draped his arm around my shoulders and leaned close as we read the handwritten note dated March 1887. In cursive lettering, with flourishes indicating the use of a quill pen, the husband wrote:

Dearest friends and neighbors,

Perhaps the sharpest among you noticed that my beloved wife needed rest after our delightful card games. She loves the flickering glow of a campfire, and I adore seeing her eyes sparkle in its magical light, but it is not good for her ailing lungs. After our bairns died, Edwina confided that she felt lost amidst the bustle of city life. Women endure tight roles defined at birth.

She told me a bold plan that shocked me at first: to abandon the constraints of her corset and follow in the footsteps of intrepid adventurers like Isabella Bird, whose accounts are infamous across the land. After these months of delighting in Edwina's happy plunges into lakes in her bloomers, and seeing her shining red cheeks on a winter day, I know I have performed the service asked of me during our wedding vows. Before we abandoned our former life and the comforts of modern society, I secured a precious commodity from my medical supplies. A means of gentle release. Her eyes are fluttering like the butterflies we collected and inspected up close, but she is smiling and nodding.

Perhaps we will be found shortly. Perhaps not. Perhaps it is best that no one will chide us during this moment when her pain and frailty have reached a point that she can no longer endure. With our fingers laced together, we will take another shining journey and rejoin our beloved bairns.

With love and thanks,
Roderick and Edwina Galbraith

"I'm glad they weren't murdered," I managed. "But it's so sad that they died alone in a cave. I get it. But it's really sad."

"*Shh,*" Dr. Clark soothed as he hugged me.

Feeling his frailty under his sweater, I held him tightly, unable to stave off tears. Antoine embraced both of us, adding his warmth to my back as we conducted a memorial service that was over a hundred years too late, and for the usual sad reasons. Life was fleeting and often unfair. Their ages weren't listed, but I sensed that they'd died too young.

"Notre Père, qui es aux cieux, Que ton nom soit sanctifié," Antoine whispered, reciting the Lord's prayer in French.

Afterward, Bertrand carefully folded the letter and looked toward us for some means of keeping it safe. Antoine slipped it into an evidence bag and tucked it into an inside pocket of my vest.

"Vivian or Kick must have known about the map," I said. "Instead of buckling, you protected it with your life."

"I purchased the map long ago," Bertrand said. "I had a bill of sale, but Vivian contrived a false paper trail. She convinced the senior staff that it was the college's property. It was shocking. The facts were on my side. I thought decency would prevail, but I was wrong."

"You're not alone anymore," I said, clasping his hand. "I want to take photos of the couple. Is that ok with you?"

Once his eyes were covered, I got to work.

Less than a minute into my macabre assignment, I flinched as Bertrand gripped my arm. Antoine was braced and rigid as well as the faint rasp of footfalls echoed in the passageway beyond the secret door that separated us from the outer cave. Antoine caught my eye and clenched his fist, a signal that I took to mean absolute silence, then he wrenched up his sleeve and tapped a scar with a jagged shape.

F-e-a-t-h-e-r, Antoine spelled out with ASL.

I froze, unable to grasp why I'd imagined that in hearing an advance warning for once, the threat would leave us in peace.

Antoine cupped my face to hold my attention, and then he conveyed with a fierce gaze that even when caught off guard, he was prepared, a one-man special weapons and tactics team all on his own.

Dr. Clark tightened the laces of his shoes. Antoine followed suit and motioned for me to do the same. My gaze implored him to tell me he was overreacting. Surely it was Dan breaking his promise to let me handle the rescue on my own. Antoine signaled that Dan or any other ally would be calling out in order to find us as fast as possible.

As I sat there, frozen with terror, Antoine took over the task of tightening my laces. Dr. Clark was shoring up our defenses with a horizontal bar that he slipped through the loops that he'd used to pull the door into place. The wood could be bashed to pieces with enough force, but hopefully, it would be overlooked as part of the wall.

To Dr. Clark, Antoine mouthed in a sub whisper, "Is there a way to loop behind the foe? You'll come back and keep her safe?"

Tearfully, I held onto him and shook my head.

"Focus," Antoine mouthed, first motioning down with his hands, then flicking his fingers. "You must not cast light."

Cupping my headlamp to keep the light and noise to a minimum, he cycled through the settings, then when he removed his hand, the chamber was the blackest place I'd ever seen in my life. Antoine pulled me into a fierce hug, conveying silent apologies and regret over the awful moment, and then he kissed my cheek and slipped away.

Choking back sobs, I covered my mouth as their departure stirred a whisper of air through the chamber, and then I was alone.

After a minute of hearing nothing but my own heart, a clacking sound in the distance prompted the approaching footfalls to stop abruptly, and then rapidly head away. I pictured Antoine using a pebble or some other means of drawing the threat toward a spot of his choosing.

I squeezed my eyes shut, desperately hoping that Dan was still at a state police facility interrogating Kick. If he went against my wishes and came back, he would assume that all was well, no idea there was a threat lurking in the shadows. When I opened my eyes again, I realized that blinking and staring and all other aspects of having eyes had been rendered null and void. I couldn't see the hand in front of my face.

I drew strength from Dr. Clark's example of using drawings to build a world to live within, a story he could return to when he felt frightened and alone. I remembered one drawing of a tree with outward rays as if Bertrand had likened it to the sun. A landmark, I decided. Another drawing showed a house with swirling smoke coming out of the chimney. I was certain that once I studied the stick figures in every scene, Kick, my father, the farmers, and other people would be recognizable. The drawings amounted to a timeline. The need to bring his recollections to light helped counterbalance the terror I felt in the dark silence of the chamber.

I tensed and held my breath, hearing the soft rasp of boots through the wooden door, shifting here and there and getting closer. Instinct told me that it wasn't Antoine or Dr. Clark. The person was prowling through the outer chamber as if he was operating with animal cunning, sniffing out my hiding place the way a wolf might do.

My heart slammed, sparking agony as I stifled the desperate need for fresh gulps of air. Panic-stricken breathing would be audible.

His hands slid across the upper wall, a deadly caress, and then I heard his boots rasp in unison as if he'd knelt next to the door and turned his knees to one side. His fingers slid along the stone floor, sweeping lightly as he studied the dirt pattern. A red glow briefly seeped through the crack around the door, causing me to shake uncontrollably.

His fingers touched the wooden door and stopped.

"Qu'avons-nous ici?" he softly whispered.

I clenched my teeth to keep them from chattering.

"Ah … do I hear a rabbit's breath?" he murmured. "I have a sixth sense when it comes to fear. Why are you alone, little one?"

Shaking, staring into the blackness, I reached to my right and choked in pain as a sharp point stabbed my palm and drew blood. Had Dr. Clark experienced similar moments of terror and left a weapon to use? I carefully lowered my hand and felt a rough board or torn length of wood that he'd armed with a nail driven through one end.

"You were fearless the first times that we met," he said. "Now you are trapped without a stapler, a flip phone, or a devoted ally. A different feel, non? It is not easy to shock Antoine. I savor his distress."

His fingers were digging at the edges of the wooden door, clawing at the seam, and then an implement was employed, maybe the edge of a sharp knife. The bar rattled slightly against the loops but kept the seal tight. My molars ached from clenching my teeth, and my heart was thudding unevenly from my forced shallow breaths.

"Do you hear the faint clack in the distance?" the man whispered. "It is a trick that was used on me a moment ago. Now I am using it to ensure that we are alone. I heard you lift an item from the floor. It cut you. Jabbed you. A weapon you hope to use against me. I am braced for it. Are you braced for the result? The death of everyone you love?"

Trembling, I flung the board away, sparking a clatter of noise that might anger him, but would alert Antoine as well.

Shifting sounds told me the man was changing position.

An explosion of noise and splinters shocked me, and then his military-style boots slammed into my curled legs, red from his headlamp. Moaning and terrified, I rolled away and felt the cruel jab of a nail raking my thigh. Somehow, the board had bounced toward me after I'd flung it. Aware that he would kill every last person in his path no matter what I did, I carefully gripped the weapon and honed in on the boot that was shattering wood again and again as the man cleared the broken doorway.

Swiftly, I swung the board down with brutal force and felt the nail snag his leg and sink deep, possibly down to his shin bone.

With a choked-off curse, he wrenched his boot out of sight, along with the board, confirming my sense that it needed to be manually, painfully released. I used the split second to return the sunglasses to my face. I dug my flashlight from my belt, paused for a moment, terrified by the prospect of getting my arm sliced by his knife, and then I shoved the device through the hole, aimed upward, and hit the "on" button.

"*Merde*," he hollered.

I engaged my headlamp to the red setting and used my flashlight in quick bursts on my way to the couple's chamber, looking for a place to take cover if he crawled through. Behind me, there was a sharp click and then a canister swept toward me, expelling gas. I wrenched my shirt from my pants and used it as a mask as I continued scrambling, desperate to inhale, but knowing it would be the worst, and possibly the last thing I would do in my life. Thoughts of death sparked an idea. I dove forward, rolling into the grave area, and gripped the carpet bag with one hand.

Items clinked inside as I swung it down on the hissing canister, containing the gas, and then I tripped and scrambled toward the fissure that Antoine and Bertrand had used, teeth clenched, eyes wide, chest hurting, suffering cuts and lashes from the floor. With a burst of power, I lurched through the opening, nearly blacking out from holding my breath.

I lost the battle. I needed air.

Choking and wide-eyed, I inhaled a sharp burst of an acrid smell as I hit the wall and landed on a hard, unforgiving surface, with my sense of the cave further and further away, swirling in a red-tinted fog.

Dizzy and staggering, I collided with a gaunt figure.

"Not safe," he moaned.

"Yes, *run*," I managed. "It's not safe. It's … not …"

S

  a

   f

   e

   .

   .

   .

28

"Mayday! Mayday!" Antoine hollered into his radio, then in a softer tone, he said, "Monsieur Clark, she's fine. Only unconscious."

Shit, for real? Jeremy's voice squawked over Antoine's radio.

"We're near the upper entrance," Antoine reported. "Monsieur Clark, please don't run away. Monsieur *Clark!* Bon sang, c'est un cauchemar. Berrichon, if you could wake, that would be good."

My eyes rolled. I was aware of my arm being draped around Antoine's shoulders, and my boots dragging on the ground.

"W's going on …?" I managed.

"What knocked you out?" Antoine asked. "Did he jab you?"

"C-canister," I slurred. "Some kind of gas …"

"Of course. I'm smelling a hint of it."

Antoine slipped me to the ground and poured water into my eyes and mouth. Choking and sputtering, I motioned for him to stop.

"How much did you inhale?" he asked.

"I put the couple's carpet bag … over the canister."

"Thank God," he said. "Well done."

I rubbed my eyes. "Where is Dr. Clark?"

"I'll fetch him once you're safe," Antoine said.

"How can *any* of us be safe?" I asked.

"I am so desperately sorry," Antoine whispered. "He changed tactics, his whole approach. I don't know how, or why. I can't advise you," he said, cupping my chin. "I will try to engage him, get through to him, but I can't advise you on what to do. He will have set traps in the forest. I am *so* sorry. Now for the pep talk. You've been here before. You've faced the worst of the worst. It is possible to walk away from this."

"How?" I asked. "What does he want?"

"Chaos. Anguish in others. If he gets past me study him. Watch for hints and signs. His mind might be skewed by drugs."

"Antoine!"

Jeremy's voice echoed nearby, and then he was suddenly there to help carry me to the exit and hoist me to their shoulder height until Sal could haul me out of the cave. The crisp night air was enriching, coursing into my lungs. Jeremy climbed out and checked my eyes.

"Is she ok?" Antoine asked, having ascended the rope until he could brace himself on the rock edge of the opening.

"Looks like it," Jeremy said. "Her pupils are mostly normal."

"You know the rules," Antoine said.

Jeremy nodded. "Yeah, I've got it."

"Hang on," I said, clutching at Antoine's arm when he turned to look down. "Don't you dare go back. *Wait.*"

With his face set, Antoine released a brake on his line and descended with a zipping sound. I heard his boots land on the cave floor.

"What is he doing?" I whispered.

"He's getting the job done," Jeremy said. "Sal, walk her around a little while I keep an eye on Antoine's bodycam feed."

"You scared us for a minute," Sal said, steadying me as my swirling head and occasional missed steps revealed that I might have inhaled more of the gas than I'd thought. The trees had a distant quality, and my sense of my feet was off as if I'd been pumped full of helium.

"How is it that you're still here?" I managed.

"I'm an outlaw," Sal said. "With you still in the cave, I didn't want to leave. You've been good to me. Kind and understanding. So, when Dan told me to wait near the EMT van, I sort of ducked away."

"Nicole left as well?" I asked.

"She was *extremely* sour over the fact that you were a part of whatever was going on down there," Sal said. "She left in a huff."

"I suppose that's one blessing," I said.

Abruptly, Sal stopped and motioned for me to walk on my own for a minute. Frowning, he signaled for me to come back.

"You're tinkling in a weird way," he said.

I looked down, worried that getting knocked out had brought on an unfortunate bout of incontinence, but my pants were dry.

"He means you're jingling," Jeremy said.

"Oh … I assume it's the stuff in my tactical belt."

"Let's have a look," he said.

As Jeremy removed my belt and started opening the pouches, I stared in shock to see gold coins gleaming in the beam of Sal's light. Tucked into other pouches were treasures that ranged from costume jewelry to currency from the 1800s, including paper banknotes.

"Holy moly," Sal murmured. "Look at that."

"Dr. Clark must have put it there," I said. "According to his notes, a lot of these items were meant as goodwill offerings as the couple traveled from town to town. There's historical value in them, but it's not the hoard of riches people imagined. This belongs in a museum."

"Jeremy told me a thing or two about the bad guy," Sal said. "As a kid, he honed his quickdraw skills through paintball. As an adult, he uses the real deal. He fears and hates and admires Antoine as the ultimate adversary. Apparently, it's been going on for years."

"I drove a nail into the bad guy's shin," I said.

Jeremy gaped at me. "You did *what?*"

"He played a mind game, telling me the consequences of lashing out, but it was hard to hold back," I said. "I landed a blow."

"Hopefully, it'll slow him down," Jeremy said, studying his phone as it dinged. "Antoine's target alert just came through. I don't know who found who down there, but he's fighting with all he's got."

I snatched the phone from his hand and held up the screen in a way that allowed Jeremy and Sal to lean in and watch.

Growls and the tumbling noise of a fight made the phone vibrate in my hands, with blasts of red light as Antoine grappled with his foe face to face. Thuds, grunts, and swirls of motion told me that Antoine was using the narrow cave walls to right himself when flipped and press forward with rapid-fire counter moves. Choked-off words blurred into constant noise, making it impossible to know who was pummeling who.

Uufff. Arrrh.

A sharp *shing* indicated a knife being pulled from a sheath, and then Antoine was cursing and slamming his opponent's arm against the rock wall until the blade tumbled to the ground.

"Stop this madness," Antoine seethed.

"Madness needs a vent."

"Explain yourself," Antoine insisted. "Why this time?"

"J'ai raté ça," his foe snarled.

Amidst the swirls of red light, a blast of clarity showed Antoine's arm aiming his flashlight at his opponent's scrambling, retreating exit in the narrow cave, and then Antoine was chasing the awful man in a half-crouch, cursing as he knocked into unforgiving rock and then pushing onward. He caught up, pitching them into a tumbling tangle of angry, hard-hitting sounds, and then they were face to face again. I winced at the thuds of hard hits and body slams, the combatants growling *merde* and *bastard* and *asshole* without missing a beat. Abruptly, the rushing noise ended with one or the other delivering a blow with a hard object that had been hidden from view, maybe left to one side as a devious move.

It wasn't Antoine who'd pulled it off.

With a groan, he struggled upward and illuminated the fleeing man. Barely visible, his foe turned and appeared to smile.

"I bought you a ticket to hell!" the menace called out, slamming his palm against a small object on the wall. "Enjoy the ride!"

I jerked in shock as a grating tone shattered the night from the cave's entrance, as if it was a prison broadcasting an escape.

"Run for cover!" Jeremy hollered.

"What is it?" I asked.

"Whatever charge he used has a timer!"

I fought Jeremy's grip on my arm, desperate to help Antoine and Bertrand if they reached the opening. Jeremy snagged me around the waist as he dashed through the trees, and then he set me down to run on my own with his hand securing my belt when I stumbled.

All the while the warning buzzer blared through the forest, echoing against the hills where Dr. Clark and my father had once roamed in the spirit of adventure. Abruptly, Jeremy stopped running and whirled me down to the thick layer of fallen leaves. He dropped onto my back, breathing hard, and covered my head with his arms.

"We can't let this happen!" I hollered.

"I'm sorry," he managed. "It's too late."

From below my torso came a deep *whump*, a jarring, explosive shuddering of the ground, as if planet Earth's heart was pumping one last blast of life-giving blood to its extremities. Horrific tongues of orange light blasted overhead, and rocks pelted through the trees, shredding leaves and severing branches with savage speed. Not far away, a pine that had stood in place for the better part of a century split from its foundation and slowly toppled with splitting, cracking sounds, its upturned roots spraying dirt every which way until its massive trunk landed on the forest floor with a second horrific, bone-shattering *whump*.

The rain of debris grew fainter, from stones to pebbles, down to a fine rain of dirt. Last of all came the leaves, buoyed by air, until the only sound in my ringing ears was Jeremy's exhausted breathing.

"Good God," he said. "Are you ok?"

"Not if they didn't make it out," I moaned.

"Sal," Jeremy called out. "We talked about worst-case scenarios. We're in the red zone. You know what to do."

"Yes, Sir," Sal said. "You can count on me."

Watching him jog away through the trees, I staggered to my feet and found myself face to face with Jeremy's intense gaze.

"I'm going to do the unthinkable and leave you on your own," Jeremy said. "You're *not* on your own. I'll be in position. There's always a plan, but—" Jeremy closed his eyes. "You'll want to crash around and see if you can find Antoine and Bertrand. Make sure to steer clear of the blast zone. We can't know if any of the explosives are still active."

"Dan is going to freak out …"

"Sonny." Jeremy grasped my face with both hands. "Get a grip and do what you do. Think. Strategize. Survive."

"Get a grip," I said. "Got it."

Jeremy pointed. "That way is best."

On shaky legs, I followed his instructions and cut a path through the forest, tripping over sticks with the night air sawing in and out of my lungs. He'd warned me to steer clear of the blast zone, but that didn't make sense. I had to search the rubble for signs of Antoine and Dr. Clark. Everywhere I looked were broken branches and stones turned upside down, ruining the beautiful moss and lichen. Raymond would be appalled, having estimated that some of the lichens in the region were hundreds of years old.

"Antoine?" I hollered, coming to a halt.

The forest was silent, etched by moonlight. I cast about for signs of Sal and Jeremy. Had they fallen into a hole?

Now it was necessary to call out to four missing men. Breathless, with a thudding heart, I held my light with a trembling hand, making a racket with every step. My beam caught a flash of movement, and for a split second, I thought Antoine was stepping from the shadows. It was a man who was built like Antoine, dressed in black and outfitted with a sidearm and gear, but with a face that I couldn't have dreamed up in my worst nightmares: painted with a camouflage pattern that obscured his features into a confusing plane of shapes that would not be easy to identify.

Limping slightly, Antoine's nemesis stepped to within ten feet of me and then signaled to me to close the distance between us.

I stayed put. If I wasn't mistaken, there was a flicker of complexity in the man's eyes, as if he'd suddenly caught onto the downside of eliminating his lifelong foe. No more chances to conduct his twisted version of fun and games. His world revolved around greed and vice and inflicting pain in others. Cheating, gambling, and hollow victories.

"I just earned myself a new nickname," he said, indicating the exploded cave. "Tison, French for firebrand. What do you think?"

"You want me to call you that?" I said dismally.

"Think it, say it. It's who I am now."

"Pain doesn't matter to you," I murmured.

"Of course it does," he said, thinking I was talking about physical pain as it related to him. "Antoine always lands damage, but I guess that's over with." Tison popped a pill into his mouth. "Want one?"

"No."

As he tossed a pill toward me anyway, I shifted my shoulders and let it pass harmlessly by and land amidst the leaves.

Tison folded his arms and studied me. "In billiards, job one is knocking the balls into motion. Again and again, you tipped the table and ruined my aim. Gerald was meant to vanish for all time to come. A disgrace to the police. Vivee was careless … uh-oh, you look upset."

"Because of the way she talked about you," I said.

"Do tell," Tison said, smiling. "I would love to know."

"Sadly, she's not here to speak for herself," I said.

"What is it from, your fierceness and bold gaze?" he asked.

"My father was an asshole," I said.

"Monsieur French?" he said. "Surely not."

"Donald Littlefield."

"Ahh, that explains a thing or two."

He tensed and looked to my right. Amidst the debris that had landed in the area from the blast, I tuned in on groaning sounds and saw Antoine's soot-darkened hands and sleeves shoving rubble aside as he crawled from the ground as if he was emerging from the grave.

"Excellent," Tison said, looking upward. "Asshole lurking in the tree. Come and help the poor man. You know I've rigged surprises in the forest. You've got a damsel here. Toss your weapons."

The snapping of branches drew my gaze to Jeremy emerging from a perch in a white pine and landing amidst the leaves with a thud. With a glare, he tossed his rifle away, and his sidearm as well.

"Hurry up," Tison said.

Jeremy pulled stones from the hidden entrance, helping Antoine first, and then they joined forces to haul Bertrand from the ground. Once the frail archaeologist was tucked against a tree, afraid and wide-eyed, Antoine gripped the water bottle Jeremy handed to him, dumped half of it on his upturned face, and then gulped down the rest of the water in a couple of swigs. Blinking away droplets, he stared at Tison.

"What now?" he prompted.

"In front of God and these witnesses, admit that it got to you, letting Isaac off the hook," Tison said. "You saw his connection to a Maine state trooper and thought, *finally*, I can upend his life."

Antoine massaged his brow, cursing in French, and then he looked at his nemesis with a mix of exhaustion and despair.

"That's what this is about?" he asked.

"Admit it. Confess your sins."

"You're quite wrong," Antoine said.

Tison pointed at him, seething with outrage. "Chloé stole heroin from my stash. I didn't plan it. Isaac dumped her when she was in a fragile state, but I was the one who went to prison."

"You're a drug dealer," Antoine said. "You broke the law."

"Luring that trooper up north proves you're not impervious to wrongdoing," Tison said. "I'm not leaving until you admit it."

"You're in luck. I think this property is for sale."

"Don't joke with me asshole," Tison hollered. "We were tight as kids. You, me, and Chloé. We got slapped together and starved together. What kind of person destroys his own family?"

"You're *not* my family, and you were the one to slap me," Antoine said. "Move on. You've let me keep my weapon for a reason."

"Yeah, here and now," Tison said. "Final showdown."

"Excuse me," I said, motioning with my hands. "I can see where this is heading. I assume I can have a last request?"

Under the glare of their disbelieving eyes, I realized the gas I'd inhaled might have dislodged me from normal priorities, like shivering in terror. Shock factored in as well. The sensation of being pumped full of helium was still in play as I pointed to the upturned rock.

"Can someone help with this?" I asked. "It's driving me crazy to know the lichen is getting crushed. It's hundreds of years old."

"Are you insane?" Tison asked.

"She's in shock," Antoine said. "With all your sins, I've never known you to gun down a woman. Let her go."

"I'm not going anywhere until this is fixed," I said.

With that, I knelt and struggled to move the smooth rock that had sat in place for eons. Left in the wake of a glacier, maybe. Tears arrived as my hands slipped on the muddy half, and then Jeremy pitched in and rolled the fifty-pound weight until the lichen was exposed. I took his water bottle and washed away the dirt. The ancient life form responded immediately, greening up, still fixed to the stone by tiny filaments.

"Your face paint reminds me of a tiger's stripes," I told Tison. "It's confusing because I dream of photographing tigers in the wild. Elephants as well. They're awesome up close. They weigh up to eight tons, but their feet are cushioned. They're graceful and gentle."

"Can you please shut up?" Tison asked.

"I'm explaining why I needed to fix the rock," I said tearfully. "Lichen doesn't have a voice. It's not beautiful like a tiger or a bird, but it's a vital form of life. Somebody has to step up for lichen. It was my father's passion for a long while. Now the job has fallen to me."

As I spoke, Antoine had stepped closer to his nemesis. Abruptly, the advantage was over. Their glaring match continued, and once again, I was too fed up with my hard luck to tremble with fear.

I stood and brushed dirt from my hands.

"Can I tell you a story?" I asked.

"I'm about to break my rule around women," Tison said darkly.

"In Costa Rica," I persisted, "I was hiking on a trail in the rainforest. A guide pointed out an eyelash viper perched on a low bank next to a hole where a bird had nested. Apparently, the viper would wait, and wait, and wait until its prey returned, no matter how long it took."

"This is dull," Tison said. "You're telling *my* story."

"No, it's about how things will unfold if you don't step away without causing further harm," I said softly. "To kill one of us, you'll need to kill all of us. If I don't come out of this alive, I will be the pit viper for the rest of your days, hounding you as a phantom. Ask around. Shit happens to people who cross me. As a ghost, I'll pull the wind through your ears like a pair of ice tongs. Even now, it's answering my call."

Nearby, a moan stirred upward, not from magic or enchantments. The cave had been drawing air all along, but it was only then that Tison noticed it because he'd relied on pills to ease his pain instead of toughing it out. I also saw Sal in a hidden spot, aiming a rifle at Tison's back. Even in his ballistic vest, a single direct shot to Tison's torso would drop him long enough for Antoine, Jeremy, and I to launch an assault.

"This is a first," Tison said. "I have gooseflesh."

"Nature's whisper," I said. "Let it guide you."

With sirens wailing in the distance, Tison simmered with menace as he unfastened his sidearm. Behind him, Sal disengaged his rifle's safety with an audible click that cut through the forest.

Tison sighed. "You ruin the game yet again."

"Focus on tomorrow, the next day," I said.

"Your talents are wasted here, Berrichon," he said. "You're chided and curbed, used and then shoved aside. I see potential in you."

I paused. "This is a job interview?"

"An upgrade-your-life interview," Tison said.

"It's a hard no."

"I'll be back when you least expect it," he said.

"The standard line," I said. "We hear you."

"*Sonny*," Jeremy hissed.

Casting a dark look toward Sal's hidden spot, Tison walked backward a stretch of paces, and then he checked his wrist for a heart-stopping moment, alluding to unseen allies or hidden tricks. With a parting glare at Antoine, he turned and jogged past the ruins of the cave.

"I'm dying to nail the bastard once and for all," Jeremy growled. "But it's too dangerous to act with Sonny and Dr. Clark here, and the fact that he left this easily means he set up traps."

"His path will be the only safe route," Antoine agreed.

With tree trunks in the way, we stepped to one side or the other to make note of the exact path the fleeing nemesis was taking through the forest. Still clearly in view, he plowed through one of the puddles on the property with a splash of boots landing in five inches of water. With a choked-off growl, he began vibrating in place for a moment, twitching and confused, and then he dropped to his hands and knees.

"What the hell?" Jeremy breathed.

"Stay put in case it's a trick," Antoine said.

With guttural sounds and growls, the nightmare of the hour appeared to be returning to hell, the awful realm where his merciless spirit had come from. His thrashing faded to a quiet rustle of leaves, and a stirring of water, and then the dark forest was silent and utterly still.

"Holy shit," Jeremy said. "He got it wrong."

"He got what wrong?" I asked.

"The compass bearing. Either he landed in his own trap, or his gear is reacting to the water. Whatever the cause there might be an electrical current over there. It'll take a drone to figure it out."

"He's definitely not moving," I said. "The puddle he landed in is ice cold. He would be shivering. We'd see and hear it."

"This has a dreamlike quality," Antoine murmured. "I was in a coma one time. It felt like this, physical pain and weirdness. I might have inhaled some of that gas from the canister. I can still taste it."

Seeing his level of shock, Jeremy held up a heart locket on a fine chain. As the pendant sparkled in the moonlight, casting gold glints into my eyes, I wondered if hypnosis was an element of Antoine's recovery system after the hard physical punishments of his job.

"You wanted this on your coffin if the worst happened," Jeremy said. "I'm off the hook for that unpleasant task."

"This is a dream," Antoine whispered. "I'm dead."

"He's the one who's dead," I said. "You can finally move on."

Antoine allowed the fine chain to be draped across his palm. With brimming eyes, a wounded, world-weary version of the youth who'd stood above Chloé's grave, Antoine choked and devolved into sobs.

When I started to slip away, he engulfed me so tightly that I couldn't breathe, shaken to the core by his vivid emotion.

"This shouldn't have fallen on you," he managed. "If I could reverse time and *not* take down his awful family ..."

"We made it," I said. "We're safe."

"You can't imagine my terror, knowing what he might do," Antoine said. "I felt the warning signal in my bones. Harsh and loud, like every wrong turn. He was bound to change tactics. I was a fool not to see it."

"He's gone," I said. "We're safe."

"Fate is never kind," Antoine said.

"It is now and then," I said. "Here we are, living proof."

"He's left a wake of death and destruction for over a decade," Antoine said, pacing away a few steps and rubbing his face. "Arms dealing, bank heists, always one step ahead of the law. He can't have been undone by *lichen*. My mind is shot. His punch rattled something."

"Focus on my voice," I said. "The night air."

Abruptly, Antoine kissed me, a scorching moment that tasted of fallen leaves and exploded cave. Dizzied, I leaned away.

"Ok, that's not cool," I managed.

"It doesn't matter," he said. "We're dead."

"Dude, let's walk it off," Jeremy said, prying me loose and taking over the task of hauling Antoine's shocked, blown-up mind into the reality he was facing: one less enemy was on planet Earth.

I stared for a moment, lost in thought, then as my phone dinged with alarmed texts from Dan, I found it more restful to watch Dr. Clark talking to his wife on Jeremy's phone. Even from a distance, I heard the excited squealing of Bertrand's sons coming through the device.

"That's nice," I said. "I'm glad for them."

"Gosh," Sal said, gingerly patting my arm. "You've had quite a week. I totally got the reference to the ice tongs. Gerald is up there smiling." Sal blinked away tears. "I'm grateful, Sonny."

"I don't suppose you can call Dan for me," I said.

"It's best you cover that angle," Sal said guardedly. "Jeremy made some confusing comments about wrangling with a supernatural foe, but if it happens, he's got an ace in the hole. We all do."

When I stared blankly, Sal motioned with one hand.

"You, dummy. A supernatural friend."

29

For the third consecutive morning, Dan and I were lingering in bed at 6:30 a.m. for all the wrong reasons. Absently, he played with my curls, and finally, as Luke yawned on the floor, I stirred and sighed.

"Is it the same concern, or something new?" I asked.

"It's tough to move on without knowing the specifics of how the guy's gear went haywire," Dan said. "He was smart and tactical. Nicole thinks it stemmed from battle fatigue. That's a relief."

"Because she's *always* right," I murmured.

"I want to believe Antoine didn't set it up," Dan insisted. "They're in a phase where she's seeing him with the blinders off."

To allow for private conversations during the rescue operation, our bodycam had cut out for short periods. Detective Allen and others on the lumbering law enforcement bus were slow to admit that Antoine's gear had provided crisp footage of every *critical* event.

I didn't want to start the day on a bad note, since Dan had been endeavoring to not end the day on a bad note. Instead of coming straight to bed, he sat downstairs, completing paperwork and writing notes.

"What's up?" he softly prompted.

"Things are weird," I said. "Tell me I'm wrong."

Dan shifted position so he faced me with his head propped up by his hand, and then he brushed his fingers over my cheek.

"When I saw the footage of you using strategy to throw the guy off, it was a moment of awe," Dan said. "Then I was steamed at Antoine. Then I dropped into terror for you. I don't like feeling helpless."

"That's why you've been quiet for days?" I asked.

"Unlike some people in the room, I'm slow to process complex feelings and events." Dan dropped a kiss on my lips. "I'm due at the blast site on the early side. What's your game plan today?"

"Curating my photos, then I'm meeting the realtor at Aaron's house at the end of the day." I studied Dan's face. "Once Dr. Clark recovers, maybe we can team up to create a museum dedicated to the 1800s couple and their artifacts. The turtle sanctuary as well."

"It's a great idea for whoever buys the property," Dan said. "What else has you looking worried? I can tell there's more."

"I heard you on the phone last night," I said.

Dan hesitated. "Oh?"

"Kevin is on your case about your dim prospects of a happy life with me," I said. "Should I bow out of meeting the realtor?"

"It's my call," Dan said. "Stop letting his attitude get to you."

While Dan showered and shaved, I followed Luke down the stairs and let him outside, and I got breakfast basics underway.

With a mug of coffee warming my hands, I sat on the porch with my feet on the top stair and basked in the shimmering rays of dawn. A clatter came from behind me as Dan grabbed a plate from the cupboard and set about warming chocolate croissants in the toaster oven.

Once the sun had risen to the point where its rays reached its fingers into the gloom at the bottom of the hill, mist began stirring upward from the stream, as had been happening all week. On that same date last year, Raymond had described the predictable north-south noodle of mist as a serpent waking from a nap. His own personal cloud.

Within three months of that note, he would be dead.

Arriving with a cup of coffee, a journal, and a plate of warmed croissants, Dan sat next to me and spent a minute petting Luke, who alternated between panting and looking hopefully toward the pastries, and chomping his lobster toy until it squeaked.

"One of your father's musings caught my eye," Dan said, offering the journal. "I flagged the page. It's halfway down."

Raymond wrote, *To pass the time when I couldn't fall asleep last night, I counted up the thoughts I'd cranked through in the dark. Let's say I had a thought per minute for eight hours. That's 480 thoughts I'd wrangled with before dawn. Add up my 16 waking hours, we're up to 1,440 thoughts I'll churn out in a single day. Some folks I talk to will get a few sentences out of me at most. When Ella was alive the notions that I shared didn't begin to reflect what had gone on in my mind. I've got to communicate more. Step up my game.*

While I read, Dan focused on pondering the sunrise.

"This feels kind of familiar," I said.

"I read it thinking Raymond's estimate is a minimum range this week," Dan said. "Upstairs, I caught onto your worry about it."

"It'll get better, right?" I asked. "Once we're past this phase?"

"Define phase," Dan said.

"You talked about quitting. Not wanting to be a cop."

"I can't leave a lot of loose ends for my colleagues to resolve," he said. "There will always be a form of survivor's guilt."

I plucked at a hangnail as he continued eating, unable to arrive at non-problematic wording to address how it felt to land in the crosshairs of his colleagues on a random basis. My friends supported Dan without question. I wished he wasn't too busy to see the imbalance.

"Well, I'm off to the blast site," he said.

"It's alarming how normal that's starting to sound," I said.

"We'll settle back into our version of normal," Dan said, not quite nailing an assuring gaze. "I don't know if we can swing a whole week, but we'll get away for a bit. A long weekend, ok?"

"Name the time," I said. "I can be ready in five minutes."

With a parting kiss, he gripped the rest of the croissant in his teeth to dig out his keys, carrying his coffee in his free hand, and then climbed into his truck. Soon, when my neighbors were back and my friend, Arlene, returned from her glorious trip to China, my heart would be pulled every which way, with Dan's parents proposing a giant gathering, and Arlene proposing a giant gathering, and my neighbor proposing a giant gathering, and *my* mind proposing a get-out-of-town plan.

With Luke bounding here and there, sniffing scent trails, I crossed the driveway to greet Dodge as he thudded toward me across the frosty grass. I paused and savored the scent of the timothy and clover hay that I tossed into the paddock, a burst of summer sweetness. On my way back to the house, I stopped in my tracks to see Antoine on my porch, admiring the view with a croissant and a cup of coffee in hand.

"Lovely morning," he said around a mouthful.

Despite the chilly morning, he'd arrived out of the mist in the usual dark, button-up shirt that highlighted his physique, and threadbare jeans that somehow never split apart. He regarded the long view as if he hadn't a care in the world, his bold features awash with morning light.

"Spanish blend?" he said of the coffee.

"Where have you been?" I asked.

"Here and there," Antoine said. "Doing this and that."

"I've been worried about you," I said, folding my arms as he continued to eat. "How are you? Be straight with me."

With a sigh, Antone pulled a crystalline marble from his pocket and held it out between his thumb and forefinger.

"My foe was thrown a curve ball," he said. "Around this size. Secret and contained, wedged into his amygdala. It was found during the autopsy. Headaches must have alerted him in recent months."

"Hence, the change you sensed in him?" I asked.

"Maybe," Antoine said. "It's telling how different we turned out. Not just criminal versus cop. I thrive on merging my mind with my hands and on knowing how things work. Tison preferred to delegate. When his crew was nabbed, he charged in anyway, with half-learned technical knowledge, driven by the need for revenge. He paid the price."

"I know your way involves dark brooding and alone time," I said softly. "It's ok to come up for air and relax now and then. I've heard Scotland has misty moors and a low crime rate. Lots of sheep as well. Not Mongolia, of course. It's too touristy this time of year."

"Stop taunting a lesser being," Antoine said, sitting down and patting the adjacent spot. "We have a matter to discuss."

"Raymond's death?" I asked. "I've decided to put it aside."

"Nonsense, you're a spaniel," Antoine said. "Born to plunge into a churning river if that is what it takes to follow a trail."

With a sigh, I sat down next to him and fiddled with a sprig of pine needles that had drifted from the stand of trees at the bottom of the driveway along the road. I pictured it twirling in the air, buoyed by a breeze for two hundred yards, and then hitting an obstacle like the porch roof. That was how my expectations felt at that moment.

"Dan is a little shut down, so it's necessary to tap the brake on what I need for a while," I said. "Plus, Isaac is painting the events in the cave as an illegal sting operation. It's stressful and unfair."

"It won't work thanks to Gerald," Antoine said. "Bless the man, he kept detailed man-hour records of the mining operation, with screenshots of the notes to ensure a business approach. He and Sal knew Kick was their secret boss. It's icing on the crime cake."

"I know it'll settle out," I said. "We'll get there."

Antoine took the liberty of securing a stray curl and smoothing it in place where it belonged. For once, there wasn't a flirtatious element in the gesture. He looked troubled and concerned.

"What about your needs, Berrichon?" he asked. "If someone has an inkling of who killed your father, how will you handle it?"

"It's a moot point," I said. "The trail is cold."

"Not for a fellow spaniel," Antoine said softly.

I stared at him. "You know who it is?"

"If you dive in to flush them out, there would be no turning back," he said. "They are likely to respond with force."

"I've been there," I said. "I know what you mean."

"Strict secrecy would be necessary," Antoine cautioned.

Hearing this condition stated out loud, I felt my stomach curl around the croissant like a clenched fist. Dan and I allowed each other some slack when it came to sharing our inner turmoil. Antoine was talking about a campaign of lies. In the end, no matter how I spun my reasoning, the truth would be plain. It would amount to my stubborn streak. My rebellious streak. My refusal to comply with what was expected of me at the expense of pursuing a goal, whatever the risk to myself.

"You're not ready," Antoine said softly.

"Things will smooth out in a month," I said.

"I won't be here in a month," Antoine said.

"How certain are you?" I asked. "Ninety percent?"

"Your turmoil is painful to watch, Berrichon."

I stared in confusion as Antoine set his coffee mug on the table and descended the porch steps in his sneakers.

"No basics?" I asked. "Like where to stage things?"

"I will check in again before I leave town," he said.

"What if I change my mind?" I asked.

He tossed a flip phone over his shoulder. I caught it in midair.

"What do I say if it rings?" I asked.

"Hello."

"It's not connected to a store?" I asked, staring as he neared the logging trail next to the barn. "No advice or parting words?"

"Enjoy your day," he said. "In case it's your last."

"That's not funny," I said. "*Antoine.*"

His shirt, ponytail, and tight-fitting jeans merged with the shadows, and then it was as if he hadn't been there at all.

* * *

Summoned to the Corner Pocket, I was startled to see Jeremy stocking shelves instead of disappearing into his role as an undercover cop. At the sound of the bell jingling over the door, Sue and Kate closed in and signaled for Jeremy to join us in the shelter of the bread aisle.

"We're fed up," Sue announced.

"I'm sorry for not stopping in," I said.

"Not with you, dummy," she said. "We heard Roy is poised to ply you with more questions. Enough is enough."

"If it means resolving things fast—"

"*Shh*, here he is," Kate said. "Follow our lead."

With her red hair in a tight chignon, a different look from her usual carefree style, Kate directed Roy to the coffee area. Flanking me as I sat down at a round table, she and Sue signaled to Roy that he should sit on the opposite side. The detective hesitated and glanced at Jeremy, who stood with his arms folded and a scowl intact in front of a wall that featured watercolors and other local artwork.

"Actually, I need a private word with Sonny," Roy said.

"Never again," Sue said. "Not on our watch."

Glancing at the shoppers who'd paused to study us with curious stares, Roy motioned for peace and calm as he sat down.

Kate leaned forward. "It's a little-known fact that I was an attorney in Connecticut before I met Sue and moved to Maine. I am now licensed to practice here. If she's willing, Sonny is my first client." Receiving my nod, she continued, "Multiple cold cases under your watch have slammed into Sonny, tanking her ability to exist peacefully in this town. Her strength can turn into her weakness. A bold gaze and refusal to be treated unfairly is a trigger for certain cops. All the while, Sonny has extended trust to the Maine State Police without seeking representation."

"All right," Roy said. "I hear you—"

"Good, because I'm only getting started."

While I looked on with wide eyes, Sue and Kate delivered a blistering assessment of how I'd been treated like a problem instead of a victim, harshly questioned in the wake of trauma multiple times, and stripped of my rights with zero concern for my welfare.

"Now, hang on," Roy said.

"As in this instance," Jeremy said, stepping forward to slide a printed photo onto the table: a shot that had been taken over my shoulder in the ambulance as I'd read Roy's note that left me with no other option than to accompany him to a conference room. "Sonny no sooner crawled out of her trashed car when you exploited her fear of hospitals."

"Given the nature of the attack on the road—"

"Is this your handwriting, Sir?" Jeremy asked.

"Sonny looked fine," Roy managed.

"I am a top cop," Jeremy said. "Don't lie to my face."

"Where did you get this photo?" Roy asked.

"A concerned EMT," Jeremy said. "Instead of letting him do his job and check Sonny for injuries, you pushed him aside."

"Ok, golly," I said. "Let's calm things down."

"There you go, she's tossing you a lifeline at her own expense," Jeremy said. "Antoine and I strongly object to your methods."

"Jeremy, calm down," I said.

"That's not his name," Roy pointed out.

"It sure as hell is, official as of today," Jeremy said. "Look it up."

"Again," I said carefully. "Sue and Kate, Jeremy as well, it's thanks to you that I've landed on my feet these past few days. If I can help get the case resolved, I'm happy to pitch in."

"That just got recorded," Kate said, pointing to the security camera. "Sonny asking for calm, despite how she's been treated."

Roy's expression reflected a laborious effort to dial down his usual tough demeanor. He turned to me with a smile.

"I apologize for any instances where you felt—"

"Thank you," I said. "What do you need?"

The detective laced his fingers on the table. "Dr. Clark is mistrustful of the police. It's no wonder. We failed him. As a consequence, he is being 'forgetful' around certain critical points, like where he got the rock sample that he gave to the geologist. Thoughts, anyone?"

"Unbelievable," Kate said. "You want Sonny to ask him."

"I won't do that," I said. "When he became a target, his only ally was Raymond. On top of that, we're talking about an age-old issue in the larger sense, people going nuts in order to make short-term gains. At some point, we need to stop gutting our precious world."

"Again, witnessed and recorded," Kate said. "Next topic."

While Roy sat there looking sour, I returned to the worry that the sample had come from the turtle sanctuary. I wouldn't budge on the point as long as Dan co-owned the land with two deeply flawed men.

"You're stewing over a detail," Roy prompted.

"She's not obligated to say anything," Kate said.

"Let's try this approach," Roy said. "You exited the cave with treasure in your pockets. Help me not see the arc as a scheme that a cagy undercover cop set up to kill his enemy and get rich."

I gaped. "You can't imagine …"

"I'm willing to believe Dr. Clark put the treasure in your pockets," Roy said. "I need to hear it in his own words, and soon."

"You've got *every* item from my pockets, and most of it is costume jewelry," I said. "Antoine almost died because he stayed in the cave to save Bertrand. To think otherwise is outlandish."

Roy shrugged. "It's hard to know for sure."

"All right, I'm shutting this down," Kate said.

"No, I've got this," I said furiously. "Do you recall the conference room, Roy? Your team cheering when I delivered evidence? Seriously, how fickle, stubborn, and blind can you be? Raymond would blast you for it. In fact, maybe you had a grudge against him because he was always one step ahead of you day in and day out. It's got me wanting to start from scratch. Where were you the night that Raymond died?"

Now it was Roy gaping at me. "You can't be serious."

"*Answer* the question," I seethed.

"You want my schedule spelled out?" Roy asked.

"To the letter," I agreed. "Jeremy, you'll take over?"

Smiling, he said, "Yes, Ma'am."

I hugged Sue and Kate, glared at Haydn Pike eavesdropping nearby as I crossed to the entrance, and pulled out the flip phone.

"I'm in," I said. "Let's get it done."

Antoine pointed out that I hadn't even made it until noon.

"It's been in motion for months," I said. "The pan is hot now, and I just outed myself as the problem to neutralize."

"Indeed," he said. "I witnessed the exchange."

"No time like the present. What's the plan?"

30

Once the realtor stepped from Aaron's house into the twilight, I crossed into the kitchen, where I'd left a photo of Aaron with a twinkling votive candle illuminating his face. Dan appreciated my plan of leaning into his best friend's memory as a selling point for the house: a first responder and deputy who'd devoted his life to keeping others safe. For now, I blew out the flame, casting a thin plume of smoke into the air.

"I'm heading home," I said in case Antoine was listening. "The realtor was late. You probably know that. To be clear, I do *not* want your mystery plan to unfold on the road in the truck that Dan renovated for me. The rollbar is a theoretical, worst-case addition."

I opened the door and collided with Isaac Munroe standing on the stoop in a crisp shirt, dress slacks, and expensive shoes.

"Steady," he said when I lurched back. "Can we talk inside?"

"Here?" I asked. "I'm not sure this is the right setting."

Isaac looked at me sideways. "For what, exactly?"

"Sorry," I said. "I'm tired after a long day."

Glancing toward the darkening windows, I retreated to the kitchen and put the island countertop between us before I faced him.

"I heard you put Roy Allen on his heels today," he said. "You and Isaac Junior have taken Dr. Clark's place as scapegoats."

"It's a complicated case," I said.

"Sonny, Dan isn't in your corner as much as you imagine," Isaac said. "He's two-timing you with the Canadian chick."

"You're trying to get under my skin," I said.

"Look at the imbalance on display here," Isaac said with a sweeping gesture indicating the house. "You've put your own priorities on hold to help Dan. Meanwhile, he's playing cop games up north. From Kick's perspective, it looked fishy. Out of concern, he set out to expose Dan as a corrupt cop. This nightmare is the result."

"Let's delve into how Raymond shamed you in public for teaming up with Vivian after she fired Dr. Clark," I said. "He took you to task on your own turf for exploiting Bertrand's hard luck."

"That's ancient news," Isaac said tiredly. "Dan is pulling it out of the shadows to pin your father's death on either me or my son. Meanwhile, Dan didn't tell you he put handcuffs on Raymond. Haydn Pike told me how shocked you were when he mentioned it."

Just then, Dan opened the door and stepped in with a disgusted look aimed at Isaac. I flipped my hands, foiled from completing my mission before I'd had a chance to regroup.

"Isaac, you were warned not to approach Sonny," Dan said.

"I didn't know it was her truck outside," Isaac said.

"This won't help your cause," Dan said. "Show some sense."

Once Isaac was escorted to his car, I was confused when Dan returned with Nicole, who looked pleased by my distress.

"My life is imploding," I said. "What's going on?"

"Antoine is meeting us an hour north of here," Dan said. "I was about to text you when I saw Isaac's car heading this way."

I blinked. "You're meeting Antoine tonight?"

"Yeah, it's last minute," Dan said. "He has intel to share."

"That's not possible," I said. "It doesn't make sense."

"I told you how she would react," Nicole cut in. "She's stung because Antoine didn't include her in the meeting."

"Please don't add to it," Dan said. "Give me a minute."

For the first time, I saw how he talked to her, with a pleading glance befitting a trusted confidant. Nicole's cat eyes cut toward me to see if I'd noticed it, and then she smiled on her way out.

"What was that?" I asked, knocked breathless.

"She takes jabs at everybody, and so does Isaac," Dan said. "I heard him putting a spin on my encounter with Raymond."

"We're here," I said. "Explain it now."

"You know your father drank for a stretch," Dan said softly. "He threw a punch in a bar. I responded to the call. Hearing his story, seeing his pain, I removed the cuffs and called a friend to pick him up." Dan shrugged. "There never seemed a right time to tell you."

"Did you resent Raymond?" I asked. "Murder him?"

"Did I *murder* him?" Dan said. "Of course not."

"Then we're done," I said. "Next candidate, please."

"I'm sure there's a reason for this mystifying tangent," Dan said wryly. "But Nicole and I are running late. I need to go."

"Here, take these back." I tossed him the keys to the truck. "A lot more than my car got trashed this past week, and Nicole was a major part of it. You promised not to buy into her crap, which makes the truck feel like a quick fix to mask a hidden problem."

"This is Isaac's fault," Dan said. "He got under your skin."

"It's not Isaac," I said. "It's you. It's me. It's us."

I tried to stop, for all the good it did because all 1,440 thoughts of the day were whirling through my head in a matter of seconds.

"How crazy is it that Antoine's nemesis saw my pain?" I asked. "The rocky road I've experienced with your colleagues. You spend all day with people who trash how I operate, and then you sit in my living room, alone, to get your mixed-up feelings sorted out. There's a new dynamic where I feel starved for connection unless we're in bed, and even that's derailed by your concerns around the case. We're living a glossed-over version of who we were a few weeks ago. I'm tapped out."

Dan looked breathless, as I must have done a moment ago.

"Wow, when you decide to share, you really share," he said.

"At least you're *hearing* from me," I said furiously. "The night your house was attacked you disappeared. In some senses, you haven't come back. Undercover Dan isn't retired. He's standing in front of me, which means you truly are a better match for Nicole."

"I've told you again and again—" Dan closed his eyes. "All right, here's the thing you don't know. She's the one who recruited me up north. You can't imagine how it felt to trade my anguish for a gig that truly mattered. She's been committed to closing off whatever went wrong to bring it here. If she's intense at times, that's what it's about."

I waited for Dan to experience an ah-ha moment, but he didn't grasp that Nicole might have recruited him because of his connection to Isaac. I pictured Antoine reacting with shock however many months ago. Far from impressing him, Nicole had saddled him with the need to return Dan to safe ground with minimal damage. Antoine had kept it a secret to avoid sparking trouble. For now, I needed to do the same.

"Sonny?" Dan prompted. "You're finally hearing me?"

"Yes," I managed. "I hear you."

"I hear you as well," Dan said, responding to my softer tone. "We have issues to sort out, but I can't promise it'll happen tonight. In the meantime, I'm not out for a joyride. I'm trying to resolve the case to the best of my ability, and escape the undercover stint for good." Dan tossed the keys to me. "You seem to forget that you need a set of wheels."

"Of course," I said. "Silly me."

"That was a southpaw catch," Dan said.

"Go to your meeting," I said. "Drive safely."

Concern touched his brow as if he sensed that he was misreading my quick smile, and then he stepped out and closed the door.

In the stillness, after Dan's headlights slipped from the front windows and the rush of tires faded down the road, I relit the votive candle and watched its soft, flickering light play over Aaron's face. What would he say to Dan after witnessing our back-and-forth? What would he say to me? Would he take a side, or advise us both to move on?

I choked and blinked back tears, wishing I'd stayed in Boston where I was disillusioned and lonely, but still had a functioning heart in my ribcage, and wasn't trashed from a lover's turbulent past.

I groaned as the power shut off, plunging me into darkness.

"Thanks for the support," I said. "Really nice."

I pulled the flip phone from my pocket, pressed the call button, and was greeted by silence instead of a dial tone. The only missing element was an announcement that another ghost was in the wings.

"I'm back to being miffed at you," I said, rummaging in drawers for a flashlight. "Apparently, you double-booked yourself."

I headed for the basement to check the circuit breaker and then halted as the beam from my flashlight touched the step where Nicole had sent me into a painful tumble. Behind me, twinkling lights said the rest of the neighborhood had power. Only Aaron's house was dark.

The votive in the kitchen flickered as the front door opened, letting in a wash of cold air, and then a floorboard creaked.

"Sonny?" Kevin said. "Why is the power off?"

"I don't know," I said. "It just happened."

As we met in the kitchen, Kevin shined his flashlight on the photo I'd left on the countertop, then he aimed the beam at me.

"I saw you come from the basement just now," he said. "You're not very bright if you think darkness will give you an advantage."

I paused. "Are you drunk again?"

"Yeah, I took a swig while I was watching events unfold," Kevin said. "The realtor, Isaac, Dan and his beautiful colleague. Based on the way she was gloating, she's in and you're out. You think if you can prove that you're as tactical as her, you'll win back his heart."

"Dan and I argued, but … why are you here?" I asked.

"You're one who arranged a private talk," Kevin said.

"There's been a mistake," I said. "I need to go."

I reached for my bag and yelped as he gripped my wrist. In that split second, when our eyes locked in the flickering candlelight, I caught onto his alert gaze, his sidearm, and the beads of sweat on his brow. Instinct seized me by the back of my neck. Kevin's fingers weren't ice cold from being outside. His blood didn't pump like mine.

"What did you do?" I managed.

"That's enough," he said. "Keep quiet."

Roughly, Kevin untucked my shirt and checked my bra for a listening device while I breathed in frightened gasps. Where was Antoine? Why wasn't he bursting through the door and issuing commands?

"No wires," Kevin said, running his hands down my legs and groping my ankles. With a grim expression, he secured my phone and tucked it into his pocket. "Come on. Get moving."

Pushed forward as he gripped the back of my shirt between my shoulder blades, I tripped and stumbled as he made a quick circuit of the rooms. His light stabbed the shower curtain, raked across freshly painted walls, and gouged holes into the darkness of closets. Tripping, moaning, I was half suspended in his grasp while he opened the basement door and swept his beam over the empty shelves and vacuumed floor.

"Calm down," I managed. "Let's talk."

I was hauled to the front door, where his breath came out as blasts of mist as he combed the darkness. Nobody was there.

Kevin continued onward, dragging me by the collar until we reached the garage door. Once we crossed the threshold, he flung me to the concrete floor with such force that my sore shoulder suffered a fresh bolt of pain. Dan's chair was there. His bottle of whiskey.

Shaking, I closed my eyes and understood why Antoine was holding back. We needed a confession with enough facts and details to put Kevin in a dark hole where he couldn't hurt anyone ever again.

Watching him pace in the darkness, I tried to recall any mention of him in my father's journals, but I drew a blank. Human frailty would be to blame. Errors in judgment. This was Antoine's ultimate foe, and mine as well: the hidden slips that left crimes unsolved.

My father's death was *not* going to be one of them.

31

The body protects itself in moments of terror. As the first blast of it settled into a vibration, a shimmering altered state, it felt like the story that I'd planned to tell buyers was coming to life, Aaron embracing me, assuring me that he was there. He steadied my legs and helped me climb to my feet. Together, we faced his father standing there in the garage.

"What was that?" Kevin asked. "You switched gears."

"I'm used to people venting at me," I said. "Pike is bitter. Roy Allen is frustrated. Why do you hate the sight of me?"

Shaking, Kevin said, "Who else knows?"

"*That's* your first question? Not, 'How much does it hurt?'"

"Don't talk to me about hurt," Kevin growled. "Anything soft in me got stripped away by my job. Dan was good at listening. He was there for Peg, even when he was young. Not when Aaron died. He disappeared without any warning. You don't know how that felt."

"Actually, I do," I managed.

"We're in a diner, Peg and I, trying to move on after Aaron died," he said. "Raymond came over to express sympathy. I was still angry from the fuss he kicked up when Bud and Birdie died, so I stepped away to pay the tab. I got back and there was Raymond consoling Peg. Holding her hand as she cried. That's the nutshell version. The tipping point."

I stared in confusion. "For what?"

Kevin's mouth twitched. "You were bluffing?"

"Take a breath," I said. "Calm down."

"The text you sent implied knowledge of the snowmobile trail I took, every detail of the night," Kevin hollered. "That was a lie?"

"I'm trying to clarify your side of things," I said.

Pacing, Kevin rubbed his brow. "I shouldn't have had a drink. My head is slamming, but sure, I'll tell my side. Peg's friends set things off, bringing her to the blasted casino, saying she was stuck inside too much, the whole empty nest thing. Peg took the betting too far and drained our cash. Came home tearful and ashamed. Then Bud and Birdie died. Raymond said it felt staged. I was like, Peg, what have you done?"

"Isaac Junior is the one who hastened their deaths," I said.

"I didn't know that at the time," Kevin said. "How could I?"

"You thought Peg was capable of it?" I asked.

"At first, but it came down to Bud being Bud," Kevin said. "When the furnace broke, he got an old kerosene heater, got drunk, and died from the fumes, and Birdie along with him. Peg almost went under from the shock. There's Raymond, diving in where he's not wanted."

"He counseled a lot of people," I said.

"It wasn't a counselor mindset," Kevin said with disdain. "Raymond was a widower looking to warm up his home life. Haydn is pulling the same stunt lately. Peg is naive about men."

"Your wife sees Haydn as a son," I said desperately.

"Not with Raymond," Kevin said. "I saw Peg light up when he was around. Once I caught onto it, my blood started to boil."

"This happened when Aaron was still alive?" I asked.

"Aaron's death put the problem on overdrive," Kevin said. "People saw my wife and your father at the church, the diner. The next thing I knew, Peg wanted us to go to counseling. Jesus Christ, why didn't Raymond leave it alone? My wife's problems were not his concern."

I closed my eyes, crushed to my core to grasp that Raymond hadn't died trying to rid the world of an elite criminal, or upend a drug gang, or any other high-stakes reason that might help ease the loss of life. My father had been murdered out of an irrational, jealous rage.

"I see you judging me," Kevin said.

"How would your son feel, seeing you right now?" I asked.

I gulped as Kevin shoved me backward until my back slammed against the wall in the lightless garage. I recognized the cold touch of metal against my temple and inhaled the familiar scent of gun oil.

"Stop—asking—*questions*," he seethed.

"Ok," I managed. "Calm down."

A muffled grunt in the yard drew his gaze toward the windows on the bay doors, and then he fixed me with a grim scowl.

"That's another problem," Kevin said. "The ally you brought in to help corner me. I've got him hog-tied out there."

My mind collapsed as I pictured Antoine trying to communicate with me, or maybe he was hollering at heaven.

"I can see that you're tortured by what you did," I said desperately. "In honor of your son, you need to turn yourself in."

"Like that can happen now," Kevin said, massaging his brow. "Aaron left this house to Dan, cold inside from things I'd said. When he was weak and stupid, I told him so." Kevin paced, caught up in his thoughts. "Aaron texted me. Said we needed to talk. I pulled into the driveway and opened my truck door. *That's* when he did it. My son shot himself right here." Kevin pounded his chest. "Right in the heart."

"Dear God," I whispered.

"Took all kinds of punishment growing up. Never came at me in return. Not until that night," Kevin added. "The lights were not off like now. I staggered out and vomited. I left him for others to find."

I closed my eyes, aching for Dan.

"*There* it is," Kevin said, pointing at me. "Regret over pushing it, but way too late. It's time for next steps. Do you love Dan?"

"It's why I cleaned this house," I tearfully whispered.

"He needs me as a father figure, and FYI, I had a different take on you back in May," Kevin said. "Dan had disappeared on us. I got wind of him being at a crime scene at your farm. I showed up in time to see him tripping over himself, transfixed by something in you. Others saw the same thing. You were a ticket for him to get back to his normal self. I couldn't believe it when you convinced him to head back north."

"He couldn't quit because of me," I said in despair.

"Now there won't be a need," Kevin said. "This week, there's a new round of people who want you dead. So, here's the deal. You're going to text him and tell him you're going to Boston."

"You can't be serious," I said.

"Deep down, you know you're the wrong woman for him," Kevin said. "He's had to haul your ass out of trouble multiple times."

"Is this the kind of logic you used when you killed my father?" I asked. "You went to his farm on a snowmobile and lured him out during a storm. You hit him when he wasn't looking."

"No, we hollered face to face," Kevin said. "He knew why I was there, and it got ugly. I thought I erased all the evidence."

"Your attitude is chilling," I said tearfully. "I would give *anything* to be Alison French. Instead, I ended up with an imposter father who hated the sight of me. Just like you're looking at me. There's no escaping it."

"It sounds like we're in agreement," Kevin said.

I nodded. "Why not? Everything is ruined."

"If you text the wrong thing …"

"I want Dan to be happy," I said. "I truly do."

Shaking, sobbing, I half-lifted my left hand to take my phone. Kevin stepped closer and manually put it into my palm.

Swiftly, I slammed my fist into his nose, sending him sprawling backward, and then I raked his forearm with my fingernails.

"*There*," I hollered. "Your nose is bloody, and your DNA is right here on my hands. You are *not* getting away free tonight."

"You've trapped me?" Kevin hissed. "Is that it?"

"It's over," I said. "Drop the weapon."

With a look of rage, Kevin lifted his gun and shattered the quiet with horrific, nonstop blasts. *Pop-pop-pop. Pop-pop-pop.*

Breathless, I looked down at my torso and didn't see blood.

"What the hell?" Kevin demanded.

Antoine was a blur, wrenching the weapon from Kevin's hand and all but lifting him off the floor as he shoved the murderer back and slammed him against the wall. There he paused, his shoulder tight and unmoving. The only sign that Antoine had delivered an unseen punch was a slight shift of his weight and Kevin's sharp gasp of pain.

"*Stop*," I said. "Don't give his lawyer ammunition."

"He was supposed to see your distress and come to his senses," Antoine growled. "To confess his sins without damage. Gutless coward, tossing you to the floor. C'est lui qui a sa place dans la tombe."

"Please stop," I said desperately. "Calm down."

Antoine relented and gathered me into a tight embrace, reflecting the tension and fury he'd weathered while the dicey, gripping plan had played out. His voice in my ear had a calming effect.

"I cut off the power so I could be a shadow, poised to act, if necessary," Antoine said softly. "After Aaron's death, Kevin divested himself of all of his guns except the one he brought. Haydn's bond with Peg was an asset. With his help, I was able to replace all of Kevin's bullets with blanks. You weren't alone, Berrichon. I'm sorry the path involved moments of terror. His capture is a done deal, his guilt beyond doubt."

"I thought he'd tied you up," I managed.

"That was an undercover cop, a tactic to give Kevin a false sense of control," Antoine said. "Kevin is well-liked in local police circles. It wasn't possible to carry out the plan with officers he knew." Antoine cupped my face until I focused on his eyes. "In the forest and here in this garage, you showed strength and courage, Alison Evelyn French. You got justice for your father. He would be proud."

"You brought in a specialized team?" I asked.

"The best of the best," Antoine said. "Just for you."

With a remote control, Antoine triggered the overhead lights to flare on, which had me squinting as the bay doors opened. Officers stepped in, looking grave and focused as they handcuffed Kevin.

"You ruined everything," he slurred, dripping blood from my blow to his nose. "You made Dan question events."

"It's time to switch gears, Kevin," I said, hovering over the slumped killer. "There's no hope for your soul until you confess."

"Come, Berrichon," Antoine said, sheltering me with his arm as he led me forward. "All is well. Let's have some cocoa."

* * *

The yard was the usual stunning blur of swirling strobe lights and officers setting up crime scene tape. A familiar man in black gear approached with a grin. He'd been a part of Dan's specialized team since day one.

"You aced it," Liam said. "Fist bump."

"Later," I said. "Right now, I can't lift my arms."

"I need to warn you," Liam said, "Dan had a sixth sense moment and returned to the house. We had to handcuff him to the van."

I gaped. "He *saw* what happened?"

"Through the video feed." Liam tossed me a set of keys. "These are for the cuffs. Approach slowly. He's as mad as a bear."

A half-block away, Dan was pacing with his right wrist cuffed to the van's back door. My hands trembled as I slipped the key into the lock, aware of the torn skin left by his struggle to break free. Dan grabbed the key, got the job done, and gripped me tightly, whispering curses against my ear, and then he studied my face with a fierce, assessing gaze. I could tell his mind was torn between fury and relief.

"You're ok?" Dan asked. "No damage this time?"

"Well …"

"You understand that we can't keep ending up here, with you in harm's way and me having a coronary," Dan said crossly. "This time you went too far. Honest to God, Sonny. It's off the charts."

"Roy accused me of stealing treasure," I managed. "He's been hot and cold on the murder theory, so I lost faith."

"I'll never get it out of my mind," Dan said, rubbing his face. "Terror, feeling helpless, then point-blank gun blasts."

"Dan, I didn't know it was Kevin," I whispered. "It's shocking, and it's got your local colleagues casting scowls at me. They didn't see or hear what went on. You need to tell them he's truly guilty."

"How can I?" Dan asked. "I'm still in disbelief."

"Dude," Liam said, jogging toward us. "Kevin has waived his rights and wants to explain. Take a breath. Calm down."

"I can't *unsee* what happened in there," Dan seethed.

"Kevin is showing remorse," Liam said. "He loves you like his own. Come on, walk it off," Liam added, striving to get Dan's blood pressure in the desired range. "You're good now? Ready to roll?"

"Yeah, let's get it over with," Dan said.

Shaking, I stifled my urge to call him back and let others handle the moment. Dan needed to confront the man who'd added to his pain after Aaron's death. He needed to release his sense of guilt and fulfill a critical, professional role in the closing hours of the case.

"Congratulations," Nicole said, coming to stand beside me.

"Can I have a blanket?" I asked, shivering in the cold. "I left my jacket in the kitchen, so it's part of the crime scene."

"Absolutely." Nicole secured a fleece wrap from a vehicle and snugged it around my shoulders. "All set?"

"Better," I said. "Thank you."

"We're friends now?" she asked.

"You have to admit," I said. "That's a stretch."

"You need to listen like that's where we're at," Nicole said with sudden intensity, her gray eyes as bright as crystals in the police lights. "I've seen how you use your influence over men. *I'm* the one with knowledge of him. Depth and history. A bond you can't begin to grasp. You're a civilian. An artist. Surely you see it's not a good match? Tempt him onward, and you will destroy what makes him unique."

I blinked rapidly. "But ..."

"End it tonight," Nicole said. "Stay in your lane."

With that, she jogged to the garage, where Dan was preparing for a sit-down with Kevin to tie up the case. As Nicole arrived by his side, Dan leaned down to hear her. Catching stray words in the night air, I knew they were speaking in French in a cadence that rose and fell like a tide, a natural phenomenon. They were equals. Sympatico on the job front. Her actions had not led to the raw wounds on Dan's wrist.

Breathless, I felt the attacks of the past year of my life collide in the center of my mind, a seamless miasma of trauma, and for a moment, all I could think about was the harsh message a murderer had whispered in my ear, *What will you remember? What will you forget?*

Nicole's fragrance was on the blanket, the same way it would be on Dan. I crossed to the van and flung the blanket inside.

Coatless and shivering, I started pacing in the glare of the strobes. A short while ago, a confession in a cold case hinged on my strength and endurance. Now I was alone and forgotten, relegated to the three words I always heard at a crime scene: "Wait over there."

The road beckoned. I left Aaron Pierce's front yard and started walking past the holiday lights festooned on the fences of nearby yards. It felt good to be free of the noise and chaos of the crime scene. I needed to process the jarring night. To stop hearing the sound of gun blasts. To escape the sight of Dan speaking with Nicole in French.

Headlights claimed me from behind, and a dark sedan eased to a halt.

Antoine's window slid open. "Need a lift?"

"Maybe," I said. "I don't know."

Antoine motioned. "Come on, get in."

My feet felt like blocks of ice as I crossed around the fender. With Antoine looking on, I wrenched the door open. Once I'd settled into place, I closed my eyes, vibrating in the warm, minty interior.

"You're not supposed to leave a crime scene," he said.

"Isn't that what you're doing?" I asked.

"Fair enough," he said.

Awash in the dashboard's soft light, Antoine put the car into gear, his sun-streaked curls unleashed, falling just short of his shoulders. Maybe, once a case was closed, he literally let his hair down.

"What now?" he asked.

"I don't suppose you can get me to China," I said. "My best friend is on a birdwatching tour. I need a hug."

"Sounds like fun," he said. "Maybe I'll join you."

I swiveled and frowned into the darkness behind the car, worried that my unexplained departure would spark a police pursuit.

"Nobody has caught on that you left," Antoine said. "Dan and Kevin are in folding chairs in front of the spot where Aaron killed himself. It's painful. Dan looks trashed, but it's necessary to sit there and take whatever comes out. Kevin waived his Miranda rights, so—"

"How can you know all this?" I asked.

"I'm listening in." Antoine shifted his hair to show an earpiece. "Liam is narrating. Kevin is talking about the night Raymond died."

"Did he suffer?" I whispered.

"Raymond was caught off guard, not dressed for a fight in a blizzard," Antoine said softly. "They fought. I don't want to sugarcoat the situation, but for the most part, your father didn't suffer. I'm sorry, Berrichon. Do you want me to convey other questions to ask?"

"My questions are for you," I said. "How you figured it out."

Antoine took out the earpiece and set it aside.

"Bars are a great setting for cultivating allies," he said. "Haydn yearns to be a cop again, so I had a colleague chat him up. Long story short, Kevin approached Haydn about getting rid of you."

I blanched. "Good God …"

"A terrifying prospect," Antoine agreed. "Haydn's bond with Peg was the clincher. He hates how Kevin treats her, so we looped him in on short notice. He might have potential as an undercover agent."

"Raymond's death would never have been solved without your help," I said. "With your skills, you could be a billionaire."

Antoine smiled. "What makes you think I'm not?"

"If so, you can retire," I said. "Your worst enemy is gone."

"Your father's murderer as well," Antoine said.

"He's detained rather than gone," I said. "I have a strict policy against fist bumps and victory laps. I don't think I'll be free of those last moments anytime soon. I thought I was dead."

"You believe you survived it?" Antoine asked. "You're alive?"

"Umm … I'm hoping so."

"You did," Antoine said. "I'm asking if you *believe* it."

"Maybe tomorrow," I said.

Antoine turned left into my driveway, sending the headlights through the pines and up the hill until the barn windows reflected the bright glare. Once the car purred to a stop near my porch steps, Antoine shut off the engine, plunging the car's interior into darkness. The only sign that we were inside a machine was the whisper of the heater.

"About Nicole's rant," he said. "When she told you to stay in your lane, it's possible she was jealous of my bond with you."

I closed my eyes, forced to reset the scene in my mind.

"Will you forgive her for recruiting Dan?" I asked.

"It's not likely," Antoine said. "She hasn't learned."

"Three words that are usually devoted to me," I said.

"You need to stop listening to critics," Antoine said. "Never question your sense of what unfolded outside the cave, and stop letting Isaac get a word in edgewise. He's another one who refuses to learn. Hopefully, his efforts will fail. His guilty son will cut a deal."

"That would be a relief," I said. "I don't want to have to testify."

"While it's on my mind …" Antoine pulled out his phone and showed me a photo of the basement wall in Bud's house. "I marveled at the kind of stone they used. Granite, maybe. Or pegmatite."

I looked up with wide eyes. "Is that where the sample of rock came from? Bud asked Bertrand to check it out?"

"By all accounts, the stone was trucked in from elsewhere," Antoine said. "Paul and Isaac are allergic to liability issues, so they excluded the old house plus two surrounding acres from the Pintail Holdings contract. Of course, if they get wind of the basement's value, they'll launch claims and court cases. I would suggest a quiet demolition process once their attention is turned elsewhere," Antoine said. "From an environmental perspective, I would bury the rubble and forget it."

"Because lithium batteries can explode?" I asked.

"And other concerns, but it's not my choice to make."

I nodded, though it wasn't my choice either. It was another clear night with flakes drifting down through the air. Dodge and my sheep were near the fence, outlined by moonlight, a reminder that however much I wanted to flee from my troubles, I had a responsibility to my pets.

"I see that you can't leave on short notice," Antoine said softly. "Your animals need a keeper. You need a keeper as well, non?"

"I think I'm destined for a nunnery," I said.

With tears in my eyes, I gripped his strong hand, unable to express my gratitude for his help in achieving a wrenching goal.

"I'm going to miss you," I managed. "Not many men have faith in my abilities. To get it from a shining star like you is special. Truly stunning. Forgive me for rushing off. I'm not at my best right now."

Antoine kept hold of my hand as I started to leave.

"Do you recall the story I told you about the hawk with a tether on its ankle?" he asked. "A creature of the wind and the sky?"

"But sort of broken, a captivating puzzle for men," I agreed. "To be honest, it's not an accurate description of Nicole."

"I was talking about you," Antoine said softly.

I focused on his soulful eyes, the emotion he conveyed as he dropped his guard, how I'd felt when he'd stolen kisses and hugged me and delivered his thousand-watt smile. I felt the pull of attraction to him, more than I wanted to admit, but we were too damaged in the same ways to imagine anything but heartache. Not to mention my mixed-up feelings for Dan. Words escaped me. I lifted my shoulders and shook my head.

"You understand that I wouldn't draw you into my dangerous world," Antoine whispered. "But it's good to have this one moment."

"I meant what I said about coming up for air. You deserve a good life, Antoine. I hope you find peace. A way to heal."

"Ton optimisme est rafraîchissant," he said.

"Here in Maine, *English* is refreshing," I said.

Antoine reached for my other hand, closing his eyes as he pressed my palm against his cheek, and when that didn't answer the moment to his satisfaction, he drew me into a fierce hug across the cup holder. I clung to him, holding on for a long moment, savoring the bond we'd forged over the week, and then I tearfully pulled away.

"Stay safe," I whispered.

"Bonne chance, Berrichon."

I left Antoine sitting in the driver's seat, watching me, and though my absence from the crime scene remained an issue, I knew the police would figure it out. I'd landed in the first place they would look.

Once I opened the door Luke milled excitedly, his tail twirling. I knelt and hugged him, apologizing for the week of shocks. For a moment, with my keys back at the crime scene, I fell into confusion, not sure why the door was unlocked. Luke licked my face and bounded to the kitchen table, where someone had set up an arresting tableau.

I hesitated in the dark room, and then I walked forward in a daze until I bumped into one of the kitchen chairs. In the center of the table was a framed photo of Raymond, encircled by votives that a mystery visitor named Antoine had arranged in a heart shape.

With a trembling hand, I picked up the lighter on the table and lit each candle until their fragile flames brought definition to Raymond's image, almost a living warmth to his smile. Luke's tail sent wafts of air over the votives, stirring angelic light across the ceiling. I pulled out the chair and sat down in a trance, afraid of breaking the spell.

"It's over," I whispered. "I know who took you from me."

It's impossible to know how long I sat in the near darkness, awash in Raymond's presence, with his journal passages in my mind.

I miss Ella so much. She begged me to reach out to Sonny, but there was always some reason I held back. Now they'll never meet.

"Stop kicking yourself," I whispered. "I'm here, now."

I've put out word that I need a sleigh. A one-horse rig, like in the song. I can't wait to see my neighbors in the back seat, grinning ear to ear.

"I found a sleigh," I told him. "And bells, just like you wanted."

We talked about cutting down a Christmas tree in the woods near the pasture instead of buying one from a lot. I liked the tree where it was. I wanted to watch it grow. *They're Christmas trees*, Raymond argued, *clipped every year so they'll achieve the perfect, fluffy shape.*

"You seem to think I'm a pushover," I said.

"That's not true," Dan said, kneeling next to my chair in the darkness. "I know I didn't handle the moment well—"

"When did you get here?" I asked.

Dan paused. "We've been talking for five minutes."

"I was talking to Raymond," I said. "Antoine did this for me."

"I figured," Dan said. "Let me start from scratch—"

"It can't be lost on you that I'm grieving," I said. "Get on with your life with Nicole, and don't disturb the candles on your way out."

Dan hung his head, looking anguished. "Except for one moment in the Box & Bag, you put on a poker face when Nicole came up. Even then, you backed down. Tonight, there's a video of the scene outside Aaron's house. For the first time, I saw how she cut into you."

"Your sense of her has been confusing," I said.

"Sonny, when you're not playing poker, your eyes guide me like no other force on earth," Dan said. "It happened tonight in Aaron's kitchen.

Nicole didn't see potential in me. She wanted to bring me to Antoine as a prize. I got more hints from Jeremy. She came at you?"

"She tripped me on the stairs in Aaron's house," I said. "She hollered at me and grilled me until I almost blacked out."

Choking and gutted, Dan pulled me into a fierce embrace, and I gave up worrying about the votives blowing out. Unlike a human life, a match could be struck, and candles lit again.

"Up north, the pressure got to me, and Nicole was a part of it," Dan admitted. "It was superficial and kind of dark, a sign of how far I'd fallen. We'd parted ways when I met you, Sonny. If she implied otherwise, it was part of a power play. That's who she is."

"I'm sorry, my mind is getting jammed by an epiphany," I said, staring at Raymond's photograph. "There's an awful downside in learning the truth and getting justice. I feel him around me amidst the candles, but he's free now. He'll slip away, and he's not coming back."

"Raymond is wherever you are, the same as me," Dan said. "Wherever you go, no matter how rash and stubborn you are, we're on the job twenty-four-seven. Luke as well," Dan added as my dog rested his head on my thigh and looked at me with adoring eyes.

"I'm not the only one who's rash and stubborn," I said.

Dan nodded. "It's possible I might be worse."

It's funny how smiles can turn into tears. We held each other, thinking about Raymond and Aaron in the flickering light, committed to helping each other absorb the reality that even when justice was served, it was a hollow victory when loved ones were gone for good.

About the Author

Nina's Sonny Littlefield novels are based on her own experiences as a photographer, and the years she and her husband raised sheep and horses on a small organic farm in rural Maine. During her travels to jungles, coral reefs, and other destinations, Nina is always on the lookout for ways to incorporate interesting characters and realism into her fiction. In writing the series, she draws heavily on her own brushes with disaster, moments when she pressed her luck too far, even the time she brought a tip to the police and ended up helping them solve a crime.

Nina's albums of nature audio tracks are available through Spotify, Apple Music, and other streaming services. Examples of her photos and videos are on her website, www.ninadegraff.com. Her Etsy shop is open when time allows. Her fabric designs, some of which are created with her mystery novels in mind, are available through Spoonflower.

If you enjoyed reading "Dead North," please consider putting your review on my Amazon book page. To stay in the loop about future books you can follow me on my Facebook page, "Nina DeGraff Books."

www.ingramcontent.com/pod-product-compliance
Lightning Source LLC
Chambersburg PA
CBHW070509310726
48976CB00002BA/390